IN EXTREMIS

A novel by

David Ainsworth

First published by Dog Ear Publishing
4011 Vincennes Rd
Indianapolis, IN 46268
www.dogearpublishing.net

ISBN: 978-1-4575-3793-6

This book is printed on acid-free paper.

This book is a work of fiction. Places, events, and situations in this book are purely fictional and any resemblance to actual persons, living or dead, is coincidental.

Printed in the United States of America

ACKNOWLEDGEMENTS

I liken the new era of self-publication in its various forms, in kind if not in importance, to the invention of the Gutenberg Press. Currently, a retrenching traditional fiction publishing industry is more and more dependent on those genre, and the stable of contributing writers thereof, known to produce needed revenues. Any experimental, untested or even cross-genre fiction by a debut author is met with a dreaded, but almost universally expected, rejection letter.

In medieval times, one had access to written knowledge only via an original manuscript or one painstakingly, lovingly, and often with artistic flourishes, copied by the hand of a cloistered monk. That choke point was removed by the Gutenberg Press, and thereafter books and other writings multiplied exponentially. Universities were founded. The Renaissance flowered. The Reformation and Enlightenment evolved.

It is presumptuous, of course, to claim that the current explosion of self-published materials may be expected to have a comparably profound effect on human kind, but, over time, by removing the choke point of traditional publishing for works of fiction and non-fiction alike, it may be expected to have a lasting and significant effect. Much, much more prose and poetry will be available to an expanding world population connected by e-documents than would otherwise be the case, *whether or not this incremental art is commercially successful.* That is a good thing. So, my first acknowledgement is of the technology that has enabled self-publication in its various forms and the flowering of creative and non-fiction writing that would not otherwise see the light of day. This book is only one such example.

Thanks go to my son, Gray Ainsworth, whose critique of the book was invaluable as well as expert. His suggestions brought the sensibilities of telling a story through film to bear on the written word in many beneficial ways. Thanks also go to David Slaby, a fellow traveler in the law and in winemaking, for his critical comments borne of a voracious reading habit. As a student of all things commercial, political and futuristic, his critiques provided essential sanity checks on my own imagination.

My final acknowledgement is related to the aforesaid self-publishing phenomenon. I needed a really good editor to work with in spotting passages in my drafts that didn't work, suggesting treatments that were missing, forcing me to adhere to professional-grade tradecraft or have a very good reason for breaking the rules, and encouraging latent strengths in the creative process. My editor, Ana Manwaring, filled that need perfectly, and I am most appreciative of her services.

David Ainsworth
Saint Helena

FOREWORD

If something can't continue indefinitely, it will stop. (Herb Klein)

If something can go wrong, it will. (Murphy's First Law)

Things tend to go from bad to worse. (Murphy's Fourth Law)

CHAPTER

1

At last light and with the mother ship a small, grey blotch on the horizon, the leader gave the signal to commence the attack. With a push on the accelerator handle, the powerful engine on each of the three special operations craft roared to life. Their composite carbon-fiber hulls pounded violently off the tops of the waves as they raced toward the large tanker in the distance they had tracked since late afternoon. The timing was perfect; the forecasted solar storms were at their peak and provided cover from satellite surveillance.

On each of the boats, six men had a hard grip on the lanyard that ran around the pontoon gunwale and prevented them from being thrown overboard by the jarring impact with the crest of the waves. An automatic weapon hung by web gear on each man's torso. Through the eye holes of their head masks, save one, the Mongoloid eye folds and dark eyes of the Asian races were visible. The leader's eyes were rounder and blue.

By now, the boats would be fixed on the tanker's radar, and they would be the focus of alarmed attention by the officer at the helm of the tanker. With his free hand, the leader pulled out his infrared binoculars to see whether the tanker was changing course. If the tanker turned to the same heading of the approaching attack boats, it would be making a run for it. The steady position of the tanker's green starboard running light told him the target had not yet reacted and was still headed southeast off the coast of Sumatra and down the Strait of Malacca. In this upper part of the Strait, ship traffic had not converged into the congested narrows to the south, and the tanker was alone.

Mariners knew the Strait to be the shortest route between Middle Eastern oil ports and ports in East Asia. Its waters formed the passageway between the coasts of Sumatra and Malaysia, forcing ships to pass the countless bays, coves and villages along each shoreline. For centuries, these places harbored pirates exploiting the Strait's waters of uncertain jurisdiction.

In his mind, the leader ran through the range of anti-piracy tactics the tanker might adopt. He had enough weapons at his disposal to take the target ship, but its cargo was both precious and flammable. He couldn't run the risk of extensive damage to the ship. It had to be navigable afterward with its cargo intact.

The tanker headed down the Strait directly at them. That meant its master was confident the ship could run the gauntlet. The leader assumed the tanker carried an armed guard and probably sound and water cannons as well. The cat and mouse game had begun.

It took six minutes for the boats to close with the large crude carrier. The leader inhaled the heavy, fragrant air of the tropical sea as lightning flashed from thunderheads in the east too distant to be a factor in his operation. The *M/V Energy Future*'s name in white letters against its black hull came into focus, and it flew the Panamanian flag of convenience. The ship likely had already reported the attack via its ship security alert system, and its location was continuously transmitted via satellite. Somewhere in Panama, the alert was registering with the ship's agents there, a matter of little concern to the leader. He judged it extremely unlikely that Panamanian monitors could communicate promptly with naval authorities in all three countries having possible jurisdiction or that any of them could manage a timely intervention, especially after dark.

He steadied himself with one hand on the lanyard of his circling boat and continued to study his quarry through binoculars. He could see a machine gun crew setting up on the stern and two others on the boat decks on either side of the bridge. At least two guns would face directly toward almost every position around the tanker's hull. The bow and the stern, both obscured by the flare of the hull, were the exceptions. The attack boats were now well within the range of the ship's machine guns, and it was not slowing down.

A flare went up from the tanker's bridge, brightly illuminating the surrounding water. The leader welcomed the light to exhibit all three of his boats. Two men on each boat stood with a rocket propelled grenade launcher in full display. He put down the scope and picked up a megaphone.

"HEAVE TO! WE HAVE INCIDIARIES AND WE WILL USE THEM IF YOU DO NOT STOP! I REPEAT, HEAVE TO." The amplified command was given in English and repeated in Chinese.

The leader directed the boats to fall off as he watched the giant tanker for signs of the master's reaction. He could see men taking cover around the machine gun positions.

It will take more than threats to get this oil, he thought.

An ear-splitting jet of sound hit the leader's boat and a green laser moved between the other two boats, but the ear protectors and goggles of the attackers, together with their speed, rendered those anti-piracy measures ineffective.

When the flare died out astern the tanker, it was replaced by another. The leader spoke into his mic, and all three of the attack boats began to run along the tanker's starboard side with the attackers firing automatic weapons at the bridge. Machine guns from the vessel returned fire, their bullets pinging off the composite hull and cockpit of the boats, and puncturing the pontoon gunwale on the leader's boat.

The tanker's water cannons surged on, creating an oscillating stream of water under pressure strong enough to knock a man overboard. The leader's boat and one other peeled off and crossed the wake close under the huge, squat stern of the big ship. The third boat fell back, aiming its covering machine gun fire at the tanker's stern gun position while the first two boats moved in under the slight flare of the blunt stern on the port side of the rudder, blocking lines of fire from the tanker's machine guns.

At the leader's order, each of the two attack boats under the stern fired a rocket propelled grenade at a water cannon directly overhead on the port side. Both were direct hits, destroying the nozzles to the water cannon and creating huge fountains forty feet apart and obscuring the view of the tanker's gun positions. The two boats then ran close alongside the hull, and men on each boat threw a satchel against the hull. Powerful magnets inside the satchels snapped onto the steel hull in two locations above the water line and remained firmly attached. Then the attack boats retreated under cover of the spraying fountains of water at the two destroyed water canon locations.

The leader's boat fired an RPG at the port wing, striking it with a violent explosion, shattering the glass on the bridge and tearing the radio direction finder from its stanchion. A hail of automatic weapons fire was directed from the other boats at the machine gun position on the port boat deck.

The leader could see the ghostly red images of the crew take cover and grinned. *Not professionals.*

He could see that there was no important damage to the ship. The leader spoke into his mic, "All boats fall off and await my order."

He stood upright in his boat as it kept pace with the tanker and again directed his megaphone to the bridge. "AHOY, ENERGY FUTURE. HAVE YOUR CAPTAIN CALL ME ON THE MARINERS' CHANNEL."

After a moment, a burst of static emitted from the leader's phone.

"This is the captain."

"Have a crewman look at your port side aft, captain. We will not shoot at him. He will see two satchel charges attached to the hull. If you do not heave to within five minutes, I will blow your rudder and propeller pods to pieces, and then we will board you. The five minutes begin now."

"You're bluffing," came the answer in accented English. "You wouldn't risk blowing up the ship or even damaging its steering. You would lose your ransom."

"Captain, if we disable your ship, we can still take survivors as hostages and still get our ransom. If we let you go, we've gone through all this for nothing. If you survive, you will have to explain to your owners and their insurance companies why you gambled and cost them hundreds of millions in ship damage, lost cargo, and oil pollution liability. Either way, we get our money. You survive with your career intact only if you cooperate. You now have four minutes."

The leader absentmindedly felt his neck for a pulse. *Sixty Eight. I used to get excited during an operation.*

A man previously a part of the tanker's stern gun crew ran to the rail and looked down at the satchels attached to the hull on the port side beside the rudder, and then ran back to take cover talking into his radio handset. In less than two minutes, the vessel began to reduce speed, finally steadying with just enough power to maintain navigational control of the big ship. A Jacob's ladder was lowered to accept the boarding party. It was over.

***

Three hours later, after the leader's reconnaissance of the tanker and its machinery and disabling the global tracking system required by Panamanian law, a lifeboat was lowered. The lifeboat, minus all lights, flares, radios, cell phones, and navigational aids and with its engine disabled, settled into the calm sea. Four oars remained on board. All but one of the crew descended the port gangway and into the life boat. All had survived the firefight with only minor injuries. Those who had sought the safety of the ship's panic room voluntarily elected to join the rest of the crew aboard the life boat rather than be taken hostage.

The crew would spend the night rowing toward the nearest shore lights without the ability to signal distress or communicate ashore. If naval or police boats from Sumatra had been alerted of the attack by radio or by the explosions, they would be ill-equipped to search in the dark for a lifeboat adrift in the Strait. By morning, the tanker would be gone.

After the lifeboat drifted off into the dark waters of the Strait, the leader turned to face the remaining crew member still aboard.

"Come with us," he said in perfect, American-accented English.

The Chief Engineer, a portly but powerfully built German named Fischer, was escorted by the leader and three men, all still wearing their head masks, to the engine control room. In the control room, an array of video monitors and digital displays around three sides of the room provided images of each of the giant diesel engines, generators, a boiler, and access passageways. The fourth wall contained the chart table and supply cabinets. The leader directed his men to tape over the clock and the digital display for compass bearing with duct tape.

"We have kept you on board for insurance, Herr Fischer. Not as a hostage as you might be thinking, but as a technical advisor. We may have questions about these controls."

"Why should I help you?" Fischer responded, his eyes wide. "You will kill me anyway."

The leader returned the engineer's gaze, but the leader's was without fear.

"You will help us because we will certainly kill you if, but only if, you don't cooperate. You have seen how we put all of the other crew safely into life boats. You have seen us cover the screen and clock here in the engine room. That is to prevent you from observing our course changes and the time. The only reason we would do that is to prevent you from reporting that information later to our pursuers. And the only way you could report our bearings and the time between course changes is if you were alive after having been set free, am I right? We just want the ship and its cargo. When the time comes, you too will be put safely into a life boat, and then you can begin writing your exciting memoir. What could be more reasonable?"

The engineer nodded after a moment. "Okay. Are these three your engineering crew?" inclining his head toward the men holding their guns on him.

"They are. They speak good English. You will be handcuffed in that chair over there and answer their questions. If you need to get up to show them something, one of them will keep his gun on you while you are out of the chair. If you do your job, you will be treated well. Clear?"

Fischer nodded.

The leader turned to one of the men in black. "We will get underway immediately. Are you and the bridge in communication?"

The man nodded. "Yes, sir. Standing by."

"Good. I'll be up on the bridge. Call me if Herr Fischer is uncooperative or you think he is giving you bad information."

The leader stepped into the engine room elevator and pushed the indicator button for the bridge. As the elevator door closed, he removed his head mask and absentmindedly scratched the scar that ran into his sand colored goatee.

Responding to commands from the bridge, the big diesels brought the giant ship to full ahead, and it resumed its southeasterly course down the Strait. One blip on the radar screen revealed another nearby vessel on course to intersect the tanker's heading. The mother ship was closing to recover the three attack boats. It had been successful and clean.

The Engineer told his captors where the ship's paint locker was, and they located a large store of black paint for the hull and several buckets each of white and green paint. At dawn, the ship eased behind an island at the mouth of the Kampar River opposite the Strait from Singapore. During daylight, the ship's homeport of "Colon" was painted over and replaced with "Vasco de Gama," an obscure port in what is now the Indian province of Goa, sometimes used as a flag of convenience. Then, the crew used black paint to cover the yellow band around the top of the stack and the letter M below it that served as a logo for the German owners. A small, ambiguous green palm tree was painted on each side of the stack. "*M/V Asian Glory*" was painted on both sides of the bow and on the stern.

The vessel now looked generic. Most importantly, it would not be recognized as the hijacked tanker by any other vessel who might glimpse it from a distance during its short voyage. The leader assumed that the lifeboat containing the crew had been found by now and that its passengers were telling their story.

After sunset, the tanker resumed its southeasterly course. Soon, the verdant coastal mountains faded into the dusk over the fantail. Flashes of lightning again illuminated the dissolving afternoon cloud cover and brought the daily showers that fed the teak forests of Sumatra.

***

The leader watched the sunrise and drank coffee from the captain's mug. He looked at his watch and picked up the handset to the engine control room.

"We'll be at the berth this afternoon."

"Yes, sir," came the answer. "The Engineer showed us how to operate the bow thruster and the mooring winches. We're ready."

The leader then took the elevator down to the engine room and pulled the black head mask over his face before stepping out of the elevator.

"Well, Herr Fischer, you will be happy to know that we have reached your disembarkation location. You should be able to reach the coastline in a few hours even without rowing. There is a strong current that runs toward land here." The leader pulled a Glock from his shoulder holster. "Let's go."

The Chief Engineer looked anxious getting in the elevator with a gun pressed into the small of his back, but seemed reassured by a glance at his captor's mask.

On deck, Fischer inhaled the fresh, salty mist in the headwind and his spirits lifted. The hazy coast line was not far and the weather was fair. He knew nothing of who his captors were or what they intended to do with the ship, but at least he could tell the authorities that the vessel seemed to steer a steady southerly course with what he thought were some turns to the east. He could tell by the change in the ship's roll as the southeast swell struck the vessel from changing directions. Brunei sounded about right.

The leader pointed to a lifeboat from which its covering tarp had been removed. The boat was properly positioned over its set of blocks rigged to lower the boat to the water. Fischer lifted his leg to climb into the boat when the bullet struck him behind the ear. He fell back to the deck coming to rest face up with a puzzled look on his face. His mouth made an effort to form words. The leader fired another round into the engineer's sternum, and the man was still.

The leader peeled off his head mask. "It was much less trouble this way, Herr Fischer. You were comfortable while you were with us, and we got your much-needed cooperation."

His men unbuttoned the front of the engineer's coveralls and inserted a heavy engine room wrench down his pants leg. Then, using his shoe lace, they tied the cuff of his pant leg containing the wrench tightly to his leg. That would prevent the wrench from slipping out when the gasses from his decomposing body gave it buoyancy later.

The leader's benediction was brief. "That should hold you down on the bottom nicely."

It took three men to pick up the heavy body and throw it overboard.

"Restow the lifeboat and clean the deck," the leader ordered. Then spill diesel fuel on the deck where the blood was. If anyone asks, the damage to the ship was caused by an unsuccessful pirate attack off Oman."

The three men nodded and fell to.

***

It was late afternoon when the pilot came aboard and guided the tanker into its berth. The crew, dressed in ordinary work clothes, lowered the ship's gangway onto the long wharf jutting out from the refinery. The leader walked down the gangway and shook hands with a caucasian man standing apart from the native men attaching the giant hoses through which the oil would be unloaded.

CHAPTER

2

The State Department's daily intelligence bulletin conspicuously stamped "SECRET" dropped into the IN basket of Captain Vincent Long, United States Marine Corps, an hour later than usual. By the look of it, it was thicker than usual too, although it been growing over the last several weeks. The American Embassy in Beijing had resumed hard copy dissemination of the bulletin after an embarrassing hacking incident indicating that the Chinese had been reading them on-line.

It was delivered by Jeff Bell, Second Secretary of the Embassy, who immediately preceded Long on the intelligence bulletin routing.

"Vincent, be glad you are here in Beijing rather than in Washington right now," Bell said. "The power outages continue. The Northeast is getting the worst of it because it has most of the oil-fired power plants."

"They must be in a world of hurt," Long responded. "No one realizes how logistically infeasible cities are until their systems break down."

"I gather that the high rise buildings pretty much have to be cleared out after a few hours without power," Bell said. "With the blowers off, the air gets stale and hot in those sealed up buildings. At least it's spring. Heating and air conditioning aren't so critical."

Bell glanced at his watch and grimaced. "Blast. I've got to go over to the Foreign Ministry and take some more crap off of those guys about our blocking their attempts to buy the Canadian oil sands."

"Well, tell them go pound sand. Pun intended," Long said, grinning. "Hydrocarbons in Canada belong to us. Monroe Doctrine and all that."

"Yeah, well, you jarheads may have to go up to Canada and surround the place before this is over. The Canadians are getting uppity about their sovereignty and their God-given right to sell to the highest bidder. Maybe we should have treated them with more respect over the years. See you later."

Bell executed a decent about-face for a civilian and left Long's small office.

Long stared at his sword mounted in its escutcheon on the wall facing his desk. It never failed to trigger a sense of the Corps' history-rooted traditions. Called the Mameluke sword, it was a replica of one presented to Lieutenant Presley O'Bannon by a desert chieftain of Mameluke warriors in Tripoli. O'Bannon led a Marine detachment in a successful assault against the fortified city of Derna in Tripoli in 1805. The raid eliminated pirate activity that had been interdicting American shipping in the Mediterranean from the "shores of Tripoli." The Marine officer's sword was the oldest weapon in the United States military arsenal.

He picked up the intelligence bulletin. It was routed to him in his capacity as commander of the Marine security detachment for the Embassy. It alerted him to developments affecting the Sino-American relationship, especially those likely to kick up security threats at the Embassy—usually in the form of orchestrated demonstrations.

America's transportation modes run on oil, it said. Small towns and rural areas in America were said to be in better circumstances than cities because locally grown food supplies would be more accessible over the coming growing season, and sparse development made housing more habitable in the current circumstances than in the cities. In the cities, acute gasoline shortages were disastrous. All subsistence supplies must be distributed by truck, rail and air transport, all of which were operating on reduced schedules. Ship schedules in port cities grew increasingly unreliable as bunker fuel scarcity choked off imports. Prices for early spring produce from the Southwest and Mexico escalated wildly if any could be found at all.

One paragraph described a conflict that had surfaced in New Jersey. A major oil company complained that the City of Newark had begun requisitioning its needs for gasoline from the company's local refinery. The company protested the City's payments for the gasoline at prices well below market price. It claimed that it was being coerced by the City's refusal to provide police and fire services to the refinery if it did not comply with the City's requisition practices. The refinery found itself continuously under siege by people desperate for gasoline, and the company could not control the determined looters without city police protection. Newark officials, in turn, alleged that the refinery's extortionate price increases violated its contract with the city.

The President was quoted excoriating those guilty of price gouging or hoarding scarce fuel and food supplies and thereby compounding the situation. They were, she said from the Rose Garden, "as un-American as any foreign enemy seeking to destroy the country." She appealed to the country for calm in what Long judged to be a mixed message after having condemned the practices of retailers in purple language.

Citing the Department of Energy as its source, the bulletin reported that natural gas, geothermal and wind farm power plants continued to operate normally, but they could not begin to meet the country's needs. Coal fired plants were experiencing frequent down time as trains that supplied them with coal increasingly struggled to procure a steady supply of diesel fuel for their engines. When oil and coal fired power plants stuttered, blackouts and regional grid failures resulted.

Long turned to his computer and did a search for "alternative power generation." An energy blog run by a charitable foundation stated that the output of hydroelectric power had been falling for years as climate change-induced drought in the Midwest and Southwest lowered the level of reservoirs below dam intake tunnels. Also, nuclear power plants around the country were forced to shut down for days at a time during more the more frequent temperature spikes in recent years.

Long picked up the State Department intel bulletin again and put his feet up on his desk.

A Department of Energy report on fracked shale gas was excerpted in the intel bulletin. Natural gas supplies on which the utility industry had placed heavy bets were facing declining production, due, in major part, to the fact that some shale rock turned out to be "tighter" or less porous than originally thought, yielding less gas. Many coal fired plants had been replaced by gas-fired ones in prior years on the rationale that gas was a cleaner source of energy. However, the fracking boom had ended after saturation drilling peaked about fifteen years earlier in the early 2020s. Gas shale reserves depleted more quickly than "conventional" gas wells because of shale's low porosity. The situation had been compounded by newly feasible LNG infrastructure that made natural gas transportable by ship, thus driving America's natural gas prices up to world market levels. Previously, methane distribution was limited to places served by pipelines within North America, the only means of delivery. Environmentally, the hydro-fracking boom had worsened the atmospheric concentration of greenhouse gasses by making natural gas temporarily abundant and cheap, accelerating its use.

Experts were saying that the current energy shortage was not self-correcting and could be expected to deepen with the passage of time.

Long looked up at his Mameluke sword.

How do we fight this enemy?

Long's attention was next drawn to an item at the top of the international part of the intel report. A large tanker carrying Chinese-owned crude had been hijacked by well-armed pirates in the Strait of Malacca two nights ago and was now missing.

Long pulled his feet off the desk and planted them squarely on the floor as he continued to read. Only yesterday, the Minister of Energy in Beijing condemned the black market for crude that had sprung up and stated that the missing shipment of crude was likely to find its way into the markets of China's Asian neighbors. The implication was that Japan, if not an actual perpetrator of the piracy, would benefit from this black market trade in stolen crude. The Minister stated that Japanese electronics manufacturers were reportedly unable to meet their delivery obligations to the American Defense establishment for essential components for missiles, smart bombs, aircraft and naval weapons systems and drones. He said that Japan could no longer count on future sales of rare metals from China to meet its manufacturing needs.

It was the talk of the foreign embassies in Beijing that China's carefully erected structure of agreements with oil-rich, volatile, middle-eastern regimes which were locked in conflict with the America and the West gave China preferential access to the production and exporting capacities of those oil-producing countries. China had also built a pipeline from oil fields in Kazakhstan over China's western border and across the entire width of the country to Shanghai and other cities on China's populated eastern coast.

Also, in a major shock to the American administration, China and Russia had recently renewed China's pipeline license from Russian oil fields in Western Siberia into Manchuria. The State Department had hoped that, upon expiration of China's prior preferential license to Western Siberian oil, that oil would become available through the new Russian pipeline to the Pacific port of Nakhodka and by tanker via the relatively short Great Circle route to the U.S. Pacific Coast. Now that China had successfully perpetuated its rights to that oil source again, the America lost that opportunity to increase its depleting sources of oil.

Long's musings were interrupted when the intel report slid off his lap onto the floor with a slap. Retrieving it, his thoughts returned to the tanker hijacking. A tanker had to be in navigable waters and would, by definition, be within the strike capability of the amphibious Marine Corps. Where was it? If the missing tanker were to be located, perhaps quick military action against energy pirates could be employed. Since the oil was apparently owned by the PRC, any such operations in Southeast Asia could be expected to involve the Beijing Government. The American Embassy in Beijing would necessarily also be involved. And, of course, the Navy and Marines.

He stood up and performed several squats to inject some life into his legs. Then moving toward the solitary window in his office, he looked down at the guard house near the entrance of the Embassy. At this time of day, there were three Marines on duty in the security office. Incongruously, directly in front of the Marine detachment's security post, on a small, raised island of concrete facing the public street, a single Chinese policeman stood guard. The great weight of the People's Republic was represented by that lone guard who stood as an ostensible protector of the diplomatic mission of America, China's ideological and economic competitor. Protector from what? Threats from whom? Only the monolith of the People's Republic and its multifariously tentacled agencies had the power to threaten the American Embassy. Long operated on the assumption that the man dressed as a Beijing City policeman was a poser. He was likely Red Army or state security. Whoever he was, he could be relied upon to report Embassy traffic to one or more state security services.

As Long watched, a Mercedes taxi pulled up at the front gate and a lean Caucasian man with a blonde buzz haircut and a short goatee stepped out of it. The Chinese police guard made no visible response whatever to the man's arrival, confirming the ambiguous nature of his duties. The man was dressed in a well-cut, dark suit and moved with athletic grace to the Marine guard office to show his passport. Shortly thereafter, having been issued the necessary pass for entry into the Embassy, the man moved quickly to the front door, turning his head to scan the mirrored front windows of the Embassy. His penetrating blue eyes glanced at the window behind which Long stood unseen.

Long turned away and walked into the corridor, following it to the office of the naval attaché. The door was half open, and the thinning hair on the top of Commander Jerry McMasters' head was visible as he hunched over some aerial photos. Long knocked and pushed the door open.

"Come in, Vincent," McMasters said, pushing back from his desk and sliding some papers over the photographs. "I wish I had some *café au lait* and a plate of *beignets* to offer you, but we are a long way from the *Café du Monde*."

McMasters referred to a favorite haunt in his native New Orleans and its signature menu items, a fondness for which both McMasters and Long shared.

"I do hope their supply of coffee beans is secure," McMasters drawled.

"Yes, sir. Those *beignets* are wicked good, alright. They haven't been outsourced to China yet, though, damn it."

"So, what's up with the United States Marine Corps, the Naval Establishment's favorite subsidiary?"

Long grinned at the jab. McMasters was emphasizing the organizational fact that the Marine Corps reports to the Secretary of the Navy and its mission is deeply rooted in amphibious operations conducted with, and under the ultimate command of, the Navy.

"Well, sir, I have a question for the even more senior agency that shall go unnamed but has NSA in its acronym and is rumored to have an operative somewhere between the offices on either side of yours."

"Oh, that agency," McMasters said, indicating his appreciation of the repartee with a wide smile. McMasters gestured to a chair facing his desk with a stack of books on it. "Take a seat."

"Thanks," Long said, dropping the books onto the abstractly patterned, low pile government carpet. He got to the point.

"In the intel bulletin this morning, there was an item about an oil tanker that was hi-jacked in the Strait of Malacca last night. The report said that pirates took it and that it had disappeared. Now, NSA's sister agencies, the National Geospatial Intelligence Agency and the National Reconnaissance Office, have a satellite system and analysis capability that could track any vessels that would have been in a certain location at a certain time—like, say, night before last at the northern end of the Strait of Malacca. Unless they've missed a step, they probably caught that incident in its data stream. What do you make of the intel bulletin's statement that the tanker has disappeared?"

"Way ahead of you, my man, but you have a need-to-know problem." McMasters referred to the rigid discipline among those to whom classified information is disclosed to disseminate that information only to persons having an operational "need to know" it.

"Well, I appreciate that, but if something is going on that might result in a crowd of angry, orchestrated people outside the Embassy, that *is* my affair. Being mindful of the confidentiality of the Embassy's paper and electronic files and the personal safety of its inhabitants—people such as yourself, for example—I would want to prepare for any such eventuality."

"Why would the hi-jacking precipitate any demonstrations here? You lost me."

"Because the oil in the hi-jacked tanker was Chinese, and China has good sources of oil, whereas Western countries, and America in particular, have a devastating shortage of it. Moreover, our Beijing hosts likely figure that the agency you represent knows the whereabouts of the tanker, while the Chinese Government likely does not because their satellites can't see in the dark very well, I'm told. And, if the American Government is not sharing its knowledge with the Chinese Government about the status of the tanker, the Chinese Government will assume that we are complicit in the affair or worse. Under those circumstances, the possibility of demonstrations, including calibrated levels of violence directed at the Embassy, can't be discounted."

"Ah, I see," McMasters nodded without expression. "That's a bit of a stretch, though. Well, suffice it to say, your security detachment should have its contingency plans at the ready as always. But we really don't know very much about this business. Apparently, on-going solar storms have been affecting the satellite transmissions. The transmissions showed some light pulses in the area that might or might not have been munitions explosions, but most of the images were just snow. By the time the images partially cleared yesterday, there were hundreds of ships in southeastern Asia going this way and that, including *beaucoup* tankers. None had the markings of the missing tanker. I gather that the Geospatial Intel people are continuing to study their pictures, but they apparently don't have any answers for now."

"Okay, Commander, thanks for the input. Maybe the situation will clear up in a day or two. See you later."

Long left the naval attaché's office and walked toward the elevator.

Solar storms? Convenient.

Long noticed that the elevator was already in operation. At the sound of the elevator's electronic bell, the door opened, and Long looked into the face of the man he had seen exit the limo a few minutes earlier. He noticed a scar that ran across the man's cheek and into his goatee.

Not a businessman coming to lodge a complaint about Chinese protectionism.

Long stood aside to allow the man to exit, and the two men exchanged nods and half smiles. Vincent stepped into the elevator, and the man in the dark suit turned down the hall in the direction of the naval attaché's office.

Certainly not to lodge one with a military attaché.

CHAPTER

3

W hen Vincent returned to his office, he checked his voicemail. There were two messages, and the voice on the first one surprised him. It was Grace's. They hadn't spoken since his home leave a year before. They'd met for lunch in Georgetown to sort out some joint stock brokerage account matters that lingered after the divorce.

He flashed back to the pick-up line he'd proudly delivered the night they met. He'd been on liberty from Quantico and seen her in a bar in Washington one Friday night talking with two girlfriends. Something about her bobbed, honey-colored hair and cameo profile was striking. Fearlessly, he walked up to her and said, "Excuse me, but you look *exactly* like my first wife."

She'd given her friends an embarrassed, wall-eyed look and played along. "Well, I suppose it's possible that we spring from the same gene pool. You marry a lot, do you soldier?" she'd asked, eyeing his haircut.

"Oh, I've never been married," he'd said pleasantly, looking into her eyes and hoping his delivery had been good. "And, by the way, it's Marine."

Grace, distracted by the eye contact, had gotten it only after her friends started whooping. After that, Vincent bought them a round of drinks, and they made room for him at the bar. Eventually, as if by an unobserved signal among single women, both of her friends pleaded a pressing social obligation elsewhere, leaving them alone. From that moment, he and Grace had been a couple.

Until we weren't any more.

Grace's message was cryptic. It just asked that he call her back when he got a chance. She wanted to talk to him about something.

Her call probably had something to do with the energy crisis. Presumably, she still lived in her apartment in Rosslyn, a high rise neighborhood in Arlington, Virginia across the Potomac from Washington. What he saw on Chinese television corroborated the speed in which the Eastern Seaboard metropolitan areas were reportedly sliding into chaos. This time, the heavy hand of the Chinese government propaganda machine wasn't needed to portray "capitalist decadence" in an unfavorable light. International business channels were also delivering the same images in their saturation coverage of the situation in America and elsewhere. The images didn't lie.

During the recent fall and winter months, Americans began to go hungry, and instances involving elderly shut-ins and the poor dying of exposure or malnutrition were reported in northern urban areas. Particularly hard hit were the growing number of refugees around the nation's rising tidewater areas. Swaths of Louisiana and the Piedmont area had been inundated repeatedly during a lengthening hurricane season worsening rising water levels caused by melting polar ice and ocean water expansion as water temperatures increased.

Vincent recalled the Latin phrase he had learned from one of his texts at Quantico—*in extremis*. It meant "at the point of death."

He assumed that, whatever Grace's fate, she was sharing it with the man she had begun to date by the time he got his orders to Beijing. Gossip emailed from a Quantico classmate informed Vincent that Grace's companion was a partner in a prominent Washington law firm. He would have some assets and could do more for Grace than Vincent could, especially from seven thousand miles away. Vincent felt guilty under his present circumstances of relative comfort, courtesy of the Peoples' Republic.

He looked at his watch and converted Beijing time to Washington time. It was way too late to call Grace now. He decided to call her just before he went to bed. That would be tomorrow morning her time.

The other voicemail message was not a surprise. It was from the assistant to Liu Chee Hwa, the Superintendent First Class of the Beijing Police section assigned to provide security for the foreign embassies in Beijing. Conventional wisdom among the foreign embassies held that Liu's monitoring of foreign diplomats extended to electronic surveillance of their private residences. Since every landlord in China is a part of the government, the Beijing government has ample opportunity to bug every hotel room, office or apartment of its choosing. Liu's secretary left a phone number at which Vincent could reach Superintendent Liu. Vincent picked up the land line phone and dialed the number.

Liu's secretary answered in English, revealing that the police phone system had a caller-ID function that revealed the foreign identity of the incoming caller.

"Yes, Captain Long. One moment please for Superintendent Liu."

After a moment, the familiar, baritone voice came on the line in excellent English acquired from his undergraduate years at Berkeley.

"Ah, Captain Long, good day. How are things back home?"

Liu was too sophisticated for his question to be devoid of sarcasm. He often chided Long for America's failure to plan for the shortages it was now facing. Countless delegations of American diplomats had visited Beijing since President Nixon "opened" China in 1972, each pointedly urging China to adopt free market "reforms" as the solution to an exponentially expanding trade imbalance, currency distortions and other problems. Those problems, however, were all America's problems, and China uniformly declined to abandon, against its self-interest, its planned economy to suit the purposes of the profligate Americans. Liu could not resist his barbed inquiry, couched though it was in an innocent expression of concern.

"Hello Superintendent," Long said. "Well, things have been better in the States as you have probably heard. Our vast middle class is preoccupied with its own problems so they haven't got much enthusiasm for buying things. I imagine China's exports are suffering as a result. Are many Chinese being laid off these days?"

Liu apparently judged that an exchange of provocations was not going to be fruitful, so he ignored Long's riposte and got to the point.

"Perhaps, Captain, you are aware that two days ago, a jumbo oil tanker from the Persian Gulf was hi-jacked in the Strait of Malacca. The news reports say that it was the act of pirates, but we know that is not true. I wonder what you have heard of this incident." Liu stopped and waited.

"Yes, I have seen some media reports about it, but that's all," Vincent lied. "Why do you say it wasn't pirates? Indonesian and Malaysian pirates have been a serious problem for shipping in the Strait for centuries. In recent years, they've taken tankers and siphoned off oil many times."

"That is true, Captain Long, but our Ministry of Transport officials have debriefed the crew of the tanker. The crew were apparently put in a lifeboat by the attackers and found yesterday morning in Malaysian waters. They said the attack boats appeared to be new and well equipped and the men in them were in a black costume with their faces covered like *ninja*. One of the crew, the Chief Engineer, was kept on board and has not been heard from. We are aware of no pirate activity that fits this—how do your police call it—MO?"

Long considered for a moment. Adding Liu's information to the solar disturbances which, according to Jerry McMasters, prevented U.S. satellite monitoring of the incident, Long's anxiety level increased from mild to medium.

"That is strange," he said finally. "Do you have any working theories about the incident? Do you need our help?"

"Well, to state the obvious, Captain, if the perpetrators are not ordinary criminals, they must be agents of a state. Some states find themselves in very short supply of oil presently. This may be an act of war by such a state against the People's Republic of China."

Liu had just raised the ante big time. *War.*

"I see the logic in your suspicion of a possible government involvement, but there must be a great number of national and commercial oil companies who are desperate for oil. Besides, that tanker can't stay lost forever. It has to be registered somewhere to operate and the country of registry will know its hull and engine numbers, where it was built and the like. Sooner or later, the pieces will come together, and you will know who was behind it."

He waited and then added, "Why would you be raising your concerns about this question with me? There are officials in your government who can discuss matters of such importance with their counterparts in our State or Defense Departments."

"Yes, of course. Your Ambassador has been called to the Foreign Ministry also, but I want to advise you at our level that the Embassy personnel of certain countries, including yours, will be restricted in their movements until further notice. They will need permission from my office in order to travel outside of Beijing. All commercial visas and activities of the American consulates in China are suspended until further notice. Americans in China on business visas should depart immediately as those visas will be cancelled within forty eight hours."

Long thought about the man visiting the Embassy. He would have to find him and relay this information.

"To be clear, are you claiming that there is a connection between the tanker's disappearance and the Government of the United States?"

Liu responded, "My government has asked yours for information tracking the hi-jacked tanker because of the satellite tracking capability your government has. None has been provided. American State Department officials said that solar disturbances prevented the American satellites from having good images in the area. Chinese satellites saw only small disturbances. This lack of cooperation from the American side is a matter of serious concern to our Government. These new measures are therefore required."

Long's urge to debate with his adversary was condition reflex. "Your government can do the tracking itself using its own satellites without assistance from the American Government. So what is the problem?"

Long was sure he knew the answer to his own question, so his asking it was merely a further provocation. His understanding was that the Chinese satellite system was not as sophisticated as that of the United States. Liu could not admit that, however.

"You have my message, Captain Long. The restrictions are in effect immediately and enforcement will be strict. We will, of course, know if any of your staff or visitors deviate from their normal routes within the city. If they do, they will be detained."

Long noted the implication in Liu's threat that the electronic surveillance of the Embassy staff and its visitors extends to the vehicles in which they travel.

"I'll report this conversation to the Ambassador immediately, Superintendent. I'm sorry about this regrettable development."

"Goodbye, Captain," were Liu's only words before hanging up.

Vincent bolted out of his chair and headed for the First Secretary's office out of his instinct for adherence to the chain of command, but the First Secretary was not there. He proceeded to the Ambassador's office and told his special assistant that he needed to speak to the Ambassador about an emergency. She hesitated and then stood up and walked into the Ambassador's office, closing the door behind her. A minute later, the door reopened, and she asked if he would wait just a minute while the Ambassador concluded a meeting.

He gazed out at the high rise silhouette of the great city across the broad roadway that ran past the Embassy. Short, iconic, wrought-iron fences lined the curb facing this and other major roadways in what would be an extravagantly expensive landscaping design element in America. In view of the abundance of iron and manpower in China, however, these decorative fences were commonplace. Immaculately pruned trees along the roadway were beginning to leaf out as spring came to North China. Soon, suffocating dust storms from the high plains of Mongolia would make their appearance as low pressure systems migrated up from the tropical China Sea and began their weather-making ballet with the dry, cold air from Mongolia over the city.

The door to Ambassador Marshall Pickford's inner office opened, and Jerry McMasters, Bill Serra, the First Secretary, and the blonde man Long had seen earlier, exited. McMasters and the blonde man each glanced at Vincent and started to walk toward the door to the hall.

Speaking to the three men about to enter the hallway, Vincent raised his voice.

"Excuse me, gents. Bill and Commander McMasters, you may want to stick around and hear the news I have for the Ambassador because it will affect you. Your guest could be affected as well."

They stopped and looked puzzled. The Ambassador looked angry.

Long extended his hand to the blonde man. "Vincent Long, Marine Security Detachment. I wonder if you would wait here for a second while we have a word."

The blond man smiled slightly and shook hands.

"Name's Sam Johnson," he said. "Good to meet you." He looked at McMasters with a puzzled expression but saw only uncertainty in McMasters' face.

"Sure, I'll wait here."

Sam Johnson, yeah, right. Every time Vincent had run into a spook attached to one of Long's units in the Marine Corps, he had been identified only as "Sam" or "Joe." *This guy has to have a passport with a name, so it's Sam Johnson. Not subtle.*

Inside the Ambassador's office, Vincent related his conversation with Superintendent Liu and recited the new restrictions.

"That's probably why I've been summoned to meet with the Foreign Ministry in half an hour," Pickford said. Vincent confirmed it by relating Liu's comment to that effect.

Getting back to the new restrictions, Vincent continued. "Of course, this is China we're talking about, and these restrictions are not written down anywhere. They can be stretched and twisted to suit the discretion of those enforcing them. So our people may be stopped by the police, and they may be harassed even if they are just traveling to and from their residences. Does anyone know the travel plans of Mr. Johnson? Is he just arriving?"

It was Jerry McMasters who answered. "He is just leaving. Literally headed for the airport. This shouldn't be an issue for him." McMasters offered nothing more in the way of information about the man. "I'll tell him about this development and make sure he makes his flight out."

The Ambassador now looked even angrier. Vincent decided to linger in the Ambassador's office after the others left to see what he could pick up. He had served in the Embassy for almost a year of Pickford's tenure, and they had gotten on well. It didn't hurt that Pickford was also an ex-Marine.

Marshall Pickford had been appointed by the President after a long and distinguished career in agribusiness, culminating with his posting as Secretary of Agriculture in the previous administration. He was a member of the other party, but the President had opted for an expert on the export of American farm products, especially to China and the rest of Asia, over considerations of patronage to major donors. Pickford had worked painstakingly and relentlessly, with measurable success, to open more doors to the importation of American farm products. China would not relent, however, on its protectionist policy to bar or severely limit foreign products from competing with those produced in China.

At the moment, Vincent wondered why the Ambassador was so obviously irritated after his meeting with his recent visitors. He decided to probe.

"What odds would you give me, sir, that Sam Johnson isn't really that fellow's name?"

The Ambassador stood staring at the papers on his desk and absentmindedly smoothing his full head of silver hair.

"Mr. Johnson's card says that he is a consultant to the energy exploration industry. He was meeting with the Ministry of Science and Technology about an exploration joint venture. Running seismograph crews out toward the Caucasus."

"That doesn't sound like the sort of joint venture the Chinese do," Vincent offered. "They have their own exploration capability. They supply half of their oil and gas needs from within the country already."

"Well, it turns out that the Chinese lack some critical technology having to do with deep seismology and fracking wells. So, to explore hydraulic fracking many thousands of feet down in tight rock, they need this technology, hence, they are considering a joint venture. Apparently, the American oil and gas industry wrote the book on it."

"But to do a joint venture with the PRC, an American company will have to give its cutting edge technology—patents, trade secrets, equipment and the like—to Chinese partners who may eventually compete with them. What do they get in return? American oil companies aren't going to be allowed to export any of China's oil."

"Apparently the American, ah, let's call them investors' thinking is that oil is oil. Participating American oil companies could earn credits for oil reserves pledged to China in places where U.S. bound tankers could pick it up, for example, in the Black Sea after moving by pipeline from the Caucuses. The market for oil is global."

"I may have misjudged Mr. Johnson, sir. It sounds creative."

"Well, that doesn't mean his name is really Johnson. Covers are always plausible. Did he look like a geophysicist to you? And would a geophysicist stop by my office to tell me—*tell* me—that the commercial officer of the Embassy would not have a role to play in the joint venture activities—that those activities would be need-to-know only."

Long pursed his lips. "Why would the naval attaché be his contact in the Embassy for a commercial drilling venture?"

"Oh, well, this stuff goes on," said Ambassador Pickford, shrugging and supplying no answer. "What irritates me is that when these black ops blow up, the Embassy and the State Department have to clean up the mess. Also, we don't know whether the work we do dovetails with what the spooks are doing or not. If their adventures turn to dust, our credibility has to be built up all over again from scratch."

The Ambassador walked to his desk and sat down.

"Okay, Vincent, you'd better get the word out on the new travel restrictions and the consular closings, chop-chop. I'll pass it on to the Secretary of State."

"Yes, sir."

Back in the elevator, he wondered what misgivings about the blond man and his activities the Ambassador had. Anyone participating in a joint venture of the kind just outlined would have access to good, timely information about China's oil exploration and planning. That intelligence would be valuable to people—or nations—vitally interested in the world market for oil. Why would such data be too secret for the Embassy?

Vincent headed toward the First Secretary's office and stuck his head in to confirm that an immediate all-hands meeting was being called so that Embassy staff could be briefed on their new travel limitations. Then he called the front gate security post and told the duty sergeant that no Embassy staff was to leave the Embassy until further notice. He acknowledged the duty sergeant's report that a male visitor has just departed for the airport.

CHAPTER

4

Vincent returned to his small one bedroom apartment late. Three of the Embassy's employees were stopped by police as they walked home, and all three called Vincent at the time as instructed. In each case, it took a phone call to Superintendent Liu to allow the employees to proceed to their nearby apartments. Liu said that there would likely be initial "confusion" about what travel would be permissible for Americans in Beijing.

He opened the window in the small, stuffy, room as far as possible. The smell of Chinese spices and hot oil pushed into his apartment along with the mild spring air. Chinese opera drifted up from another apartment's open window facing the concrete courtyard at the rear of the building. Three boys were kicking a soccer ball in random triangulation under the dim light of the courtyard and loudly taunting each other. The high whine of an underpowered motor scooter passing in the alley momentarily drowned out the courtyard noise and then faded away.

A glance at his watch told Vincent that the neighborhood restaurants would be closed now, but the aromas of fried food made him acutely aware that he was hungry. He settled for some instant noodles from the cupboard above the microwave. As he slurped the noodles with chop sticks, Chinese style, he wondered if Grace wanted to talk about something that he didn't want the Chinese state security apparatus to know about. He judged it unlikely. Any government eavesdroppers would probably enjoy a narration about harsh living conditions in Washington, but he didn't care about that. It seemed unlikely that she would get personal.

He keyed in her number. After four rings, he got her answering machine. That meant she had electricity at her place, at least at the moment. If the phone had been out of order, he would have heard a busy signal. He left a message that he was returning her call, that he hoped she was coping well in the circumstances, and that she should call him back on his cell phone or, if he did not answer, his office land line again. He left his cell number.

After hanging up, he opened his small refrigerator and pulled out two bottles of Tsing Tao beer. The first one went quickly.

***

"If I were running for President of the United States …," he paused for the laughter and applause that followed his trademark opening. "I'm not, of course, as I have made clear many times."

The amplified sound of his voice overrode the dying laughter and filled the Empire Room of the Intercontinental Hotel in Los Angeles.

"I couldn't possibly get elected, saying the things I do. That's why I can't be considered a candidate. But if I were, I would use the emergency powers of the Office of the President to turn this thing around. Thirty dollar a gallon gas is obscene!"

Aaron Grey, the senior Senator from Oklahoma, fairly screamed the current price of gasoline, and the World Affairs Council audience roared its agreement.

"And that is if you are lucky enough to find some on your assigned day and have the stamina to wait in line long enough to buy it. That price only partly reflects the true value of oil; it also reflects the market's perception of scarcity. The Russians are rationing their oil and gas partly to inflate the world market price to which their contracts with Europe are indexed, and perhaps partly to conserve their resources in the face of forecasted long term shortages-its oil industry being the only important industry it has. The Saudi regime's collapse in an orgy of Wahhabi-driven revolutionary jihad capped the perfect storm of oil shocks that propelled us into this crisis. Wahhabi extremism is destabilizing the Emirates and Qatar as we speak and has curtailed their oil exports.

"The Saudi regime's collapse may or may not be a short term problem. Their successors in power will eventually need to sell oil in order to support themselves, but in the interim of unknown duration, the shortfall in oil on the supply side is considerable. If the Emirates go the same route, the picture is even uglier. Recall the so-called Arab Spring twenty years ago. The Shi'a-Sunni civil wars that grew out of America's destabilization of the region by replacing a secular Sunni regime with a fundamentalist Shi'a regime in Iraq continue to this day unabated.

"Like an ocean swell that feels the gradient of the shoreline and builds into a breaking wave, oil prices rose suddenly as the markets perceived scarcity. And with the violence of a breaking wave, the market broke and roiled. In just eight months, the great American economy went from the envy of the world to a shambles. We hit peak oil two years ago enabling the experts to project consumption and production rates into the future. Scarcity was already upon us and the ship of state has been scraping along the bottom ever since. When you add energy shocks like these to chronic scarcity, we're toast."

Grey detached the mic from its stand on the lectern and walked out to the edge of the stage. He stared at the audience without speaking long enough to make them uncomfortable. Taking advantage of this rapt attention, he delivered the centerpiece of his speech.

"The oil and natural gas industries, indeed, all mineral rights to energy sources in this country, must be nationalized."

In the audience, heads shook in disagreement and shock, and the sound of hissing could be heard. Grey raised his voice.

"Not regulated like a public utility. Not subjected to price controls. Nationalized!"

A scattering of applause broke out, interrupted by catcalls of "No! No!" A shout of "Socialist!" punctured the falloff of applause.

"Yes! Yes!" Grey challenged his deniers. "Those industries and mineral rights must be owned by you, the public, and operated by the Federal Government as is the case in many other countries. This crisis has been building steadily for years. The energy industry has done nothing to prepare for it because energy companies have a powerful incentive to exploit the assets they have at high prices. Their soaring profitability confirms this fact. They do it because they can, and it's in their interest to do it. That has to stop.

"We have long known the ugly underbelly of unrestrained capitalism. It has been regulated over the years to curb its excesses since the late nineteenth century. But it has been allowed to continue as the basis of our economic system because of our belief that private ownership of the means of production and free markets are the most efficient and most beneficial aspects of our economy. However, we have learned the limits of that faith. We now know that private ownership of mineral rights does not meet our requirements for equitable energy resource allocation and conservation. Imagine an oil company's managers increasing its R & D budget for the development of alternative energies and selectively dialing back production to conserve its reserves. Why, they would be hung in effigy by the shareholders."

Strong applause broke out this time, overwhelming the level of hissing from those disagreeing with Senator Grey. Grey smiled and made no gesture to quiet the applause.

"To state the obvious, energy industry management was unprepared for this day. These companies have extracted oil and gas from the earth as fast as they possibly could. And we are complicit. We have obligingly consumed their fuels in ever increasing amounts. Well, we have all been hoist on our own petard."

Grey wagged his finger in the air to emphasize the cliché.

A florid-faced man and his wife conspicuously stood up and awkwardly climbed over others in their row. Grey watched them struggle out of their row and then hurry up the aisle to the exit door. A scattering of others around the auditorium followed their lead.

Gray watched them, smiling, and whispered, *sotto voce*, to laughter, "They must be late for the theater."

He quickly resumed, spreading his arms as if appealing to his listeners.

"We don't blame the industry. It has done nothing it hadn't been incentivized to do. We are *all* to blame. We have unwisely delegated to these companies an unwarranted amount of power to manage our precious energy assets in the collective interest—something they don't know how to do. But we're in crisis mode now. Going forward, the use of existing energy assets and future energy development must accomplish two objectives. First, non-essential uses of energy should be discouraged in order to conserve energy and mitigate ongoing environmental ruin. Second, alternative energy technologies must be implemented now by government initiative whether or not the cost of their output can initially compete with that of fossil fuels."

The Senator from Oklahoma paused and stared over the heads of the audience as the applause built. He knew the effect his words would have in his home state of Oklahoma—a state whose economy is defined by oil and gas. He knew also that the energy industry would turn on him with all their fury to prevent his reelection after this. He would have no more than the remaining eighteen months of his six year term to accomplish his objective.

"Remember folks, we've had a lot of bad training. Central planning by government has long been an object of ridicule. Not only have we failed to do the acutely necessary strategic planning for this era of shortages; we are hostile to the very idea of planning for it!

"Many nations reserve mineral rights to the sovereign. They do it irrespective of their democratic forms of government, civil rights protections, and economic systems granting the liberty to conduct other businesses privately and for profit. The old paradigm that all collectivist policies were discredited by the collapse of the Soviet Union has itself been discredited by the success of the collectivist policies of China in planning for energy shortages and implementing remedial programs. China's economy is headed for recession as its exports decline precipitously in this downturn; however, it shows no sign of collapse. That cannot be said of America."

A collective gasp arose from the audience.

"It is a simple fact that there are too few resources to support the earth's populations. Housing and office space for them eliminates productive land. Heating and cooling them pollute our air with greenhouse gasses and skew our climate. Transportation systems connecting all those buildings and supplying the people in them with consumer goods, themselves manufactured with vast expenditures of energy, do likewise.

"Increasingly, world populations must be fed industrial food—crops grown by energy intensive monoculture dependent on fertilizers that create ever-expanding dead zones where our rivers empty into the ocean.

"All we have to do to see our country completely dissolve into chaos, anarchy and a mass die-off is to keep doing what we are doing. Perpetual resource wars will likely be our fate—if we survive as a nation. Charting the course I am suggesting involves wrenching change—a one hundred eighty degree turn away from many of our traditions. But it is a necessary response to a world that we have created. We have failed to consider the consequences of our actions, even though they were readily foreseeable to anyone who cared to see them. The course correction that I am urging is a giant step backward in the right direction."

Grey's audience was now murmuring loudly. Many angry faces looked back at him in the sea of faces talking excitedly among themselves.

"I'm just the messenger folks. But, to assure our continued survival as a free and democratic nation, my message is: elect a President and like-minded Senators and Congressional representatives who can be trusted to do the right thing. If I were running for President, you may be sure that I would work to that end. Thank you."

A scattering of applause started up and dropped off to the same loud crowd murmur, accented by booing. The booing, in turn, triggered competing applause and shouts of "hear, here" as the progressives and conservatives in the audience vied with one another. Grey was joined from the wings of the stage by the President of the host World Affairs Council who attempted to make herself heard over the din.

"If I could have your attention please ....Your attention please ...."

Eventually, amplified audio triumphed over the crowd noise as she invited those who had a ticket for the reception to proceed to the adjacent room of the hotel.

Grace Long scanned the faces of the audience and tried to overhear comments of those near enough to her to be audible and lip-read those who were not. She could perceive only uniform anxiety on their faces. Many of the reactions that reached her were angry, but much of that anger seemed to be more directed toward the current state of the country and the imagined effects of the extreme proposal they had just heard than toward the speaker himself.

An elegantly dressed woman remarked to a cluster of people in the aisle nearby that the Senator's speech was "something that needed to be said." Her remark drew no rebuke from those around her. Grace would be certain to make that point in the article she would shortly forward to her editor.

CHAPTER

5

Back in the hotel room after the reception for Senator Grey, Grace called her apartment in Rosslyn for messages. Vincent's, returning her call, was the first. She wrote down his mobile number. The other one from her mother in Denver had been cut off in mid-sentence. That told her that the power in her building had gone out while her mother was speaking, but that it was on again now.

A card placed on top of the mini-bar unit next to the desk apologized for the absence of refreshments, citing "ongoing interruptions" of deliveries to the hotel. She rejected the thought of walking to a convenience store in the next block to stretch her legs and pick up some snacks. A woman on the street at night alone, especially a well-dressed one, became a magnet for the desperate. Besides, the store was probably out of much of its inventory even if it was open. Grace looked in her purse and found the mints she purloined from the reception and sucked on one of them while she sorted through the evening's events in her mind.

At the reception, Council members eager to challenge the Senator's views on the need for nationalizing the energy industry had pressed around him, overwhelming his staff's efforts to limit each one to the standard two minutes. Grey had stood at the center of the throng looking as relaxed and pleased as his staff looked uncomfortable. He seemed to relish his new notoriety, no doubt aware that this level of attention and buzz translated into political capital that even money couldn't buy.

The mainstream media, fearful of being judged disreputable by its peers, had previously dismissed him as idiosyncratic and too underfinanced to be taken seriously. Now, however, she was going to have to compete for access to Grey. Grace had heard comments among Grey's staff that contributions were flowing slowly into his campaign. Perversely, the contributions he did receive were from oil and gas interests eager for access to the Senator to lobby against his proposals and monitor the threat that he posed. She wondered whether this speech would kick-start a flow of contributions from the environmentalists and progressives.

Grace had positioned herself just outside the jostling crush of bodies surrounding Grey, but close enough to overhear exchanges with the Senator. He caught her eye and grinned once as if to say, *How about this?*

Questioning of the Senator by the ticket holders cycled within a narrow range of discussion points. Grace heard many exclamations that there had to be a better way to respond to this crisis than the un-American course the Senator was proposing. To this, Grey would challenge the speaker by saying, "And that way would be what?"

After the Senator's staff finally extricated him from the crowd and they left, Grace sat down with her tablet at a table on the periphery of the Empire Room where her racing mind emptied itself into an e-document describing what she had seen and heard. With a click of the send button, she met her deadline for the next series installment for *Insider On Line.*

Grace's arrangement with Grey allowed her to follow him around and acquire the deep background needed to write an authoritative series on "What Makes Senator Grey Run?" She was attracted by the fact that his calls for government controls of energy seemed to fit the current crisis, and by the fact that it ran exactly counter to the views of his constituency. She had sold the proposal to Grey's staff as an intimate portrait of this extraordinary non-campaign by the quixotic Senator from Oklahoma. Grey and his staff accepted her proposal, probably because no well-known reporters seemed to want to cover him at the time.

Her association with Grey had enabled her to get on the plane with him to Los Angeles. The shortage in aviation fuel made private charters impossible, and the scheduled commercial airline flights had been booked for weeks. The influence of Grey's staff with the airline's government affairs office in Washington, however, got them enough seats for their small entourage.

Whatever calories provided by the meager hors d'oeuvres at the reception had long since burned off. Now, with only coffee and wine in her stomach, Grace felt light-headed and shaky. She called room service and learned that the only thing available was a meatless quesadilla. The hotel had a supply of cheese on hand and they were still getting tortillas from Mexican suppliers in Los Angeles. She ordered two.

Grace next dialed Vincent's cell phone number. He answered after the first ring.

"Hi. It's me. Sorry I missed your call. I'm in LA."

She felt the need to slow down and get her nerves under control.

"Gracie, it's good to hear your voice. How are you getting along? Are things as bad there as we read over here?"

"They're bad in Washington, and now it's getting that way here on the left coast. Nothing really works anymore, and all the stuff you need every day is in short supply. The crime is the worst part, though. It's like Dodge City sometimes. I may get myself a cute little pistol and start packing. I hear they make them in pastel colors."

"I see your sense of humor is intact, so you must be toughing it out okay."

"It's just gallows humor. Toughing it out is for Marines. I didn't sign up for that." She regretted that comment as soon as she said it.

Vincent changed the subject. "Well, you must have plenty to write about," he said. "Oh, by the way, in case you are about to reveal any state secrets, you can't assume that this conversation isn't being monitored by the Peoples' Republic."

"Great," she said. "Terrific."

"It goes with the territory, so to speak. Anyway, it is actually kind of fun to give them a zinger once in a while. Drop something like 'I hear that China has won its bid to hold the next Winter Olympics on Hainan Island.'"

Grace laughed and relaxed.

"I get it. It's the tropical island in the South China Sea, right? I wonder if they get your sense of humor. So, what are you doing for female companionship over there, Vincent? Are you able to date the locals?"

"Not really. The Chinese ministries I deal with have plenty of government girls around, but the obvious inhibitions are mutual. I meet the occasional foreign embassy staffer or American businesswoman who has contacts with the Embassy, but it's not a deep pool. How about you? Are you still with your lawyer friend?

Grace wondered how Vincent even knew about him. *Jungle drums.*

"No. There were too many sharp elbows in that relationship. Most of them mine, probably." She laughed.

"Get outta town," Vincent said. "Impossible."

Neither one of them could think of anything to pursue on that subject. Vincent spoke first.

"You said you're in LA. You can get on commercial flights?"

"Well, celebrity reporters like me can. I'm doing an in-depth piece on Senator Aaron Grey from Oklahoma for *Insider On Line*. It is kind of a big break for me to get this access. I pestered Grey's office for an up-close-and-personal piece ever since he made his first If-I-Were-Running-For-President speech to the American Medical Association convention in Baltimore last year. He finally relented because he knows the only way to reach young voters—the demographic that seems to be most open to his radical views—is on line. Anyway, I get constant access to his office, and I'm serializing my reporting. Because he is so controversial, my reporting has a decent following—she says modestly. Grey's staff got me on the plane to LA for his speech before the World Affairs Council in LA tonight. Would you believe he proposed nationalizing the oil and gas industries along with all of the country's energy mineral rights? He proposed it to all these establishment types. Sucked the air right out of the auditorium, it did."

"Hey, I'm impressed by your scoop," said Vincent. "I always knew you were a gamer."

Vincent's gracious comment was a shift from his attitude when they were divorcing, a fact not lost on Grace. The root cause of their divorce had been his expectation that her career would be subservient to his when the two conflicted. She was told that a Marine officer needs a wife who understands and supports the demands of his career. His call to duty becomes her call to duty. Grace simply refused such a role. Now, he was acknowledging her independent success.

"Why, thank you Vincent. That's sweet."

"Not at all. I'm happy for you, and I'll be on pins and needles to see your report. I haven't seen *Insider On Line*. I'll check out its archives. We don't hear too much about Grey over here."

Grace shuffled through her papers and removed a page on which she had made some notes.

"I wanted to talk to you about some background on China. If any of this is subject matter that seems like something we shouldn't talk about over the phone, just say so. I don't think any of it should be cosmic top secret, but what do I know?"

"Let's find out. Shoot."

"Senator Grey makes a point of saying that China has a big advantage over the U.S. in accessing oil on the world market. I was wondering whether that strikes you, a resident of Beijing, as true. Not for attribution, of course, but do you agree with him?"

"Yes, I do. America has its own domestic sources of oil for maybe seventy percent of its needs—that's up from sixty percent before the fracking boom—and is bidding on the world market for the rest. I gather that some domestic oil isn't going to domestic refineries at all. The oil companies have an interest in selling it on the world market at the highest prices they can get and can get permits to export it. Since oil is easily transportable, domestic oil prices roughly track world market prices.

"The Department of Defense invites bids from the country's oil companies to supply its needs, but it pays discounted world market prices. I gather that the companies sell it on a preferential basis. So what is available for domestic civilian use is limited and is much less than what is needed.

"China, on the other hand, has long cultivated the Persian Gulf suppliers, along with Russia and some other oil regimes with which the American Government has had troubled diplomatic relations. China signs long term contracts with those countries and doesn't give a rip about their politics. It gets preferential access to their oil. China also built pipelines into Siberia and the Caucuses and has long term contracts for those sources. And, it uses dollars from its vast trade surplus with America to outbid us. So, because of its forward planning, plus its still heavy use of coal, China has a much larger percentage of its energy requirements being met than does America."

"Okay, so why is the U.S. so slow to lock up its own sources?"

"Washington didn't try to counter China's acquisitiveness at first, because it seemed natural. Even Washington recognized that it handed the role of being America's manufacturer over to China beginning as far back as the mid-1980s. Whatever the wisdom of that policy, our government knew that China needed large amounts of energy to manufacture the goods consumed by Americans."

"So we were surprised by this trifecta of shocks to the world oil market?"

"Pretty much. Hitting peak oil recently got their attention, but it was too late. The recent shocks then turned scarcity into this crisis, especially the Saudi collapse. My personal opinion is that there are several combinations of shocks that could coincide to cause these conditions. There isn't just one perfect storm scenario; there are several. The Federal Government, though, seems to lack the capacity to think these things through and then take action. On the corporate side, our behavior is based on short term rewards—you know, produce and consume for fun and profit to the exclusion of all other things. Shame on us."

"China uses coal, why don't we use coal too?"

"America has coal, but coal fired power plants are environmentally less desirable so we've been phasing them out and not building more new ones or working on cleaning up coal combustion. The hydraulic fracking hustle twenty years ago figured into that. I say hustle because the fracking pioneers launched a massive and successful PR campaign to trash coal so that the market share for gas would increase as power plants shifted from coal to gas. They argued that gas combustion produces less carbon dioxide than coal combustion. But everyone forgot to factor in all the methane being released directly into the air by fracking. The drillers say their well construction methods are proven, but they aren't. They fail all the time. Methane is a way worse pollutant than carbon dioxide as a greenhouse gas, but it doesn't have the sulfur pollutants that coal does.

"Anyway, China knows that it needs coal, and it builds thousands of coal plants, to hell with the environment. We can't convert oil-fired power plants to coal overnight, and even if we could, we can't reliably get the coal to the power plants by train without diesel fuel from oil required by train locomotives. Bottom line: China can meet its energy needs, but they breathe sulfurous air. Our air is better, but we have to freeze and starve in the dark."

"What about Japan? Does America compete with Japan for oil?"

Vincent paused. Grace assumed that he was sorting out what of his knowledge was acquired from classified sources and what was not. While she waited, Grace took a bite of quesadilla and chewed it unenthusiastically.

Finally, he responded. "I heard a talk here by an economist for a Japanese bank in the Mitsubishi *keiretsu*—sorry, it means family of companies—in which he said that America has recently supplied some oil to Japan stipulated for use in making electronic devices and parts for the U.S. military. So, it's a cooperative arrangement to some extent."

Grace noticed the suddenly abbreviated nature of Vincent's commentary, and made a mental note that it occurred when talking about oil supplies to Japan and the Department of Defense. If this subject matter is laced with classified information, it would be pointless to press him on it now.

"So, you confirm that America isn't faring too well in the global market, at least compared to China. Is that the oil companies' fault? Would nationalizing mineral rights increase America's oil supplies?"

"Well, you are going to need a more authoritative source than me on those questions. I'm just a geology major and military grunt that follows this stuff. But it is a truism that nationalizing the industry would insure that use of the domestic supplies could be prioritized as between domestic users and the Defense Department, including their foreign suppliers of critically needed items like Japan. Also, nationalizing energy assets would allow total control of all of them for conservation, environmental, pricing, and allocation purposes. That's in place of private companies seeking to extract and sell the reserves they have to all comers, foreign and domestic, as rapidly as possible."

"Okay," Grace said, "That fits with Senator Grey's ambition to be President. If he were to be elected with a mandate to nationalize the energy industry, he would be one powerful, revolutionary, populist dude. And the country's voters are desperate. I can see something like that getting done. The industry and their lobbyists will flip out, hell, are flipping out, at the idea. I got a whiff of that earlier tonight."

"So, when Grey gave his speech, he did it before a hostile group of fat cats? He's taking it to them?"

"Well, it was to the World Affairs Council, an enlightened bunch, and it was in California. The Hollywood contingent was on board with it, but the Orange county crowd didn't like it one bit. I'm guessing that the country will pretty much split the same way. We'll have to see what happens to Grey's coffers to judge how his idea is playing. The polling business has pretty much withered because the pollsters can't reach people with the power off a lot."

Grace found herself wishing that they were having this conversation in person over dinner in Beijing. Vincent would know some good neighborhood restaurants in Beijing, and she loved Chinese food. She flashed back to their dinners at the Double Happiness Café way out on Sixteenth Street in Washington. On hot nights, they had tables in the alley with a funky canvas cover that protected diners from the rain. She sighed, her mouth watering.

"Tell me something, Grace. Your Senator is from Oklahoma, isn't he? His support, by definition, comes from the oil patch, doesn't it? So what's up with nationalizing the industry that supports his voters and funds his campaigns?"

"I have no idea. It makes no sense to me either. That's one of the fascinating aspects of this guy's non-campaign. A strategy to win the Presidency by turning on his home state business base?"

"Wow. I don't think Niccolo Machiavelli's handbook has a chapter on that."

"Well, Vincent, it's late here, and I've got two cold quesadillas on a tray waiting for me. I'd better sign off and tuck into them before I faint with hunger. Thanks for your input."

"Glad to be of help, if I was. You've got me interested in what you are writing about. This is stuff that is affecting all of us.

"Take care of yourself."

"You too."

CHAPTER

6

A white Toyota pickup truck idled on a track beside Lake Aibi around which the pipeline passed after its descent from the Alatav Pass. Four men dressed in traditional Uighur clothes stood beside the pickup with binoculars scanning the welded pipe strapped on to the tops of pyramidal steel supports. One of the four was not Uighur. He went by the name of Ali, but he was a white foreigner with sandy colored facial hair. He spoke Chinese with the others as they selected portions of the pipe that would be easily accessed when it came time to rig the pipe with high explosives.

The new pipeline snaked over six hundred miles from the Aktobe oil fields in Kazakhstan westward into the Xinjiang autonomous region in northwestern China. Most of it was buried underground, wrapped in its creosote preservative coating, but much of it traversed sand and rock and remained above ground. It was destined for the PetroChina refinery at Dushanzi. At its capacity, it contributed only five per cent of China's oil needs, but the fact that it represented a marginal increase made it an incrementally very valuable share, especially now.

The project had been an important accomplishment of China's central planners. China had to pay the high premium demanded by the Kazakhs to build the pipeline to its Western border, but now the pipeline surged with oil, just as China's need for it peaked. It was production that would now be permanently unavailable to BP, Shell, Chevron, Exxon-Mobil and the other oil majors.

The new pipeline ran over the ancestral homeland of the Uighurs, the last remaining Muslim population to live under Communist rule anywhere in the world. The yoke of the Han Chinese government did not sit easily on the Uighurs, and the on-going enrichment of distant Han Chinese overlords in the east from world trade—riches in which the Uighurs did not share—caused growing conflict. Muslim tribal leaders approached the local Communist party leaders with numerous demands for water projects for irrigation, improved roads and new schools, but the dusty, barren villages remained as they had for centuries.

A new dynamic had been introduced to this mix in recent decades by the Taliban activity in the tribal areas of Pakistan not far away. Uighurs who had been recruited to fight against the Pakistani army in the area grew restive when they returned to China, and a resulting militancy bled over into Xinjiang. Armed bands of radicalized Muslim Uighurs seeking to purify their land from the godless Han Chinese regime had formed spontaneously.

"When can you blow this section?" asked Ali, his blue eyes fixed on the pipeline.

"The high explosive is coming over from Kyrgyzstan through Yining by pack train. Once it gets to Yining, we can use vehicles, and it should happen quickly after that. Assume four days' time. Naturally, we expect our payment first."

Ali patted his satchel.

"Here is the bribe, er, inducement money. In dollars."

He handed the satchel to the Uighur man who had spoken.

"If you call your contact in Peshawar, you will be able to confirm that the rest of the funds have already been received."

The Uighur who spoke for the others said, "The Chinese will be able to rebuild the pipeline within a year. What do you expect to accomplish by this attack on the pipeline?"

"We are sure that the Kazakhs will be anxious to take advantage of the current price spike by selling the oil that would have moved over this pipeline. During the period this line is out of commission, the diversion should be worth many tankers out of the Russian port of Novorossiysk on the Black Sea. That oil would be outside the pool of oil the Russians are rationing and we can do business with Gasprom. And what about you Uighurs?" asked the foreigner. "The Red Army is going to assume that you were involved."

"God willing, we will teach those Han dogs a lesson they will not forget. When our brothers were extradited back to China after being captured by the Pakistani army, Beijing arrested them as terrorists. They were shot in the soccer stadium in Urumqui.

"We will blow up six miles of their pipeline and the last of their welding machines—the only one within a thousand miles. As they bring in replacement pipe and more welding machines, we will pick off a few dozen of their officers to let them know what happens when they insult Islam. Then we will melt away."

Ali nodded. "*Allahu ackbar.*"

The Uighur gave the foreigner a hard look to see if the man's praise of Allah was sincere.

Stoically, the foreigner added, "May Allah guide you in this life and the next."

That seemed to satisfy his companion.

***

At precisely 0400 five days later, a Chinese security guard was reporting for his shift change at the guard house beside Lake Aibi when a series of six explosions occurred at one mile intervals along the pipeline leading to the east. The oil in the pipeline ignited in a series of orange fireballs that illuminated the chaparral like noonday. A column of acrid black smoke boiled off of the fires and then bent toward the east along with the prevailing winds. The two guards looked at each other in amazement. Then, with the dull roar of the fire in the background, one of the guards reached for his radio.

***

Ambassador Pickford returned from his meeting at the Foreign Ministry to which he had been summoned at 10:00 pm. His first action was to put in a call to Foggy Bottom and brief the Deputy Secretary immediately of these developments. His next act was to summon the senior secretaries and attaché staff. Vincent Long joined the meeting in progress after receiving a call from the Embassy while at dinner with his counterparts from the Embassies of Great Britain and Germany.

"Well, Vincent, it looks like we get some unexpected R & R," Commander McMasters said. "Our hosts have given us the boot."

"Who's us? And for what?"

"Us is the military attachés at this embassy."

The Ambassador indicated the northwestern part of China on the conference room wall map.

"The Chinese have a new pipeline that runs from the oil fields in Kazakhstan through the Xinjiang area. Muslim locals that live out there have been pushing back against the Beijing Government on a variety of subsistence issues. Beijing has neglected their needs for decades, probably because the Uighurs don't have anything to give local party officials by way of payoffs.

"Anyway, Vincent, that pipeline was blown up night before last. The Foreign Minister just told me that a party chief in the region was caught with a stash of dollars under his fireplace hearth. He was apparently dealing with some Taliban sympathizers in the local community suspected of blowing up the pipeline. That fellow will no doubt meet his end in one of the local soccer stadiums. Minister Li said the fellow had the distinct impression the perpetrators were being financed by foreigners."

"That's it, sir?" Long said "Because some party boss in Xinjiang was on the take and some home-grown jihadis in their Muslim population, whom they mistreat, are insurgents, they are going to expel American Embassy attachés? That sounds a little crazy."

Pickford folded his lanky frame back into his chair and ran a manicured hand over his hair.

"Minister Li said their Kazakh partners have advised that until the pipeline can be repaired—something that will take many months—the oil consigned to the pipeline for China will be moved by other pipelines to ports on the Black Sea and sold there on the world market. That means the oil majors will buy the crude and no doubt take it to refineries in the West. Minister Li said that this sabotage of their pipeline, as well as the hijacked tanker in the Strait of Malacca, both point to Western beneficiaries. That, in turn, he said, suggests that Western—he used the word Western but he meant American—military adventurism is involved. Beijing doesn't believe that this is all just a drunken walk among lucky pirates and aggrieved nomadic peasants. That is how they get to us."

Long attempted to draw a distinction now between himself and the other attachés. "I'm just a company grade officer in command of a security detachment of Marines. They can't forbid the security detachment from protecting the Embassy, can they?"

"Vincent, as you know, under our law and tradition, the Navy can assign *enlisted* Marines to the Embassy to act under the direct authority of the senior authority present—that would be me. You are an officer and technically not part of the security detachment. You are here as an attaché, and, as an attaché, you can be thrown out at any time. If the American Government doesn't choose to sever relations with China over this development, which I am advised by the Secretary of State that it does not, then we will lose the pleasure of your company until further notice."

Pickford stood again and gathered up his portfolio.

"Of course," he said, "the Chinese military attachés to the PRC Embassy in Washington will also be asked to leave our country. The consulates in both countries remain closed, pretty much choking off bilateral trade that hurts the Chinese side more than ours. Anyway, the tit for tat will taper off and life will go on.

"Meanwhile, you are all on leave, commencing immediately. You can check with your respective headquarters for your next duty assignment. You have to be out of the country by midnight tomorrow night."

Vincent and the other three attachés stood at attention. McMasters and Vincent both spoke in unison. "Aye, aye, sir."

Out in the hall, Vincent couldn't resist taking a shot at McMasters.

"So, Jerry, what do you hear from your friend Johnson? Sam was it? Wasn't he conversant with the subject matter of oil ventures in the Caucuses and Western China?"

The lips on McMasters' pasty face curled into a snarl.

"Watch your mouth, Captain. We all work for the same sovereign. You would do well to assume that others have a broader view than you may have from the counter at which your enlisted men whomp documents with rubber stamps. Have a nice trip home."

McMasters turned and walked toward his office.

Vincent smarted from having been dressed down by McMasters. He had it coming, though. He popped off to a superior officer, and he really didn't know anything for certain. Still, unilateral acts of aggression by the United States against the PRC to obtain crude oil, which the National Security Agency attaché had just failed to deny, didn't pass the nose test.

What the blazes is going on?

Back in his office, he saw a message to call Police Superintendent Liu.

Stand by to get rammed.

***

Police Superintendent Liu was matter-of-fact when Vincent reached him.

"I just want you to know, Captain Long, that China Airlines is able to ticket you and your associates on flight number 312 to Tokyo tomorrow evening. Your airlines can manage only a small number of flights into China these days because of jet fuel shortage in America, and so they have no flights that meet the deadline."

Long already knew that to be true.

"Fortunately, Chinese airlines are able to fly their normal inter-Asia routes because China has adequate fuel stocks locally."

Long could think of no good riposte, so he tried diplomacy.

"Superintendent Liu, I'm sure you know that I have not engaged in any military operations directed against the Peoples Republic. I'm sure you also know that our two countries have a mutual commercial dependency that will keep the U.S-Sino relationship intact despite these temporary problems. I hope we have the opportunity to work together in the future."

Liu was not able to switch gears as nimbly.

"Expulsion of military attachés from the American Embassy will not be the end of the retaliation. Goodbye, Captain Long," Liu said and hung up.

CHAPTER

7

The China Air flight departed Beijing on time and landed three hours later at Tokyo's Narita Airport. An American military escort met the attachés for transfer to the air base at Misawa. As Vincent and the others walked to the ground transportation exit to board their van, few passengers were visible in the vast airport and most food service counters sat dark behind locked security shutters. This glimpse of the spreading economic downturn that frustrated the world's cities constituted the men's re-introduction into a world under which the ground had shifted.

At the Misawa Air Base, each man was on his own in arranging transport back to the United States. Vincent was able to hop an Air Force aerial refueler to Hickam Field on Oahu that same evening. Hawaii seemed as good a place as any to sort out his plans for the next two weeks while he awaited orders. He figured he might as well spend his down time on the beach.

During the flight to Hickam, Long joined the cockpit crew at the invitation of the pilot, an Air Force captain named Parsons. Parsons explained that they were taking a load of aviation gasoline to Hawaii. Over the whine of the engines, he said that the core mission of the squadrons on Hawaii consisted of patrolling the vast expanse of the Pacific Ocean. The Pentagon didn't want any surprise military developments in the Pacific, especially under the current circumstances, so it continued to allocate enough resources for the squadrons in Hawaii to minimally fulfill their mission.

"You're taking aviation gas from Japan to Hawaii?" Vincent asked. "Wouldn't that fuel normally be supplied by refineries or ships in Hawaii?"

"Roger that," Parsons replied, "but these days it's scarce, and we are getting it where we can get it. Japan has been doing some cutting edge work in using biofuels to supplement the hydrocarbons needed to make quality aviation fuel. I think the Defense Department and the Japanese Government do some bartering to try to overcome our respective shortages these days. All I know is that DoD got this allotment, and they want it delivered to Hawaii. So, that is your ticket out of Japan."

And Japan is about to get another big parcel of oil to work with, Vincent thought.

"You'll be surprised when you get back home," Parsons added. "The civilians are really taking it in the shorts."

"I've been reading intel reports and have some idea, but I'm sure experiencing it will be punishing," Long said. "It's not like the weather in Hawaii is going to be a problem, though. And your beaches operate without gasoline."

"Yes, they do, but you're thinking about beaches from the tourist magazines—where they serve you mai-tai's under the banyan tree and all that happy horsefeathers. The beaches ain't like that anymore. In fact, they can be downright dangerous. The Resort at Turtle Bay on the North Shore, for instance, has been taken over by locals who are poaching the turtles up there and selling turtle meat to anyone who will pay their price. The big turtles went from a protected species to stew meat overnight."

"Where the law? Who's minding the store?"

"Local police don't have enough gas for their cars. Oahu officials talked to the Commanding Officer at Schofield about having the army go in and secure the place. The army would have to continue to occupy it or it would just revert back to chaos, so they passed on that. Anyway, the perps are just trying to survive. Most of them are native Hawaiians who think the land is theirs anyway. No one has the stomach to go wage a pitched battle with the squatters and then occupy the place long term. So, it's the Wild West up there."

What was it Grace said things were like—Dodge City?

Vincent sat back in his seat and marveled at this news. It was beginning to dawn on him that his country was not a country at peace anymore. It was more like a rapidly deteriorating battlefield.

His thoughts ran back to his boyhood growing up on the ranch near Los Alamos, New Mexico. He admired his father, a stoic Westerner like the other ranchers in the area—men of few words and an intensely held code of conduct. A man's reputation for honesty, dependability, and competence was never to be squandered by drink or malfeasance. He followed his father's lead by becoming capable in the myriad skills demanded of a rancher—in animal husbandry, crop growing, mechanics, construction and the government programs and financial markets that affected ranching. Vincent's model was a fiercely independent man who was responsible for his family and never breached faith with them or his neighbors.

His father and the other men were mostly military veterans from the days of the draft, and they exchanged stories of their service from time to time—always in seemingly fond, or at least respectful, terms. Their sense of community had been expanded by their military service. They served with people from other parts of the country—people who worked in different fields, came from different cultures, and had different interests. All had pledged their lives for their common good in the abstract, but more immediately, for each other. The men spoke, too, of their time spent in foreign countries in Asia and Europe.

Vincent had an inquiring mind and did well in high school. Later, at the University of New Mexico in Albuquerque, he double majored in geology and political science, specializing in international relations. He spent summers working on seismograph crews in West Texas and New Mexico as a "jug hustler," a worker who placed geophones on the ground in patterns so that a seismic charge could record sonar waves as they bounced off subterranean rock formations, thus mapping them as possible reservoirs for oil and gas. As graduation approached, and not having much of an idea how to use either of his undergraduate degrees, a Marine recruiter gave him the idea of joining the Marine Corps as an officer. Unlike his father's generation, he had no mandatory military obligation, but he had taken to heart their conversations among themselves to the effect that doing away with the draft had been a mistake. Few Americans knew what war meant; and politicians sometimes misused the volunteer military for unjustified purposes. It wouldn't happen, they said, if all American families had a stake in American military adventures like they did when everyone's children served.

When he told his parents of his interest in joining the Marines, his mother was shocked. His father questioned him at length about his motivation and awareness of what was involved, but his father's final words on the subject conveyed approval. "You might as well fly with the finest," he'd said. So Vincent visited the recruiting office in Albuquerque and signed up for the officer candidate program at Quantico. Upon graduation and satisfactory completion of the boot camp for officers, he would be commissioned a second lieutenant.

Boot camp was as grueling for officers as for enlisted men, since the training had the same objective—the making of a basic rifleman. He had been in shape and handled it well. What he hadn't anticipated was his yielding to the Marine mindset. During boot camp, he and his fellow recruits weren't Marines. They were "dirt bags" and "numb nuts." Those that made it through, however, became Marines. It was like achieving immortality. They were in the company of the ones who had gone before them—the ones who had achieved so much at Belleau Wood, at Tarawa, Iwo Jima and Okinawa, at Chosin and Khe Sanh and the rough terrain in Helmand. The ones that had gone before were the ghosts that accompany all Marines for the rest of their lives. They were taught that a Marine would do anything, would die, before failing those who had gone before, before failing his fellow Marines, before failing the Corps. Vincent embraced that tradition like any other Marine.

His first assignment after eight months of officer's basic training was as an infantry platoon leader in Okinawa. A year's duty schooled him in infantry tactics and command protocol for a company of "grunts." After making first lieutenant, he was posted to a company of security troops for the Naval Air Station in Rota Spain. That, in turn, led to a company executive officer's billet in Somalia which had been made vacant by an IED.

The Sunni Arab zealots had continued to morph from one failed state in the Middle East to another over a time span of thirty years. After being driven from Afghanistan and Pakistan, an amalgam of Wahhabi, al-Shabab, Muslim Brotherhood and other terror groups had surfaced in

Syria's civil war and then attempted to establish a caliphate state in Syria and western Iraq. American-led NATO forces and the established governments of both Shi'a and Sunni regimes combined to suppress them. They merely moved to Somalia, another failed state, and resumed their anti-modernist quest. After successfully engineering terrorist attacks in Chicago and Omaha through the recruitment of American passport holding sympathizers from the Somali community in the upper Mid-West, America again invaded the host country-this time Somalia. Vincent's battalion saw action in the Nugaal Valley as the Marines fought to keep the recently discovered oil and gas deposits there from falling in to the hands of the al-Shabab-led terror groups. He won a purple heart when his company came under fire by insurgents who ebbed and flowed across the Ethiopian border in hit and run raids. During his last battle, he was shot twice but wounded only once, as he took one round in the shoulder outside his Kevlar vest protection. The second had been stopped by the vest.

While recuperating in Germany from his shoulder wound, he received word that his parents had been killed in a car accident. They were broadsided by a drunk coming out of an Indian casino outside Tesuque north of Santa Fe. He was granted leave to attend the memorial services with his arm in a sling. In Los Alamos, he made arrangements with a long-time ranch hand, a Pueblo Indian named Joe Martinez, to be a caretaker at the ranch in his absence.

He returned to his unit in time to be rotated back to Camp Pendleton in California with his company where he made Captain. His next orders were to command a training unit at Quantico. He'd been on liberty from Quantico one weekend when he met Grace.

Sudden shaking of the aircraft made him aware that the aircraft was descending to land. The refueler landed roughly in crosswinds at Hickam Field just after sunrise. Once the tanker was secured, Vincent followed the crew to the operations room to check in and from there to the mess hall. The array of hot, plentiful, breakfast food on the chow line steam table looked irresistible. His boot camp discipline quickly returned. *Take what you want; eat what you take.* It was a mantra he'd adopted the day he first heard his drill instructor bark it.

He checked into the BOQ mid-morning, took a shower, and changed into civilian clothes. The Honolulu TV station reported dismal tourist numbers. Commercial flights to and from the mainland and Asia were sharply curtailed. Desperate budget cutbacks forced on the county of Oahu because of severely reduced hotel and restaurant tax revenue crippled services. Even worse, the island's shipping lifeline was not bringing in nearly enough food and other supplies needed by the State's inhabitants. Groceries and supplies were accumulating on the docks at West Coast ports as rolling electric blackouts interrupted the operation of port cranes. Gasoline shortages also delayed truckers shuttling cargo to and from the ports, further increasing the time needed for loading and unloading the ships. These conditions greatly reduced ship turn time. Statements from shipping company management defended their rapidly escalating rates, saying that their high fuel surcharges merely passed along price increases for increasingly scarce fuel oil.

A news clip showed the Director of the State Consumer Affairs Department complaining that hoarding contributed further to the scarcity and high cost of food and consumer goods in Hawaii. Honolulu's mayor was quoted as threatening anyone engaging in such activities with prosecution "to the fullest extent of the law."

Good luck with that.

A live feed of a reporter standing in front of the Mayor's office came on. The reporter quoted the Mayor as urging the military bases at Schofield, Pearl Harbor and Kaneohe in Maui to expand their resupply operations to include civilian goods. The Mayor's message stressed how unseemly it was for the military personnel on the island to be getting their food and medicine needs met at the taxpayer's expense, but the island's civilian population was falling into hyperinflation, deprivation and chaos. The Defense Department, in turn, contended that it lacked the capacity to replace the island's commercial shipping with equivalent airlift, a mode that consumes far more fuel per unit of cargo than the fleet of container ships that serves the Island. The DoD pledged, however, to work with the State of Hawaii's Congressional delegation to develop an emergency relief capability for the State.

Good luck with that, too.

The news broadcast concluded with a series of clips from the outer islands, indicating that conditions there were even worse since most of their consumer goods were shipped via Oahu and at less frequent intervals. The reporter said that outer-island residents were migrating to Oahu in the hope that food and other subsistence goods could be more readily had there. The migration, in turn, worsened the situation in Oahu.

Vincent turned off the television and called the front desk. He learned that to get from Hickam Air Force Base to the Marine Air Base in Kaneohe where he could report for whatever duty they had for him would require a bus to downtown Honolulu. From there, another bus over the Pali highway would take him to Kaneohe.

The next bus downtown was scheduled to leave at 3:45 pm. He was told that most of the buses operated on compressed natural gas. Newer ships that brought LNG to Hawaiian power plants as cargo were also powered by LNG. The older plants that burned fuel oil operated intermittently as oil supplies ebbed and flowed. Since the newer power plants in Oahu were natural gas fired and the community depended on their output, the power plants had priority on natural gas, leaving the supply of natural gas for busses unreliable. Vincent inquired about a car rental, but the person at the front desk just laughed. He said the rental companies stopped renting to tourists. Too many customers abandoned their rental cars if they were unable to find gas.

He hung up and opened the door to his mini-lanai all the way and stretched out on his bunk, luxuriating in the trade breeze. He recalled the threat uttered by Beijing Police Superintendent Liu as his departing benediction. *Expulsion would not be all the retaliation.* He visualized a pipeline snaking across the desert in Northwest China as it exploded and burned when sleep overtook him.

***

Senator Aaron Grey picked up the hand mic and walked out from behind the lectern to face the standing-room-only audience at UCLA, his second major address in Southern California.

"Today, this country is facing a possible paradigm reversal—from private ownership of energy to public ownership. I hope this reversal will occur as the result of reasoned discussion and sound judgment early enough for orderly remediation of this crisis. If not, it will occur hastily, in disorderly collapse as the country's response turns to panic. I stand before you advocating the former. You are free to agree or disagree, as always, but I do urge you to think this problem through, and don't delay too long. This country needs a united response to this new era of shortage in natural resources. The private sector, in the case of energy resources, is the problem. Government, in this case, is the solution. Only government can provide the central planning and public policy driven goals that we desperately need."

A few catcalls and some hissing floated up to the stage. Grey only raised his voice more.

"We can no longer afford to have critical resources ...."

The lights in the auditorium suddenly went out plunging the vast space into compete darkness. The audience murmured in the blackness.

Grey tried to speak into the microphone to urge the audience to stay seated and remain calm until the lights could be restored, but the microphone was dead. He could not make himself heard over the growing din. After thirty seconds, the house lights went back on as the emergency generators kicked in to provide backup power. People on the ends of their rows stood up and began to move to the exits. Then the auditorium was plunged into compete darkness again. This time, the lights did not come back on. After a full two minutes in the pitch dark, shouts arose from the alarmed crowd.

Grace Long stood still in the dark wings of the stage wondering what was happening. Then she remembered that her car key fob had an LED light. She dug the ignition key out of her purse and switched the light on. It emitted a surprisingly bright beam of light, and she moved onto the stage and over to Senator Grey on the stage.

"Senator Grey, it's me, Grace. My guess is that the auditorium security folks are going to take over crowd control, so why don't we get you and your staff off the stage? Who knows what is going on here?"

"Good idea, Grace, and thank you very much for your alert help. Maybe somebody doesn't like my message," he said cheerfully.

Grace laughed. "Could be. You're messing with the electricity gods."

They walked to the stairs at stage left.

One of the university's security staff spoke to the audience via a battery driven bullhorn.

"Ladies and gentlemen, please remain in your seats so that we can evacuate you all safely and in an orderly fashion. Our staff will lead you out with flashlights by row, starting in the rear in just a few moments.

As Grace and the Senator reached the stairs, they ran into Chief of Staff Chuck Haden and Press Secretary Flor Alonzo who had felt their way up to the edge of the stage and along the stage to the stairs in the dark.

"Ah, Senator. Outstanding! I didn't know how we were going to find you in this mess," Hayden said.

"Well, we have my guardian angel, Ms. Long, to thank for that. She appeared at my elbow as if by magic with her cool little light as soon as the power went out the second time. Memo to the file: If we're elected, Ms. Long for Director of FEMA."

Haden had never seemed comfortable with the uncontrolled proximity Grey had granted to Grace. After all, she was a virtually unknown journalist and a potential loose cannon as far as Haden was concerned. Still, her on line news postings had been well written, insightful and, on balance, helpful to the campaign. Now, she had been better prepared in this mini-emergency that he had. He seemed impressed.

"Well done, Grace, and congratulations on the FEMA Directorship," he grinned.

"Not so fast," she countered. "Hanging out in hot, humid, disaster locations is not what floats my boat. I was thinking, like, maybe Paris."

Flor Alonzo took her cell phone from her ear. "This blackout is all over the City and maybe beyond. It appears to be total. Channel 4 says they have no idea yet what the problem is."

"Ah, well then, it couldn't have been a response to my speech," Grey said rubbing his hands.

"No, but it sure underscored your message." Haden pointed out. "Okay, how about we ease over there toward the stage exit where we came in. Flor, call the driver and tell him to come back to the same door as before and pick us up now. I'll tell the university security people so they won't have to worry about you. Then let's see if the hotel has back up power so we can function until the power comes back on. Man, this stuff is getting old," Haden said, picking his way carefully toward an approaching flashlight.

The others grouped around the arc of dim light provided by Grace's key fob and walked over to the door and out into the cool marine air flowing in from the Pacific Ocean. Until they breathed the fresh night air, they hadn't noticed how hot and stale the air inside the auditorium had become.

The limo Hayden had managed to corral from a major donor was waiting outside the door, and they all climbed in as Hayden rejoined them. Grace and Flor sat on the jump seats across from the Senator and Hayden. Flor was back on her cell phone and the others were listening intently to her side of the conversation.

"The whole grid is out? That's pretty much the whole western U.S. isn't it? Wait, you said that power demand wasn't particularly high today, so how does this happen?"

She mouthed to the Senator, "Computers are down." Then she continued talking to her source.

"I thought that's why the World Wide Web was invented, so this crap couldn't happen."

CHAPTER

8

S teady rain, mixed with road grit, deposited an opaque film on the bus
window. Vincent peered out, but it was hard to see where the soaring
Pali ended and the sky began. The bus had been an hour late, but it finally
arrived at the Hickam stop. Its driver announced that there would be one
bus returning from Honolulu that night departing from Bishop and King
at 9:00 pm.

Vincent didn't know what to do in Honolulu. He just wanted to wan-
der around, have a drink, and eat something good. The bus rolled down to
the Nimitz Highway past the Honolulu Airport and then along the light
industrial marina into downtown. The afternoon rain had tapered off on
the leeward side of the island and the sky was clearing. He got off and
walked down Bishop Street to the Aloha Tower. A micro-brewery and
restaurant faced Sand Island across the harbor. He could see a server waiting on some seated people out on the patio. *Perfect*. He walked to the patio
bar and slid onto a stool.

The bartender placed a coaster in front of him almost immediately.
"Afternoon, pilgrim. Want to see a menu?"

"Let's start with whatever ale you have on tap, John, and then we'll
see." Vincent read the barkeep's name off the tag on his aloha shirt.

John brought a tall glass of the brewery's amber martzen and set it on
the coaster in front of Vincent. "We don't see many military in here. They

don't seem to get off the bases as much nowadays, and the beer is a lot cheaper on the base."

Vincent was sure the bartender was reading his Marine haircut. It was cut right down to his skin on the sides and cropped short on top.

"That so? I've been out of the country for a while so I'm not sure how things work with this energy flap going on."

The bartender gestured around the patio and restaurant inside. "Very little happening here these days. We get a few people from downtown in for lunch. Beyond that, it's onesies and twosies. No tourists at all, which was most of our business. They just went poof," he said, snapping his fingers. "This is our flagship joint, so the owner is reluctant to close it, but ...." His voice trailed off. "So what brings you out for a brewski?"

"Enforced idleness. I'm waiting for orders, but everything is running in super slow-mo."

"Well, hang ten and enjoy the wave, as we say here in paradise. But be careful. Especially in the parks."

"Thanks for the tip. Say, John, do house rules permit me to make a cell phone call?"

"Sure thing, bruddah. I don't see anyone close enough to even notice," he said, discretely walking away.

Vincent dialed 411 and took a sip of the draft ale. Eventually his call got through to Marine Corps Embassy Security Group in Quantico. Since he was no longer involved in Embassy security, he was referred to a major on the staff of the G-1 Manpower office at the Pentagon headed by a Lieutenant General reporting to the Commandant. Vincent identified himself by name, rank and serial number. He gave the major a sketch of his situation, and asked whether there were any orders for him. The major put him on hold. After several minutes, he came back on the line.

"Captain Long, we have you in the system, but there are no orders for you yet. We show you on leave. The State Department is still trying to get the military staff of the Embassy back on station in Beijing, but things don't look good on that score. We think it is premature to assign you to another duty station long term, and, as you probably know, it isn't easy to move people around these days. This failure of the power grid out west hasn't helped things any, either. You are on a Marine base now, so you've got three squares a day and a flop. You're temporarily off the radar. Just stand by while they figure this out. Enjoy your leave. I'm sending an email to the Kaneohe base commander as we speak telling him of your presence there and your situation."

Vincent interrupted. "I'm at Hickam Field in Oahu because that's where the Air Force plane landed. I plan to migrate over to the Kaneohe air station by bus tomorrow."

"Fine. Check in with the base commander's office when you get there, but you are pretty much on a frolic of your own. We know how to reach you. Any questions?"

"Yes, sir. You said something about a power grid failure out west. What were you referring to?"

"Well, just tonight, all the western states, except Alaska and Hawaii, lost power. They still aren't back up, and it's causing some problems for the other grids as well. The media has this on its twenty four-seven news cycle. I haven't heard anyone who's able to explain it."

"So everyone is in the dark about it, so to speak," Vincent quipped.

"So, groan, to speak." Vincent could tell that the major enjoyed his pun. "*Semper Fi*, Captain."

"Aye, aye, sir."

"Oh, hang on. I see a note here to have you call Navy Commander Gerald McMasters ASAP." The major gave McMasters' phone number to Vincent and then repeated it. "See you on the beach," he said. "So to speak."

Vincent grinned appreciatively. It was a double entendre referring to both the core mission of the Marines to conduct amphibious landings and Vincent's current location.

Vincent wondered if Grace was alright. Then he wondered why McMasters was trying to reach him. He looked at his cell phone and considered whether to call Grace or McMasters first. If Grace were still in LA, she might be in trouble.

Not that I can do anything about it.

He tapped in Grace's cell phone number first, and after one ring tone, she answered.

"Hey Grace, it's me."

"Vincent! Wow. Twice in one week. How are things in China?"

It was friendly. He liked that.

"Actually, I'm in Hawaii now, and I just heard about the grid failure out west. Are you still in LA or did you get out of there before it went dark?"

"No, I haven't been able to leave, and it's making me crazy. Senator Grey and his chief of staff got a ride on a military plane back to Washington yesterday, but the rest of us are still here coping. Hawaii? What are you doing in Hawaii?"

"Well, the short answer is that the PRC Government ordered all the military attachés out of the country. They think America is conducting military actions against them."

"Well, everyone else is paranoid these days, why not the Chinese government?"

"Even a paranoid schizophrenic can have enemies," he said ambiguously.

Grace laughed.

"Say, Grace, you ought to come to Hawaii. There's no one here, and I'm sitting in a scenic waterfront joint right now having a suds and getting ready to eat a pulled pork sandwich."

"You have food? God, we can't get any decent food. I'm eating nothing but industrial quesadillas. This is just subsistence eating. And everything is *soooo* hard. I couldn't get to Hawaii if my life depended on it. Why don't you come to LA and get me the hell out of here."

"Not much chance of that either, I guess," he said. "I'm waiting for orders in place. So tell me what's happened? What are you doing?"

"I'll tell you what I'm doing. I'm sitting in the lobby of the Los Angeles Museum of Art because a very nice lady in the office is letting me recharge my cell phone. They have a generator that runs on diesel or something, and so they have a bit of power in their office. My life revolves around my cell phone because it is the only way I can be in touch with the outside world. And because it is on all the time, it needs to be recharged all the time, so I spend my waking hours trying to get that done, which isn't easy. And, naturally, the museum cafeteria is closed, so I'm chewing on the biggest carrot that I could score at a Chinese market on the way over here."

Vincent could hear that she was on the verge of tears.

"Blast. Sorry to hear all that. Come to think about it, just because it is printed on this laminated menu I'm looking at doesn't mean they actually have any pulled pork. I may be eating taro roots for dinner for all I know." He couldn't think of anything helpful to say. "Are you still in a hotel? You have a place to stay don't you?"

"Oh, yes. The hotel is keeping open for us and some others drifting in from the local area—stranded people. Their computers are down, the air conditioning is off, the housekeeping staff doesn't show up for work and the hotel cafe serves whatever they can find in the way of food. No one knows anything. The last time I spoke to my editor, he said he heard a rumor that the power outage was triggered by a cyber-attack and the technicians are trying to debug the grid's computers. He said there was some evidence that the grid's computers are being remotely controlled from computers in Asia."

Vincent was stunned. His mind again replayed Commander Liu's threat. *"This will not be the end. Expulsion of military attachés from your Embassy is not all the retaliation!"* Of course! Hundreds of China's computer engineers and software experts would have been engaged in systematic hacking and electronic spying for years, compiling a catalogue of vulnerabilities in America's infrastructure operating systems. China would have developed a cyber-attack capability that our government may or may not know about, and vice versa. And it was likely scalable to increase the amount of disruption to its enemy with each level implemented. *So, this is how war is going to be fought!*

Grace's voice had been in his ear for several moments, but he now began to hear her. "Vincent? Can you hear me? Are you still on the line?"

"Uh, yeah, Grace. Still here. I was distracted for a minute. Look, so your immediate plan is to maintain in LA until things sort out, and then you're trying to get back to Washington, right? You have enough money?" That sounded oddly possessive.

"I'm alright. You can't use credit cards sometimes because they can't clear the charges electronically when the juice is off. My hotel works with me on that, but taxis and groceries require cash and lots of it. The ATM usually works when the power is on, but it's not on now. Anyway, thanks for asking."

"Listen, Grace, I've got to return a call to someone who outranks me. This may be useless advice, but you might try ingratiating yourself at the Chinese market and find out when their deliveries are made so you can be there. They probably have Chinese suppliers who are different than the supermarket sources. Maybe you can even broker some sales to the hotel restaurant as soon as the deliveries arrive and be a hero at the hotel. The restaurant might scratch your back in return. Bartering is primitive, but it works. They do a lot of that in Asia."

"Wow. So that's what the slogan 'think globally, act locally' means. Thanks, I'll see what I can do."

"And if that doesn't work, try bribes. They do that a lot in Asia too. Good luck, Grace."

"When will I ...." Grace caught herself. Asking when she would hear from him again assumed that they had a relationship. Vincent heard her slip of the tongue and answered her unfinished question.

"Let's talk again when either one of us has some news."

He punched off when she did.

He sat staring out at the harbor entrance at a tug pulling a barge piled high with refrigeration containers approaching the harbor entrance.

John the bartender walked back over. "That's the barge from Maui. Here come the pineapples."

It sat low in the water and moved steadily with a following swell. Vincent assumed that the Maui growers were selling into a rapidly rising market and that they were eager to get their pineapples to Oahu and the mainland.

Vincent was having a hard time getting focused for his call with McMasters. *What have these guys started? Did they game out the Chinese reaction at all? Were wise men running the country?* He had no answers. His duty was to defend his country, something he was proud and determined to do. But right or wrong?

He called McMasters at the number he'd been given by the G-1. The area code told him McMasters was in Washington. The electronic ring tone stopped after two rings and Jerry McMasters answered.

"Good evening Commander. Vincent Long here. I got a message that you called. I know it is late there, but the message said to call ASAP."

"Yeah, its fine, Captain Long. I'm glad you called. I'm hoping you are still in Hawaii?"

Vincent remembered telling McMasters before they separated in Japan that he had picked up a flight to Hawaii.

"I'm still here. HQ is telling me to sit tight. I gather our return to the embassy isn't going to happen anytime soon."

"Ah, no, no. I don't expect so." McMasters sounded distracted. "Listen, Vincent, I know this is a little off the wall, but we need for you to do something while you have this down time. You'll have to trust me that we can square this with the Corps later if they start looking for you."

Vincent did not miss the switch to informality in addressing him. He would do likewise.

"I'm happy to do you a favor if I can, Jerry. Just name it. Want some chocolate-covered macadamia nuts?"

"No, it's not a favor; it's more like a mission. We want you to go to LA and pick something up from a mutual friend. Remember Sam who came though the Embassy on the day the Chinese started limiting our movements? He's there and has something that we need to have picked up chop-chop. He is needed elsewhere and can't deliver it to us himself. We don't have anyone in position to make the exchange and you—you have an idea already of the sort of operation that we have been helping a sister agency with."

Great, just great. Now they want to suck me into their goofy black ops.

"Jerry, I don't think I can get to LA. I can check with base ops at Hickam and Kaneohe to see …."

"Well, we can make that happen. A reconnaissance flight from Hickam to Miramar Marine Air Station can be arranged tomorrow. It would be just a routine flight on their books; it's what they do out there, only you would be a passenger."

"Okay, so I get to Miramar. Then what?"

"You pick up a drop," said McMasters. "Then you bring it here, to Washington."

"What is this item and why me?"

"Hey, you are a Marine officer. You accomplish your mission. Did you ever read Elbert Hubbard's *A Message to Garcia*?"

"Let's see," said Vincent, thinking out loud, "President McKinley hands a man named Rowan a message for General Garcia who is battling Spain in the mountains of Cuba. The President says, "Take this message to Garcia." Rowan doesn't ask 'where is he?' or anything else for that matter. He says only "yes, sir," and three weeks later, Rowan hands Garcia the message in the jungles of Cuba. It's one of the great personal motivational stories of all time. Alright, you don't have to hit me over the head with a two-by-four. I get it. You want me to just shut up and make it happen."

"That's pretty much it. Of course, we're not giving you the mushroom treatment entirely. You already have an inkling of what the context is, and we suspect that the power grid failure in the West is part of it now. You will appreciate that you are on a need-to-know-basis. This is the way it's done."

Vincent switched back to the formal way of addressing McMasters for his next comment. "Commander, what I do know, suspect rather, makes it as likely that some renegade elements in the intelligence community are on some *sub rosa* mission as that this is national policy set by the President and his national security team. And if it is the former, I want no part of it. So you are asking me to take pretty big leap into the dark. Besides, you are not in my chain of command. I don't have to follow your orders. In fact, I probably shouldn't."

McMasters chuckled softly and drawled, "There are no flies on you, Captain Long. Your concerns are perfectly sound, and you are dead right about the chain of command. But, we are asking you to do this anyway, and you are still on a need-to-know basis. All I can do is tell you that this is something that you need to do. Your country is engaged in a strange new kind of war, and it is threatened now as surely as if bombs were being dropped on it. You already have a sense of the nature and scale of the problem. That is why we called you. Are you in or not?"

Vincent thought a short time before answering. *Discipline in the military is crucial.*

"Aye, aye, Commander. Tell me what I need to do."

McMasters then explained that Long would be contacted by someone in flight operations at Hickham and directed to an aircraft. He would be flown to Miramar Air Station near San Diego whereupon he would exit the base without contacting anyone on the base. He would catch the Amtrak train from San Diego and take it to the end of the line at Union Station in Los Angeles and await further instructions which he would receive via his cell phone and which should remain fully charged.

"By the way, Jerry, in my last telephone conversation with Commander Liu of the Beijing police, he was yelling at me that expulsion of military attachés would not be Beijing's only response to what he claimed were the acts of war being perpetrated by the United States against his country. He said that there would be additional, unspecified measures. I mention it now in case it tends to corroborate what I understand may be a cyber-attack involving computers in Asia that are remotely controlling or disabling the Western power grid."

"Hmm. Interesting, but we're all pretty sure about that connection anyway," said McMasters. "Anything else come to mind?"

"No, nothing else."

"I'll be in touch Vincent. Happy trails."

Long hung up. *What the fuck?* Oh well, he had been wondering how to fight this new enemy of his country. Maybe this is how it will go. Then he circled back to the thought that had come to him while listening to McMasters' instructions. *Grace is in LA.*

John the bartender confirmed that the pulled pork sandwich was indeed not available and bar snacks didn't sound good, so Long paid his tab and left. He exited the Aloha Tower complex and turned toward Waikiki. John had told him about a local restaurant called the Back Street Inn that was hard by the Ala Moana Shopping Center. He said it's a place where local chefs go to eat on their off hours, so it might be as well stocked as any place in town. Long was determined to have a good meal, and he had plenty of time before the last bus left for Hickam.

As he neared the Ala Moana area twenty minutes later, the edge of the park appeared on his right in the gathering dusk. The scent of plumeria was heavy in the close air. There were only a few lights showing at the giant shopping center ahead of him on the left, and all but a few of the park's street lights had been disabled to save power.

Suddenly, four young men materialized at Vincent's side from among the rooted trunks of a huge banyan tree at the edge of the park.

"Hey brudda, where you goin'?"

The speaker was a huge native Hawaiian teenager. His three companions looked like the melting pot that is Hawaii. One slight boy who might be Philippino, one stocky, goateed boy who might be of Portuguese descent, and a tall boy who looked Eurasian. They all had on their game faces, scowling and bouncing on their toes in a ghetto affectation.

Vincent decided to be diplomatic and observe the boys' demeanor. "Just doin' my thing, friend. What up with you lads?"

"We the toll collectors, soldier. And I see toll all over you. Dat a good watch you have bruddah. Rolex, right? A diving watch, right? Then, too, you have a cell phone in dat shirt pookah an' I bet a wallet. All dat be yo toll ... friend," the large boy added mockingly. "Then you can be goin' do yo thing."

Vincent knew he couldn't lose his cell phone or his ID in his wallet. He was going to need them where he was going, and didn't have time to replace them. He didn't much want to lose his Rolex Submariner either.

"I'm afraid not, lads. Now, I'm going to give you some advice. Know your enemy before you mess with him. That's it. So, I'll tell you this just once. Step aside. There will be no tolls taken here."

Vincent spoke calmly but with his eyes locked on those of the big Hawaiian boy. He knew this was his adversary. The other boys were window dressing.

The Hawaiian smirked and returned Vincent's gaze. He lifted his shirt with one massive hand and pulled a large boning knife out of a leather holster.

"Hey guys, this *haole* talks like an officer or a sergeant. Wha'cho think? Maybe we show him how we filet officers and sergeants and shit— jes' like a grouper." He glanced at the tall mixed-race boy and jerked his head to Vincent's left side.

Vincent unbuckled his belt and slid it out of his pant loops. The belt was woven leather with a heavy brass buckle. Vincent grasped the tip end in his palm and wrapped the belt around his right hand a couple of loops leaving the buckle dangling.

The tall boy reached into his cargo pants and pulled out a switchblade, opening it with a clean snap. He grinned and began to toss it from hand to hand as he circled around to Vincent's left.

Catching the boy in the middle of a toss of the knife, Vincent lunged to his left and swung the belt overhand, bringing the buckle down hard on the boy's left eye. The boy yelled in pain and jerked his arm up to his face to protect himself. The knife fell to the sidewalk. Vincent lunged again and kicked the inside of the tall boy's left knee. The crunch of tearing ligaments was audible. As the boy's leg folded and he fell, Vincent reached down quickly and picked up the switchblade.

The shorter, stocky boy turned and started to run back into the park.

The Big Hawaiian yelled after him, "Lupe, you'd betta get yo' ass back here!"

The fleeing boy only answered, "Come on, man, let's get outta here," and kept running.

Vincent looked at the Hawaiian, then at the small Philippino standing wide-eyed and frozen beside him, and then back again at the Hawaiian.

"And then there were two," Vincent said evenly.

The tall boy on the ground was on one knee, but couldn't get up. His left eye was shut. "Hey, Ihe, gimme a hand, man. We betta get lost. My knee hurts like a sumbitch, man."

The Hawaiian began to advance on Vincent with a swagger. "Shut up, pussy. You watch and see how to handle this *haole* fucka."

Vincent began to walk backward, and the Hawaiian advanced faster. Vincent increased the speed of his retreat but at a slightly slower rate than the Hawaiian's advance. When the big native boy closed the gap enough to be within striking distance, he raised the knife overhead and brought his big arm down with the knife pointed at Vincent's neck. Vincent raised his arms overhead and caught the descending arm at the wrist with his belt stretched between his two hands. He grabbed the boy's wrist tightly as he fell into a backward somersault, pulling the Hawaiian forward and down. As soon as Vincent's back hit the ground, he planted both feet on the Hawaiian's sternum and lifted him off the ground. In the split second they were face to face, mutually locked in the continuing roll, Vincent saw a startled look on the Hawaiian's face. Their inertia caused Vincent to complete his backward roll, and as he did, he let go of the Hawaiian's arm and shoved the big boy's body away from him with all the strength in his legs. This motion catapulted the Hawaiian backward several feet with his feet to the sky and his head down. Upside down, his back struck one of the tendril trunks of the Banyan tree, and the boy slid down the tree trunk and landed hard on his head, his heavy body crumpling to one side. When he came to rest, the Hawaiian lay on the grass, jerking and silent.

Vincent's backward somersault left him standing in a crouching position facing the last boy. Then adrenaline-induced fury in him propelled him forward. The Philippino was quick. He turned and sprinted away in the same direction that the first boy had taken.

A lone car had stopped on Ala Moana Boulevard just past where Vincent stood with two bodies on the ground near him. Vincent could see that the driver, a man, was on his cell phone. When the man looked back at Vincent, their eyes met for a minute, then the man accelerated toward Waikiki.

Vincent's mind returned to his situation as the adrenaline began to subside. He knew he could forget his mission if he waited for the police. What he did was self-defense, but he didn't know whether there had been any witnesses or which parts of the altercation might have been observed. It would take days to work through the police investigation, even assuming he wasn't arrested. The man likely calling 911 solved one of Vincent's problems, though. Now he wouldn't have to call for an ambulance for the boys that were down and try to do it anonymously. If he called from his cell phone, he could be identified.

The tall boy laying on the ground and holding his knee stared at Vincent with one frightened eye.

"Congratulations, ass-hole," Vincent said. "Maybe you and Ihe and Lupe and the gang can think of a better way to spend your time than collecting tolls."

Vincent turned and began to trot across Ala Moana Boulevard, turning up Pi'ikoi Street toward the café that had been his destination. Knowing he was still in the line of sight of the boy he had just left and was being watched, he then crossed the street and walked into the shadows of the covered garage that surrounds the vast Ala Moana Shopping Center. The police would spend all night looking for him in the Center and its endless encircling parking lots. Once in the parking structure, he walked parallel to Pi'ikoi, pausing only to duck into a T-shirt shop on the street level to buy a baseball hat with the logo of the Oakland Raiders. Outside, he put the hat on backwards to partially hide his haircut, recrossed Pi'ikoi a block up and headed for the Back Street Inn. It was the only place he knew in the area, and he should get off the street.

He jogged the two blocks to the cafe, almost passing it by entirely. The façade of the place was industrial looking, painted black, with several exhaust vents punching through the front wall onto the street. A single neon beer sign appeared above a glass door with decal numbers stuck on it. The numbers were the same as the address he had for the café. Four people stood outside by the door talking enthusiastically about fried rice. He lowered his head and looked away from the group as he entered. Inside, the café was a crowded, noisy place consisting of several awkwardly connecting rooms full of booths. One of the rooms had a bar with an empty seat. He sat down, still wearing his Raiders cap and asked the server for a menu.

Vincent stared at the menu without seeing it, collecting his thoughts. *God damn it. I hurt those two boys, maybe badly.* He knew they had been a serious threat to him, and he had his orders. He was not about to let some dumb-ass thieves interfere with national security. *One thing is for sure; the enemy isn't some punks in a Honolulu park. How did that fucking happen?*

The server reappeared. "What'll it be for the silver and black?"

Vincent quickly scanned the menu. "I'll have some fried rice, chicken *okusan*, and a draft beer."

"You got it."

Vincent looked at his watch. He had plenty of time. Alone with his thoughts he waited for his food to arrive and smelled the scents of Pacific Rim cooking, wondering how this obscure eatery managed to exist. When his food did arrive, the portions were mountainous. He dug into it, ravenous, as though he hadn't eaten in a week. When he finally put his fork down, he had managed to eat all of the chicken but only half the fried rice. He asked for a doggie bag for the rice. It might be his breakfast tomorrow.

He left the café and headed down Auahi, a narrow, dark street that paralleled Ala Moana Boulevard, back toward the foot of Bishop Street and the Aloha Tower. At the Aloha Tower, he waited only fifteen 15 minutes before boarding an empty bus back to Hickam.

CHAPTER

9

G race sat in the Starbucks across the street from the Hilton Checkers hotel sipping a surprisingly good cup of French roast. Starbucks was able to make coffee by boiling water over propane and then pouring the hot water over ground coffee.

Back to the future.

She wondered whether to call Sarah, her boss's secretary, again. No, that would just waste phone battery power and irritate Sarah without accomplishing anything. If they could get her a reservation on the Amtrak from LA to Washington, they would and, if so, they'll call. She'd ridden the bus to the train station and stood in line for two hours just to be told that there were no reservations to be had for the next five days. No cars could be rented, and no plane reservations could be made because of the fuel shortage and power outage. She felt helpless. She *was* helpless.

Her mood alternated between exasperation and resignation, depending on the proximity of any obstacle to her personal comfort. Right now, she had scored an armchair in Starbucks and had a hot cup of good coffee. Things could be worse.

Her phone began to play a tinny, electronic version of Pachelbel's Canon in her purse announcing that she had a phone call. *Now what?* She fished around in her bag for the phone, swiping it on. It displayed "Vincent Long."

***

70

"Hi Grace. It's me. 'ssup?"

Grace laughed. "You must be in a good mood. You're probably lying on the beach eating papaya and thought you give me a call just to mess with me."

"Actually, I'm getting on Amtrak in San Diego, and I'll be pulling into Union Station in LA in a couple of hours. I moved heaven and earth to come rescue you."

"You're kidding, right? I mean, you said you were stuck in Hawaii just yesterday. I don't ...."

"I'm not kidding. It is a long story, but I caught a flight to Miramar early this morning. It's a Marine Corps Air Station down here. First, I have some official business in LA, but after that I'd like to come pick you up. Maybe you can treat me to one or two of those carrots you've been getting at the Chinese market. It's the least you can do to show your gratitude."

"Yeah, I'm livin' large on carrots all ri .... What do you mean it's the least I can do? In exchange for what?"

"Well, you may want to saddle up and get ready to fly to Washington. I think I can get you on a military flight with me. I'll have to give you the particulars when I see you, but it will be sooner rather than later. Maybe even tonight. Are you in?"

"Absolutely! I can be ready anytime you say. But what ... how ...?

"Can't go into that right now, but I should be able to get to your hotel early evening. I'll call and give you a heads up when I have a better idea when I can get there. Does that work for you?"

"Is a bluebird blue? If you can get me out of here somehow, I will owe you more than carrots!" Grace's spirits soared.

"Pledge your firstborn to the Corps?"

"Ah, well, I'll have to see about that ...." Grace could hear the sound of an incoming call on Vincent's end.

"Whoops, gotta take this call," he said. "Talk to you later."

***

Caller ID confirmed McMasters as the caller.

"Vincent Long here."

"Okay Vincent, here's the deal. We're going to make it easy for you. Sam will meet you at Union Station for the handoff. He'll be in the bar area in the waiting hall. You can't miss it. No cloak and dagger stuff. You will just be a couple of guys meeting and have a cup of coffee or whatever. He will hand the envelope to you. It is a set of USB drives. Just so that you know the significance of what you are doing, I can tell you that the data on them has been supplied by one of our sources in Hong Kong who used to work in the cyber arena in the country of your last duty station. The data reveals how our electric grids can be hacked and controlled offshore. That's a key to unblocking the malware. We will get a sanitized version of this information to the utility companies' servers for the western grid. We're guessing they can have the grid up and running within the next couple of days. Those drives promise to be very useful to us in countering future cyber-attacks by the same folks and perhaps by others. All of this is top secret, of course.

"When you get the packet, you can then get yourself out to LAX and proceed to the Pacific Zenith Air Cargo office in the Cargo Complex on Century Boulevard. To be safe, be there by 10:00PM. The flight to Washington leaves at 11:00PM. It belongs to our sister agency in McLean. If you can get yourself to the airport, fine. If you have any trouble getting a cab or limo, call this number." McMasters recited a local phone number and Long duly wrote it down on the margins of his *San Diego Tribune*. "Give them at least an hour's notice, and they will pick you up at your location and take you to LAX. You arrive at Washington's Reagan Airport where you will be met at the arrival gate by me. I will relieve you of the flash drives."

"If Sam doesn't show, then what?"

"He's already there. Any other questions?"

"Not really. This seems like kind of a raggedy-ass way to get some very urgent intelligence from the field to headquarters, but what do I know?"

"Yeah," McMasters said, laughing. "Welcome to our world."

"Oh, one more thing." Vincent said it with authority, as though it wasn't open for discussion. "I will have a passenger with me. It's my ex-wife, Grace. She's a journalist and got stuck in LA covering Senator Grey's campaign when the power went out. She has to get back to Washington. She knows nothing about any of this. I'm telling her that I am reporting to be reassigned by HQ Marine Corps and that this is a Department of Defense charter flight."

This news was met with silence on McMaster's end. Then, "She's not with you now? She won't see Sam?"

"No, no. She is at her hotel in LA. I will pick her up on my way to the airport."

"Okay. Helps with your cover. You were entrusted with the country's secrets at the Embassy in Beijing, so you know how to keep things to yourself. Meeting Sam for a pop and taking your ex-wife along on the flight fits the pattern of this thing—sort of raggedy-ass."

"*Touché*, Jerry."

"After all, Grace divorced you because she had no taste for this kind of life anyway. She probably won't even ask."

Zing. McMasters let Vincent know that they knew all about him. It was a shot across Vincent's bow to stay in line.

Vincent ignored the comment. "I won't call you again, Jerry, unless something comes up that I can't handle. I'll see you at Reagan in the morning."

Vincent put the cell phone in his pocket and climbed aboard the Metro Liner car. It was still a half hour before the train was due to leave, so he had his choice of seats. He flopped into a window seat on the left side of the car—the ocean side going north, and the car began to fill up.

***

A little over two hours later, the Metro Liner funneled into underground tracks leading into the arrival platform at Union Station. When the crush of passengers handling their luggage permitted, Vincent stood and pulled his duffle from the luggage rack. He made a note to email the Embassy and have them airfreight the personal effects he had left with the Embassy guards in Beijing upon his abrupt departure. He would have them sent to … where? Grace's place? He'd have to think about that.

The walkway from the arrival track to the Alameda Street exit had a sign pointing to the "Waiting Room." He headed for the stairs, taking them two at a time. The exertion felt good. He'd been sitting ever since the incident in Ala Moana Park.

I should have found a way to avoid hurting those boys. But how?

The stairs opened at the top into a vast, mission-style room with a high, dark, wooden beam ceiling. Massive art deco chandeliers hung overhead, and the room was filled with oak chairs and benches polished into a lustrous patina by many thousands of traveler buttocks. The room was divided into halves by an ornate marble tile walkway that ran the length of the waiting room and into the more austere ticketing hall beyond. In the middle of the waiting room on one side was a bar surrounded by armchairs. In one of them, a fair, athletic-looking man sat watching him. Vincent recognized him immediately. Vincent walked to him and stuck out his hand.

"Sam Johnson isn't it? Thanks for making this so easy for me. Talk about a convenient place to meet." Vincent shook hands and dropped his duffle beside the chair opposite Johnson's.

"Captain Long, good to see you again." They sat down together. "It didn't make sense for you to be running around trying to cope with all this power outage nonsense," Johnson said, absent mindedly rubbing the scar above his goatee. "Taxis and busses are pretty scarce. So, we wanted to make the handoff of the baton clean and certain. Speaking of the baton, I'll give it to you shortly, but for appearances sake, let's get something from the bar and chat for a few minutes." He scanned the area in his line of sight facing Vincent. For his part, Vincent surveyed the area behind the man's back. Vincent guessed that Johnson saw no one who registered as suspicious either.

"What's your pleasure, Vincent? It's on me. I think I'll have a beer."

"Just ice tea, thanks."

"New broom sweeps clean, eh?" Johnson grinned as he got up to walk to the bar. Vincent took the remark to mean that Vincent was taking his clandestine task so seriously that he would err on the side of avoiding alcohol. He had to admit that Johnson was not wrong.

The blonde man returned with the drinks and took his seat again.

"Would a cyber-attack from a distant computer involve risk of live agents following either one of us around?"

"Well, the handoff in Hong Kong was from a live source, and that always involves risks. The baton is something that we don't want intercepted or compromised. It merits caution, and perhaps you won't be offended if I mention that you are not trained to spot people following you. I just don't want anyone watching me to pick you up as a target. They don't wear uniforms."

"I dunno, Sam. There are a lot of Chinese faces in LA. I don't know how you can reliably sort out the citizens from the spooks by eyesight. But, that is probably the least of the inconvenient effects of provoking the Chinese."

Vincent's companion focused his ice blue eyes on Vincent and frowned slightly. "I'm not sure I follow. Provoking?"

Vincent knew that he was on shaky ground, but his lingering concern about which side's operatives triggered this crisis and who his real enemy might be compelled him to continue.

"Well, if a heavily energy-dependent country has been out-maneuvered by another country with a strong, long-range, strategic plan for energy sourcing, and the former decides to interdict a few tankers and pipeline parcels of oil belonging to the latter and take them for its own use, then the pirating country can expect a certain amount of blow-back."

Johnson seemed to feign surprise. "Oh, I see," he chuckled. "You suspect that American security services are behind all of that?" His chuckle was heartier this time.

"The Chinese think so too. In fact, they put the idea in my head."

Johnson leaned forward. "The pipeline explosion was the work of the Uighurs. That is pretty well documented now. The Chinese have got confessions from a regional party boss who was taking money—dollars—from them. The Uighurs have been unhappy with the Han for a long time. You don't need a conspiracy theory to explain the pipeline explosion. The locals want a share of the pipeline riches out there so the locals let Beijing know they are serious."

Vincent's face remained impassive and the blond man continued. "The tanker hijacking is just as easy to explain. Where did it occur? The northern entrance to the Strait of Malacca. What navy controls the entrance to the Strait? The Indian navy. What country is China's biggest rival for power and influence in Asia? India. Is India energy-poor and dependent on foreign sourced oil? It is. And when the Chinese complete their canal across the Isthmus of Kra in Thailand, China's navy will have short route into the Indian Ocean. China's navy will then confront India's navy, which makes India nervous.

"India is the obvious culprit for that hijacking job. Where else could the hijacked tanker have disappeared to, if not to the east coast of India?

Our analysts have noodled that one big time, and that is their conclusion. And just because some excitable police bureaucrat in Beijing blames it on the Americans doesn't change the facts. Hell, everybody blames us for everything. You shouldn't fall for that one."

Vincent had listened attentively to Johnson's *prima facie* case. It made sense, and any American diplomat would feel comfortable using it to defend America against charges of involvement in the tanker hijacking and the pipeline explosion. Vincent thought it prudent to soften his probe.

"Your scenario is plausible, er, Sam. I hadn't thought of the possible Indian connection. Anyway, you understand that I was answering your question hypothetically as to why China, believing *as it does* that America is the culprit for both incidents, might take this step. I mean, you and I wouldn't be sitting here if China's beliefs hadn't been manifested in a cyber attack."

Sam shrugged. "Anyone in Asia who helps themselves to Chinese oil can be expected to whisper in China's ear about American involvement. And, we don't have good ways to find out about such things. Short of the serendipity of turning one of their key agents sometime in the future, we may never know who is responsible for these incidents, and we may never convince the Chinese that it was not us. You can be certain, however, that we will put the Chinese on their inquiry about that. Maybe if we shut their stock and commodity markets down with an attack of our own, that would give them an incentive to be more careful next time."

So that's how this is going to go.

Johnson reached into a leather portfolio at the side of his chair. He pulled out a copy of the *Financial Times* commodities section, folded it in half, and handed it to Vincent. Vincent could feel extra bulk in the paper.

"Here is the article we talked about. Please pass it on to our colleague in Washington when you see him. It may give him some ideas," Johnson said in a strong voice, standing up. "It's a pleasure doing business with you."

Vincent stood also. "Will do. Thanks for the tea."

As Johnson walked away, Vincent unzipped his duffle and shoved the folded magazine inside to the very bottom. He sat down again and sucked on an ice cube from his empty glass. He was still thinking about the scenario Johnson had posited. It didn't compute. Not just anyone could pull

off a large tanker hijacking anonymously. For the American satellite surveillance technology to be affected by solar radiation at precisely that time
could be coincidental. But there was no doubt that American oil companies would be able to obtain several tanker loads of what should be Chinese oil while the pipeline is out of commission. America, more so than
India, would be the beneficiary of the pipeline sabotage.

The ship canal being constructed across the Isthmus of Kra can be
readily explained in terms that have nothing to do with challenging the
Indian Navy in the Indian Ocean. The canal would cut hundreds of miles
off the route to China for China's shipments of oil from the Middle East
and consumer goods to and from Europe. It would also avoid the demon-
strably real piracy and blockade risks inherent in ship transit through the
Strait of Malacca. That was a red herring.

Nope. I'm not buying it.

This little chat he just had with "Sam" was more than curious. Why
had it been necessary for them to sit and talk here in the waiting room at
all? The only thing that took place here was the monologue that Sam had
delivered to Vincent tending to deflect any suggestion that American
agents had committed overt acts of war against China. McMasters must
have told Johnson about Liu's threat of retaliation. How else would he
know about the "excitable police bureaucrat" who blamed America for the
oil thefts?

It sure looked like McMasters and this Sam character concocted this
meeting for the purpose of neutralizing Vincent's suspicions. Was that the
only reason? Did the flash drives really contain the antidote for the attack
on America's power grid? Or were they props in a scheme to distract, iso-
late and neutralize him? He had no way of knowing, but he had no choice
other than to do his duty as he understood it. The record would show only
that he accomplished his mission.

***

Walking out of the front doors of Union Station facing Alameda
Street, Vincent looked up and saw the top of Los Angeles City Hall. He'd
seen images of it on countless television dramas over the years. Designed
by the same architect that designed Union Station, the building was iconic

of the City of Angels. He strolled onto the green belt in front of Union Station with its line of very tall, thin palm trees and called Grace.

"Hello?" Grace answered immediately.

"T'is I. Let's see, you are staying at the Hilton Checkers Hotel on South Grand, correct?"

"I am. Do you know where that is?"

"Well, the tourist map I picked up says that it is about fourteen blocks away from Union Station and it is a fine, Southern California evening. I don't see any cabs around here, so I think I'll just walk to the hotel. I should be there in about half an hour."

"Okay. It will be good to see you, Vincent. I really appreciate this. I am going to Washington with you, aren't I? Please say yes."

"You are indeed. We'll just have time to get something to eat—I hope your hotel restaurant is offering something yummy—and then head out for LAX. The plane leaves at 11:00 tonight."

"That's wonderful! Oh, I can't believe this is happening! It is the first decent break I've had in four days. I'm going to do a whole article on how Captain Vincent Long of the U.S. Marines landed on the beaches of Los Angeles and liberated me."

"Ah, well, don't do that without talking to me first. See you shortly."

"Bye, Vincent."

***

The Pacific Zenith cargo plane descended to 3,000 feet on its approach to Reagan National Airport across the Potomac from Washington DC. As it dropped though the cloud cover leading a front working its way east from the Great Lakes the plane hit turbulence that awoke Grace in the seat next to Vincent. She straightened from her slump against Vincent's shoulder. They were side by side in the two seats at the rear of the cockpit that the management kept rigged for the occasional courier hitching a ride.

McMasters said Pacific Zenith Air belonged to a "sister agency". That would be CIA and it would link NSA and McMasters to the CIA, which, unlike the NSA, ran agents of the sort Sam Johnson appeared to be.

McMasters had been right about Grace. When Vincent told her that he had been ordered to report to the Pentagon for a new duty assignment and he was able to get her a seat on the plane as his wife, she asked no questions about it, other than whether he thought he would be stationed in Washington now. He had said, quite truthfully, that he didn't know.

Their view through the windshield at the front of the cockpit revealed only the dark grey color of the rain cell in the early morning light.

"Are we going in?" she asked groggily.

"Yup. The plane has been descending for about fifteen minutes so it shouldn't be much longer. I don't know about you, but my chicken croquettes are wearing off."

He was referring to the meal they had shared at the hotel before they left for the airport. The restaurant featured frozen chicken croquettes sourced somehow. The wine was the best part of the meal, and they polished off a whole bottle of Sancerre while Grace related her experience with the strange campaign of Senator Aaron Grey and then with the blackout. Around nine o'clock, they were picked up at the hotel by an airport shuttle that still operated hybrid vehicles to LAX by appointment.

At the Century Cargo Center, the Pacific Zenith dispatcher had been expecting them. They were introduced to the pilot and crew in the waiting room. When the plane took off, the half bottle of wine caught up with Grace, and she fell into the deep sleep from which she now awoke. Vincent envied her. He never could sleep sitting up. Bleary-eyed and tired, he was now trying to figure out how to deliver the flash drives to Jerry McMasters at the gate without Grace being present. He decided to be straightforward.

"Grace, I'm being met at the gate by the Navy attaché who served with me at the Embassy in Beijing. His name is Commander McMasters, so he is two ranks above me. I will be accompanying him to the officer's quarters at the Navy Yard. You and I will have to split up here, so you will have to get yourself home on your own. Okay?"

"Oh, sure, Vincent. I'll just head on out then," Grace answered quickly. She looked somewhat relieved at this bit of intelligence, probably because it foreclosed any question about whether Vincent had a place to stay. He wondered what this adventure they had just shared meant for their personal relationship.

The pilot raised the wing flaps all the way at the last minute, and the aircraft touched down smoothly on the wet runway. It taxied to an outlying hangar that serviced cargo planes well away from the busy commuter aircraft and other commercial passenger gates, and the pilot cut the engines. They could hear the top of the mobile stairway bump slightly against the open door behind them. The refreshing smell of warm spring rain flowed into the cabin.

"You folks will have a short walk to the terminal, but it isn't raining hard," the co-pilot said to them. "Just head for that door with the yellow light overhead."

"Okay, Vincent. I'll say my good-byes here. I'm going to the loo and freshen up a bit before I go into the terminal. You can just go ahead and meet your colleague. Maybe we can catch up in the next day or two. I owe you big time for getting me on this flight."

"I accept your IOU," Vincent grinned, rubbing his day-old beard and glancing at the yellow light. "I'll call you when I know what I am going to be doing. It's been real."

They hugged goodbye without awkwardness. Then, Grace entered the cabin bathroom, and Vincent walked stiffly down the mobile stairs. As he stepped onto the tarmac, and looked toward the door with the yellow light, he thought he could make out the uniformed figure of Commander Jerry McMasters waiting on the other side.

CHAPTER

10

Grace scored a day-old tuna salad sandwich in the terminal by way of breakfast and got the last seat on a hybrid bus headed for Arlington. The rain showers tapered off, and the sun came out on the short trip from Reagan. It was already hot and muggy. She walked the few blocks from the bus stop to her apartment wheeling her carry-on behind her and arrived sweating and red-faced. Power was off at the building, but the elevator still operated off of an emergency generator.

In her apartment, she started to make a cup of tea, but then realized she couldn't. The units in the high rise building came uniformly equipped with electric stove tops for reasons of safety and economy. She envied people who had gas stoves. They could cook when the electricity was off.

When Grace took her shower, the water was warm, indicating that the power had gone off recently. As she scoured off the real or imagined road dirt and sweat, the tepid water felt bracing until it went completely cold.

Because of the power outages in Washington during her absence, her refrigerator had been off much of the time she had been gone, and all the food in it had spoiled. In a cupboard, she found a package of instant noodles—the kind Vincent liked—and poured them in some water to let them hydrate. If the power came back on, she would heat them. If not, she would eat them at room temperature anyway.

Deferring the unpleasant task of cleaning out her refrigerator, she sat down and opened her laptop. Hoping that the battery pack would last until she was finished or the power came back on, she edited the report of her experience with Senator Grey's Southern California appearances. She'd written different parts of it while she marked time in Los Angeles, but the whole article now came together as she wrote. The Senator's controversial speech in juxtaposition with the power grid failure that occurred almost on cue during the UCLA appearance made it uniquely compelling. Within ten minutes after emailing it to her editor, Raj Patel, he called to say that he loved it and that it was being immediately posted on the e-magazine.

As she put the phone down, she heard the noises electric appliances make when the power comes on. Instinctively, she plugged the cell phone in its charger and then warmed up the noodles. After eating her meager fare and unpacking, she opened the sliding door to her bedroom deck and, feeling a slight breeze, lay down on top of her bed spread to think.

Mid-afternoon, she awoke to the odor of spoiled food and spent the rest of the afternoon evacuating the refrigerator and placing its purged contents into the garbage chute. Just before it closed, she dropped off her dry cleaning at the shop down the street. The woman at the counter couldn't tell her when it would be ready. The problem, the woman said, was the pressing machines. They were electric, and when the power went off, nothing got pressed.

At the corner market operated by Eritreans, Grace was able to buy some survival groceries; rice, canned tuna and canned tomatoes. The fresh produce looked terrible, but she bought a bunch of radishes, some mildly wilted kale and a bruised honeydew melon at twice the price of produce the week before. She felt almost exhilarated by the meager bounty filling her grocery bag.

In the lobby of her building, she ran into her girlfriend Jody, an editorial assistant at *Insider On Line* who lived one flight below her on the fourth floor. Jody said she had some fresh eggs and invited Grace to come over. True to her Italian heritage, Jody made a delicious meal out of toasted ciabatta bread and eggs poached in a sauce made from Grace's tomatoes. Grace, famished, was nearly in tears as she sat down to the fragrant meal after having been deprived of tasty, nourishing food for so many days. In a superbly gracious gesture, Jody even pulled out a bottle of Prosecco from the refrigerator which had been on long enough to chill the wine. They drank it slowly throughout the evening as they related to each other their recent experiences coping with the creeping dystopia around them. When the power went off, they made do with candlelight.

Jody told Grace that the advertising revenue on which the e-magazine depended had nearly dried up. With so many power interruptions, people were not turning on their computers nearly as much and the viewing audience had dropped precipitously, in turn, causing advertisers to insist on lower fees. Some just pulled their ads altogether. When Grace and Jody called it a night, they were both certain that their employment at *Insider* would end before much longer unless the power situation was somehow fixed. Jody opined that Grace's job would last longer because her articles provided content and attracted the eyeballs advertisers require.

***

In the kitchen the next morning, Grace waited for her tea to boil. If the pattern held, the power would cut off late morning when the demand exceeded the limited power being generated by the curtailed grid. Then it usually came back on in the late afternoon when office demand tapered off, although, when it was hot and air conditioners were turned on as people returned to their homes, the power could stay off until ten or even later on weekends as people went to bed later.

She turned on a morning television show. There was a demonstration how housewives could salt and dry their meat to preserve it during the frequent power outages. Another report called attention to the rise in accidents where traffic lights were out. Finally, a breathless, this-just-in, talking head reported that an unnamed Pentagon source forecast that the Western power grid would be restored sometime the following day.

Grace shook her head as she reached for the phone and dialed the pre-programmed number. Senator Aaron Grey himself answered the phone.

"Hi, Senator Grey. It's Grace Long. I'm back in town after our interesting sojourn to the City of Angels last week, and I'm wondering whether we can pick up where we left off with my coverage of your campaign."

"Grace! It's good to hear from you!" he boomed. "Charlie showed me the article you filed on the *Insider* yesterday. I liked it a lot. Say, I'll bet you have a greater appreciation of electricity now. Without it, your medium can't exist."

"That's true. Nor can I enjoy air conditioning in sealed buildings, lights after dark, a hot shower, or even a cup of tea for that matter."

"You're right, Grace. These days, we get only degrees of terrible. I can't get all my work done because it's such a big production just to communicate and get transport."

"I gather the western grid may be up and running tomorrow some time. The explanation why it happened will be interesting to hear, if we ever do."

"It's a great teaching point for the country, though. A voter would have to be pretty dull not to see why there is urgency to conserve our fossil fuel. I liked the part in your article about the audience being electrified, so to speak, by my startling vision for the future, accented as it was, by the wholesale failure of the grid. How it will play in Peoria is indeed the question before the house. You wrote the same article I would have tried to write—crisp, clear, and astute about the excitement of my colorful, ah, non-campaign."

"Well, your vision for the country is *the* story, for sure, Senator. That's why I need to keep those revelations coming."

"Absolutely, you're access remains active. Just let Charlie know when and where you would like to hook up with us again. I'll tell him we spoke. Say, I'm giving a speech to the American Bar Association annual meeting in Philadelphia day after tomorrow. You'll want to catch that."

"I'm there, Senator Grey, if I can figure out the travel bit. I'll talk to Charlie about logistics. Good luck with the speech."

Grace refilled her tea cup. It was Limoges and had been a present from her mother. She hadn't spoken to her mother in several weeks. It was still too early Mountain Daylight Time to call now. Her mother wouldn't be up, and she didn't want to get her dad.

As she looked out at the partial view of Georgetown University in the distance across the Potomac, her thoughts turned to Vincent. What were they going to be to each other? After their divorce, things seemed clear. Their differences had indeed been irreconcilable. His rigid professional code probably shouldn't have come as a surprise, but it did and she'd felt suffocated by it. She returned to the continuing question whether to change back to her maiden name. Ambivalent, she just sighed.

Her relationship with her father had always been difficult. A railroad lawyer in Denver, he judged her severely, as though he were preparing the son he never had for great things. Her response was passive-aggression in the face of his criticism. She spent her high school and college years disappointing him by refusing to follow his dictates to prepare for a career in business or the law. Instead, she ran with fine-arts-major friends and, as a journalism major, wrote for the student newspaper at Boulder on political subjects.

After college, she felt the need to stretch her legs. She joined the Peace Corps and spent twenty seven months in Botswana teaching English and basic computer skills. Her experience with the school children had been enchanting. The people of Botswana were friendly, cheerful and dignified, and they took pride in the success story Botswana represented in sub-Saharan Africa. She would never forget her occasional excursions into the bush on field trips and holidays.

Feeling estranged from her home in Colorado after being absent more than two years, she spent her severance pay from the Peace Corps on rent for a studio in Georgetown and looked for work in the nation's capital. A job in the Public Relations Department at National Geographic opened up, and she got the job. After writing copy for two years on Nat Geo's web site, Grace joined a political blog, editing submissions from a stable of stringers who wrote by assignment.

She dated as much as she wanted to in the pool of men in Washington—Congressional staff, lobbyists, lawyers, and civil servants. Then one Friday night, she met Vincent, a young Marine Captain stationed at Quantico. He was different than the men she had been dating. He was worldly and less partisan. Vincent shared with her an upbringing in the Rocky Mountain West as well as wonkiness in all things political. And, she found his dark hair, green eyes and athletic gracefulness striking.

After six months and under the time pressure of orders Vincent expected at the completion of his training program, they decided to marry. Vincent managed to get leave during a break in his training program, and they went to Denver to be married at Grace's parents' home. It was a joyous occasion.

Grace's father took to Vincent instantly, but she felt conflicted by having satisfied her father with her choice of husbands yet hurt that he showed no pride in her own career.

Vincent and Grace honeymooned at the ranch in Los Alamos he'd inherited from his parents-a bittersweet experience for Vincent. The high desert sunsets were, as advertised, enchanting for Grace, and she loved the scent of pinion in the clear, still, silent air.

Shortly afterward, Vincent received orders to Camp Lejeune, North Carolina, to join a unit that would be deploying to Somalia. At Lejeune, Grace experienced for the first time what life was like on a military post. She immediately began to chafe at the role that was expected of her as a Marine officer's wife. It was subservient and accessorial to her husband's career. It assumed that a Marine's wife shared the same paradigm of Corps, country and tradition that her husband did. She had no indoctrination for such an unliberated view, and seeing no opportunities for a career in journalism, spent hours in the public library in Jacksonville just to escape the isolation of Lejeune. Her alienation had been perfected when the wife of Vincent's commanding officer made her a present of a manual for wives that featured rules of command etiquette and counseled unqualified support for her husband's duty. Grace said it could have been written for the Stepford Wives in an argument with Vincent about it.

The same passive-aggressive response she had adopted in response to her father's domination she reprised with Vincent. In the few short months before his unit deployed to Somalia, she became convinced that she'd made a mistake in marrying him. She felt guilty leaving her husband as he headed into harm's way but saw no point in prolonging their misery and wanted to settle it before he left. She decided to return to Washington and her work. They both recognized that her resolve would make her marriage to a career Marine impossible, so they agreed to divorce.

Her father was appalled by the divorce. His daughter had disappointed him yet again, and Grace bitterly resented his judgment of her. She remained largely estranged from him.

Now, things seemed much less clear. She had to admit Vincent's assistance and companionship over the last several days, however extraordinary, had endeared him to her again. On the plane from LA, she had felt like they were couple—so much so that she fell soundly asleep on his shoulder. And he seemed to genuinely be interested in her work. This time, she was not subservient to his position. It was a more mature and matter-of-fact intimacy, something felt naturally arising from their common ground. But what were their feelings? *Love?* Was there such a thing as segueing back into love? Or, had she never actually been out of love?

Her thoughts returned to the candidacy of Aaron Grey. She called Raj Patel and told him she was covering Senator Grey's speech in Philadelphia he next day. Patel was enthusiastic and asked to have her report as soon as possible after the event. Her reports were being widely read and the webzine desperately needed the following Grace's writing attracted.

She wondered whether Vincent would like to come along. He could get the flavor of this remarkable campaign first hand. Maybe he would even have fresh input for the candidate. She called him.

"Hi, Grace, can I call you right back," he said. "I'm just finishing up something."

"Sure, Vincent. I'm going out for lunch in a little while, but ...."

"Where are you going?"

"Well, I feel like celebrating, so I thought I'd take advantage of one of the best benefits of my membership in the Smithsonian Society. I'm going to walk over the river to the Smithsonian Administration Building. They have a very nice dining room. I love the ambience."

"How about I join you? Will they let in just anyone?"

"Well, if you are wearing your dress blues, there isn't a receptionist in the world that would turn a poster Marine like you away. If you're in civvies though, just say you are joining me as my guest. Since you are dining with a budding media presence, they will no doubt do a lot of bowing and scraping, but don't let that intimidate you. Just come on in and look for me."

Vincent laughed. "We do bowing and scraping in the Corps. I'm very comfortable being on the receiving end of it. See you in, say, an hour and forty five or so."

"Perfect. 'Bye."

Grace retrieved her *Washington Post Digest* from the lobby and returned to the sofa. The mailed version was a weekly digest of the voluminous news items carried by the media company on its website. Looking at the front page, her half smile quickly morphed into a frown. The securities markets continued in free fall because of declining corporate earnings caused by lack of consumer confidence and spending. Investor fears of being unable to execute trades as the power outages continued were perversely manifested in increased trade volume when the markets were open. The volume consisting disproportionately of fearful sellers ordained market free fall.

Transportation difficulties were keeping more and more shoppers from visiting stores. Consumer goods ordered on line when computers had power were disappearing into the nation's logistical holes as deliveries became less and less reliable. This, in turn, meant that the earnings of retailers and businesses in the supply chain for consumer goods were dropping dramatically toward unknowable levels.

She noticed an article in the City section that made her heart sink. Kidnapping of children off the street was on the rise. Schools were closing at irregular hours due to difficulties for students and teachers getting to and from school, unreliable schedules for lunch program food, and black outs that interrupted air conditioning and lighting. This meant that more and more children were unsupervised as working parents endured longer and longer commutes, and predators were taking advantage of the situation. The article said the Police Commission was meeting every day with school boards, and parent-teacher associations to try to develop solutions.

Grace tossed the paper down on the coffee table and got dressed. Glancing in the mirror, she combed her hair with her fingers, smoothed the crisp, white, short-sleeved blouse that fit into the waist of her tailored khaki slacks, and applied fresh lipstick. Out on the street, she decided not to waste time trying to put together a bus route to the Smithsonian. Taxis were nowhere to be seen. The adrenaline build-up she had felt from thinking about the divorce and from reading the newspaper left her jittery. She needed to walk that off.

Heading south on Wilson Boulevard to Memorial Bridge, then across the river and turning right at the Lincoln Memorial, she walked to the Smithsonian about a mile away. When she got there, the Smithsonian restaurant was closed.

Idiot! I should have called first, she thought and started to tear up. *Vincent is going to fight his way down here and find out I've screwed this up.*

She walked over to a female security guard eyeing her from the museum entrance.

"Excuse me, do you know why the restaurant is closed?"

"I guess things got too difficult for them, ma'am, with their supplies and all. Couldn't keep up their menu. They closed about a week ago. The Air and Space Museum has a snack bar that they've been keeping open, though, so people can get something to eat. It's just down the street. They have hot dogs and sandwiches and the like."

"Thanks for the tip," she said, looking around. "Is it always this quiet these days?"

"Yeah, pretty much. Some of the museum executives still come in and try to work, but it's sporadic. We close today at 4:00 o'clock. So does the snack bar, I think."

"Well, hang in there, Rita." Grace read the woman's name from her ID card. "This too will pass—I hope."

Rita grimaced. "Well, I don't know, the way things are goin'."

Grace walked out the front door of the Smithsonian headquarters building and took a seat on a shady bench facing the front door so that she could not miss Vincent when he arrived. She didn't expect him for another fifteen minutes.

Grace called Senator Grey's chief of staff, Charles Haden. "Hi Charlie, it's Grace Long. I'm going to cover the Senator's talk in Philadelphia tomorrow.

"Yeah, he mentioned it. I assume it will still come off."

"What do you mean?"

"Off the record?"

"Sure. What's up?"

"Well, he gets these severe migraines sometimes, and he's got one now. Sometimes it takes a day or two for them to clear up and they are pretty debilitating. The doctor thinks it is just stress. Anyway, he says he's going to make it to the ABA Convention."

"I just talked to him earlier this morning. He sounded fine."

"Uh huh, it just started coming on. It does that after … well, after he gets too stim- … ah, works too many hours. You know."

No, I don't know.

Grace didn't know what to say, and Hayden didn't volunteer anything more. *Is something wrong with Grey?* She made a note to follow up with Hayden when they had a private moment.

"So, assuming he does make it, is your office going to take a van or something up to Baltimore, and if so, can I hitch a ride?" On impulse, Grade added, "Oh, and I may have a friend with me, I'm not sure yet."

"A friend? We don't let members of the public ...."

"He is a Captain in the Marine Corps, and also my ex-husband. He is, or was until a week ago, an attaché at the Embassy in Beijing and has some unusual perspective on these energy issues and how they bear on the US-Sino relationship." She was free-associating now. "I thought he would enjoy hearing Senator Grey speak, and the Senator might like to hear his perspective."

"Okay, if we can't trust the Marines, who can we trust? Besides, we owe you for your help when the lights went out in LA, and you wrote a good article on that speech. Yes, we have corralled a van to take us all up there tomorrow, and there will be seats for you both. We will leave the Senate Russell Building about 11:00 am. Meet you in the lobby about ten of."

"Got it, Charlie. Thank you for the lift. Getting around these days is just a bitch."

"Yes, it is. I expect Senator Grey might mention that at some point tomorrow."

Grace laughed. As she looked up, she spotted Vincent walking down Independence toward her. He was in civilian clothes, but his walk was ramrod straight and his eyes were fixed on her.

"I hope the Senator feels better," she said into the phone. "So long, Charlie."

"See ya, Grace."

Vincent turned up the walk toward the front door of the red brick Smithsonian building and then took the side path that led to Grace's bench opposite a lush bed of yellow bearded iris.

"Aloha," he said, and gave her a hug as she stood up.

Grace could feel the hard muscle across his back as she hugged him in return. It was a moment that lasted perceptibly longer than a casual hug. As they released each other, she raised her palms in supplication.

"Well, Vincent, in the Corps they probably court-martial people who screw up like this, but the Smithsonian restaurant has been closed for a week. I didn't check first. I'm just not used to this ... shit. The only thing open around here that serves food is the snack bar at the Air and Space building over there." She pointed at the modern steel and glass building down the street. "It closes at 4:00 I'm told."

Vincent mock scowled. "Since it is your first offense, we won't drum you out of the Corps just yet. Besides, I've never seen that museum, and I'd like to." They started walking toward it. "Anyway, we don't worry too much about gourmet food in my world. With us, there is only good chow and bad chow. Hot dogs can be very good chow."

"Eeuwh. Tubes of smushed nitrates. I'm *so* hungry for a great Crab Louis salad."

Vincent feigned a dreamlike trance. "Crab Louis? What is Crab Louis, mother? I've heard of Crab Louis."

Grace socked him weakly in the arm.

At the Air and Space Museum snack bar, all of the tables were empty. They ordered from the laminated menu. Vincent asked for a hot dog while Grace studied the meager menu, not liking anything she saw. Finally, she selected a pita sandwich with cucumber, garbanzo beans and yogurt.

Sitting at a table facing the lobby, Vincent stared at the historic plane models suspended from the trusses high over the first floor. "Hey, there is the *Enola Gay!*"

"I know," Grace said. "I took the tour once."

"Chill," he said vaguely, looking around, distracted by the sights overhead.

"So tell me. Did you get orders? What's your situation now?"

"Well, funny you should ask ...." His voice trailed off and he appeared to think carefully. "To tell you the truth, Grace, I've no bleeping idea what my situation is right now. Nor do I know how much I can tell you. Actually, not much, but let me speak in generalities. Assume, hypothetically, that a man who is steeped in a code of discipline and service to his country has reason to question what he is being asked to do for his country. Imagine his confusion and distress if, based on his core beliefs, he disapproved of actions that are being taken in his country's name and in which he is involved peripherally."

"You don't mean, like, *coup*-type activities? Nothing like that, right Vincent?"

"No, no, well, I hadn't formulated it in those terms. I don't know. I'm not in a position to know. I may never know. But not being able to rule it out is … problematical."

"Holy crap, Vincent, you're scaring me. Has this got something to do with all the energy shortage stuff?" Grace didn't know why she asked that question. It was just a feeling.

"Yes, it all fits under the same hat. As I said, though, there is a lot that I don't know. I do know enough to be way beyond saluting smartly and saying 'yes, sir.' For the first time in my career, I question what I see my country doing—correction—what is being done in my country's name. And that is the one mindset that I cannot have and do what I do." Vincent eyes were a mirror into his angst, and his gaze into Grace's eyes were a mix of beseeching anxiety and anger.

"Feelings are running very high all across the country about this energy crisis. Things are getting desperate in some quarters, but do you mean something else?

Vincent's eyes hardened and he seemed to find resolve.

"My telling you these things seems completely inappropriate to me, Grace. It goes against all my training and my obligations as a recipient of classified information. I ask you to keep this to yourself, not to mention it to anyone—not anyone. I can't even rule out the possibility of harm coming to you if you wrote about it. But I wanted you to hear it so that you will keep your journalistic eyes and ears open. Perhaps being around a Presidential campaign—I guess that is what your man Grey is up to—you may hear something, see something, that looks out of line, or … warlike. If so, I'd like to hear about it."

"But you can't tell me what you see and hear?" Grace queried, her tone sharper.

"Now don't get all competitive on me, Grace. Classified information, if disclosed, is a felony. You're not in that position."

"Okay, fair enough. Sorry. Anyway, you can eavesdrop yourself if you want. I got permission for you to join me tomorrow in Senator Grey's campaign entourage for his address to the ABA lawyers in Philadelphia. The van transporting us all leaves in the morning at eleven. That is, if you are free tomorrow."

"Hah. I am not only free; I have nothing to do. Did you ever hear of a military officer with no orders and no duty station? Me either, but you're looking at one. I'd love to tag along and hear the Senator first hand, though. He sounds a little squirrelly from the media coverage."

"Well, not from *my* media coverage. He is saying many things that are likely to trigger powerful opposition and so may not be politically smart, but the things he is saying are thoughtful and sound rather like the truth. He is pretty interesting."

"If you like him, I'll like him. Uh, by the way, is he personally interested in you? Has he made a move on you?"

Grace was not comfortable with that question. She tried not to let it show.

"I understand that he is married, but I've never seen his wife on the campaign trail, and he doesn't refer to her in his speeches. I don't get any vibe one way or another whether there is a close relationship there. And, no, I'm not dating him."

Vincent noticed the slight evasion, but said nothing.

"So, where are you staying?" Grace asked.

"Another good question. I was at the Navy Yard bachelor officer's quarters last night."

Grace said it instinctively. "You want to stay with me? I've got two bedrooms, so we have ... options," she added ambiguously.

Vincent suddenly looked exhausted. A wan smile came over his face. "That would be great. If it's no trouble."

CHAPTER

11

The battery-operated travel alarm went off at 7:00 am, and Grace mashed the stop button down with her palm. She turned to the other side of the bed. Vincent looked back at her.

"*Allo, bahbee-uh*," he said, affecting a French accent. She'd heard that shtick before, but it sounded good.

"*Allo* yourself," she smiled and rolled over into his arms. His closely cut hair was as neat after sleep as when he was wearing his uniform. "That's not fair when you look as good in the morning as you do at night." She grabbed her own hair and tossed it carelessly into a broad golden halo around her face. She rubbed the stubble on his jaw.

"Well, except for the beard." She touched her own lips. I seem to have a whisker burn I didn't have yesterday."

"I'd be happy to apologize for that, but I think you kissed me first."

"Umm. Yes, I did. It was after you said that I am an essential part of you. Like a pancreas, you said."

The night before, Vincent had told her about his dealings with Jerry McMasters over the last two days. After she questioned him about his career doubts, he confided that he'd been a courier for certain Federal agencies by ferrying classified information supposedly helpful in restoring the Western power grid. That's why he'd traveled from Hawaii to Washington at McMasters' request. Yesterday morning, he went in person to the Pentagon to talk to the major in the Manpower office he had spoken to in Hawaii and explained his presence in Washington as being the result of an extraordinary mission undertaken covertly for the NSA. Vincent was in that office when Grace had called. The G-1 major called McMasters and received confirmation of Vincent's story, but nothing more. The major showed irritation at these developments and at the mushroom treatment from McMasters. He told Vincent to be available by phone until HQMC had orders for him.

Grace had remarked that his mission was surely something to be proud of. Why was he so downcast about it? Why was he questioning his military service when it had meant so much to him? Vincent couldn't explain about the tanker hijacking or the pipeline sabotage or Sam Johnson. He had direct orders from McMasters to keep quiet about that.

He did tell Grace that he suspected his involvement may have been engineered, perhaps as a cover-up for matters he couldn't talk about. His whole role as a courier may even have been a sham for unclear reasons.

She'd asked how he could tell her this much if his activities were so hush-hush? "Good question," he'd said. "No good answer. I shouldn't have."

Grace traced a figure eight in the hair on his chest with her index finger.

"When you told me things that you weren't supposed to last night, I felt like we were a couple again—that you and I were a team. Not that you and the Corps were a team and I was an ... adversary. At LeJeune, I felt like I was being controlled against my will. Now, it's like we are equals. We respect each other, we depend on each other. Can you know how important that is to me?" Grace asked.

"I understand it a lot better than I did before the divorce. I also understand that my own sense of mission and self-importance is a lot blurrier than I thought then. It seems like we are just trying to make our way now. Nothing is certain. We face big problems all of a sudden, and we are stronger together than apart."

He stroked her back with his fingertips as he talked, then pulled her toward him more purposefully.

"And I love getting you in the sack," he said, "Not to put too fine a point on it."

Grace chuckled into his neck, "I've missed you too—in and out of the sack."

"Oh!" Grace remembered the time. "We have to get up. I have to review some news clippings about Senator Grey from last week before we go up to the hill."

With difficulty and a good deal of squealing, she pried Vincent's fingers from her backside and skipped to the bathroom.

"You are going to see a lot of lawyers today," she called back.

Vincent groaned, swung his feet to the floor and sat up.

"I'll take my shark repellant."

***

Aaron Grey let the polite applause die down and walked out to the front of the stage, clasping his hands behind him. He bent his body forward and peered at the audience in a professorial manner.

"I see the Dow broke below 6,000 today," he said. "Not only that, but the price of oil is trading $12.00 a barrel lower than yesterday's close. Consider that fact for a minute. High oil prices have caused the world's economies to tank. Oil scarcity drives prices up sharply, but only if there are buyers. Everyone one needs gasoline, but more and more of us can't afford to buy it. So we quit buying it. Then the price goes down, but distribution has been interrupted. Markets are beginning to fail. That, by the way, is how you define collapse—when markets fail."

He extended his arms toward the crowd.

"Do you know when that happened last? In the Great Depression. Let me tell you a story. My great uncle was a cattle rancher in the Flint Hills of Kansas before the Depression. His cattle fed on the lush prairie grass native to the Flint Hills—they call it tallgrass—and his cattle was in great demand. By 1933, however, with people everywhere hungry but without the means to buy beef, the market for it fell to basically nothing. He couldn't sell his cattle because the market collapsed. He had no income so he couldn't pay his taxes. The government foreclosed on his ranch for unpaid taxes, and he lost the ranch that had been in his family for generations. The government didn't want to incur the expense of buying feed for the cattle during winter—cattle that had little market value—so they slaughtered his cattle in the field. The carcasses rotted there. And all this happened despite the fact that people everywhere were hungry, in fact were desperate for meat. That's what it means when markets collapse. And all the wealth in those markets just vanishes. The ranchers, the distributors, the transporters—they just disappear.

"My great uncle never got over his experience. He earned a living in a small town in Kansas for a few years as a water well driller, but he just couldn't accept what had happened. He put a bullet in his head one day in his tool shed."

The lawyers assembled in the conference center auditorium looked back at him in silence. Some of the older ones nodded sadly, but the younger faces were blank. They didn't appear to get it. The wholesale disappearance of wealth along with markets was beyond their experience and comprehension.

"Our markets are rapidly, repeat, rapidly, headed in that direction again. You'd like to think it will be a gradual process, that you will see it coming and have time to react. But when it happens, it happens suddenly. You don't have time to react, and you are unprepared for desperate living conditions. That is the state of affairs toward which our nation is sliding."

A collective murmur went through the convention hall, punctuated by shaking of many heads as if scandalized by these remarks. Grey unclasped his hands from behind his back and sat down on a stool—the lone piece of furniture on the stage. Then he slowly extended his right arm and pointed to the audience.

"And it's your fault," he said, stunning the lawyers.

This time they smiled at each other and raised their eyebrows at the preposterous charge.

"The Bar Association makes up a substantial part of the establishment in this country. You lawyers hold political office, you sit on Boards of Directors, you are prominent and influential members of your communities, and you let this happen without showing any kind of awareness that this state of affairs, though perfectly foreseeable, was coming. You did it without raising any alarm or taking any action to head off this disaster."

The audience started to murmur again, this time in protest.

A woman called out, "You were in the Senate. You are paid to safeguard the commonwealth. Why didn't you raise the alarm?"

Gray raised both arms toward the lawyers in acknowledgement.

"Ah, thank you for that. You are correct. I cannot exclude myself from my own indictment. I stand before you even more culpable than yourselves. I have been a good, bought-and-paid-for Senator from an oil producing state, loyal to a fault to my constituents. A lot of Oklahoma voters work in the oil patch. My oil industry contributors generate good jobs at good wages for many people, and they pay taxes that permeate Oklahoma's and the nation's economies in countless beneficial ways."

Grace saw that Aaron Grey's countenance had grown ashen, and he was sweating profusely as he rubbed his left temple. She glanced at Vincent and saw from his expression that he noticed it too.

"We knew that reserves of hydrocarbons and other raw materials were finite; we knew that land and fresh water and clean air were finite; and we knew that the sources of our food supplies were finite. But, with relentless population growth, we continued to accelerate our use of these finite resources—resources on which long term human survival depends. We continued to exhaust these resources even past the time when we began to experience shortages. I am—but so are you—we are all guilty of this malfeasance."

Grey tilted backwards on the stool, off balance for a moment, and then grabbed the front of the seat to right himself. He raised a hand to his forehead and winced. Several heads in the audience turned to their neighbors with inquiring looks. Grey paused for a long moment and then seemed to collect himself. He stood up and leaned heavily on the stool with one arm as he faced the audience. Grace looked over at Charlie Hayden and saw him run his hand over his face and shift in his seat, wide-eyed.

Grey's voice rose again, firm and demanding. "This is not one of those proceedings to determine culpability that you lawyers are used to. That's already been determined. You well know the Latin phrase *res ipsa loquitur*. The evidence speaks for itself. We all walked blindly, stupidly up to this precipice. Now we are bound up in a frightening exercise in adaptation that, though foreseeable, came upon us too suddenly to prepare for. Unfortunately, we were handicapped by our own paradigms. We've received a lot of bad indoctrination as the result of decades of confrontation with international communism. We were taught that all forms of collectivism are a bad thing because Soviet and Chinese communism was a bad thing. Ayn Rand told us that in her novels. William F. Buckley told us that in his essays. Federal Reserve bankers and Presidents have conformed to that notion. Generations of Congressional representatives have legislated it. However, we all missed a crucial piece of the puzzle. Capitalism, with its free, open and privately held markets, has an inherently short range view designed to maximize near term enrichment of the holders of wealth *to the exclusion of all other things*—the very essence of greed.

"Notwithstanding the many undesirable permutations of collectivism, our bias should not confound us and turn us away from long term strategic planning that is essential to our survival. In an era of shortages, a capitalist system requires that capability as desperately as a collectivist one. It is an article of faith in this country that the allocation of resources by the free market produces the best possible distribution of those resources. But, as events that have overtaken us bear out, our faith has been misplaced. Right now, the People's Republic of China is much better positioned to ride out the economic shocks that are presently churning the world order. The PRC has, through centralized, strategic planning, systematically pursued and secured sources of energy and raw materials for decades.

"America has taken no such precautions beyond the already exhausted Strategic Oil Reserve. We did not build nuclear power plants. We did not create clean coal. We rely on oil for power and transportation well past the peak of terminally declining production. Private interests are squandering our large supplies of natural gas resources by exporting LNG as quickly as the now extensive LNG infrastructure permits in order to take advantage of high world prices.

"We were all there, you and I, and we let it happen. We have proven ourselves to be feckless as well as reckless. And what do we hear from our President in the face of this crisis? How does she use the bully pulpit of her office? Stay the course, she says! We will work our way through this period of difficulty, she says, as though overpopulation and exhaustion of needed natural resources are somehow self-correcting. Well, the bad news is they are self-correcting only by collapse. Overpopulation is self-correcting only with an horrific and unthinkable die-off of humanity. A collapse and a die-off on that scale would put those who survive it back where human existence was before the Industrial Revolution.

"I suppose the Easter Islanders realized that they were consuming their resources at an unsustainable rate, yet they persisted with their social habits, finally fighting with each other over them, to their everlasting ruin."

Grey's hands trembled as he pulled out a handkerchief and mopped his brow. Grace could see two uniformed men carrying emergency medical kits arrive and stand at the base of the stairs at stage left.

"Even lemmings, I suppose, on some level, know that running toward the sea at top speed in a swarm is inherently risky, but they do it. How much DNA do you suppose we share with the lemmings?" he queried the audience with a crooked smile.

Grey mopped his face again, took a sip of water, and then stood up straighter.

"That is why, my fellow citizens, we have to admit our past errors, cede more power to the Federal Government, and do the hard work needed to survive. If I were running for President …."

Grey waited for an appreciative laugh at his trademark line, but it didn't come.

"… as I have said before, the first thing I would do is seek authority from the Congress to nationalize all energy mineral rights and all petroleum and natural gas exploration and production assets in the United States and its territorial sea. Because this crisis was precipitated by the oil sector, I would ration oil and refined oil products in an equitable way. I would ensure that our national defense requirements for energy were met, but I would reduce the scale of the defense establishment and its energy allocation to clear, identifiable levels. We can no longer afford pork-driven defense industry consumption of resources. The ban on exporting crude oil enacted after the OPEC embargo in the 1970s was terminated more than a decade ago at the urging of oil producers who wanted to make more money by selling our oil overseas. I would reinstate that ban and expand it to cover gasoline and other refined oil products which have never been controlled.

"The next thing I would do is seek a constitutional Amendment that strengthens the emergency powers of the Chief Executive, including the power to declare a national emergency and the scope of it. With such powers, the President could intervene in any market in the public interest."

By now the audience was murmuring audibly and some shouts of protest were reaching the podium. Grace rolled her eyes at the outrageous breadth of Grey's stated goal, but Vincent was staring intently at Grey and didn't notice.

"Oh, I know that these proposals strike you as radical and dangerous. Yet, these things need to be done. I know this President will simply stall until the people of Oklahoma throw me out of office for the things I have said. But, I need people of your stature to support me. I may be able to gain the support of many working men and women of the country—those who are below or close to the subsistence line now as their jobs evaporate, their houses grow cold, and their cupboards are emptied. But you represent the establishment. Without your support and the influence you and other prominent people in society exert on the Congress and your communities, I can't save this country. I challenge you as you leave this hall today to reflect on whether anything I have said is without merit. Don't regard my speech through the distorting lens of party ideology or short term self-interest, but do so fairly, with an open and independent mind. That is what I have learned to do in the face of this crisis, and it is quite liberating. If you admit to yourselves that I spoke the truth today, I ask for your immediate support. Time, as you say in your trade, is of the essence."

Aaron Grey gathered up the speaker's notes that he had ignored on the lectern throughout his speech and walked to the wing of the stage where his staff waited and down the steps onto the auditorium floor. Two men in the audience walked up to Grey, shook his hand, and urged him to persevere in his campaign.

A woman called after Grey, "Traitor! Lunatic!"

Grey and his entourage, including Grace and Vincent, exited through the side door as the ABA President was thanking the Senator for his thought provoking remarks. Outside, as the group walked quickly toward the waiting van that would take them back to Washington, Vincent found himself walking alongside the Senator with Grace hurrying to keep up.

"I must say, Senator, I'm in complete agreement with you about the need for planning and rationing. From my job in Beijing, I could see the advantage China has over America."

"I'm very glad to hear that, Captain. Can I look forward to your transfer to our Corps of Salvation?" His smile was wry. It was a test.

Vincent grinned back appreciatively, "Well, I'm not free to switch Corps just now, as you will appreciate. But I will look for opportunities to, er, advance this idea."

"Ah, you just waffled, Captain. You know the truth, but aren't ready to jump. That is just where the great majority of Americans are on these issues—including the folks in that hall today. It is one thing to have an insight, but it is another to take the leap of faith that it requires. It's probably something about how the brain functions. It would be better for everyone, of course, if I or someone likeminded were elected president and Congress immediately did an about face, as you might say. But that's not how things work. America doesn't know how to pivot on a dime. It will take however long it takes, if it happens at all, and we just may not survive as a country."

"What you just said to Vincent wasn't off the record, Senator," Grace interrupted from behind him, "May I quote you?"

Charlie Hayden turned to Grace. "Not so fast, Grace. This isn't gotcha. Let us vet that and get back to you."

"Okay, Charlie, but on line journalism is pretty much real time," Grace said. "That's how we roll. Don't take too long."

They arrived at their van and climbed in. "I hope we have enough gas to get back, George." Grey spoke to his driver.

"Yes, sir. I checked the range of this vehicle before we left. Its battery power will get us nearly back, and then the engine will kick in. We should be in good shape."

"Senator, you seemed to be a little wobbly there toward the end. Are you feeling alright?" Grace asked.

Grey glanced quickly at Charlie Haden before answering, but Haden's eyes were averted and his face impassive.

"I'm fine, Grace, just fine, thanks. I just have to remember to hydrate myself a little extra before I walk into those lights. It was pretty hot up there."

George turned the van onto to the I-95 South on-ramp for the three hour trip back to Washington. Charlie Hayden reached into his portfolio and pulled out a copy of the Senator's schedule and began to confer with Grey.

Grace started typing the draft of her article onto her pad and listening to the conversation as best she could. It seemed like the Minority Leader was threatening to remove Grey from the Committee because of the radical positions that Grey was taking in his campaign. Grey and Hayden seemed to think that they could hold off his party's leaders with implied threats. If he became the party's standard bearer, they would need him and he would remember their disloyalty. They would likely wait for the political yeast to rise before taking any action.

The schedule included a floor debate and voting on an urgency bill to have U.S. Government-guaranteed bonds finance the construction of eight small nuclear power plants by local public utilities in six states, and four more built on public lands in the Southwest.

Just south of Baltimore, Grey and his chief of staff concluded their schedule review, and Grace judged it an appropriate time to raise the question that was foremost on her mind.

"Senator Grey, you said in your speech that you had experienced a change of heart, to put it mildly, about the nation's energy practices and in particular, your role in fostering those practices. It was a dramatic moment in the speech along with the plea to help you save the country from, and I'm not trying to be flip, *le deluge*. That is pretty strong stuff, and it is going to be the central theme of my article. Do you have anything you'd like to add? I take it that you thought it timely to make your personal metamorphosis known at this time. And do you have any comments about the growing movement in Oklahoma to remove you from office on the grounds of ...," Grace checked her notes quickly, "breach of trust?"

Charlie Hayden answered first. "I think the speech itself contained all the explanation necessary ...."

"It's all right Charlie. Grace gets to ask her questions, and we should answer them as best we can. Charlie didn't think this was an opportune time to offer any *mea culpas* about past votes, but I was asked a direct question and I felt obliged to answer it. There simply comes a time when you are faced with overwhelming evidence that a position you have taken is wrong. Maybe it is changed circumstances. Maybe it is a fresh insight. I think this crisis we are in and the absence of any clear way out of it are the factors that did it for me. Being from Oklahoma and having an oil patch constituency doesn't alter the facts. As for the talk about removing me from office, you can quote me as saying that I intend to serve out the unexpired part of my current term. It is very difficult to remove a U.S. Senator from office in the absence of moral turpitude. And it wasn't me that started down that path …."

Hayden quickly interrupted. "So, what Senator Grey said in his speech was unambiguous. We can stand on his plain words." Hayden looked at Grey who merely shrugged.

Aaron Grey's cell phone ring tone began to play "Oklahoma", the eponymous tune from the musical. He looked at the display screen and answered it.

"Yes, Diane?" He listened for several moments with a stony countenance. "You heard about my speech already?" He looked at Hayden. "Yes, those are my views, seriously."

He listened for a minute, then grew impatient and interrupted. "Look, Diane, I'm in a bus with a passel of other people so I'll have to call you back about that. No, not tonight. I've got things going on. Maybe tomorrow." He listened for another minute and then pulled the phone from his ear and looked at it. He raised his voice and spoke toward the phone's mic, "Gotta go, Diane." He punched off.

Grace knew that Grey's wife was named Diane. She jotted down "Bad Marriage?" on her notebook and showed it to Vincent. He nodded, then took the notebook and wrote "Got Stress?" before handing it back to Grace.

George slowed down and pulled the van alongside the curb in front of the Russell Senate Office Building. Everyone piled out and said their goodbyes on the sidewalk. Grace thanked Senator Grey and Charlie Hayden for allowing her and Vincent to ride along and giving her so much personal time. Grey shook hands with Vincent and wished him luck in his career. Then, the Senator's group walked toward the Russell Building and Vincent and Grace walked down the sidewalk to look for a cab.

As they walked, Grace looked at Vincent out of the corner of her eye. "Well, *that* was interesting!"

With her pad phone, Grace logged onto the municipal driverless car service operated jointly by the District with the States of Virginia and Maryland, but got only a "none available" message.

"So, how long are you going to wait on Hayden to get back to you on Grey's revelations," Vincent asked.

"I'm not going to wait. I'm going to finish writing this up, and if I don't hear from Hayden by the time I finish, it's going out. Then I'm going to find out more about Grey's wife. Did you catch that half sentence about moral turpitude and his not being the one to start whatever it was he almost said before Hayden cut him off? Whoa! There is a story there."

"Well, I'll tell you one thing," Vincent offered. "The guy is a little too shaky for me to want him as my Commander In Chief. And the bit about granting him emergency powers to do whatever he sees fit is from outer space."

At the corner of Delaware and Constitution, Grace stepped into the street with her hand up directly in front of a hybrid taxi pulling away from dropping a fare at the Russell Building behind them, and the cab braked just before hitting her.

"Extreme circumstances call for extreme measures," she said, moving toward the cab's rear door. "You coming? I've got to get back and write my article."

Vincent looked shocked by her dangerous move. "No, you go on back. I'll meet you at your place later today. I've got something to do. But I wish you wouldn't step in front of traffic like that. I just got you back. I'd like to enjoy you for a while."

"That's sweet, Vincent." Grace blew him a kiss and hopped into the cab. "I don't know what we are doing for dinner," she called through the window of the cab as it sped away.

It sounded so routine.

CHAPTER

12

Vincent walked across the grounds of the Capitol building toward New Jersey Avenue. He thought of walking up Pennsylvania Ave to the White House. He'd never done that. Turning his cell phone back on after having silenced it before Grey's speech, and he saw a missed call from HQMC. He sat down on a bench overlooking the Botanic Garden and returned the call.

"Major Howell speaking."

"Afternoon, major. This is Vincent Long. Checking in as directed, sir."

"Where are you Captain? You need to get here immediately."

"I'm at the Capitol Building, sir. You want me to come over to the Pentagon now?"

"What are you doing at the Capitol? Having lunch with the Speaker?"

Vincent took his sarcasm to mean that the major was still smarting from the treatment he got from McMasters yesterday.

"No, sir. I'm ...." He decided to abbreviate his answer. Howell would probably not like to hear about his day on the campaign trail with Senator Grey. "I'm just doing a little sight-seeing."

"You are out of uniform, I suppose?"

Yes, sir. I could go back to my, ah, quarters and put it on."

"Hell, no, that would take forever. Do you know where the Navy Yard is?"

"Yes, it's just down New Jersey a few blocks from where I am."

"Okay, run, don't walk, to the Navy Yard main gate and tell them who you are. I'll arrange to have a car standing by to drive you over here. If you are in your civvies, we'll just have to explain the circumstances."

"Aye, aye, major. What is this about?"

"Yours not to reason why, Captain. Just get here," barked the major. Then he relented. "The Commandant wants to see you."

"The Commandant. Of the Marine Corps? General Forest? Wants to see me?"

"Are you still on the phone, Captain? It doesn't sound like you are running."

"I'm on the way, sir."

What the hell?

He started to jog. In ten minutes he slowed to a walk at the main gate and approached the Marine sentry.

"Is the Sergeant of the Guard here, Lance Corporal? I'm Captain Long ...."

A First Lieutenant stepped out of the guard house and saluted. "Captain Long, I'm the Commander of the Guard. If you will follow me, sir, we have a military police vehicle standing by to take you to the Pentagon."

Vincent was unable to return the salute because he was out of uniform, that is, he wore no hat. Marines do not salute "uncovered." His clothes were wilted from sweating profusely in the humid June heat after his run. He assessed the impression he would make on the Commandant and hoped that impression would not find its way into his personnel file.

The MP lieutenant opened the back door of a black Ford sedan, and Vincent sat down in the welcome shock of air conditioning. The car pulled quickly out onto M street and sped up New Jersey Avenue to I 395 heading southwest toward Arlington across the Potomac.

The driver was a Marine staff sergeant. Vincent caught the sergeant looking at Long's limp civilian clothes through the rear view mirror.

"We'll be there in just a few minutes, sir. There isn't much traffic on the road these days. In this town that's saying something."

"That's the good news," Vincent said absentmindedly.

He was lost in thought trying to puzzle out why General Forest wanted to see him so urgently. He wondered whether it had something to do with McMasters. Could the major in G-1 have reported Vincent's mysterious movements up the line? He tried to reconstruct events from the time he learned of the tanker hijacking to the present.

Screw McMasters. I'm not going to keep anything from General Forest.

General Forest was known for his bull-like physique and his demanding nature. His neck was almost indistinguishable from his head except for the rolls of flesh that his tight collar pushed up framing his head. His nickname among the troops was "General Foreskin." God help the Marine who ever had a slip of the tongue in his presence. Vincent tried to put the nickname out of his mind. He would address the general as "sir" to make sure he didn't make that mistake.

The military police sedan pulled off Pentagon Access Road and up to the door facing the massive parking lot of the Pentagon. As he did, Vincent's cell phone played *Ruffles and Flourishes*, announcing an incoming call. It was Major Howell again with labyrinthine directions on how to get to his office. Howell would escort him to the Office of Commandant. Vincent's name would be on the list of authorized visitors at the entrance security station.

After passing through security, Long proceeded to Howell's office via an elevator ride up one level. He then traversed a hall which connected the concentric pentagonal corridors with each other. Finally, he walked down a long corridor to a door marked Adjutant, G-1, Office of the Deputy Commandant, Manpower, Headquarters Marine Corps. Major Howell was waiting for him.

"Good to meet you Captain Long. Unless you need to use the head, we will go directly up." Vincent demurred, and they started walking. "You should consider everything that is happening to you today as classified and need-to-know only. I reported your covert activities with the NSA to my intelligence contact in the G-2's office. Apparently, the G-2 briefed General Forest about it this morning. The General said he wanted to see you ASAP. The Joint Chiefs' meeting is tomorrow morning and he wanted to talk to you before that. That's all I know."

"Thank you, sir," Long said. "You can imagine my astonishment."

"Well, no, I can't. I have no clue what you've been up to."

Howell was not going to let go of the way in which one of his officers had been appropriated by another agency and then his being dissed about its purpose.

"Uh, major, given these developments that tend to be above my pay grade, and in the interest of full disclosure, I might mention that I spent the morning in Philadelphia with Senator Aaron Grey and his entourage. He was speaking to the American Bar Association and his remarks will likely get some press. I spoke to him about some of his, ah, controversial ideas. I can't think of any way my presence there or anything spoken between us would be disclosed or reflect unfavorably on the Corps."

"Of course you were with Senator Grey in Philadelphia this morning! Of course you were! Whisky-tango-foxtrot … what next?" Major Howell's voice rose, but he was too flummoxed by this news to have a further response. Also, they were in flag rank country. Howell checked his irritation. The Commandant himself had asked for Long.

"From here on, you are on your own," Howell said. "Anything else we should know?"

"I don't think so, major. Sorry to be stepping outside the chain of command so much. It's really just happenstance."

They arrived at the polished walnut doors of The Commandant of the Marine Corps, General Richard Burston Forest. Major Howell opened the door and walked in with Long in tow. A middle aged civilian woman with stylish, chin-length grey hair looked up from her desk.

"Major Howell and Captain Long?"

"Yes. Captain Long to see General Forest."

"One moment, please." She stood and walked to a closed door, opened it and closed it again after her.

"Well, Captain, you are up on the skyline now. Check with me before you leave the building, that is, if it doesn't interfere with your busy schedule," he added dryly and left the room.

It took some effort on Vincent's part not to smile. He was beginning to feel exhilarated by what was happening to him, and the new deference from his G-1 contact was downright enjoyable. Still, he knew he was out of his depth. This was going to be a test of his growth potential.

The receptionist reentered the room, leaving the door open this time.

"Captain Long, follow me please."

They walked a few steps down a carpeted hall and into a paneled room. The unmistakable countenance of General Forest appeared behind a broad polished desk as he looked up from a stack of papers. He was flanked by the flags of the United States and of the U.S. Marine Corps.

Vincent felt a powerful urge to salute. However, even if he had been in uniform, he was indoors. His only option was to stand at attention.

"Good morning, sir."

General Forest put the top sheaf of papers in a folder and stood. Glancing at Vincent's wilted street clothes, he walked around his desk.

"I apologize for my appearance, sir ...."

The general made a dismissive waive of his hand and stared into Vincent's eyes with an intensity beyond Vincent's experience. "Don't worry about it, skipper. Sorry to spring this on you. He addressed Vincent in the informal way of the Marines. A captain in the Marines is given the same moniker as the "skipper" or captain of a Navy ship, although the latter carries a much higher rank.

"We just didn't have time to let you get all starched and ironed before coming in."

"Yes, sir," was all Vincent could think to say.

Just then an Asian-American one star general entered the room. General Forest handled the introductions. "Captain, I've asked Brigadier General Yin, my intelligence officer to sit in on this discussion. Captain Long, General Yin is the G-2."

"Pleased to meet you sir," Vincent said as they shook hands.

General Forest pointed a finger at a leather sofa off to the side of his office against the wall. "Take a seat."

The Commandant sat down in one of two matching armchairs on either side of the table in front of the sofa. General Yin took the other arm chair. Vincent was in the gunfighter's position.

"Okay, skipper, I understand you have had some unusual interface with the NSA recently, and I'd like to hear about it. Do you have a problem with that? They swear you to secrecy or anything like that?"

"Well, yes sir, I was asked not to disclose certain things, but I don't interpret those instructions as binding where you are concerned."

General Forest nodded. "Good. Fire away."

Vincent related his association with Commander McMasters in the Beijing Embassy, the incident concerning the hijacked tanker in the Strait of Malacca, Vincent's encounter with Sam Johnson afterward and Johnson's association with Commander McMasters, the Ambassador's reaction to Johnson's visit, his own exchanges with Police Superintendent Liu, and his expulsion from China along with the other military attachés at the Embassy.

He described his irregular travel to Washington via Hawaii and Southern California, omitting only the episode with the young gang bangers in Honolulu. He explained his ex-wife's presence in Los Angeles when the western power grid went down during her coverage of the campaign of Senator Grey there. Finally, he related his recruitment by McMasters to courier some UCB drives, personally delivered to Vincent by Sam Johnson at Union Station in LA, his and Grace's subsequent flight to Washington aboard military aircraft arranged by McMasters, and finally his delivery of the memory storage devices to McMasters in Washington. Twice during Vincent's recitation of his recent history, General Forest and General Yin exchanged glances. Both occasions involved his discussion of his contacts with Sam Johnson.

"Very interesting, Captain Long. That's an odd bit about the flash drives. What's that about?" he asked ambiguously. General Forest was looking at General Yin, but the G-2 shrugged.

"So where have you left things with this Commander McMasters? Do you expect to hear from him again or do you think you are finished with that bunch?"

General Forest hunched his shoulders and peered intently at Vincent, punishing his shirt collar greatly.

"I don't know, sir. He didn't indicate one way or the other. I don't have any reason to think that McMasters will be in touch again, but then he may have manufactured the last reason to contact me. By that I mean that I'm wondering if that flash drive delivery business was what it appeared to be or whether he wanted Johnson to spin the hijacking and pipeline episodes to quiet my suspicions. Or maybe to assess whether I represented a threat to him. I may be flattering myself, sir."

"Well, Captain, I'd say your instincts are pretty good. General Yin, would you please arrange for some new orders for Captain Long? As of right now, he works for you, no, make that me. A special assistant to me can be anything, but you are the G-2 so that means intelligence. It should be confidential so that if McMasters talks to Personnel again, they don't mention it to McMasters. You never know."

The G-2 nodded, "Roger that, sir."

General Forest looked back at Vincent. "I'm going to let you in on some highly secret stuff, Captain, or at least give you a window into some things. I'm doing it so that you will have some context that might help you appreciate what to watch for and what may be at stake if you have any more contacts with your spook friends. This information may not, repeat, not be discussed with anyone besides General Yin and myself. Got that?"

"Aye, aye, sir. I'm clear on that."

Vincent wondered how he had gotten sucked into all this. Would he be able to handle himself?

"We've got a Joint Chiefs meeting tomorrow, and one agenda item concerns a report that has come out of the NSA. It details the strategic advantage that China has over this country in energy because of its systematic efforts over the years to exploit anti-American feelings in the Middle East, North Africa, and Venezuela. The strategy won long term energy contracts, joint ventures with oil production firms in Russia and the Caucuses, and pipeline and refining infrastructure that will serve their needs well into the future. NSA argues that the last time one nation embarked on such an industrial strategy was the 1930s when Hitler's Germany rearmed. NSA thinks China's preparations reveal an intent to use its energy assets in a warlike manner, and that the United States should preemptively interdict those assets. They point out that America's defense forces run on oil.

"In their view, the Marine Corps should put together a contingency plan as the point of the spear in joint invasions of Venezuela and Saudi Arabia along with the Army airborne. In other words, what they are thinking about is too big a job for some one-off special ops teams. They are talking about major naval and land-based offensive operations resulting in control of those countries. These would be attacks by the United States, but pre-emptive ones for defensive reasons, if you can follow that reasoning. Any thoughts so far, skipper?"

"Well, yes, sir. Unless NSA's got some smoking gun evidence of a warlike stance by China's leaders, I'd say that NSA has misread or misstated the situation. My dealings with the Chinese tell me that they have battalions of central planners, and those folks foresaw the commodities shortages we are now seeing, the most important of which right now is oil. They are merely being smart about what they saw coming. They see it as economic competition, not preparation for war. I know for a fact that they think we are, well, stupid, for not doing likewise, and they have for some years marveled at America's reliance on China as its source of needed man-ufactured goods. America's reliance on them implies that China's energy sourcing practices are to be expected, even required—you know, to con-tinue to supply America with what it needs but no longer makes. China's leaders would not see anything out of the ordinary about doing just that. That may be why the Chinese were so upset by the apparent American fingerprints on the tanker hijacking and the pipeline demolition. It took them by surprise. If it was us," Vincent added.

General Yin's face creased with a smile, and his head nodded in agreement.

The Commandant looked angry.

"It galls my ass to say it, but the Chinese are right. We are stupid. We should have been doing something like that ourselves all along. It's pretty clear that, as a country, we don't know how to respond to this threat now and are locked into some kind of desperation politics.

"The NSA people are panicking because they are responsible for national security and have egg all over their faces. The best response these cowboys can come up with is to dust off Manifest Destiny. They think America is fundamentally entitled to have plenty of energy, so America must use its enormous military capability to take somebody else's.

"I think the tanker hijacking and the Western China pipeline episodes are the leading edge of that policy. But these guys are speeding. At least a cadre of them are. This Sam Johnson guy is a cipher, though. The NSA doesn't run field agents like him. That's normally the purview of the CIA, so there is a piece here that we're not understanding. Who are these special ops people?"

General Yin spoke in a surprisingly commanding baritone.

"Well, the NSA's budget is huge and not carefully reviewed by the CBO, so they might just do it through contractors. There is a big pool of those people out there left over from the Gulf Wars and Afghanistan when the DoD used them extensively. Or, the CIA could have an oar in the water on this operation."

"Good point, Jasper," addressing his intelligence officer informally. "The CIA itself is a part of this or the NSA uses contractors. But these little grab-ass stunts still only get them puny oil scores, and they invite embarrassing retaliation like the western power grid hack. These geniuses need large scale military operations to get where they want to go. I expect that's why they are coming to the Joint Chiefs now."

Vincent's mind was reeling at this news. It was wild, but everything seemed to fit.

If the resource wars are going to start, I hope America isn't going to become the aggressor. Vincent caught himself before he said what he was thinking. *I didn't sign up for that.* He didn't want to be insubordinate. Besides he hadn't been invited to join in this discussion between the flag rank officers.

General Forest stood and walked to a map of East Asia on the wall.

"Well, I can tell you one thing. The United State Marine Corps is not going to be the point of that spear unless this becomes official policy. I don't know where the President sits on this. She has to know about NSA's overture to develop these invasion plans, and I'll wager that there are people on her staff that think something like this is going to be necessary to avoid economic catastrophe and an avalanche of political fallout. Also, they seem to have forgotten that the war power is vested in the Congress. They probably think Congress can be rolled into delegating its power to start wars to the President like they did with Bush 43 in Iraq. But unless this is a *coup de e'tat*, they have to put it to a vote in the Congress. I should find out tomorrow how the other services are leaning.

"You keep all this under your hat, skipper. I'm not going to keep you informed. I'm sticking what passes for my neck out a mile by bringing you into this. You've got the top secret clearance, but you don't have the need-to-know. So you don't know anything, right? On the other hand, you are to report back to me through General Yin if you have any more contacts with these friends of yours that could indicate they are still out there speeding. Agreed?"

"Absolutely, sir."

General Yin stood up. "I'll walk out with Captain Long, sir."

"Good," said the Commandant. "One more thing, Jasper. Long here needs a little more *gravitas* than a company-grade rank to be serving at this level, and I think he's earned it. Tell the G-1 that Long is now a major, will you Jasper?"

"With pleasure, sir." General Yin grinned at a clearly astonished Vincent.

General Forest extended his thick hand to Vincent. Vincent's move to shake it was just short of a jump.

"Thanks for coming in, Major Long." Then the Commandant offered the traditional Marine benediction. "See you on the beach."

"Yes, sir. Thank you, General Forest."

Out in the hall, General Yin took Vincent's arm.

"You just continue with your liberty, major, until we contact you or until you have something to report. Don't initiate contact with McMasters on your own. If they suspect that you are stalking them, it could be hazardous for you. These appear to be true believers that think starting a war is good for the country. Here is my card. Contact me for any reason. The after-hours number will reach someone who can reach me at any time."

"Aye aye, sir. I'll stay in the Washington area and just stand by."

Vincent made his way back to Major Howell's office as instructed before leaving the building. Howell was on the phone. When he hung up, he looked at Vincent as though expecting an explanation of some sort. Vincent offered none.

Finally, Howell said, "I've just been told that your temporary reporting relationship is to the Commandant's office, so you needn't check in with me anymore. If the Embassy attachés are allowed back into Beijing, I will pass the word up to the Commandant's office. Doesn't seem like that is going to happen, though. Anyway, your new rank isn't a good fit now."

Vincent tried to be ingratiating.

"Thanks very much Major Howell. I hope the rest of the people you look after aren't so difficult."

"Good luck, Major Long, and congratulations."

CHAPTER

13

Grace obtained a vast amount of personal information about Senator Aaron Grey just by doing on-line searches for articles about him in the archives of Oklahoma newspapers. He grew up in Ardmore, a small town in southern Oklahoma not far from the Red River that formed the border with Texas. The Red River, according to a local bumper sticker quoted in one of the articles, "keeps an Okie from being an asshole."

Grey went to public schools in Ardmore. His grandfather worked as a fireman on the Santa Fe Railroad out of Ardmore during World War II. His father had a career with Northern Energy in the booming oil industry, starting out as a driller and then, over the course of a long career, winning a series of promotions up to middle management. His mother worked as a librarian in the Ardmore public schools. Her influence inclined the Senator-to-be, their only child, to studiousness, and he excelled in grammar and high school, graduating at the top of his high school class and winning a National Honor Society designation.

Under a scholarship to The University of Oklahoma in Norman in chemical engineering, he built a perfect four point average. Grey had the same grade point average as the valedictorian in his graduating class, but Grey had been absent from graduation for medical reasons and was not similarly recognized.

One article described Grey's subsequent attendance at Georgetown University's graduate school of political science as having been paid for by educational grants, supplemented by part time jobs as a go-fer for a lobbying firm. While at Georgetown, his mother died suddenly of a stroke. Northern Energy fired his father for an unexplained assault upon another manager at the company's headquarters, after which his father moved to Los Angeles and remarried. The Senator and his father were said to have a "cordial" but not close relationship. Grey distinguished himself at Georgetown as a member of the debate club as well as student body president and graduated *cum laude*.

It was during the Georgetown years that he acquired a powerful case of Potomac fever. He believed the United States Senate was the greatest debating forum in the world, and joining that elite body became his driving ambition. He returned to Oklahoma and joined the staff of his elderly Congressman. He successfully ran, in turn, for the State legislature, and when his Congressman retired, for his Congressional seat as a Republican and won easily. After three terms in the Congress, and with the support of a leading kingmaker in his party from Ardmore, he was mentioned for both Governor and Senator, but he opted to run against a long-serving but aged Republican Senator in the primaries. When he won the primary and defeated his Democratic rival in the fall election, it was the fulfillment of his dream.

All of the movers and shakers in Oklahoma business were Republicans, and Oklahoma farmers were preponderantly Republicans. Grey himself explained in an interview that his ability to work across the aisle with Democrats was because he deemphasized ideology in favor of practical solutions. The Oklahoma Congressional delegation delivered on farm supports and energy industry benefits. That "brought home the bacon" in Oklahoma, and that is what the electorate kept score with. The industrial worker and minority constituencies in the State that leaned Democrat were too fragmented and poorly financed to challenge the Republican platform. Left-leaning academicians in the State's colleges and universities were not influential in Oklahoma, owning chiefly to the fact that they were seen by most Oklahomans as intellectuals and "different" with "funny ideas."

Grace's cell phone ring tone went off. Caller ID told her it was Vincent.

"Hello, Vincent. How go the wars?"

"Interesting choice of words, my girl. I'll just say that the U.S.-Sino relationship hasn't returned to warm and fuzzy yet."

"Are you nearby? What's happening?"

"I've had my ticket punched by those who pay me, and I remain a man of leisure. Speaking of money, I don't make enough on my salary to rent myself a place to live in Washington indefinitely. Ah, can we discuss the possibility of my bunking with you on an on-going basis? I have to give the Corps my address and home phone number."

"Discussion over. You can bunk with me indefinitely. The fact that I love you aside, it is the least I can do to repay you for getting me out of LA. But, I'm not as naive and innocent as I look. I see now that you re-seduced me just to get into my good graces and score a place to crash."

The pun was set up for him. "If I'm in Grace's good graces, I'll take it, and we can hold any discussion of my motives in abeyance. Anyway, I'm walking back from the Pentagon so I should be there in thirty minutes or so. There was a guy on the parkway selling produce out of the trunk of his car when I came over. If he's still there, I'll buy whatever he has. Maybe we can make a meal out of it."

"Sounds good. I found a can of tuna in the kitchen cupboard this morning. We have overcome the biggest obstacle between us and the future—another meal. I'm so relieved," she said lightly.

"Oh yeah. It just doesn't get any better than patty melt. *Ciao.*"

Grace turned back to the computer screen, and just as she did, it blinked into the black screen of death. She could hear the refrigerator turn off and then back on and then off again.

Exasperated, she got up and went in search of a nail clipper to attack the hangnail she had been scraping all morning. She found one in her top dresser drawer next to a matchbook that read "Piero's Fine Italian Cuisine, Manassas, VA." She and Vincent had lunch there one delightful Sunday afternoon when they were first married. He'd promised her they would have a bright future together.

Well, maybe, allowing for some ups and downs. It's not over yet.

She took a diet cola out of the refrigerator before it warmed up. There wasn't much else in there because of the unreliable power.

The can was half empty when she heard the knock on the door. She opened it to see Vincent in his wilted clothes holding a wrinkled paper sack.

"Got to have a key made for you," she said and set the bag on the kitchen counter. They kissed purposefully and then stood in a tight hug for a long time; as though they were taking a drink of each other.

"Wow, how about you go out and come back in again," she said. "That was nice."

Vincent grinned and pulled the fabric of her blouse tight across her breast, revealing its lovely half-moon contour.

"Aren't there studies that show spikes in the birth rate nine months after big storms and other events that keep people housebound?" he said looking at her chest. He dropped his hands and pulled her hips toward him, kissing her again. Then the ring tone on the phone in his pocket erupted.

Vincent screwed up his face and looked at the caller ID.

"It's McMasters."

Immediately, he was all business, releasing his grip on Grace and stepping away. "Good afternoon, Commander. What can I do for you?"

Grace went back to her cola as Vincent listened to a monologue by the caller. The expression on his face told her that this call held his complete concentration. Then his expression changed to surprise and embarrassment.

"Yes, that is where I am staying. It's her apartment."

Grace felt a wave of irritation. She didn't like the idea that this McMasters person knew about her.

"No, I didn't write up a report on my contacts with Superintendent Liu at the end. Things were happening pretty quickly if you recall..." Another long pause. "Oh, a debriefing ... yes, okay, I've got it. Check. Tomorrow morning at eight. How is it that you have all these vehicles at your disposal and the rest of us are taking shanks mare all over town?" Vincent immediately wondered if his tone was inappropriate with a superior officer.

Then he laughed, but Grace could tell that it was not genuine. "National interest does go to the head of the line, yes. See you in the morning."

Vincent hung up and looked at Grace who returned his gaze. The vibe between them couldn't have been more different than it had been immediately before the call. He looked out the window at the Rosslyn skyline for several moments and then walked over and joined her at the table as the refrigerator powered back on and her computer lit up.

"Let's back up a bit," he said. "I actually have a fair amount to fill you in on."

Grace nodded. "Would you like me to heat up the water for tea?"

"What? Sure, let's have some tea. I used to drink tea in Beijing all the time," he said absentmindedly.

Grace got up and put the kettle on and returned to the table. "Before you get started," she said, "tell me how this McMasters knows about me."

"Ah, yes. Well, the military transport we flew back on was arranged by Jerry, so he would have had a passenger list. And, when he was briefing me before we left LA, I asked him, well, told him really, that you were coming with me and about how you got stuck out there in LA with the Grey campaign and all."

Grace nodded again. "Of course. That makes sense." She seemed more at ease.

Vincent hesitated, and then went on. "However, McMasters let me know that he knew we were married, were divorced, and that the reason for the divorce was that being a Marine Officer's wife was not, dare I say it, your cup of tea. I don't know how he knew all that 'cause I didn't tell him."

Grace's eyes widened.

"This … situation involving questionable activity by some parts of the government continues. There is much I still don't get about what is going on, but I seem to have a role to play in it. I will tell you two things at this point. First, I don't think you are personally exposed to any sort of danger or threat, although I can't say that for a certainty since there is so much I'm not privy to."

"Oh, well, that's comforting," Grace said unsmiling.

"Second. There is an important story here which needs telling. And ironically, it sort of fits in with the stuff that Aaron Grey is talking about. You would be a good person to tell the story when the time is right. But for now, I owe it to people I trust, not to mention legal requirements, to keep quiet. As soon as I am able, I may leak some stuff to you."

Grace, now intrigued, asked, "Can't you leak it now on a not-for-attribution basis?"

Vincent shook his head. "If you write something about this, I'm the source. It's not like Deep Throat, where lots of people could have been Deep Throat. If I disclose it and the wrong guys win, I would spend the rest of my days in Leavenworth. I may blab anyway, depending on what happens, but not right now."

"So ...." she jutted her jaw forward and waived her left hand in circles questioningly. "What are we doing? Where do we go from here, Vincent?"

"The dialogue I am having with myself, Grace, is whether to just remove myself from your life until ...."

Grace interrupted. "Look, we had a heartfelt talk the other night about having a new relationship that would be between co-equals. Facing life together and all that. Remember? We'll decide what to do together, after we talk it though. You don't make any big, fat judgments on your own about me or us, right? Not before we talk it through."

Vincent made a face and scratched the short hair on his pate.

"I guess Faulkner was right. The past isn't dead; it isn't even past. This sounds like the conversations we used to have before we split. Only now, I get it. I surrender."

Grace's face softened. "It sound like you went up the mountain in China and found enlightenment. This is great stuff. Would you repeat that? And speak into the microphone please," she joked, holding out her can of cola.

"Hah. Since we are going to have this endless conversation about all facets of matters at hand, we should probably find some comfortable seats. We could either save the bottle of Gigondas I picked up on the way back to drink with the tuna and spinach casserole—I found that vegetable cart guy and he had some spinach left—or we could drink the wine now and worry about food later. I vote for opening the wine now."

"The glasses are over the sink, and you can find me on the sofa."

Sitting closely together and holding hands, they each took their first sip of the wine simultaneously, and then sat silently for a time.

"So where were you this afternoon, Marine? What happened to bring this stuff, whatever it is, to a head today?"

"When I walked over to the Capitol Building after you threw yourself under the wheels of that taxi, I got a call from Headquarters Marine

Corps. They wanted to see me immediately about … a new assignment. They sent a car to pick me up at the Navy Yard a few blocks away, and I got to the Pentagon out of uniform and all sweaty. Because of some stuff I was privy to in Beijing, and because of my courier assignment for McMasters, which I had reported to the G-1, someone has taken an interest in me. That someone, who has chicken guts all over the visor of his hat, had me personally report in. Bottom line, I now report to this, ah, general. I will have this assignment until further notice, and during that time, I will remain in Washington at the pleasure of the Corps."

"I surmise that your new boss is concerned about the same sort of conspiratorial things that you mentioned the other night that made you uncomfortable. And this McMasters guy figures into whatever the dark side is up to. You are in contact with McMasters, so somebody with chicken guts all over his hat—let's call him Maximum General—knows that and thinks your input is useful. And, I'm guessing Maximum General is not yet aware that you are meeting with Commander McMasters bright and early tomorrow morning."

Vincent was dazzled. He looked with fish-eyed admiration at the woman next to him.

"Girl, you are a quick study! You have a talent for intrigue."

"Thank you, thank you, but I am, after all, a journalist. And that all follows from what you've told me." She adopted a less accommodating tone. "Maybe you can find creative, deniable ways to keep me posted, especially if anything comes up that is in the nature of a threat against you, which I gather could translate into a risk for me as well. Until then, Vincent, I will wait, semi-patiently, for my Pulitzer Prize-winning scoop."

Grace refilled their wine glasses and walked to the kitchen with hers. He sat looking out at the dark swath in the distance that was the Potomac River separating the bright lights from the Virginia side from the smaller, indistinct lights in Georgetown.

"I can't figure out why McMasters and his associates want a rehash of my conversations the Beijing Police Commander" he said, loud enough to be heard over the sound of chopping in the kitchen. "Those conversations have been overtaken by events. Or maybe this is another diversion—like the UCB drives delivery maybe was."

Grace returned from the kitchen and sat down again. "What I don't understand, is if McMasters is centrally involved in the fix to the power grid cyber-attack by China, if it was China, then why isn't he one of the good guys?" She was halfway through a sip of wine when the expression on her face changed. "… unless he was involved in the events that caused China to retaliate with a cyber-attack in the first place."

Vincent looked at her wide-eyed again. "No comment."

Vincent took her left hand, and traced the veins on it with his finger as his mind replayed the events that confronted them. Then his facial expression changed. He noticed that she wore her wedding ring.

He kissed her hand and then her lips. Again, he reached over and pulled the fabric of her blouse against her breast, accenting its French curve-like elements.

"Now where were we before that damn phone call?" he said.

"The tuna and spinach thingy is on a slow bake," she said standing up and holding out her hand to him. "Come along, dear. We can have it as a midnight snack."

"You mean, come along, major dear. I got my gold oak leaf clusters today. Sort of a battlefield promotion."

Grace turned and dropped her jaw. "Well, major dear, that's wonderful. Being the incorrigible punster that you are, you'll appreciate that it will be my pleasure to join with you in celebration."

CHAPTER

14

At 7:55 am, Vincent waited at the curb in front of Grace's apartment building in civvies. He looked at the points he'd jotted down about his conversations with Superintendent Liu while Grace cooked oatmeal for breakfast. It seemed clear that the Chinese were certain of America's perpetration of the tanker hijacking in the Strait of Malacca and the pipeline sabotage in Xinjiang province. The question Vincent had was, what other retaliatory measures would China undertake before its outrage moderated?

The answer to that latter question could determine whether America would soon find itself in a full blown, modern war with China.

He could only speculate about the nature and scale such a conflict. It likely wouldn't involve battlefields with conventional weaponry. It would almost certainly involve reciprocal cyber-attacks on national infrastructure and civilian institutions. Except for possible missile strikes, it promised to transcend the traditional armed forces of the two countries.

Vincent's working hypothesis held that Liu was more than a municipal police official; he was almost certainly a ranking member of the PRC's intelligence community. That factor alone would explain why McMasters' unidentified cohort would want to debrief Vincent closely. The debriefing could supply pieces that fit together in ways Vincent could not know.

An olive drab sedan driven by Commander Jerry McMasters pulled up, and, through the open driver's side window, McMasters invited Vincent to get in.

"Morning, Commander," said Vincent.

"And the same to you, Major Long. You must be enjoying your extended liberty here in Washington. Congratulations on your promotion."

Vincent quickly calculated that there were two possible explanations how McMaster could have known about his promotion so quickly. Either the NSA bugged Grace's apartment, or the G-1 told him. He decided to ask.

"Thanks. How in the world did you hear about that so fast? I just found out about it yesterday myself."

"I got a call from a Major Howell at Headquarters Marine Corps office yesterday to ask about the prospects for readmitting attachés to the Beijing Embassy. Apparently he wasn't getting anything useful from the State Department on that. He referred to you as Major Long and said you likely would not be reassigned to your former post. You are on the young side to make major, so I gather that your fitness reports have been glowing. Maybe the brass figures that if you are aggressive enough to get yourself thrown out of China, you must have potential."

"Yes, according to the Peter Principle, apparently I haven't risen to my level of incompetence yet."

McMasters pulled the car into the traffic and headed south toward Arlington Boulevard.

"All of these power outages are really putting my family through some changes. My wife says shopping's a freaking ordeal out our way in Bethesda. How are you coping?"

"The same," Vincent said. "Maybe worse, since the malls and big stores are few and far between the closer you get to the District."

McMasters turned into the exit lane for North Meade Street short of the George Washington Parkway and the Potomac River. This surprised Vincent.

"Where to? I thought the NSA was in Fort Meade, Maryland, not Meade Street in Arlington."

"Hah. That's good. I didn't put that together. I just thought you might feel at home here."

McMasters circled around the perimeter drive of the Marine Corps War Memorial until the Lincoln Memorial, the Washington Monument and the U.S. Capitol Building across the Potomac were in precise alignment with their present location. There, on a rise behind them, stood the iconic statue of six Marines raising the flag on Mount Suribachi on the Pacific Island of Iwo Jima. The view of these four landmarks aligned down the entire length of the Mall reminded him that he was in rare air.

"Been here before?" McMasters asked.

"Yeah. I always thought the story of the Navajo Marine, Ira Hayes—the one at the end reaching for the flagpole—was a compelling story. Joe Rosenthal took the photo from which the statue was made. Of the six, three were killed on Iwo. Hayes was one of the three that made it back, but he was tormented by guilt at having survived and being paraded around to sell war bonds. He froze to death one day up on some mountain on the rez when he was drunk. That was before they had a name for post-traumatic stress. You probably knew all that."

McMasters nodded. "Let's take a walk, Vincent. We're meeting a guy here who shares my interest in your parting exchanges with Superintendent Liu in Beijing. There he is now."

McMasters indicated a rumpled, gray haired man sitting on a park bench away from the path on which the tourists were already beginning to circle. Oddly for a summer morning, the man was wearing a wool herringbone suit with a bow tie and was smoking a pipe while his thumbs worked the keypad of an electronic device.

Vincent put his hand on McMasters' arm and stopped him. Vincent decided to push for some information. Since McMasters had called him by his first name, he would do the same.

"Jerry, before we get there and I start disclosing confidential information to yet another person unknown to me and whose need-to-know is unestablished, at least to me, which you constantly raise as a barrier to explanations to me, a word please. As a matter of serendipity perhaps, I have been privy to a good deal of secret goings-on having to do with a very serious developing conflict between America and China. You are outside my chain of command, as we have discussed before, and yet we have this continuing relationship that has no parameters that I can see. I'm not entirely comfortable with it, since I have no clue what my role in it is. The emblems on your uniform are those of the U.S. Navy, but my working intel is that you are NSA. The little I know about the NSA tells me that it doesn't have field operatives like our friend Sam Johnson running around in or out of this country. How about bringing me up to date? Where does Sam Johnson, or whatever his name is, come in? Who exactly is that guy over there—the one who looks like he's been dropped into his suit from a great height? Give me a reason to cooperate."

McMasters put on his best Clint Eastwood face and squinted at Vincent with a threatening intensity. "Wrong questions, Captain. The question is what you can do for your country. You've sworn an oath and ...."

Following McMasters' lead again, he would switch back to formality. "It's major, remember? Yes, yes, I know all about my oath and my duty and my nationality, Commander. But I also know my job description, and, no offense intended, you aren't in it. So unless I get some answers, you can contact your counterpart in the Marine Corps, or have your boss contact his counterpart, or whatever it takes to get someone in my chain of command to order me to cooperate in the manner you are requesting. I want to emphasize that I do not mean to be insubordinate. But these are matters having to do with national security, and for all I know, you could be working for Hamas. So, set the stage for me, please."

McMasters' demeanor changed again, a little too quickly. "Look, Vincent, I take your point. But you can appreciate that I am part of the military intelligence establishment, I am carrying out a mission, the general nature of which, as you know, is to advance and protect America's interest in secure energy supplies and to counter foreign-sourced efforts to defeat our energy objectives. You don't have a need-to-know the kind of information you have asked for, and you know very well that, in the absence of that need-to-know, you aren't going to get your curiosity slaked. It's natural enough that you would like to know more, but it ain't going to happen."

"That's it?" said Vincent.

"I'm afraid that's it. Now will you talk to Doctor Mahdi, please?"

The speech McMasters had just made contained valid points. However, the words spoken concerning his military intelligence mission could also describe the role of the cadre General Forest suspects of leading a coup of sorts. Vincent's suspicions increased. He decided to raise the stakes.

"Sure, Jerry," he said, following on McMasters' earlier first-name informality.

They resumed their walk toward the seated man who was now watching them. Vincent was introduced to "Dr. Mahdi, a government security contractor."

"It's good to meet you Captain Long," he said shaking Vincent's hand. "Shall we sit?"

McMasters interrupted. "It's Major Long now, doctor. His career is on a fast track."

Vincent wondered where the listening device was. Dr. Mahdi shifted to the center of the bench facing Vincent on one end. McMasters sat at the other end, his eyes scanning the crowd.

"So, Major Long, Commander McMasters tells me that you had some exchanges with one Superintendent Liu of the Beijing Municipal police. We have reason to think that he may be a more important figure than that. Our working assumption is that he is in charge of the state security surveillance of foreigners in Beijing. He bugs the hotel and meeting rooms of foreign visitors and eavesdrops on the Embassies. Anyone in his position has to be able to evaluate what is overheard in light of China's most current and most important policy objectives in order to know what is helpful to the Government. He is believed to have quite a stable of analysts under his direction to parse through all that surveillance material. So, in a time of stress like the one which got you and the Commander here bounced from the Embassy, spontaneous words he spoke in anger are of interest to us. So, with that as background, I wonder if you can recap your exchanges with Liu using the exact words used by both of you. And also the tone of voice used, such as angry, shouting, that sort of thing. Okay? Start at the beginning of the first exchange please."

Vincent nodded that he understood. "Well Doctor Mahdi, it's been awhile since that happened, and a lot has gone down since then. I just remember him yelling that America wasn't going to get away with it, whatever "it" was. And that the attachés were being expelled. That's pretty much it." Vincent stopped talking.

McMasters' face flushed red as he glared at Vincent. He knew then that his speech hadn't been good enough. Long was going to stonewall them.

"Well, there must be more details that you can remember, for instance, who made the first call to whom?" The professor hadn't yet picked up the *kabuki* that he was involved in.

"I'm not sure. But Liu said that we attachés were going to be expelled because the Embassy wouldn't give them satellite images. Something about an act of war against China. His English wasn't so good. Would you mind telling me what your need-to-know is?" Vincent stopped again.

The inquisitor looked uncomfortably at McMasters. This information was useless. What was his need-to-know? Why was his time being wasted here?

McMasters looked furious now. Vincent had thwarted whatever purpose there was to this meeting. Vincent had a general idea that his actions would reflect badly on McMasters in the latter's circle of conspirators, but he didn't have any reason to fear McMasters' wrath. He just wanted to make the point that he wasn't going to be at the end of McMasters' yo-yo.

"Let's go, Dr. Mahdi. Major Long has developed selective memory syndrome because he wants something that we are not prepared to give to such a marginal asset." McMasters was gratuitously insulting Vincent for the double cross.

Vincent was delighted. Before the conspirators would tell him anything, they must first believe that they would get nothing further from him unless and until they demonstrated their bona fides. They may opt not to tell Vincent anything more and disappear. Vincent was fine with that. He would go back to enjoying his newly reborn love affair with his wife, all courtesy of Headquarters Marine Corps and his peculiar circumstances.

When Commander McMasters walked away with a confused looking Dr. Mahdi, Vincent glanced at his watch. It was only ten o'clock. McMasters hadn't offered him a ride home. No matter. Arlington Cemetery was just across from the Pentagon. He would call first to make sure General Yin was in the office, and if so, he would walk over and relate the morning's developments to General Yin in person.

As he left the Memorial, he saw park police setting up barricades and connecting them with police tape. A sign was posted on the barricade in the middle of the circle drive reading, "DUE TO CONTINUING SHORTAGES OF MANPOWER, THE MEMORIAL WILL BE CLOSED UNTIL FURTHER NOTICE."

Vincent stood with his hands on his hips, glowering at the sign. *This is beginning to piss me off.*

***

As arranged in his phone call forty five minutes earlier, Vincent's name was on the authorized visitor list at the Pentagon entrance. He received directions to General Yin's office, which Vincent soon learned was in the same hallway as that of the Commandant. General Yin's receptionist, a Marine staff sergeant, showed Vincent into the general's office without any wait. He could tell from her look at his casual civilian clothes and his rank as a field grade officer that she saw his visit as out of the ordinary.

General Yin rose to shake hands and motioned Vincent to a small conference table. The general took the chair with the note pad and pen placed on the table in front of it.

Vincent related in careful detail the developments of the morning at Arlington Cemetery and his attempt to elicit more information from Commander McMasters. Vincent half apologized for free-lancing in the manner that he did. Being unschooled in such matters, he wondered whether he should have checked in with the General as soon as McMasters had called him to ask for the meeting.

The general had filled up two pages on his yellow writing pad when he put his pen down at Vincent's question. "I'd say you handled that extremely well, major. You may not have any training or experience in matters of intrigue, but you have an aptitude for it. The reasons you gave McMasters for wanting to know more were plausible, and I expect he took them at face value. The tactic didn't work, at least not on the spot, but I doubt that he suspects you of being on their trail. Now we'll find out whether they see you as an indispensable party in finding out what the police commander in Beijing knows about their activities. If so, they will likely contact you again and be more conciliatory this time. If so, your improvised strategy may pay off yet, and we'll learn something. If not, it might meant that they are just walking you around to keep you hooked. I'll pass this information on to General Forest as soon as he gets back from the Joint Chiefs meeting.

"As information for you, we have asked a source in the Defense intelligence community if this Sam Johnson character can be identified. If we can find him in the Langley organization or the FBI or on the contractor side, it would identify another dimension to this conspiracy. Your Doctor Mahdi's name will go into the same hopper for the same reason, so you did manage to move the inquiry along just a bit. You may yet learn more.

"If we get any hits on either one of them and get lucky with photos, we will want you to ID them. Again, well done, major. Oh, and as far as contacting me anytime you get a contact from them, I will leave that to your discretion. I wouldn't have been able to add value if you had called me first this time, so it was fine. If they contact you again for a face-to-face and you have the opportunity, you might let me know. That would be a heads up that we might be learning more, and that might help General Forest. It will also provide us with some ability to trace your whereabouts."

He omitted the implied words "in case you were to disappear," but Vincent heard them loud and clear.

"Anything else?"

Vincent shook his head. "No, sir. Not unless you have the name and address of a well-stocked grocery store nearby with reasonable prices."

"I hear you there, major. My wife wants me to order an amphibious landing on whatever island it is where they are hoarding all the food. The PX out at Andrews Air Force base probably has more stuff than most grocery stores but you need a car to get out there. Do you need to borrow one from the motor pool?"

"No, sir. My wife has one, so we can use hers. Filling it up with gas is the problem. But that is a good tip about the PX. Thank you. I'll just have to spend a few hours in line at the gas station and remember to bring my wallet."

General Yin stood up, signaling that the visit was at an end. "I know you didn't sign up for this, but the times are challenging. Keep up the good work."

"I'll be in touch when I have something, sir."

Outside, the endless hallway ran to its vanishing point. Vincent walked to the junction of the hallway he was in and another that connected the other rings of the building. He wondered how many miles of halls there were in the Pentagon and in NSA and CIA facilities and whether all the people who inhabited them were under control. He already knew the answer to that one.

He continued on to the elevator and asked a Navy corpsman where the nearest cafeteria in the building was. At least he could get some chow before going back outside to sweat through his clothes again. It was even muggier than the day before.

CHAPTER

15

Aaron Grey exhaled deeply into the phone.

"Diane, I'm simply not going to do it. Your beloved and his CEO pals in The Hydrocarbon Council had better understand that. I know they are hiring all the political consultants in the country, and that they are playing for keeps. I understand that they may get me eventually, but, by God, I will go down in flames before I will quit. I'm not going to be a handmaiden in the destruction of our country any longer."

His speech was clipped and staccato, and he punctuated each declaration with a punching motion of the hand holding a highball glass, sloshing small quantities of scotch onto his lap.

A cultured voice answered. "Aaron, this just isn't … decent. It is embarrassing to all of us, including the children. It goes against your roots and the interests of the community that sent you to Congress."

"Interesting choice of words, Diane. You weren't so concerned with decency and embarrassing the children when you were sleeping with Jack for four, count 'em, four years. All the while, he and his wife were holding Cherokee Basin's fund raisers for my campaign and passing to me a long list of Washington priorities. I wonder how the pastor over at the Methodist church you all go to would think about that."

His estranged wife's voice lost some of its softness. "Oh, grow up, Aaron. These things happen. You were gone half the time, carrying on with who knows how many government girls. I fell in love; it happens all the time." She paused. "Are you seeing Doctor Geiser like you are supposed to?"

Grey ignored the last question. "You could have been ethical, Diane. You kept your little affair for four, repeat, four years secret and all the while lobbied me for Cherokee Basin's agenda. In our home, Diane. In our bedroom. I delivered their tax breaks even when I knew that they were unsound." He brushed some of the spilled drink off his sleeve. "Christ, it makes me feel dirty when I think about it."

"You didn't answer my question about Doctor Geiser, Aaron. Are you seeing him?"

"It is lovely that you are concerned about my well-being, Diane. If I were a betting man, I'd wager that Jack and his forces of evil are already planning ways to use my ... my history against me, guided by your valuable, not-for-attribution, input no doubt. But that isn't why you called. You are fishing about my campaign for the nationalization of the oil and gas industries. Jack is having you do it because I am not returning the calls of his lobbyists and he lacks the *cajones* to call me himself. Well, you can tell him that I am going to continue my efforts to create a grass roots movement to take over those companies. I am doing it because it is right and because, as even you people must realize, we have a national emergency. Tell Jack not to worry though; we will give the energy companies fair compensation for taking them over, say, by paying them the book value of their reserves after accelerated depreciation and depletion allowances."

The voice at the end of the line was stronger now. It conveyed fury.

"Aaron, that is so stupid. They are going to ruin you personally and professionally if you don't ... the children will be humiliated ...."

"Diane, this conversation is over," he said and hung up.

Grey took a long swallow from his glass, emptying it of what was left of the amber liquid it contained. He took a series of deep breaths and felt his anxiety subside. The deep breathing was about the only thing helpful that he had taken away from his sessions with his therapist, Solomon Geiser. *What the hell does Geiser know about energy policy? What is talking to him about it going to bring to the party?*

He grinned at his threat to compensate the energy companies according to the confiscatory book valuation method. He enjoyed the sweet irony of paying them at the low valuation the companies carried on their books because of their tax breaks.

He knew that his chances of getting that far were remote, but he would make good on his pledge. He would make sure that every thinking man and woman in America would understand where their interests lay.

He refilled his glass, dimmed the lights in his hotel room, and sat down to think.

***

When Vincent let himself into the apartment after his visit to the Pentagon, he found Grace on the phone. She waived excitedly to him and mouthed *Washington Post* silently. He went into the bedroom to change into a dry shirt and made a mental note to get some more short-sleeve shirts. He put on a fresh t-shirt and noticed that the air-conditioning was not on. He flipped a light switch and nothing happened.

Grace hung up just as he walked back into the living room. She stood up and kissed him enthusiastically.

"We have a lot to talk about."

"Tell me everything," he said.

Grace proceeded to tell him about a call from Mary Salter, syndicated columnist for the *Post*. Grace was as excited as Vincent had ever seen her.

"Get this," she said. "'Salter has been following my posts on Grey's speeches in LA and Philadelphia. She gave me the name of a TV news channel producer who is doing a special on Grey's candidacy and said to expect a call from him. How about that?"

"That's wild, darlin'. You are going to get the first of a long string of quarter-hours of fame."

Her face and arms were shiny with perspiration.

"Hey, dude, you wanna go out? I can't stand it in here. By the way, they invited me to appear on Capitol News Tonight at eight. No preparation needed. I would just regurgitate my *Insider* posts and take part in a panel discussion about the Senator's positions.

"Absolutely, let's get out of here. There must be a shade tree nearby. You're on at eight? I should drive you. It is getting more dangerous in the District at night."

"That would be wonderful. Maybe you can listen in from the wings or something."

"Yeah, I'm your security. I'll wear an ear bud and some Ray Bans."

They found the elevator inoperable. The emergency batteries must have been depleted. They walked down the five flights in the hot, still air of the stairwell into the late afternoon sun. Outside, they headed for a nearby playground where a solitary mother sat in the shade fanning herself while her child dug in the sand, red faced, but otherwise oblivious to the heat.

They took a bench under an elm tree, its leaves gently shaking from a light breeze out of the west. Vincent was the first to speak.

"So, the Senator's ambiguous warnings about meeting the Government's energy needs tie in with the stuff I've been dealing with. That really shivered my timbers. He knows something too."

"It looks that way. I thought it was an odd thing for him to say." Grace swabbed her face with tissue again. "What do you think it means?"

"Hard to say. I sounds like someone is whispering in his ear. You should ask him why he's emphasizing the Defense Department's need for oil. What happened to the public's need for conservation?"

The westerly breeze freshened perceptibly. Both of them luxuriated in it.

"Whose idea was it to build the nation's capital in these Chesapeake swamps, anyway?" Grace asked.

"I believe it was Washington himself who picked the exact location. Of course, it was in his 'hood just down from Mt. Vernon. Jefferson was involved in the implementation, so the Virginia mafia can wear that one. The whole town was laid out by a French engineer named L'Enfant as a grid with radial avenues cutting through to the center. I gather the North agreed to a location in the South, and the South contributed the land and the slaves to build the buildings. In those days, they were kicking the slavery can down the road after the Three-Fifths Compromise."

Grace faced Vincent in mock amazement. "Brainiac. I know you majored in political science, but you must have actually studied."

136

He mugged. "You read, you hear things."

It was Vincent's phone that rang this time.

"Long speaking. Oh, hello Commander." He looked sideways at Grace who rolled her eyes. Then he listened for several moments. Finally, he said "Okay, that's what I need. See you there."

Grace looked at him. "Talk."

"First things first. I didn't tell you about my morning," he said.

"Oh, yes. I meant to ask and then we got off on Grey's speech and all. Sorry. What happened?"

"We drove over to the Iwo Jima Memorial and met with a professorial type who materialized just for the occasion. McMasters wanted me to go into great detail about my exchanges with the Beijing police commander who tossed us out of the country. That guy, who is more than a police guy, probably knows something about the electric grid hacking on the Left Coast. Or he knows people who do. I declined to cooperate unless they gave me some background on what they are working on. I said they weren't in my chain of command, and I needed convincing that they were on the up and up. McMasters refused and we broke off. McMasters was pissed. I then went to the Pentagon and told my story to my superior. Now McMasters concedes that I should be briefed and wants to meet again."

"When? Can you still go with me to the studio?"

"Sure, absolutely. My meeting is not until tomorrow morning. They're going to pick me up again. It will be like *Groundhog Day*."

"Well, major dear, I'm going to follow up with Senator Grey's office first thing tomorrow and ask him what he had in mind when he issued that warning. I'll play Mata Hari and get it out of him."

"Yikes, I'm pretty sure that Mata Hari had to take her clothes off a lot and ended up in front of a firing squad, so you might want to rethink that idea."

"I think you would be the first to admit, big fella, that the sight of my naked body would give him the whips and jangles. Who knows what I could find out."

"Don't I know it, don't I know it." He was wide-eyed and grinning.

"You do what you have to do as a professional," Vincent said. "Hell, I'd pimp you out myself to find out what the threat is."

"Charming. Just what I wanted to hear."

They stood up and walked back inside. Mercifully, the air conditioning was blowing cold air when they got back to the apartment, so Grace dressed for her TV appearance in comfort. Vincent took her car key and walked down to the parking level to check the gas gage. The gas gage showed just under a quarter of a tank. It was a hybrid and would run on electricity for the local run over into the District. He made a mental note that, time permitting after his meeting with McMasters tomorrow, he would have to endure hours in line to get gas somewhere.

CHAPTER
16

Vincent woke up early thinking about how Grace had just been struck by lightning, professionally speaking. Her performance on the television news panel the night before had been remarkable. She appeared relaxed and photogenic, and her characterizations of Senator Grey's background and startling viewpoints in contrast with those of his constituency were gripping. Her currency as a journalist had taken a leap into the upper media sphere.

A glance at the clock told him he had to get ready. McMasters would pick him up at eight for the do-over meeting with Dr. Mahdi. That suited Vincent fine. He also got to reshape his responses to McMasters. Today, he determined to reach.

***

Waiting at the curb, Vincent wore his summer khaki uniform. On his collar points were freshly minted gold oak leaf clusters. He also wore his campaign ribbons from the Somalia campaign, a purple heart from the shoulder wound, and his expert shooting medals. McMasters would immediately see that he was "showing the flag."

The same sedan pulled up precisely at eight o'clock, and Vincent got in. He and McMasters exchanged greetings. The tension between them was palpable. Vincent slipped off his "piss cutter," the soft, folded cap that opens in the middle and fits closely over the head.

McMasters spoke first. "I see you are in uniform today. Have you got new orders?"

"No, but I have to go to the Pentagon and check in with G-1 later. They might be sending me to school next month for littoral combat training," he lied.

"How about you?"

McMasters shook his head. "I'm still a China hand, which brings me to the subject *du jour*. We'll take the same drive as before. We meet Doctor Mahdi at the Iwo Memorial as before, but you and I will have our conversation in the car before we rendezvous with him, alright?"

Vincent nodded. "Fine, but I'm still wondering why, with all the diplomats, Secretaries of Defense and State, *eminence grise*-types, old China hands, and the like around, a lowly Marine major keeps getting sucked into these—I'll use the term again—raggedy-ass, off-the-grid missions?"

McMasters grinned. "You have a way with words, Vincent. Has it occurred to you that maybe you have become an *eminence grise* yourself."

"Right. And as Lyndon used to say, 'he pats my wrist as he reaches for my jugular'."

"Okay, here's what you want to know. The Dr. Mahdi involvement was partly, but not completely, subterfuge. It is true that we would like to have the best possible read on the spontaneous, angry utterances of Police Superintendent Liu. You will be interested to learn that his outburst to you is the only communication from the PRC our government has received implying that America is behind the hijacking and the pipeline explosion. China's diplomats and leaders only refer to 'those who would recklessly wage war on China.' And given China's likely responsibility for the cyber-attack on the western electric grid, we would be pretty dull not to make the connection. Intelligence types like to study words carefully, so they want the best record they can get as to what exactly Liu said and in what context. All arrows therefore point at you for that information."

The car turned onto the perimeter drive around the Iwo Jima Memorial and McMasters pulled up to the new traffic barrier. They again sat facing the Mall looking at three of the most iconic buildings and monuments in Washington lined up before them like a row of corn.

"You said subterfuge. What was the subterfuge?"

McMasters resumed. "Well, it is debatable whether the desire to have Dr. Mahdi debrief you on your exchange with Liu was itself sufficient cause to bring you into this, ah, operation. But, there is another, more important, reason to recruit you. That is, to see if you can get back into China and meet with Superintendent Liu. You would deliver intelligence that he and his organization would like to have, and that we would very much like them to have. That information tends to show that America had nothing to do with the tanker and pipeline incidents. Also, to the extent that their cyber-attack was intended as a response to those perceived hostile acts, it might motivate them to cease and desist. We would be derelict if we had relevant information which could make them stand down and not provide it to them. You are the logical person to do that, given your unique relationship and prior history with Liu, the only senior Chinese operative we have identified who has shown himself to be personally involved with this business."

"This information," Vincent asked, "What is it?"

McMasters opened a leather portfolio and produced two files. The file marked "Tanker" contained satellite photos showing a plan view of several Indian Navy warships traveling close to and parallel with an oil tanker. McMasters explained that these photos obtained were obtained by spy satellites after the solar disturbance at the time of the hijacking, but that they showed the Indian warships escorting a single tanker of the type hijacked on the day after the hijacking. The photo had what purported to be a Greenwich Mean Time date and time automatically stamped on the print by the photo software.

"What did the crew tell us about the attackers?" Vincent queried. "Did the attackers look like Indians?"

"No, they didn't. But Indian accents are readily identifiable. That is the last thing Indian perps would do. They had an Anglo type as a leader and seventeen others, all Asians. They all wore hoods. It's pretty obvious that they were mercenaries. Who knows where black ops mercenaries come from."

Vincent was skeptical.

"NSA must have technology that reveals whether an image like this has been altered." *NSA must also have the technology to do the altering.*

"Yes, and it looks legit."

The second file was marked "Pipeline." It contained bank records, emails and news reports implying that the Xinjiang pipeline was blown by Pakistani-based terrorists affiliated with the Uighur militants in north-western China.

Taken together, the two files pretty much supported what Sam Johnson had hypothesized to Vincent in the Los Angeles Union Station.

Very convenient.

"I'm not buying it, Jerry," Vincent said after a few moments. He had stopped addressing McMasters as 'sir.' "The notion that I alone am the right man for this important work is counterintuitive. The President, who is in charge of foreign policy, could have his Secretary of State or any number of diplomats or military types with great China credentials, arrange a meeting just as easily and a lot more credibly. His emissary could present this evidence to the right people in China. Using me is laughable. I think you are bullshitting me, Jerry. Why, I don't know. No deal."

McMasters looked angry. "I've told you before, that you don't have a need to know the entire operational plan ...."

"And last time, I told you that Dr. Mahdi doesn't have a need to know that I can see. So, this isn't getting us anywhere."

"That's cute, very cute. Look, if the Chinese decided to put you in the slammer as a spy and torture you, the country's intelligence function could be damaged if you told them about us, and, trust me, they can get you to tell them everything you know. Now, your detachment from active duty is awkward so we don't have any appropriate superior in your chain of command to go through. However, I'm your superior officer under these circumstances, and I'm telling you that you've got an important mission for your country."

Vincent's smile was more knowing than amused.

"Jerry, first of all, let's knock off this pulling rank shit. Parsing rank between you and me in this business is like parsing virtue among whores. Second, I want a cogent explanation why you and your fellow operatives aren't using normal channels for this approach to China. Now I know there is a lot at stake here, and what you want me to do may be an appropriate response. But what appears to be a systematic avoidance of normal government channels bothers me a lot, repeat, a lot. I know when I am being diddled.

"All I know for sure, Jerry, is that to have access to sister spy agency documents; to have cars and aircraft available all over Asia and the States in an acute energy shortage for clandestinely transporting yours truly around; and to run guys on your team like Sam Johnson, who is most certainly not NSA; it all adds up to a lot of people from multiple agencies having a lot of resources. Moreover, all these activities seem to focus on critical energy-related matters. Now if that is all going on outside the purview of the normal government chain of authority, then it is an unauthorized conspiracy. Hence, my reticence. Care to try again?"

McMasters' countenance seemed to sag perceptibly. He gazed at the vanishing perspective of the Lincoln Memorial, the Washington Monument, and the Capitol Building in the distance while drumming his fingers on the steering wheel, and then spoke.

"Alright Vincent. You're very sharp. Maybe too sharp. I'm authorized to bring you in a bit if you refuse to cooperate on my say-so alone. But, you understand, that when you become privy to sensitive information, you expose yourself to new, ah, obligations."

"I'll take that in the manner in which it was intended, Jerry, as a threat. But you don't have to tell me squat. I'm fine with that. I'll just walk away."

"No, no. We want you to do this. It's not too complicated. You are a student of government and politics. Look, you know how hard it is to get anything done in Washington. It takes forever to take action that requires bipartisan support between the Congress and the President. That's why the war power has incrementally gravitated to the President during emergencies, even though the Constitution expressly says that it belongs to the Congress. There is a full blown energy crisis, not just in this country, but worldwide. We have lots of energy sectors—oil, gas, coal, solar, wind, nuclear, hydroelectric, geothermal, biomass, whiz-bang batteries, you name it. The problem is, the non-hydrocarbon energy forms don't come close to meeting our needs. Coal is dirty, although coal will get another look going forward. Besides, there isn't a Navy ship afloat, much less an aircraft, or a tank, truck or Humvee that can use coal. They all need oil.

The country just isn't set up to run on coal anymore, so coal isn't a fix to a short term or even a medium term energy crisis.

"Fracking technology was good for deferring the crisis for a few years, but that was mismanaged. As you know, because it was plentiful and cheap, it caused us to use up our reserves faster. Fast forward, our unabated dependency on hydrocarbon energy continues to this day, but the world's oil and gas supplies can no longer match the world's needs going forward. We're past peak oil and looking at peak gas after that. Production of oil is now declining rapidly. Gas shale fracking is hard to finance anymore because the industry finally had to admit that they don't know how to construct wells so they don't leak neurotoxins and methane all over the place. All the litigation over their operations exposed the fact that the companies knew it was harmful all along and lied about it. Now the fracking people can't get insurance, and Congress can't get a bill passed that either limits the industry's liability or provides government insurance."

Vincent chuckled without humor. "Where is Dick Cheney when you need him?"

McMasters gave Vincent a blank look.

Vincent explained. "The so-called 'Halliburton Loophole' was inserted into in routine legislation that was enacted during the Bush-Cheney years. That law exempted fracking from the Clean Air Act, the Clean Water Act, the Safe Drinking Water Act and the superfund cleanup law. So, the immunized frackers drilled like crazy and created a big environmental mess. Eventually, their liability underwriters were handed the bill in the form of lawsuits brought by the thousands of people and communities whose properties and lives were ruined as a consequence."

McMasters shrugged. "Cow pies happen. Shame on Cheney or whomever. Shame on the tobacco companies for knowingly causing lung cancer and lying about it. Shame on the NFL for knowingly enabling concussion injuries. Can we get back on point? You don't have to run completely out of oil and gas to have their markets crash. If the energy market perceives that there isn't enough oil or gas, free market pricing drives prices up exponentially. When energy costs surge, recessions happen and currency deflates. Oil and gas are commodities that can be monetized so holders of dollars and euros buy oil and gas futures driving up those prices even more. Markets don't work anymore. Utilities can't get reliable deliveries. When electricity demand gets close to crashing the grids, which is often, the utilities just turn off the power. That causes black outs. Without air conditioning, heating, and most importantly, gasoline for transportation in all modes, people at the margins die. Cities—hell more than half the people in America live in cities—become uninhabitable."

"I know all that, Jerry. I agree. And none of that is classified information," Vincent interrupted.

McMasters nodded impatiently. "The crisis at the moment is in the oil market. The defense establishment runs on oil. Without gasoline products, we can't fly planes, sail ships, operate tanks and trucks, or transport missiles or guns or ammo. We're out of business. The country is naked."

Vincent was fascinated by McMasters' narration. He was hearing some of his own thoughts recited back to him. This was a speech he could have delivered himself.

So am I a fellow traveler after all?

"I'm with you so far, Jerry. Let's vote for Aaron Grey for President and let him bring the majesty and resources of the Federal Government to bear on these issues."

McMasters seemed to give Vincent a double take at the mention of Grey's name, but then continued.

"Because we have an emergency, we can't wait for a new Congress to make new energy policy that takes over energy allocation and pricing over the objection of the industry. Hell, even this President can't make up her own mind on this stuff. If you wait for the normal channels of government to formulate energy policy that takes account of the new reality, we could wait years or decades. By then, the country will be a shambles and the military, without a reliable source of oil, will not be able to protect it.

"Not surprisingly, Vincent, there are a group of like-minded people across the national security agencies who are prepared to take action to safeguard the country's interests to bridge this emergency. Yes, our methods are unauthorized in a legal sense, but only in the absence of *any* authority. We hope that the institutions of government catch up at some point. In the meantime, leadership is required."

McMasters was sweating as the hot, humid, summer air settled over the Potomac Valley. He started up the car's engine and turned the air conditioning on high.

"See, we can't even have this conversation without oil."

Vincent leaned his face forward into the cold flow of the passenger side air vent. "So there is a group of conspirators exercising its own notions of what emergency measures should be taken. Measures which likely emphasize military energy procurement and not so much on civilian supplies."

Then he thought of Aaron Grey. Grey warned against exactly such responses to the energy crisis; that is before he seemed to reverse course.

What did Grey know?

"Why are you telling me all this, Jerry? What if I were to go to the FBI or HQ Marine Corps and blab? You already know that I'm not keen on rogue operations that are disloyal to the chain of command."

"Well, there are multiple answers to that very good question, Vincent. First, I know what you think about our lack of a reality-based energy policy. You know how dangerous that is. Heck, you are even consorting with Aaron Grey's campaign. Second, what we are asking you to do is a no-brainer that keeps you outside of all this activity altogether. You go talk to Liu and give him information ...."

"Or disinformation," Vincent interjected.

McMasters rolled his eyes and continued, "... information that is reasonably calculated to make the Chinese less inclined to wage cyber war on America. What American, in or out of uniform, wouldn't do that? Third, what would you tell the FBI or whomever? That a bunch of military types are concerned about the capacity of the military to protect the country without oil supplies? That you and I, colleagues of long standing, have had such a conversation? I would of course deny or qualify any characterizations of our talks as being improper or conspiratorial. I would also liberally invoke the secret nature of all information relating to the hijacking and pipeline explosion. You see? Blabbing doesn't go anywhere that can't be handled, and it would end badly for you. By the way, I know you aren't wearing a wire. This car is equipped to detect such things."

Vincent hadn't expected that. They were way ahead of him.

"No, Vincent, I don't read you as unpatriotic or reckless. It isn't likely that you will blab, but if you do, we are not concerned about it. Now, if you would just pick up your God damn phone and call Superintendent Liu—his number is programmed into that handy little smart phone in your pocket—and ask for a visa to come and meet with him about matters of mutual interest, then that would be the right thing to do. Oh, and I'm sure you can see why it would be a mistake to tell your media-darling ex-wife any of this."

Vincent expected it. "You aren't threatening physical harm to her are you, Jerry?"

"Good Lord, Vincent. We don't do strong arm stuff. No, it would just be an effort to discredit her. And you. It would probably affect her career prospects. And yours."

"So, you've thought this thing through, Jerry. I actually take some comfort from that. If, as you say, the information that you want me to convey is sound and what it purports to be, I do think it should be given to Liu and his cohort to minimize the risk of more cyber-attacks against American utilities. I wouldn't have any reason to question that if not for your friend Mr. Johnson."

McMasters waived his hand dismissively. "So you're shocked, shocked to find a spook in the picture? There are spooks all over the place all the time. Look, as the lawyers say, I can't prove a negative. It is impossible to prove that Johnson wasn't involved in either of the tanker or pipeline incidents. I'm just telling you that so far as I know, he was not."

The two officers stared hard into each other's eyes for some sign of weakness or prevarication. Vincent, for his part, saw none.

"Alright, Jerry, I'm your man. I'll do what you ask. I'll call Liu this evening and ask for a visa and instructions on how to provide him with this information. And, assuming I make the trip, I will report everything that he said back to you when I return. Okay? Does that do it?"

"Excellent, Vincent. That's it exactly."

McMasters clapped his hands together and rubbed them confidently.

"So, let's go talk to Dr. Mahdi and get that formality over with. Then he can check off that box on his list."

McMasters put the car in gear and started to pull out onto Memorial Drive and then stopped.

"One more thing. I'd like to have your answer on this. Are you going to blab, as you put it?"

Vincent intended to relate all of his conversation with McMasters to Generals Yin or Forest as quickly as possible.

I should have seen that coming.

"No." Vincent lied. "I've got no reason to do that. I don't have anything beyond suspicion anyway."

He wondered if McMasters' denial that the tanker hijacking and pipeline explosion were American operations was any more truthful.

***

After Vincent had answered Dr. Mahdi's questions about Superintendent Liu's outburst in Beijing, each one rephrased and asked again several times in varying ways in exhaustive spy-craft manner, Jerry McMasters dropped Vincent back at the apartment. Vincent said he would call when he had gotten through to Superintendent Liu.

Vincent used his cell phone to call General Yin. It would be harder to monitor than a land line call.

General Yin answered on the second ring tone. "Major Long?"

"Yes sir, I have a lot to report, and I am under some time pressure. Is this a good time? Should I come over?"

"Is it important?"

"Very."

General Yin responded, "I'm meeting with the Commandant for a working lunch. I'll order a sandwich for you. Twelve noon."

"Aye, aye, sir." Vincent hung up and wondered how the blazes he should act while having a private, conspiratorial luncheon meeting with two generals, one of whom is the Commandant of the Marine Corps.

***

Sitting at General Forest's conference table and unwrapping the tuna salad sandwich he had chosen, Vincent was acutely conscious of being the sole cause of an unmistakable fishy smell diffusing into the Commandant's conference room. On the other hand, he felt that he had earned the right.

Vincent related the entire conversation with McMasters first to General Yin and again to a late-arriving General Forest in a condensed version when prompted by General Yin. General Forest smiled broadly and delivered a hammer like blow to the table with his fist.

"This is great stuff, Long. First, what they are asking you to do may actually slow the Chinese down in the cyber warfare department. It is a worthwhile mission and you've got my direction to proceed with it. Second, the rationale and even the words used by this McMasters guy and what I'm hearing match exactly. Not the unauthorized conspiracy part, of course, but the policy basis for it. That confirms the breadth of it spanning multiple agencies. They are well-enough organized to have coordinated talking points. Third, it fits some contingency planning the Corps is being involved in. I can't really go into that. You are going to be exposed to the risk of detention and interrogation in the PRC. What you know now is consistent with what you are going to be telling them. That will protect both you and the country.

"Lastly, I want you to deliver a message to the Chinese through Liu that will get their attention. They won't expect it and it will give you more credibility. It is a message that, in my opinion, they should have."

The Commandant went on to explain the message that Vincent should deliver to Liu after presenting the tanker hijacking and pipeline explosion portfolios. He directed Vincent not to write it down now or later and to deliver it extemporaneously. It was simple enough, but would serve to put the Chinese side on notice to exercise care; that there was a rogue cadre within the American Government which may be working at cross-purposes to official American foreign policy, and that any future hostile developments should be reality tested in light of that possibility.

Vincent polished off half the tuna sandwich while General Forest talked. Then he noticed that neither of his companions had touched their food, and he stopped.

"How's the chow, major?" General Forest asked, amused.

"Great, sir. Intrigue makes me hungry ... apparently." Vincent wondered if he were being too flip for present company.

Still ebullient, the Commandant took a powerful bite out of his sandwich and dropped it back on its wrapper with a thump. Chewing vigorously, he aimed his index finger at Vincent.

"I'm very impressed with your acumen, major. You've done very well and shown initiative in this free lancing role you've been handed. I'm ashamed to say that I don't frequently get to enjoy the company of my young officers. This infernal Pentagon has got so many layers of rank and bureaucracy that I rarely get the opportunity, but I'm always inspired when I do. Well done, Long. When this is all over, I'll figure out a way to get something appropriate into your personnel file."

He looked at General Yin who made a note on his pad.

"Do you have all the input from me you need?" General Forest asked.

Vincent thought of Rowan's response to President McKinley.

"Yes, sir."

Vincent realized that his presence was no longer required, so, abandoning the other half of his sandwich and the tea, he stood up at attention. Both generals stood and shook his hand.

"I'll be in touch when I get back, sir," addressing General Yin.

Vincent was waiting for it.

"See you on the beach, major," General Forest said.

CHAPTER

18

The Grey organization hadn't been running television ads, so the one Grace was watching surprised her. Ads like this cost money. The chart graphic on the screen showed a diving line indicating an unusually steep decline in the number of barrels of imported oil over the past year. Under it was a drawing of a spigot with a single black drop coming out. That image was followed by another chart showing a more gradual decline in the supply of domestic oil and natural gas. The voiceover said that the global oil market was chaotic, and pointed to America's increasing inability to import enough oil to supply its immediate needs. Natural gas supplies exceeded demand, but fracked shale reserves were depleting faster than expected.

The only avenue open to restore order in American life, it said, was for the Federal Government to take control over the production and supply of oil and gas in this country. It would do so, the voice said soothingly, by means of a new National Hydrocarbon Commission proposed by Senator Aaron Grey. Under the plan, with the guidance of its bipartisan governing board and staff of experts, the Commission would formulate a fair and balanced plan for the allocation of scarce supplies for the benefit of all sectors of the economy and consumers. The implementing details of the plan would be initially established and then annually reviewed jointly by the President and a Committee of the Congress having appropriations power over it. The ad closed with an image of a confidently smiling Aaron Grey with an aerial view of the full circle of flags around the Washington Monument in the background. Superimposed on the image were the words "Strength Requires Strong Measures."

When she last spoke to Charlie Hayden a week ago, he led Grace to believe that Senator Grey would be spending a few days attending to personal and constituent matters and not to expect any fireworks from his office during that time. It seemed to her that this ad qualified as fireworks.

She muted the TV morning news program and called Charlie Hayden.

"Hi, Grace," he said brightly. "See the ad that's running on TV?"

"I certainly did, Charlie. This is a full-throated confirmation of the Senator's candidacy and his intent to take over the industry. So much for the non-campaign."

"Sorry we couldn't give you a scoop, Grace, but we wanted all the media to get it at once."

"No offense taken. I gather that you have some serious money in the coffers to be able to afford ads like these?"

"That would be a fair assumption. Our website contributions page lit up a week ago and continues unabated. We're not sure what triggered it, but grass roots support has been building rapidly. The Senator's message seems to have caught on."

"Well, congratulations to all of you, Charlie. It looks like your rocket is launched. Any background you want to whisper to me?"

"Not really, no. Aaron's due back this afternoon. We have some planning to do on how to capitalize on this new notoriety. The phone hasn't stopped ringing, and there aren't that many of us, as you know."

"These are problems you like to have, Charlie. More money means more staff. Let me know if there is any way I can get the Senator to answer some questions about this development. It seems like a game-changer, and his passage from a sort of, well, political novelty, no offense intended, to a well-financed, popular reformer in a time of crisis should be memorialized."

"I agree about the transformation. Gotta go. I'll be in touch about putting questions to him."

Hayden hung up before Grace could say anything else. This story was moving too fast; Grace couldn't afford to just sit and wait for a call from the campaign. She grabbed her purse off the end table and reached for her wallet. From a side pocket she pulled Senator Grey's card on which he had written his cell phone number when they were in LA coping with the power outage. She was reluctant to go over the staff's head since they could make things a lot harder for her. Nevertheless, she decided to push her luck and ask him about this development. If he got mad, she would apologize and play dumb.

She keyed in the number and didn't have long to wait.

"Hi Grace," Grey's voice was friendly. "Me first. Let's get together for dinner and get to know each other off the record. And we could talk about whatever you are calling about. Does your relationship with your ex preclude that?"

Grace hadn't anticipated it. Off balance, she ad-libbed.

"Well, Senator Grey, I wouldn't be comfortable with that. It would raise disclosure issues if I were to write about your campaign while having a, um, personal relationship with you. I am deeply committed to you in my professional capacity. I find your candidacy fascinating, and I want to observe it and write about it for as long as you will let me."

Why didn't I say my relationship with Vincent was also a reason?

"Bummer," Grey said. "Then I have no choice but to treat you professionally right back. I'm at the airport in Ardmore, Oklahoma trying to get a ride back to Washington. The airline flights are cancelled today due to fuel shortages, and for some reason, my oil company constituents don't seem to have any of their executive jets available. Odd, they used to make them available all the time."

She could hear the irony in his voice. He seemed to be thoroughly enjoying the discomfort he was causing his former supporters.

"Anyway, I need to get off the phone, so …."

"Senator, one quick question. Your television spot urging nationalization of the energy industry is Topic A as we speak. Where are you raising this kind of money? I realize that if you are going mainstream from non-candidacy, I can't very well expect preferential access to your campaign, but I sure do need to be up to speed."

"Well now, you've given me an idea, Grace. If I keep you in the dark so you can't write about me, that will remove whatever conflict of interest issues you have and we can have dinner and get to know each other like civilized people."

Grace remained silent.

"Okay. Question asked and answered. When I get back to Washington, if I *can* get back to Washington, I will have a press conference and you will be invited. And it may be as soon as tomorrow. Happy now?"

"I'll be on pins and needles, Senator. Thanks."

"Oh, and Grace, please don't use this number just to get better info than the office is giving out. I live my personal life on this phone. I do have a personal life, you know, although it seems to be a bit prosaic right now." His laugh sounded forced.

Grace winced. *Busted.*

"Message received Senator, I apologize for using this number. I got carried away when I saw the ad."

"Fine. Catch you later, Grace."

Grace tossed the phone on the sofa and tallied what she had just learned. He has been in Ardmore. That could be personal or constituent-related. He was overt in pursuing a relationship with her and hinted at his marital problems. The oil companies are unhappy with him and are applying pressure. No news flash there. She should call the Big Oil trade association and get its statement.

She resumed her on line research on the Senator's legislative record, but soon the desk lamp went dark. Within minutes of the power outage, Grace could feel the deadness of the air in the apartment. She left the apartment and walked down the five flights of stairs into the humid heat and looked for a shade tree. A soft maple spread its branches over a wide swath of the parklet beside her building. The sprinklers had wetted the dirt at the base of the tree, but she sat down on it anyway and leaned her back against the trunk. The moisture from the ground began to wick up through the denim of her jean shorts and cooled—what did the fitness gurus call it?—her core.

Damn, this country is coming apart.

***

Airport management gave him the postage stamp-sized Osage meeting room at the Oklahoma City airport, and Aaron Grey was happy to have it. He sat with his back to the window so as not to attract attention.

He had driven himself the hundred and ten miles from Ardmore before his staff in Oklahoma City reported that the last commercial flight of the day had been cancelled, and he was rebooked to the red-eye that night. Usually, the oil companies would arrange for one of their jets to touch down at the Ardmore Downtown Executive Airport to pick him up, but, as one of Grey's staff euphemistically put it, there were no oil company corporate jets "going his way."

His Oklahoma City staff told him about the irate phone calls from past supporters that deluged the office demanding that their Senator abandon this fossil fuel nationalization madness. The near-identical content of the messages told him that the call-in campaign had been orchestrated by local oil patch companies. He gave his staff talking points to handle these calls as well those from the local media. For the media and for low-dollar contributors, staff members were to point out that the country was now in a crisis mode, that this crisis was not self-correcting, and they were invited to join his effort to more efficiently manage the country's energy assets for the general welfare and for national defense reasons. It should be pointed out that such a move would be good for, not harmful to, oil and gas producing states, including Oklahoma. Better that Oklahoma's remaining energy assets be strategically rationed according to long term national priorities than quickly exhausted in a free market panic. For big contributors and investors, his staff were to emphasize an additional point, namely, that Senator Grey pledged to do his utmost to see that owners of any oil industry assets ultimately nationalized would be fairly compensated.

His cell phone's ring tone erupted. A glance at the screen told him it was Bud Haskell, Chairman and CEO of Cherokee Basin Energy Company in Tulsa.

This should be good.

"That you, Bud?"

"Yeah, Aaron, none other. Say, I hear you are trying to get back to that rattlesnake nest in Washington and not having much luck. Where are you?"

"I'm at Will Rogers Airport. I'm due out on the red eye tonight."

"Well, good buddy, the Cherokee air force is going to help you out. We've got a jet that can be there in a half hour and take you to Reagan

National. I don't know why I'm being so magnanimous given the positions you been takin' lately, but you can have a ride on one condition."

"You mean you expect some sort of *quid pro quo* for your generous act, Bud? I don't think that's ever happened before in the political arena. I've always told the media that your loan of airplane seats was purely due to your love of good government."

Grey was genuinely jovial.

"*Quid pro quo* is mother's milk, my friend. The tariff for this luxurious and timely ride is that I am goin' to ride along with my old high school chum, and we are going to have a heart-to-heart over this confiscation bidness that I'm hearin' about."

"Oh, is that all. Why, I welcome the chance to go through it with you, Bud. If I can win you over, my fight is half won."

"In a pig's valise, Senator," Haskell said evenly. "I'll call you when we touch down at Will Rogers."

"Okay Bud. Say, you weren't close to that Hinkley kid in grammar school were you?"

"Hah," Haskell chuckled, getting the joke. John Hinkley, would-be assassin of President Ronald Reagan, was one of the more notorious people born in Ardmore. "Naw, he moved away before I got to grammar school. Anyway, if I shoot you, I won't miss."

"That's good, Bud. I feel much better."

Grey stood up from the plastic topped conference table and stretched his lanky frame, feeling every bit of his fifty-two years.

Damn, I've got to get some exercise. If I'm ever going to get Grace Long interested, I need a—what was the Italian expression for making a good impression? Una bella figura.

He wondered about her involvement with the Marine officer he'd met on the drive to Philadelphia. Her ex-husband she said. He certainly made *una bella figura*. Obviously, they maintain good relations. Grey would need to get a better read on that situation.

He rode the escalator up to the passenger embarkation level and walked over to the counter at Java Dave's. The young woman behind the counter recognized him as he ordered a cup of black coffee, and wished him a good morning.

"Are you on your way back to Washington, sir?" she asked.

"Trying to, Julie," Grey said, long practiced at reading name tags, "but it's a struggle."

"Well, we need you back there fighting for us, sir. I hope y'all are able to solve this oil problem, uh, so everyone is happy ...," she trailed off ambiguously, aware of the raging controversy he had started.

"Julie, if making everyone happy is the objective, the Congress couldn't hang up its coat in the cloakroom. But I know what you mean, and I thank you for your good wishes."

He took his cup of coffee and retraced his path. The smell of roasted coffee reminded him of mornings in the kitchen of their Washington apartment with Diane. The best ones, usually Sundays when he wasn't appearing on some television news program, were some of the most comfortable moments of his life. He and Diane talked about news and politics and family and life after politics. He took for granted the trajectory of their lives together.

Guess again, you delusional schmuck. Diane was thinking altogether different thoughts those mornings, and they didn't involve you.

He paused at the bottom of the escalator and took a pull from the opening in the plastic lid of his coffee cup and jerked back as the too-hot coffee burned his mouth, spilling some down his shirt. Swearing to himself, he walked back to the counter where Julie, having observed the accident, nervously smiled and handed him a fistful of napkins.

Get a grip.

Bud Haskell called again about the time Grey drained the last of the coffee into his sore mouth, and he walked to Gate 12 as instructed. Once there, he watched the sleek Jetstream pull up and idle its engines while an airport worker pushed a small mobile ladder up to the door of the jet just as it opened. Grey walked out onto the tarmac, and Haskell's bald head stuck out of the jet's door. He waved for Grey to come aboard.

Inside, the jet was the picture of luxury. A row of plush armchairs clad in soft, ivory leather marched down each side of the narrow jet, spaced so that each seat could be rotated to face the ones across the aisle. At the front of the cabin, a door in the wood-paneled wall of the cockpit stood open. After shaking hands with Grey, Haskell made a go-ahead motion with his index finger to the pilot through the cockpit door while holding a phone to his ear. Then he pointed to the seat across from him, and Grey took the seat. Synchronized with the click of their seatbelt buckles and the closing of the cabin door by a pretty, uniformed woman named Kristi, the jet began to taxi away from gate. Haskell was on the phone making changes to his schedule necessitated by his impromptu trip to Washington.

Once airborne, Kristi's face appeared at Grey's side. "Welcome aboard again, Senator. Can I get you something to drink? We have the Illy *caffe* you like."

His mouth still sore, he shook his head.

"I'll pass on the coffee, Kristi, but maybe some ice water?"

Her smile was brilliant.

"Of course. Right away."

She glanced at Bud Haskell who, still talking, pointed to an empty highball glass on the tray table beside him and made a pouring motion.

Haskell finished his call and turned toward Grey. Leaning on his knees looking down as he appeared to gather his thoughts. When he looked up, Aaron Grey's eyes were coolly fixed on his.

Grey spoke first.

"So, Bud, you *really* don't like my proposal to nationalize your company's assets. It won't surprise you to hear that I already know that. Maybe we can fast forward to the question: How can the nation best deal with this energy emergency? I understand that your company and the others are making a ton of money out of this scarcity. And you no doubt see that this scarcity will be with us going forward. Cherokee Basin will enjoy huge earnings for as far out as you can see. You have the best of all worlds. You can even sell domestic reserves to foreign markets freely now. I also know you have a huge personal stake in having this situation continue indefinitely.

"But it isn't going to go that way, Bud. Surely you can see that. The sovereign U. S. of A. won't let it. It's not the job of Cherokee Basin to worry about conditions faced by ordinary Americans, but it is the job of the sovereign. So I'm asking you. Join in. Contribute to the debate. Help operate the assets after they are nationalized. Those operating contracts are going to be valuable."

Haskell was shaking his head before Grey had even finished. "Aaron, you need to understand. We go back a long way, but this is war.

If you persist with this horseshit, it's going to be the end of your career. We are going to ruin you. You won't be able to order a *latte* in this state when we are through with you. And it's not just us at Cherokee; it's all of us—the whole industry. The fact that you have undertaken this idiocy on your own without ever vetting it with any of us is unforgivable."

Haskell leaned on the word "idiocy." Grey's face flashed instant rage.

"Oh, you would have preferred that I keep Jack Gamble in the loop? The man with whom I have such a close working relationship?"

Grey sneered, referring to Cherokee Basin's head of Government Relations in Washington and the man who had cuckolded him for four years.

"I don't know what kind of beans you've been chewing, Bud, but that idea is fucking laughable."

Grey's eyes were molten, and his body language jerky.

Bud Haskell was taken aback by the force of Grey's outburst. Then his expression changed to one first of realization and then of astonishment as the tumblers fell into place in his head. That lasted only a moment and then his face, too, convulsed with rage.

"IS THAT WHAT ALL THIS SHIT IS ABOUT?" he yelled and stood up. Kristi looked up, frightened.

Haskell clenched and unclenched his fists repeatedly.

"I've heard whispers about Jack maybe having, you know, a thing with Diane in the past. Is that true?"

"For four years now, according to a leading environmental lawyer who shall go unnamed but who was anxious to turn me against the oil industry."

"That stupid son-of-a-bitch. With all the government girls he can boff, he's got to pick the wife OF OUR U. S. SENATOR? When I was a buck private in the Army, my drill instructor told us it was stupid to piss on the flagpole. It's too close to headquarters! And Jack doesn't know that? Well, he's about to learn it."

Haskell pulled his cell phone out of his pocket and thumbed a speed dial number.

"Jack, this is Bud. You been having an affair with Diane Grey? Yes or no? I'm waiting, Jack. Don't bullshit me. I thought so. Well, you're fired, you dumb screw. Clean out your desk and leave. If you aren't out in an hour, I'll have security frog march your sorry ass right out to the curb. Oh, and you know all those severance benefits you negotiated so carefully in your contract? Well you ain't getting any of them. You are fired for cause. SHOVE THE FUCK OFF, YOU HEAR ME? MORON!"

Haskell stabbed at his phone buttons several times, apparently missing the desired end-of-call button in his anger.

Kristi had disappeared into the cockpit and the cabin was quiet except for the whine of the engines.

Aaron Gray picked up Haskell's glass and sniffed it, confirming the traces of bourbon. Grey walked up to the cabin area where Kristi had prepared their drinks and poured two stiff ones from the bourbon bottle he found in the cabinet. He walked back to his seat and handed Haskell his drink.

"Bud, I can't deny that eavesdropping on that call was the most pleasurable thing that's happened to me all week. However, Jack's liaison with Diane is not why I'm proposing the nationalization of your industry. Of course, his, ah, mistakes do put some negative atmospherics into the mix, but that isn't the cause of it, and if their affair ends, that won't affect my position. Nationalization is necessary, Bud. That's why I'm proposing it."

Haskell looked tired.

"We have a private enterprise system in this country, Aaron. The freedom to conduct business is one of the most fundamental freedoms we have. It has served this country well. The profit motive is what motivated wildcatters to go out and find oil and gas in the first place. It's what motivated the entrepreneurs that perfected hydraulic fracking to start a new oil and gas boom in this country just when it was needed. You and everyone else have been living off of that *private enterprise* for the last umpteen years. We're still here; the Soviet Union isn't," Haskell said. "How many ways can I put it, Aaron. Enterprise here is privately owned. The idea that big government is going to solve commodity shortage problems is laughable. The way out of this is to get more oil and gas."

"You're depleting source rock now, Bud. After this, there isn't any more. You know that as well as I do. You're in denial. Government control of industry that affects the public interest in important ways has been in the Federal Government's tool kit for a long time. The mail, Medicare, passenger trains, and mortgage lending, to name a few. When circumstances warrant and when private ownership of critical industries fails the public need, government steps in. You correctly point out that the Soviet Union's collectivism is dead, but China's isn't and they are waxing our skis right now, in case you haven't noticed. Besides, most democratic oil producing countries reserve mineral rights to the sovereign. In emergencies like this one, governments either react nimbly or they collapse in chaos. My job description puts me in the chaos avoidance business. Yours puts you in the profiteering business. In divorce court, that's called irreconcilable differences. So, you and I are going to reach disagreement on this."

Haskell waived his hand dismissively.

"It is a lot easier to stop legislation in Washington than to enact it, especially some new and radical program. You should know that, Aaron."

"Where did you get the fuel to fly this plane to Washington, Bud? I saw one regional passenger plane at a gate in the airport and no activity going on around that one. You could shoot elk in that airport because of fuel shortages and the skyrocketing cost of airfares due to fuel surcharges even if the airlines find some fuel."

The hubris of a Big Oil CEO was condition reflex. Leaning forward, Haskell pumped the thumb of his hand toward his chest.

"We're the goddamn oil company! We *find* the oil. We *make* the fuel! We're *always* going to have fuel."

"So you fly one guy, a Senator who can potentially put limits on your great wealth, to Washington to try to influence him. It's a small incident, but it couldn't be a better example of how private versus public management leads to different results.

"Bud, you are a very rich man. Salary, bonuses, stock options, investments over the years. Your net worth is pushing, what, a quarter of a billion dollars? Your assets can take care of your family and their progeny as far out as you can see. How much is enough, Bud? In your own mind, I know you suspect that your actions run contrary to the needs of your country. You don't need to finish your career as a grasping Fifth Columnist."

"Fuck you, Aaron," Haskell answered, gazing out the window. "If government bureaucrats start allocating fuel, the shortages are going to get even worse."

After a moment, he added, "Yeah, I think about packing it in sometimes, but I always stay because I enjoy the action. This here don't feel like fun, though."

He swallowed his bourbon in one gulp and sank back in his seat.

"Anyway, it makes no difference what I do or don't do. The others are going to stop you. They will do whatever it takes. Your mental history will be an issue, Aaron. You can bet everything right down to your cufflinks on it. You are going to lose, Aaron. You are one guy out of hundreds in the Congress, many of whom are on the take. And we've got money."

"Don't be too sure, Ben. I've raised nineteen million dollars in the last two weeks from grass roots contributions. Corporations may be fictitious people for some legal purposes, but when I last checked, they can't vote."

Haskell did the math and whistled.

"So, that's how it's going to go."

After looking out the window for a few minutes, Haskell stood up and made himself another drink. He stuck his head in the cockpit and said something to Kristi, who reappeared in the cockpit. Haskell sat down in another seat further up, took a sheaf of papers out of his briefcase and began to read.

Apart from a single, awkward inquiry from Kristi whether he would like anything else from the bar, Grey was left alone for the duration of the flight. When the plane landed at Reagan, the plane taxied to a stop and the jet door opened. Kristi's look invited Grey to debark the plane so he gathered up his things.

"See you, Bud," Grey called.

"You're welcome, Senator," came the reply from Haskell, not looking up.

CHAPTER

19

Two men in People's Liberation Army uniforms were present when Vincent presented his passport and visa to the immigration officer in the sparsely populated international terminal at the Beijing airport. One of them stepped forward and looked over the shoulder of the immigration officer as he scrutinized the visa issued to Vincent by the Chinese Embassy in Washington. The photograph in Long's brand new passport showed him in his green "service A" uniform with the gold oak leaf rank insignia of a major plainly visible; however, he was in civilian clothes as he stood before the immigration booth. The immigration official stamped his passport and stapled his visa onto the stamped page, then handed it back to him with a dismissive nod. His arrival had clearly been expected.

After clearing immigration and customs, he hailed one of the Chinese-made hybrid taxis queued up outside.

No one at the American Embassy knew of his trip. Ironically, his stealthy return on a mission for the NSA was not unlike the earlier presence of Sam Johnson that had irritated both Vincent and the Ambassador. He hoped to save the Ambassador any further unpleasantness by avoiding contact with the Embassy.

The early evening air in Beijing was yellow and thick with the omnipresent smog and dust that blows in from the Mongolian desert before a storm. He hoped it would rain hard. When light showers come in these conditions, the rain drops are a mud slurry that fouls the urban land-scape. If it rains hard, though, it cleanses the air and runs off into wel-coming reservoirs.

As the taxi circled out of the airport, Vincent replayed his instruc-tions in his mind yet again. In setting up this trip, as instructed by Jerry McMasters, Vincent phoned Police Superintendent Liu directly and requested a face-to-face meeting in Beijing. He overcame Liu's objection to permitting an expelled military attaché to return by saying that he was carrying a message that might "clarify" the "misunderstandings" that may have arisen after the tanker hijacking and Xinjiang pipeline sabotage. Such information, Vincent said, might prevent more unfortunate "interrup-tions" between the two countries. His handlers chose the word "interrup-tions" rather than "difficulties" because it covered both oil shipment interdictions and power grid cyber-attacks.

The idea that a Marine officer known to the Chinese to be in charge of a security detachment at the Embassy should represent the American Government in a significant diplomatic and intelligence operation rather than a ranking State Department diplomat or a Presidential envoy still seemed laughable to Vincent. McMasters overcame Vincent's skepticism by pointing out that the Chinese would perceive his visit as being under the auspices of the Department of Defense and therefore potentially credible. His increase in rank to major at a young age further suggested that he was held in favor by the American military. Keeping the State Department and the White House in the dark was, however, consistent with McMasters' own narrative that the NSA and its co-conspirators were acting on their own.

Vincent suspected that McMasters likely had another, unspoken rea-son for using him for this mission, namely, deniability. If something embarrassing came out of it, the NSA and CIA could play dumb and even ridicule the idea. It was absurd on its face. Moreover, they wouldn't have to blow the cover of one of their agents in the process of making this con-tact or to reveal the unauthorized operations taking place. Vincent was under the radar on the American side and yet the Chinese side would see him as credible.

Maybe this mission isn't so raggedly-ass after all.

In a double-twisting added irony, there was yet another reason for his acceptance of the secret mission proposed by McMasters-one of which

McMasters was wholly unaware. Instead of Long's apparent on-leave status that permitted him to make the trip to Beijing without the knowledge of the Marine Corps or anyone else as McMasters assumed, Vincent had instead been directed by the Commandant of the Marine Corps himself to undertake the mission and to deliver an unwritten second message to Superintendent Liu.

Vincent carried the two files McMasters had given him to pass to Liu. The first he'd seen at his meeting with McMasters in the Arlington cemetery. It was the set of the satellite images purporting to show Indian Naval vessels escorting a tanker headed north out of the Strait of Malacca toward India. The second file contained what appeared to be a bank account statement recording the wire transfer of US$190,000 sixteen days before the pipeline explosion in Xinjiang from a bank in East Turkistan. The name on the account was that of a Uighur exile well known to the Chinese security services as a top commander of the World Uighur Congress, a terrorist group affiliated with Al Qaida in Pakistan. Appended to that file was an excerpt from a speech by Abdul Haq al Turkistani, its leader, which had been delivered to the Al Jazeera office in Islamabad by video. In it he said:

"The Chinese must be targeted both at home and abroad. Their embassies, consulates, centers, industries, and gathering places should be targeted. Chinese men should be captured and used as leverage for the release of our worker brothers who are jailed in Urumqi by the Han tyrants."

The natural inference was that Al Qaida-affiliated Uighurs were solely responsible for the pipeline attack.

Vincent was free to phrase General Forest's message as he saw fit. He decided to tell Liu that now, more than ever, it would be vital that China maintain and cultivate its official diplomatic contacts with America and communicate directly with those contacts. The POTUS, his Secretary of State, or their known envoys and Embassy officials should directly be made aware of all serious issues between the countries, especially those having to do with energy matters.

The Commandant's message, if somehow disclosed or revealed by coercion, could not be seen as stepping on his civilian bosses' authority. The message was a benign and obvious recitation of American governance. However, General Forest was counting on the fact that the delivery of that message in this unorthodox context would put the Chinese security services on notice that the possibility of rogue actors on the American side may exist. If Liu had any questions about that message, Vincent would have to demur.

Vincent wondered what would happen if a Chinese diplomat, making reference to the message and documents Vincent delivered, were to ask for a clarification from a high ranking American diplomat at some future time. The Chinese could easily pass along his name. It was an obvious concern for which there was no good answer. He was exposed and he knew it. If approached by the White House or Defense Department about it later, Vincent would claim that his activity had been top secret, and say nothing more unless the Commandant of the Marine Corps or his superiors, the Secretary of Defense or the Commander-In-Chief, directed him to speak of it. Beyond that, he had no answers other than the truth.

At the New World Hotel, he surrendered his passport to the front desk during registration and went to his room on the eighteenth floor. In the eighteenth floor elevator lobby, he noticed a series of four photographs of Beijing taken in 1989 from the top of the then new and grandly named skyscraper. The photos revealed a city of low, concrete, industrial buildings interspersed with one-story ramshackle dwellings as far as the horizon in every direction. Across the street in the foreground, a squat, gray, Soviet-style building carried a large red banner proclaiming itself as Beijing Machine Shop No. 40 in both Chinese characters and in English.

There were few traces left of the crude architecture of the city before modernization. Towering new office and apartment buildings ranged thickly over the plain on which the great city stood south of The Great Wall, one of many ancient defensive walls that snaked through north China. Seemingly numberless construction cranes protruded interstitially throughout the maze of high rise buildings. An exponentially growing city recast itself into modernity from an out-of-the-way "North Capital," the English translation of *Bei* and *jing* that had replaced the historic "South" capital of Nanjing.

It was over this vast, homogenized municipal and business enterprise that Superintendent Liu exercised the police power of the monolithic

PRC government, including the reciprocal foreign intrigue naturally tributary to this unique city. Vincent realized that he was very likely outclassed in the mission he was attempting to perform. He knew nothing of the capabilities and resources of the PRC state security apparatus.

He was pretty sure he wasn't going to die in the course of this mission, even if someone was blundering, but it was hard to figure out what the stakes were. If his role was only that of a remote player adrift in the vast kinetics between these two great powers, then this mission could be interesting but inconsequential. However, if his mission were to avoid an escalating cyber war, then it mattered a lot. He wished he knew which it was.

A knock on the door surprised him. A woman in a hotel uniform handed him an envelope addressed to Major Vincent Long and then walked away. He opened it and removed a note, a brochure and a map of the Summer Palace grounds some 15 miles outside Beijing. It was from Superintendent Liu. The note proposed a meeting at the Pavilion of Purity and Ease on the northwest shore of Kunming Lake at noon the following day, the location of which had been circled on the enclosed map of the grounds.

The brochure explained that the Summer Palace had been used by the Tang and Qing dynasty emperors to escape the north capital's searing summer heat. The heavily ornate pavilion, constructed entirely of marble in the form of a barge two decks high, was erected on stone supports and did not float. It had been built just before the turn of the 20th century on orders of the Dowager Empress with funds ironically embezzled from the budget of the Chinese Navy. Popularly known as the Boat of Purity and Ease, it had been used by the Dowager Empress as a personal lakeside pavilion.

The Summer Palace sprawled over a large area and served as a popular park for the teeming residents of the city. Among the crowds here, a Chinese man accompanying a foreigner would not be out of the ordinary. Being distant from the city reduced the likelihood of them being recognized or overheard, other than by Liu's watchers. It was a good choice of venues.

Vincent carefully folded and placed Liu's directions in the fold of his wallet. He then took a shower and brushed his teeth. He was sleep deprived but felt clear-headed. Looking at his watch and doing the calculation of subtracting time zones, he saw that it was very early in the morning where Grace was, and she would be asleep.

The phone in his room rang, and he answered it. It was Liu.

"Welcome back to China, Major Long. I see they promoted you for getting expelled."

"Yes, Commander, they did. They must have thought, wrongly I should add, that I did something to earn being thrown out."

"Did you get my note?" Liu asked. "Is the meeting convenient?"

"Yes, sir. The Summer Palace is one of my favorite places in Beijing, and I will be glad to meet you there."

"Excellent. I will see you there tomorrow." Liu hung up before Vincent could say anything else.

He dressed and went down to the hotel's western restaurant. Among other things, it featured, in true international fashion, a pasta bar. He chose fusilli pasta Bolognese, featuring a meat sauce in the style of the gastronomic capital of Italy, Bologna. He washed it down with a half carafe of local "Great Wall" red wine. The wine was plonk—vegetative and astringent—but he drank it anyway. Back in his room, he watched CNN and the BBC until his body clock and the wine told him it was time to sleep.

***

In the hotel's fitness center the next morning, he picked one of a long line of mostly idle treadmills to work off the pasta from the night before. He ran two ten-minute miles on the path to nowhere and then jumped into the pool for a few butterfly laps. Afterward, his head again clear of jet lag, he dressed in dark cotton pants and a white short-sleeve shirt-the sort of clothes that a Chinese man might wear in Beijing in his leisure time.

He asked the front desk how long a taxi ride to the Summer Palace would take, allowing for the traffic. Then he allowed additional time to walk from the main entrance to the Boat of Purity and Ease.

At the calculated departure time, he collected his files in a black leather portfolio and set out. The traffic getting to the ring expressway that circled Beijing was congested as usual. Getting to the ring road on city streets involved proceeding from one grid-locked intersection to another. A mass of cars, bicycles, motorbikes, trucks and the omnipresent pedi-carriers merged and circled, pulsed and braked as they flowed in slow motion. The tricycle-like pedi-carriers carried a small platform for cargo over the two thin back wheels—a bed that permitted an astonishing amount of material to be lashed onto it for a trip across the city. Here, one with a mountain of bok choy; there, another with a teetering stack of cartons. On one, in an achievement of stowage and balance worthy of the circus, two sofas were stacked.

The taxi followed the northwest highway to the exit for the Summer Palace. At the entrance, Vincent disembarked, paid the considerable fare in *yuan* and entered the park. Passing a moon gate leading to a side garden, he glimpsed a young couple holding hands and behind them an elderly woman transported by the slow, precise motions of her *tai chi*. When he approached the Pavilion of Purity and Ease, he recognized the figure of Police Superintendent Liu standing beside the stone barge, constructed stern-to against the shoreline of the lake. On both the upper and lower decks, grinning locals mixed with tourists taking pictures filled the air like parrots.

Vincent assumed Liu would want to speak with him someplace else. He didn't notice any watchers, but thought it likely that they were there. He wondered if they would be subordinates of Liu's or of others.

As Vincent approached, Superintendent Liu turned to greet him as if on cue. "Good day, Major Long. I trust you are well rested?"

"I am, sir, thank you. And I must say, I am delighted to be back in this beautiful city."

Liu motioned for them to walk away from the pavilion and toward a stone quay that curved out along a promontory into the lake, affording a view of the marble "boat" from the front. A fleet of excursion boats lined up along the opposite shore predominantly bore the color of golden yellow—the Imperial color.

On the quay, the two men came to a bronze statue of a popular Chinese mythological animal figure which stood on a broad concrete pedestal. The pedestal made a seat on all sides of the beast upon which to rest.

"Do you know this figure, major?" Liu asked his guest.

Vincent shook his head. "I've seen it many times, but no, I don't."

"It's called a Chi-Lin. In English they are sometimes called Chinese Unicorns or Dragon Horses. They are thought to protect against negative words and malicious gossip. They bring dignity to all who encounter them."

"I am impressed by your selection of this location for our meeting. I hope the protection of this Chi-Lin extends to the information that I am going to give you."

"I hope so too," Liu answered.

Vincent was somewhat unnerved by this exchange. He was delivering a message to Liu that seemed to him to be of questionable veracity. However, he had been asked to do so by his country's National Security Agency. The Commandant, General Forest himself endorsed the mission. Vincent had no choice in the matter, but his personal integrity was invested and that made him uncomfortable.

Did Liu suspect?

"Do you still write poetry, Superintendent?"

Vincent remembered sharing a table with Liu and others at one of the diplomatic banquets the year before in which they shared some personal pleasantries. Another Chinese official had announced to the table that Liu was a talented poet. Liu said then that he had one book of poetry published and that writing poetry was his favorite pastime.

"Ah, yes, I do. It's kind of you to remember. The bigger and more crowded the city gets, the more I enjoy writing about pastoral themes. If I had an English translation of my poetry I would present it to you, but it is difficult. The literal translations do not make good poetry in English, and adapting them to English is beyond my skill."

"I understand. Perhaps one day I will be skilled enough to read them in Chinese. It must be a good tonic—we say tonic, the word means a cure or antidote—your poetry must be a tonic for police work."

"Yes," Liu said. "And you, major, what is your antidote, your tonic, for your warrior work?"

"I am embarrassed to say that I don't have one. That's why I am impressed that you are a talented poet. In America, we sometimes think that constant work is so admirable that it is enough to live for. But, we can learn something from older cultures."

One of the excursion boats cruised by them filled with school children in uniform singing a song with obvious pleasure. The words were in Chinese, but the tune was unmistakable: the Happy Birthday song.

Keying off the song, Liu asked, "Did you bring us something today, major? Something useful?"

Vincent nodded. "You and I had some conversations before the attachés were expelled. You seemed to think that America was involved in the hijacking of an oil tanker in the Strait of Malacca and then later, pipeline sabotage in Xinjiang."

Liu continued to gaze after the boat with the school children.

"I, of course, related that exchange to my superiors, and I heard nothing more of it. Later on, after our Western power grid failed, apparently by a cyber-attack from computers located in China, I was contacted by an officer in the National Security Agency. He said that your remarks to me were the only ones from a Chinese official that seemed to accuse the U.S. as being responsible for the hijacking and pipeline incidents."

Vincent watched to see if Liu reacted to that comment. He did not.

"So, they asked me to contact you and give you some documents that might help identify those responsible for the hijacking and pipeline incidents. They asked me to do so, even though I am not in the intelligence services. They also think that you are more than a municipal police officer; that you are a state security official. They want me to point out that America used restraint in response to the attack on its power grid, and they hope that our two countries do not descend into a spiral of cyber-attacks or worse, especially when they are based upon misunderstandings. So, I have been asked to give to you, for whatever use you see fit, some documents. Is it appropriate that I give them to you now, here?"

Liu didn't hesitate. "Yes, major, you can give them to me here. It is not a problem if someone watches," he said, seemingly secure in his position.

Vincent opened his portfolio and removed two file folders. The tab of one was marked "Tanker" and that of the other folder was marked "Pipeline." Vincent opened the first folder and showed Liu the photos McMasters had shown him at the cemetery in Arlington.

"Your experts can look at these and make their own judgments about what they show, but I am told that they show the hijacked tanker being escorted to the north by Indian naval vessels. Apparently, unusual solar storm activity that was occurring at the time prevented the satellites from having earlier or later photos that would have revealed the hijacking and where the tanker was taken."

Liu pursed his lips at this comment but said nothing, Vincent resumed his monologue by opening the second file.

"Regarding the pipeline sabotage, bank account records controlled by a Uighur terrorist well known to your government show that funds were received by him a few weeks before the explosion from known terrorist funding channels. The money was more than enough to fund an operation of the kind involved with the explosion. Moreover, this terrorist is the leader of the World Uighur Congress. He has made public statements about attacking Chinese targets. Your own experts can verify those facts."

Vincent stopped and handed Liu the files.

"We have a saying that it is impossible to prove a negative. So it is impossible to prove that America did not participate in these incidents, but this evidence points to others as being the ones responsible. Our side wanted to make certain that you had this information. I am also instructed to say that any further hostile actions directed toward America from China will likely be met with countermeasures."

Vincent leaned back against a leg of the Chi-Lin and watched another excursion boat go by.

Liu turned and looked at Vincent with steady eyes. His demeanor was the opposite of his telephone call with Long at the time of the attaché expulsion.

"We can all agree that bad information is something to be avoided," he said. "That is all? There is nothing more?"

Vincent still had to discharge his obligation to General Forest.

"There is one thing more that I have been asked to emphasize. Our two countries find themselves in the most serious confrontation in recent decades. In addition to our respective arsenals of conventional and nuclear weapons, both sides have recourse to cyber measures which, in many respects, can be even more destructive and which transcend our military establishments. They involve war waged directly upon our civilian populations with unknown effects.

"This means that both sides should exercise the utmost care in evaluating intelligence on which important policy is to be based. Specifically, if the Chinese side perceives events which appear to be hostile to Chinese interests or sovereignty and involve America, it is critically important, especially now, that China's concerns should in each case be communicated to the American side at the highest levels and within normal diplomatic channels. One can never rule out the possibility that unauthorized actors may be involved in such matters that are entirely unknown at the highest levels."

Liu's countenance reflected intense interest.

Didn't expect that, did you?

Vincent recalled that Chinese officials tend to view America as the monolith that China is. They don't understand how someone could be working at cross-purposes to the American President without being locked up or worse.

Liu waited several moments after Vincent finished speaking before responding.

"I see. Any such concerns on the Chinese side should be addressed to your Ambassador, your Secretary of State or your President. That suggests a dangerous state of affairs that should be brought under control." He was staring hard at Vincent's profile.

Vincent said nothing.

He gets it now.

Liu continued. "Of course, your warning is itself being delivered outside normal diplomatic channels. You do see the—what is the English word ...?"

"Irony." Vincent finished Liu's thought. "I do see the irony, Superintendent, and I have no explanation to give you. I just wanted to alert you to certain possibilities that I can see from my perspective so that you can take appropriate action as circumstances warrant."

Liu's gaze never wavered. "You will keep us informed about any important developments, major?"

Vincent met Liu's gaze.

Is Liu trying to turn me? I should have seen that coming.

"You said it yourself, Superintendent. I am not someone who would normally be authorized to speak about such things. I may not have a future role to play in matters affecting our governments. The Chinese side should rely on its direct, diplomatic contacts with the United States Government at the highest levels."

Superintendent Liu pursed his lips again and looked away, apparently satisfied. He glanced once more at Vincent questioningly.

"I have nothing more," Vincent said.

Liu stood and straightened his back.

"I'm afraid the expulsion directive is still in effect, Major Long. Your return flight is tomorrow night, I believe." It wasn't a question.

"Unless you plan to conduct any business with the American Embassy here, there is nothing to keep you. We can get you on one of our flights out tonight if your airline can't accommodate you."

Vincent guessed that Liu was fishing to see whether he was in contact with the Embassy. If not, that would indicate that Vincent was not operating within official channels. He responded matter-of-factly.

"No, I have no other duties here. I welcome your idea about leaving tonight. I'll let you know if I need any help with the reservations. My plane was two thirds empty coming over so there should be plenty of space. The economic shock caused by this world energy crisis has suddenly put our economy into a deep recession, as I'm sure you know. Few American business people or tourists can be expected to visit until things get better."

"Have a safe trip back, Major Long."

Holding the files, Superintendent Liu strode off toward Longevity Hill, a rise of land built with the spoils dredged from the entirely man-made lake. On the hill stood a warren of buildings and pavilions, and Liu soon disappeared in the crowd moving among them. A group of four fit-looking young men got up from a picnic table he passed and drove off in an unmarked van that had been parked near the pavilion. Liu had enough force with him to take Vincent into custody if desired.

Vincent sat for a time reflecting on his exchange with Liu, finally standing to look at the Chi-Lin parading above him.

Did you detect any negative words, horse dragon? Did you confer dignity on me today?

He walked back past the Summer Palace gardens to the line of waiting taxis outside the front gate.

CHAPTER

20

G race had just spoken with the staff member in charge of Senator Grey's website. He confirmed what Charlie Hayden said about the tens of thousands of small donations the campaign had been receiving. It continued unabated.

The young man managing Grey's website made a spontaneous observation of his own. All of the contributions had been bundled by environmental groups and political action committees, he said. The bulk of the funds were wire-transferred into the campaign's bank account via the website's pledge software. The campaign received only a scattering of individual checks and small credit card transactions. That was unusual, he said. It seemed odd that lots of individual contributions would come in bundled from a few groups but few directly.

Note to self: what's up with that?

She checked her email and saw one from Vincent. It said that he had concluded his business in Beijing, was on a stopover in Tokyo, and should be back in Washington late tomorrow afternoon if he could make his connection in San Francisco. That's all it said.

Vincent had said little about his trip before he left. On their flight back to Washington from Los Angeles courtesy of the NSA, he'd seemed defiant, anxiously disclosing his thoughts to her. She loved that. Now, the wall was up again. Was he protecting her? This time, she would be patient and trust in his judgment. Whatever his preoccupations, they clearly involved the energy crisis and intrigue at levels he wasn't comfortable with.

Just then a new email arrived. It was from Charlie Hayden stating that Senator Grey was holding a press conference at his Senate offices this afternoon at three o'clock. She looked at her watch. It was noon.

She called her friend Jody, wondering whether she would be at home or at work.

"Hello, you," Jody's voice said. "I was just thinking about you. You want to grab a bite at Taqueria Frida tonight?" she said, referring to the neighborhood Mexican restaurant. "Or do you have plans with your man?"

"My man is in China and I'd love to. Say, I wonder if I can borrow your bike. I have to be at the Russell Senate Office Building at three this afternoon, and it is too far to walk. If the Metro is running, I can do that, but if there is a black-out, I'm dead. Busses from here take too long, and it can take forever to get a taxi."

"Well ...," Jody hesitated.

"Oh, if you are using it, I withdraw my request, I only ...."

"No, Grace, I'm not using it; it's just that I can't afford to lose it. It's how I get around. Bikes get stolen all the time now. Can you take it into the building with you?"

"Wow, Jody, I didn't think of that. I *will* take it in with me, and if security says I can't, I'll just come straight back with it."

"Okay, I'll give you my kryptonite lock in case you have to step away."

"I hoped you'd be working at home today? How lucky is that for me?"

"I was going to tell you. They cut me back to two days a week. Raj says the company is losing money. They give me a full workload, but I only get paid for two days and I work at home. It's understood that I will do as much as I feel is appropriate. I can't make it for long on those terms, so who knows? They probably aren't going to be in business much longer." Her voice trailed off.

"Oh, I'm sorry Jody; that's really crappy. This is getting very scary. No one seems to know anything or have any fixes. I'm afraid to project this crisis into the future because if I do, it looks like the abyss."

A long silence followed. Finally, Jody said, "And on that happy note, why don't you come get the bike now and keep it in your place until you need to take off. I'm going out for a while to try to find some batteries and lighter fluid. Can't be sure when I'll get back."

"I'm on the way," said Grace and headed for the door.

***

Grace pedaled up to the Russell Senate Office Building thirty five minutes early. She was able to take the Metro with the bike from Arlington all the way to the Capital South station. She rode the bike the remaining six blocks.

She walked the bike up the steps to the corner doors of the building and explained to security that she was a reporter covering Senator Grey's press conference at three o'clock and needed a place inside the building for her bike. The security guard said they get that request a lot, and she was directed to some a nearly-filled bicycle racks inside the hallway where she parked and locked the bike.

A number of reporters and cameramen were maneuvering their equipment in the Caucus Room to stake out a good location for their viewing of the podium. Grace took the last seat on the first row and waited as the room filled with media people. At precisely three, Chief of Staff Hayden and Media Director Alonzo swept into the room and stood flanking the podium. As the last minute shuffling of reporters and their crews subsided, Senator Grey entered and walked to the podium.

"Welcome everyone," he said. "I'll make some opening remarks and then open it up for questioning."

He caught sight of Grace and smiled perceptibly.

"As you know, I have proposed nationalizing the hydrocarbon energy resources of this country as well as the distribution systems for those resources. I have also proposed that the Federal Government form an expert energy conservation and allocation regulatory body that would establish controls over the production, distribution and pricing of hydrocarbons and other energy resources. Today, I am announcing that Senators Roark and Sanchez have joined me in co-sponsoring legislation that will carry these proposals into effect. This legislation, the Emergency Energy Powers Act, is being placed before the Senate as we speak, and a synopsis of the bill is available to you today. Please see Media Director Alonzo if you would like a copy. We have also posted the text of the complete bill on our website."

A knot of reporters rushed to Flor Alonzo to obtain the document, and Grey waited until that commotion subsided before continuing.

"There will be a lot of gnashing of teeth and wringing of hands in some quarters because of what we have initiated today. Predictably, this opposition will reflect the views of those favoring the status quo. That, of course, is because they are profiting handsomely from the current situation. This opposition is vocal and its leaders are well connected. They have lawyers and lobbyists and economists and media consultants who are skilled at media campaigns and public opinion manipulation. All of that is to be expected because that is the way of American politics. The First Amendment guarantees all citizens the opportunity to speak out for their own interests.

"On the other hand, there are also people who support our efforts, and, based upon our email count and social media posts, there are more supporters than opponents by a wide margin. No doubt that is because our supporters are consumers of energy—those who need dependable supplies of energy to travel to their schools and workplaces, to the store, and to the doctor, and those who need warming in their homes in winter and cooling in the summer. More than fifty percent of our population lives and works in our cities, and high rise buildings are largely uninhabitable for either work or residential living when the power goes off. And, not incidentally, our national security establishment needs reliable sources of energy to safeguard our nation in an increasingly dangerous world."

There it is again. Grace made a note of Grey's last statement.

"Clearly, the current situation cannot be sustained. Free market allocation of energy resources results in a random walk of frivolous uses of energy along with appropriate ones. Large quantities of both American crude oil and refined gasoline are being exported into the world market to those who can pay the price. Local utilities are advocating a flood of new coal power plants over the environmental objections of their communities because coal is plentiful and relatively cheap. Large-scale hydraulic fracking operations have been constrained in recent years as several states enacted an eminent domain process that compensates those whose properties are made uninhabitable by fracking operations. Those delayed fracking operations are resuming now under the pressure of scarcity. Much of this new fracking takes place in Midwestern and Southwestern states in which severe drought brought on by climate change continues. Vast amounts of scarce fresh water are used in those operations, forcing a painful trade-off of water for energy in those states. None of these developments provide immediate relief, and all need to be regulated. Exporting oil and derivative fuels worsens the crisis here.

Grey looked confident and relaxed.

"Let me address one aspect of the hue and cry that has been raised by the oil producers and traders who stand to be adversely affected by this bill. They claim that the proposed action is an unprecedented abuse of Federal power and that the free market has been shown time and time again to be the best method of allocating scarce resources—far better than any government central planners could manage.

"Nationalization of an industry is not unprecedented in this country, so they are wrong on that score. During World War I, President Woodrow Wilson nationalized the entire railroad system in America. It was in financial ruins and failing at a time when it was critically needed. Sound familiar? Wilson consolidated the railroads under an agency of the Federal Government and operated them successfully during World War I. Over time and after the war had been won, the nation's rail system was restored to health and re-privatized. Again in the railroad industry, a too-big-to-fail Penn Central railroad was in collapse when the Federal Government took it over. Federally operated Conrail went on to serve the entire northeastern part of the United States until it was re-privatized. In the auto industry, the Federal Government twice took control of Chrysler and once of General Motors, resulting in needed new capitalization, reorganization and subsequent financial success. In the energy industry itself, under the unflagging efforts of President Theodore Roosevelt, the Anthracite Coal Strike of 1902 was settled by inserting the Federal Government into labor-management relations. It successfully arbitrated wage and working conditions issues that kept the railroads and consumers alike in reliable supplies of coal, the then dominant form of energy.

"So, on the basis of long standing and successful precedent, we see that the exercise of emergency Federal power to intervene in dysfunctional, but critically important, sectors of the American economy is the norm, given emergency conditions.

"Only an ignoramus, or someone with a strong financial interest in the outcome, would contend that the free market for energy is currently working effectively, or even acceptably, under these emergency conditions. There is no relief in sight other than what we propose. I'll take your questions now."

Aaron Grey took a drink of water and looked serenely at his audience as they clamored for recognition. He pointed to Grace with her raised pen.

"Yes, Grace?"

Grace was acutely aware that his recognizing her by name and first in the questioning reinforced her newly established *gravitas* as a Washington reporter. It was thrilling.

"Senator Grey, you just said that one of the reasons why Federal Government control over energy production and distribution is needed is to assure the Defense Department a reliable allocation of energy to meet our defense needs. You have suggested in the past that the Defense Department's energy consumption habits may merit more restraint. Would this new energy allocation regime you want to establish trump the wish lists of the Defense Department? Is this to be a super agency that has a bigger vote than the other Cabinet posts?"

She sat down.

"Good question." Grey said. "Who is to be the final arbiter of energy allocation questions where national defense is concerned? It is early in the process, but the answer likely boils down to a Congressional mandate. The new reformed Department of Energy will have to make allocations that conform to standards and objectives set by the Congress. What better branch of Government to set those standards than the branch of government that has war powers? It's the branch where the competing interests of the voters and the Defense Department and its contractors in each state must be decided. How well that happens may be a test of the viability of our form of government going forward."

Grey answered questions for another fifteen minutes before a signal from Charlie Hayden triggered Grey's exit. Then it was over.

Grace packed her things into her rucksack and walked rapidly down to recover Jody's bike. She pedaled to the South Capital Metro Station only to find that train service had stopped due to the now-predictable afternoon power outage. Sweating, she traversed back across the front of the Capitol Building. At the Peace Circle, she pointed the bike up Pennsylvania Avenue and began to pedal faster. Where Constitution Avenue meets Pennsylvania Avenue she pulled over at the crosswalk in front of the Canadian Embassy. The traffic lights were out and the intersection was clogged with traffic trying to sort out a crossing pattern for the three way stream of cars.

A small group of young black men materialized around her, blocking her way and placing her out of the view of Pennsylvania Street traffic. A muscle-bound young man wearing a Wizards jersey grabbed her front handlebar.

"We be takin' dat bike and dat pack on yo back, white meat. Unless you wan' call the po-lice." He looked around at the others laughing appreciatively.

Grace was furious. She dismounted from the bike and tried to push it through the group of men.

"Get out of my way! I have to have these things. I'm a reporter and I have to ...."

The one who had been talking grabbed the collar of her blouse and dragged her over to the edge of John Marshall Park under some trees. Hands behind her yanked the shoulder straps on her pack off her shoulders. She tried to fight for her possessions, but the stocky one placed his open hand on her face and pushed her to the ground.

"Look, bitch. You see anyone here who is goin' rescue yo skinny ass? Dat bike and dat pack are gone, knowwhatI'msayin?"

He placed his shoe on her neck while she was surrounded by the others screening her off from view.

"Dey be goin' round ol' Mistah Marshall there right now. So, shut up if you know whutz good for you."

Hands were inserted into her pants pockets and then into her crotch amid raucous laughter. Her fury had been replaced first by fear when she was thrown to the ground and now by terror as she helplessly endured the assault against her. A knife appeared and cut her bra in the back as she was dragged further onto a grassy section of the park. More hands went to her chest, but there was no laughter anymore. The eyes of her attackers were predator's eyes. Grace was numb with disbelief that this could be happening where it was at the beginning of the commute hour. She was invisible.

"A'ight," said the stocky one. "This takin' too long, let's go."

Grace's fury returned in a wave and she twisted free of the hands that held her and from the ground kicked one of the men whose hand had been in her crotch.

"Who do you think you are?" she screamed. "You're animals!"

The blow to the side of her face jarred her. She felt the shock of it in her bones, and it emptied her mind. She no longer knew what was happening. She rolled on her side holding her arms up to protect her face. She lay there with no sense of balance, no instinct to right herself, finally becoming conscious that she was lying on her back and looking up into the canopy of the trees. Several minutes passed before she remembered what had happened, that she was alone and that her face hurt. She saw none of the men who assaulted her, but sensed that they had disappeared in the direction of the park space leading to G Street to the north. Turning her head to face Pennsylvania Avenue, she saw the traffic rolling by oblivious to her. If anyone saw her from that distance, they wouldn't have seen her torn clothes. They would see a woman relaxing on her back in the grass on a warm summer afternoon.

Grace struggled to kneel, then stand up. She was dizzy but, gaining her balance, walked toward the street. There, she was clearly visible as a disheveled woman with a red and swollen face clutching a torn blouse around her chest. Her shock subsiding, she dissolved into tears and stood waving at the passing cars. Scores of them passed her, some with passenger faces looking out at her in alarm but not stopping.

They took my phone. Vincent isn't here. What can I do?

Eventually, a District police car pulled up alongside, and two officers, one female, got out. The female officer said they got a 911 call from a motorist and asked her what had happened, carefully writing Grace's answers in a small notebook. The officer asked whether she wanted to go to the hospital ER. Grace didn't answer, confused. Her cheek bone ached painfully now. The officer again asked where she should be taken and who they should notify.

"I don't know. Vincent is away." She looked for the bike, confused.

"Ma'am we're going to call an ambulance and have you checked out, okay?"

Grace had a vacant look on her face, and she shivered in the warm afternoon air. "Ma'am, is there someone we can call? Can we call Vincent?"

Grace shook her head. "No, ... he's not here ...."

"Is there someone else we can call?"

"Oh, yes, maybe." she said. "Aaron Grey. He's a Senator."

CHAPTER

21

Grace sat in a wing back chair in the living room of Aaron's Grey's apartment aware of the gathering dusk. She sipped from a cup of English breakfast tea that Flor Alonzo had found after they came back from the hospital. The mugging ran through her mind but was not in clear focus. An ambulance had responded to the police call, medical personnel had performed triage on her face and questioned her enough to develop a working diagnosis of mild concussion, and took her to the ER at Metro Hospital. An X-ray showed no broken facial bones, and neurological tests were inconclusive. Grace was adamant about not wanting to be being admitted to the hospital for more tests. The ER doctor told her that rest was imperative. A concussion scrambles your brain functions, he said, like shaking a snow globe. He explained that things have to settle down in her brain, and that can take time

The emergency room called Senator Grey's office and reached Flor Alonzo, explaining that Grace had given the Senator as a party to notify. After some confusion in the office on how to react, Alonzo came to the hospital and assured the ER nurse that she would keep an eye on Grace overnight. She was briefed on the danger signs that would call for Grace's admission to the hospital.

Grace felt deeply embarrassed and said little in the process, partly because she didn't know how to explain the fact that she had given Grey's name as an emergency notify party, and partly because her mind wasn't working properly. She remembered that she needed to write up her article on Grey's speech, but she didn't have it clearly in mind and her notes and recorder had been stolen.

Riding in the car after being discharged from the ER, she slowly and deliberately explained to Flor that Vincent was in China and she had no family in the area. She explained how she had been attacked just after leaving the press conference and when pressed for someone to contact, she had given the Senator's name because she was confused.

Alonzo looked skeptical but assured Grace that she understood. She said that the Senator had asked for Grace to be taken to his apartment until things could be sorted out.

Now, they sat and waited for Aaron Grey to arrive to see what should be done.

Flor turned on the television and started surfing the news programs. They watched two segments reporting on Senator Grey's press conference that afternoon and one of them even featured Grace's question about who was to be the final arbiter of energy allocations between Defense and civilian use and Grey's answer.

"We should be hearing this from you, Grace," Alonzo said. "The crime of those hoodlums is being compounded. No one is hearing the story from you."

The sound of a key being inserted in the front door was followed by Aaron Grey's entrance. He had a concerned look on his face. Dropping his briefcase on the sofa he saw down in the matching wingback chair opposite the one in which Grace was sitting and leaned toward Grace.

"How's the patient?" he asked.

Grace's eyes began to tear up with embarrassment and relief.

"Senator Grey, I am so sorry to be here and troubling you. I got a knock on the head and when they kept asking who they should call, I had a brain freeze I guess. I knew that Vincent was gone and yours was the only name I could come up with. I had just left the news conference ...." The tears were flowing now.

Flor Alonzo was watching both of them intently, her own questions unanswered.

"Grace, don't concern yourself about this. And don't be embarrassed. I glad that we were here and in a position to react. I had Charlie and Flor arrange to bring you here in case there is no place else that you would like to go. We couldn't set you up with a hotel room by yourself because you need looking after. Charlie has found a private nurse who can stay with you tonight right here, so you can just relax."

Grace jerked upright.

"The bike. Jody's bike! Oh, no! It belongs to my friend—in my apartment building. She was afraid something might happen if I took it out into the District ... I promised her ... Oh, no," she said again. "She has to have it to get around. Oh, shit! I forgot. She and I were supposed to go out for dinner tonight. She's probably been calling me."

"Is your friend someone you'd like to be with tonight, Grace? Do you want to call her?"

"Could I please call her? Can I use your phone?"

Grey made a move toward his briefcase, but Flor produced hers first.

Grace stared at it and looked confused.

"I have her cell number programmed in my phone, and those ... scum have it. I don't remember her number. She doesn't have a land line so I can't call 411 or look it up." She handed the phone back to Flor.

Flor Alonzo started punching some keys and then waited.

"I'm calling your cell number."

"'Lo," she heard.

Alonzo went on the attack.

"You shitheads stole my friend's phone ...."

"Don't be callin' here again, fool. Get off da line," his voice rising.

Alonzo persisted.

"Has somebody else been calling? What did they say?"

Now guy on the phone was screaming.

"I said doan' be callin' here, bitch!" Then the line went dead.

"The bad guys are using your phone Grace. Better call your phone company and tell them to cut service. Do you have a kill switch?"

"I think so. I'll check with the wireless company ... later."

"How do we call Vincent?" Grey asked. "You know his number?"

"Oh, yes. Here, let me dial it."

She did and it immediately went into his recorded message.

"Vincent, ah, I've been in an accident. I'm okay, but my phone has been stolen, and so you can't reach me at that number. Also, I'm not at home. Call me at ...." She looked up at Flor and spoke the number that Flor mouthed to her.

"Call as soon as you can."

"Where is Vincent, Grace?"

"He's in China, or maybe Tokyo. I think he's on his way back—tonight or tomorrow I think." She touched her face and winced.

Grey's lean, sensitive face registered concern.

"It's getting late, and you need rest. In fact, I'll bet they told you to rest. I got my clock cleaned a couple of times in high school football—too skinny—, and they kept telling me to rest. So, you'll need to stay here tonight."

"Thank you so much, Senator Grey for all this. And please don't call in a nurse. I don't need that kind of attention. Tomorrow, I'll be able to go home, and Vincent will be back. I really am dizzy now though."

Flor Alonzo turned and picked up her things.

"Aaron, do you want me to check back here on my way to work in the morning? Then we can figure out when and how to ferry Grace back to her place or meet up with Vincent."

Lightheaded or not, Grace picked up the suspicious vibe from Alonzo.

She thinks there is something going on between me and Aaron.

"Sounds like a plan, Flor," Grey said. "See you in the morning, and thank you for all your help. It is beginning to look like the fabric of our country is developing a few tears in it. We'd better hurry up and get it stitched back together."

***

Grace awoke the next morning when the pain killer Grey kept for his headaches had worn off, and the cumulative soreness in her body was stronger than her need to sleep. Her face hurt where her attacker hit her, and her bruised hip ached from her fall to the ground. The recollections of her attack were quickly replaced by her awareness of being in Aaron Grey's apartment. When she sat upright, the exertion and pain made her queasy. Sitting on the edge of the bed for several minutes, the nausea subsided enough to stand and walk to the bathroom. From her perch on the toilet, she remembered that she hadn't written an article about Grey's latest speech and that she had missed the news cycle.

Is it today that Vincent gets back? God, I hope so.

And she had to reach Jody.

The phone rang elsewhere in the apartment, and a man's voice spoke. It sounded like Grey's. After splashing water on her face, gingerly on the right side, she saw that a new toothbrush and a travel size toothpaste tube sat on the lavatory counter. She brushed her teeth and looked in vain for a hairbrush. Finding a man's short comb, she ran it through her hair and then realized that she had no makeup. It was in the pack with her wallet and computer equipment. Walking back into the bedroom, she eyed the clothes she had been wearing during her ordeal. They were draped over the armchair and were torn, soiled and bloody. She salvaged the pants, but her bra had been cut in the back and discarded in the ER. She put on a tee-shirt that had been left on the chair. It was oversized and long, so it must have been one of Grey's. She put on the too-big man's robe she was given the night before and walked out into the living room.

Aaron Grey sat on a stool at the kitchen counter looking at one of several newspapers piled in front of him. Hearing her approach, he turned with his face partly masked by the back light of the morning sun shining through the window behind him.

"Hey, welcome back, Grace. Let me take a look at you. Ouch, that's a big bruise," he said, reaching for but stopping short of touching her injured face.

Grace clutched the robe together at the throat and looked around, her queasiness returning.

"Good morning, Aar ..., Senator, I'm so sorry ...."

"You were right the first time. Call me Aaron. Surely we've graduated to first name basis. How do you feel?"

"Really crappy. My face hurts, and I'm dizzy."

He got up to fetch the pain killers.

"I'm supposed to ask you to do a few things to test for concussion effects." Grey had her respond to several simple requests to follow his finger with her eyes, make facial expressions and answer simple questions, all of which she was able to do.

"Good. No reason to question the initial diagnosis of a mild concussion. You are supposed to check in with your own doctor as soon as you can. It's basically good news, but you will be sore for 4-5 days and you are to take it easy. As in rest, alright? Promise?"

"Thanks, er, Aaron. I promise. You are a good nurse. You can add that to your *curriculum vitae.*"

Grey took her arm and guided her to the sofa.

"Coffee?"

"Please. Black. That would be great. I need a hit." She grinned weakly with half her face.

"Wordplay! Gallows humor! That's a good sign that you've got all your marbles."

Grey beamed and handed her the coffee.

Grace took a careful sip from the cup with the unswollen side of her mouth. Some of the hot liquid touched her fat lip, and she winced.

"Okay, Grace, let me bring you up to date. The police said it's very unlikely that you will get your stolen bike and stuff back. Muggings are commonplace now, and the police can't even investigate all of them.

"Charlie Hayden called your land line and got your recording. He also called *Insider* and also got only a recording. He left a message on both saying where you are in case Vincent or your editor get them. There must be people you need to talk to. You can use this phone as soon as you feel up to that. And you can stay here as long as you like."

"Thank you so much Aaron," she said, touched by his thoughtfulness. "This is really above and beyond the call. You've been a life saver. I don't know what I would have done without you ... your kindness."

"Not at all, Grace. In fact, I'd be lying if I said I didn't enjoy taking care of you."

Grace did not want Grey to go there. Certainly not now.

"I would like to make some calls, and then I should go."

Grey ignored her remark and sat next to her on the sofa.

"Grace, I see in you a kindred spirit. I can tell from your reporting that you get it. You see what my calling is." His eyes were open very wide. "This isn't the best moment to declare myself, but I want you to hear it so you can think about it. It's hard for us to have time alone together to talk. I want you to think about the possibility of us. You are smart, political and very attractive. I need you. I have enemies, Grace, and they are gathering for the attack like wolves."

Moisture formed on his upper lip, and it seemed to Grace that a tremor was now affecting his hands as they moved in a circle that represented the wolves.

"Aaron, I'm flattered. This is very sudden and my head hurts ...."

"Yes, yes, I know, Grace, but your head will be fine, just fine, and I want you to hear me out so you can think about it. There is so little time."

Grey's face was rapt with a trace of panic about his eyes.

"It's the oil people. They've got a strangle-hold on the country. There's this one guy; he's a big player and represents the industry in Washington. I've been on to him for a long time now. You know how in *Tinker, Tailor, Soldier, Spy* by Le Carre, the Soviet spymaster Karla had the mole seduce Smiley's wife so that Smiley wouldn't see the mole clearly? Well, it's like that. I'm amazed that they would be so obvious as to use that tactic. This guy was sleeping with Diane for years, you know, to throw me off their track. These wolves are powerful, Dia...., ah, Grace, but I'm powerful too. They forget that. I'm a United States Senator, and I can run for President. I'm beginning to close in on them too. But I need you with me. You will complete me and cover my back. You can be my wife and partner, and they don't have their hooks into you. You're too smart for that. Hell, Grace, we're talking First Lady here."

Grey took one of Grace's hands and held it palm down. His other hand stroked the top of hers repeatedly as he continued to stare wide-eyed into her eyes.

"When I was in Ardmore this time, I went to our high school and tried to get a transcript of his grades. You know, to find out whether he's as smart as he claims."

Grace knew that he was having a cerebral event of some kind, but felt like she should try to engage him.

"Aaron, are you saying that you went to the high school of this man who had an affair with your wife? To look at his transcript?"

She hoped that he would realize the irrationality of his actions if hearing it recited by her. She was disappointed.

"Damn right, Grace, only they wouldn't give it to me without his consent. That's how far their reach is. But I looked at the front steps for a long time and got a good feel, you know, a pretty good read on what ... ah, he's about." Grey seemed to be running out of steam. His eyes were downcast and his stroking of Grace's hand had stopped.

"So you see, Grace, I've got this desperate fight on my hands, and the fate of the country itself is at stake. With you at my side, I would have the ... wherewithal ...."

Then, he sat bolt upright.

"They think I'm just Don Quixote tilting at windmills, you know, like I'm crazy. What they don't know is that I've got the entire Defense establishment with me. All their carriers and missiles and bombers are with me, not them. Why, even your ex-husband, the Marine, is on board. I can tell."

"You mean people in the Department of Defense are supporting your candidacy, Aaron? Can they do that?"

Grace's question triggered a reflex that brought Grey back from wherever he had been. His eyes narrowed into a squint and shifted from side to side. He appeared to be mentally transitioning back to the self-preservation instincts that are cultivated by a lifetime in politics—or to paranoid cunning. He realized that he had said too much, and to a reporter.

His laughter didn't sound genuine.

"No, no. Good Lord, no. It's just that ... say, this is off the record, background stuff, right."

Grace felt sorry for Grey. She had just witnessed a very personal episode of mental breakdown, and she had no intention of publishing it or anything he'd said.

"Yes, of course, Aaron. This is absolutely off the record. After your kindness to me, it would be a churlish thanks to use anything you said to me in confidence. I would never do that."

"Great. I knew you were on the team. My office has normal contacts with the military brass in appropriations matters and about Oklahoma bases. That's all. They share my concerns about a disorderly energy market. Just like you and your ex."

Grey stood and pulled Grace to her feet. He put his hand on her bare neck above the collar of the robe, and the weight of his hand pushed the collar down, exposing more of her skin. He tried to pull her close, but she placed both hands on his chest and resisted.

"Aaron, your proposal is very sudden, and I am not at my best right now. I just don't think ...."

"Right, right, I know, and I'm sorry, Grace. My timing is terrible, but I wanted to you hear me out so that you know my intentions. You need to chew on it. It could be quite a ride. I'd be good to you, and I'm egotistical enough to think that you could come to love me. But, I'm a man in a hurry, so think on it."

"I will, Aaron." Grace relaxed her arms and let Grey pull her close. He kissed her on the side of her mouth that was not swollen, not with passion, but sweetly, affectionately.

Grace was touched by his vulnerability and his tenderness. She knew him to be a man of intellect and distinction, and he cared for her. A proposal of marriage from a candidate for President of the United States didn't come around every day. He needed her. Perhaps she could help him manage his neuroses, whatever they were. She'd glimpsed a mental disorder in an otherwise gifted and visionary man being seriously considered for the Presidency.

Grace patted his chest with her hands.

"You know, my squash feels better. I'd like to get a cab back to my place, if I can borrow cab fare, and break the news to my friend that I lost the bike she desperately needs and was kind enough to loan me. I expect my employer is wondering where I am too."

She looked around.

"I seem to have a clothes problem, though."

"Good news on that score," Grey said, instantly rational and polite again. "Flor stopped by earlier and dropped off some work-out clothes she thought would fit you. She seemed anxious that you should not be trapped here in my apartment in the altogether."

"Oh, that's sweet of her. One sist'a taking care of another. I owe her."

Grace picked up the outfit and took it into the bedroom. As she dressed, the sensations of having been beaten and robbed in public on the Mall in the nation's capital followed by a proposal of marriage by a Presidential candidate who had revealed himself to be mentally unstable flowed through her shocked mind. All she wanted to do was talk to Vincent.

CHAPTER

22

The wait for a taxi wasn't long, probably because the call was placed by a U.S. Senator. Since Grace's keys had been in her rucksack, she had no way to get into her apartment other than the spare key she'd left with Jody to water Grace's plants while she had been in Los Angeles. Grace was in luck in two respects. The building's standby battery-operated system that allowed the elevators and intercom to operate for several hours during a power outage still had life, so the intercom at the front door still worked. And Jody answered the intercom and let her in.

Jody was shocked to see Grace's face. She said she had been worried when Grace didn't return for dinner and didn't call. She called the police, but hung up while on interminable hold waiting for someone to tell her whether a Grace Long had been involved in an accident.

Grace provided Jody with a long description of what had happened to her, and, unfortunately, to Jody's bike. She explained that her head was too addled to overcome the problem that Jody's unlisted mobile number was programmed into Grace's stolen cell phone.

Jody found the key to Grace's front door and gave it to her, promising to check on her periodically. Inside her apartment, Grace couldn't listen to her messages. She called Raj Patel at *Insider* on her land line with its battery charged. Patel told her that there were several messages on her machine inquiring of her whereabouts that she could disregard. After receiving the phone message from Charlie Hayden, Patel was alarmed, but confident that she was being taken care of. Since they missed the news cycle on Grey's news conference, Patel no longer needed a report on it, but he told her that *Insider* had a new feature on the increasing crime rate and the breakdown in police protection people were experiencing due to fuel-short patrol cars. He asked her to do an article about her own mugging and the irony of it in light of her prominence as an investigative reporter on the Grey campaign that was focused on the subject. She agreed in principle, but made it clear that she would have the final say over any editorial revisions. She was anxious that her overnight stay in Aaron Grey's apartment be cast in the correct light so as not to embarrass her or Grey.

She needed to have some keys made, get a new driver's license, make a doctor's appointment, and get new debit and credit cards. Also another cell phone. She forgot about calling the wireless company to trigger the kill switch.

Grace thought of calling her mother. Her mother would be concerned and would likely urge her to come for a visit to rest and recover. It would be sound advice, but it wouldn't take into account the maelstrom in which she found herself professionally. Anyway, her mother didn't know she was with Vincent again. She just didn't have the strength to have that conversation.

Her jaw pain was worse. She took the last pain killer Aaron had given her "for the road" and lay down on the bed. It quickly took effect, and she fell into a deep sleep.

***

On the nearly empty aircraft, Vincent was able, for the first time in memory, to stretch out across five empty center aisle seats and sleep fitfully on China Airlines' red eye to Dulles. When he disembarked, the bright, morning light hurt his eyes.

He exchanged the *yuan* he carried back to dollars, and he still had the cash that McMasters had given him in case he had to extend his trip or buy new plane tickets for some reason. It amounted to nearly ten thousand dollars. McMasters said he didn't want to go through the awkwardness of travel expense accounting with the bean counters at the Pentagon, so they would just handle the trip with cash.

Feeling flush, Vincent caught a limo at Dulles and directed it to the apartment. A call to the apartment phone number got a busy signal. Grace would be on the phone or the power could be out. He checked for messages on his cell phone, but had none. His wireless carrier's procedure for calls made to a phone not in the range of its towers was to store them, so Grace's message went unposted on his device until after the system detected the phone's use within the carrier's system.

He called Grace's cell phone number.

"'Lo?" It was a man's voice. Vincent asked for Grace.

"Ain't no Grace at 'dis numba." Then the line went dead.

Wrong number? He had speed dialed her. He dialed again. This time he got no answer.

What the hell? He could check that out with Grace when he saw her.

He dialed McMasters' line next, and McMasters answered after one ring.

"Vincent, you're back?"

"Yes, and I can report that all went according to plan. Nothing out of the ordinary at all. I met Liu in public and delivered the files. He was non-committal, but I seemed to have his attention. He thanked me for the info, reminded me that I was still *persona non grata*, and suggested that I leave immediately, which I was happy to do. I can go over it in detail with Dr. Mahdi if you think that is necessary."

"Excellent. That's excellent. That ought to slow them down. Probably no need to meet with Mahdi. Well, you can resume your basket liberty, and good luck with the littoral combat school if you go."

"Thanks, Jerry. And don't call me. I'll call you."

McMasters could be heard chuckling as Vincent hung up.

That ought to slow them down? What did that mean?

Next, Vincent called General Yin. His administrative assistant said that he was away from his office, so Vincent left a cryptic voice message. It said that he had returned, that everything went as planned, and that he would make himself available if a more detailed oral or written report were desired. Vincent doubted that he would be asked for a written report. It was not the sort of document that anyone would want in his possession.

Damn, I forgot to ask McMasters about the money.

***

Grace heard Vincent's key at the door, and she ran to it. When it opened, she was in his arms. Just before she buried her face in his neck and began to sob uncontrollably, he glimpsed her bruised and swollen face.

"What the ...? Grace, what's happened?" He tried to push her shoulders back so he could look at her, but her arms were locked around his neck, and she clung to him even tighter, her sobbing unabated.

He held her closely for a long time, stroking her hair and waiting for her crying to subside. It did, and when she opened her eyes she saw a neighbor pass by in the hallway through the door propped open by Vincent's suitcase. She relaxed her grip and took a step back.

"Maybe I could let you all the way in before I throw myself on you," she said trying to brush her tears from his shirt, her voice catching. "Sorry, it just all washed over me. I'm really glad you're home."

He saw that her eyes were red and wet and that the entire left side of her face was puffy and deeply discolored.

"Jesus, Gracie, what happened to you?"

She saw the concern on his exhausted face and led him by the hand to the sofa, unconsciously sitting so that he would not be looking directly at the wounded side of her face.

"I got mugged. In broad daylight on the Mall just down from the Capital Building. They took my pack and Jody's bike that I borrowed to go to Aaron's news conference ...." She started to cry again.

Vincent put two pieces together.

"Was it some gang banger types?"

"Yes, how did you know?"

"I called your cell phone from Dulles and some player answered it. They are probably using it for drug business. Did you do the kill switch?"

She shook her head. "I don't know how to do it remotely, and I ... I haven't made any calls to the wireless company ... or anyone yet." she said. It was one confounding frustration too many, and she started to cry again.

He hugged her and made her take deep breaths.

"You've been to the ER? What do the doctors say about your injuries? What are your injuries?"

"Listen, Vincent, I've got a lot to tell you, and I can see you're beat. Let's just get in bed and talk. If you fall asleep, we can finish when you wake up. I just want to feel you next to me."

Just then, his wireless phone signaled the arrival of a message recorded the day before by his wireless company as he was roaming out of their service area. It was from Grace saying she'd been in an accident and asking him to call her.

***

He made it through Grace's narration about Grey's news conference, the bike ride necessitated by the Metro outage, the attack, the police assistance, the trip to the ER, and the extraordinary events at Aaron Grey's apartment. He picked up on Grace's embarrassment at having given Grey's name as her emergency contact.

Then, Grace got up to answer a call from Jody who needed a copy of the police report on the bike theft for insurance purposes. While she was up, Grace waded through all the messages on the answering machine from Jody asking about her whereabouts, from Raj at *Insider* about missing her press conference report deadline, some junk calls, and the sole message from Vincent earlier in the day. When she returned to the bedroom, Vincent was asleep. She lay down facing him with her uninjured side of her face on the pillow and she, too, fell asleep.

***

Vincent awoke before his eyes opened. He saw the Chi Lin on a giant pedestal in the Mall. The Chi Lin and the Great Emancipator faced each other across the long length of the reflecting pool like two giant bookends. Both indicated that he should approach, but he stood anchored in a pool of oily sand. He struggled ever harder against the force that held him immobile until his eyes opened with his heart racing.

Grace was already up and sitting at the kitchen table, a notepad in front of her containing a long list of pen and ink notations. He padded in wearing only his regulation white boxers. When he saw the side of Grace's face, he winced. It was now midway to what would be its full-on eggplant zenith.

She looked discouraged.

"This is a list of all the crap I have to do because those assholes stole my pack and wallet. Only I can't seem to actually do any of them. Is that what concussions do?"

Vincent rubbed his chin and felt a good start on a beard. He grabbed a bottle of warm water from the refrigerator and sat down across the table from Grace.

"Don't worry about it, pilgrim," he said, channeling John Wayne. "I'm going to help you do all that drill, and it will get done quickly and effortlessly."

"Oh, will you Vincent? Help me with all that? That would be huge."

"Don't give it another thought, little lady," he said. Then his face became serious.

"Your hypothesis that Grey's campaign is being funded by the dark side seems right. Grey's spontaneous insinuation to that effect, however unbalanced his mind may be, is very credible. Anyway, if it is true, I guess it needs to be discovered and reported."

Grace stirred the dregs of a cup of tea with her spoon.

"If you are talking about me, I see your point, but I agreed that it was off the record. I don't have the stomach for hardball, gotcha journalism."

Noting her testy response, he continued carefully.

"You can't be held to that statement, given the circumstances," Vincent said.

She crossed her arms in front of her and glared.

"Now which circumstances would those be that don't merit keeping a confidence? That he is my news source? His proposal of marriage? His mental breakdown, which would destroy him if made public. The fact that he took me in and cared for me after a beating? Or, the fact that you are jealous?"

"Okay, okay. I'm sorry. I didn't think that through. It was insensitive and maybe unethical." After a moment, he added, "And maybe I am jealous."

Grace reached over and grabbed his hand.

"Well, you can relax on that score, major. You are my one and only. But I'm not about to rat Aaron out. My scruples may eventually keep me from ever going to the top of my profession, but so be it."

Vincent nodded. "I am, whew, glad to hear that, and I respect your ethics. Still, we can't entirely lose sight of the fact that someone is trying to steal the government and a leading populist candidate for President seems to be, at best, a tool of the conspirators, and, at worst, a part of it. That is a full bubble out of plumb."

Grace absentmindedly tested the swollen underside of her mouth with the tip of her tongue.

"True, but I am still not about to rat Aaron out. Anyway, the insinuations of a man who is experiencing a cerebral event aren't exactly credible. And don't forget that you know all this stuff too. You have as much responsibility as I do. In fact, you should try to corroborate Grey's involvement on your own through your contacts at the Pentagon."

"Don't I know it, pilgrim; don't I know it," he said, lapsing back into John Wayne.

"Is there a schism over there at Defense, Vincent? What's up with your nefarious goings and comings?"

"Oh, yeah, I fell asleep before I got to my latest adventures in spook land."

He then proceeded to tell Grace about his mission to China. He left nothing out. When he finished, he quoted Jerry McMasters' pregnant, but ambiguous and probably unguarded, comment about the information he provided to Liu perhaps "slowing them down."

They both turned to look out the window and regarded the imponderables that had, through no fault of their own, taken over their lives. A squall brought a bright flash of lightning against the suddenly darkened sky, followed closely by a deafening clap of thunder. Then a thick veil of rain enveloped the green space outside in the explosive whiteout of a microburst. The curtain over the open dining room window instantly stood out sideways, and they could feel rain hitting them at the table in the middle of the room. Vincent leaped to his feet and closed the window with some effort. The curtain hung wet and limp.

Vincent picked up a dish towel and wiped the water from his face and torso.

"This is a real toad soaker," he said. "You can see why airplanes taking off or landing in one of these microbursts get hammered into the ground."

Grace looked alarmed. "Will the building, the windows, hold up?"

"Apparently they did," he said looking outside. "It's already over."

"Do you suppose it's an omen, Vincent? I mean how many once-in-a-lifetime events can you jam into a couple of days? Is something coming?"

"Yeah, it does feel like we haven't had the main event yet. The problem with conspiracies is that they lead to a result."

***

After Grace had gone to bed and the power was back on, Vincent sat staring at the television screen with the audio on low. The local newscaster was reporting that the Washington Nationals had revised its schedule for the balance of the baseball season. The team would thereafter play nothing but day games, given the unpredictability of power for stadium lighting, the gasoline shortage, and the spike in muggings, especially at night. Attendance at night games had entirely disappeared. He said the local channels intended to broadcast the day games recorded earlier after ten o'clock at night when power was more reliable.

In another segment taped earlier from Hollywood, a prominent film critic reported that the major studios had ceased making feature films due to poor attendance at movie theaters throughout the country because of the gas shortage. The industry's ability to downstream its movie programming over the Internet would also be curtailed because of power outages and computerized billing difficulties. Going forward, movies on demand would be available predominantly late at night when the power was on and the Internet accessible. The public could anticipate, he said, an increasing amount of how-to programming dealing with survival under various extreme circumstances. More content based on graphic novels could be expected also. These films increasingly featured a Chinese soundtrack with English subtitles, reflecting the preponderantly Chinese market for Hollywood's special effects.

Vincent groaned and turned off the TV, making his way to the bedroom in the dark.

CHAPTER

23

Vincent had nothing but time on his hands, and Grace seemed to lack the will or the confidence to cope effectively. That was unusual for her but a normal symptom of her injuries. He made good on his promise to run interference for her with the to-do list. Together, they ranked the priority of the actions needed, and he addressed each one in order. She made a doctor's appointment to follow up on her concussion.

At his urging, she called her mother. Grace led-off with the news that she and Vincent were together again. She outlined the circumstances that led to their reconciliation, and Vincent gathered that her mother was delighted. Then she related the facts about her mugging as matter-of-factly as she could manage, assuring her startled and worried mother than Vincent was taking good care of her.

Vincent phoned her bank and credit card companies, navigating the daisy chain of automated menu choices that passed for customer service in corporate America. Then, when he had a live humanoid who professed to be able to help on the line, Vincent gave the phone to Grace. Her old debit and credit cards would be cancelled and replacement cards reissued and mailed to her on an expedited basis. The credit card company advised that "suspicious activity" appeared on her account, but that in view of her injury and prompt call, she would not have to worry about those charges and they would be reversed.

The next open item on the list was her driver's license. Vincent was unable to reach the motor vehicle department office in Arlington by phone, thanks to the omnipresent "extremely high volume the office was experiencing." The department's website announced that the office was closed two days a week due to a furlough of government workers as the result of a projected severe budget shortfall.

Grace said she wanted to make headway on the article her editor asked for putting the latest Grey speech into perspective with reference to her own experience with crime. She didn't need him to babysit her writing, so he decided to visit the scene of Grace's mugging out of curiosity. He excused himself telling Grace that he was going out "to reconnoiter," and she should call him if she needed him.

The power was on, so Metro was running. Vincent loped down the stairs into the station at Rosslyn and took the train to the Archives Metro station. A short walk brought him to John Marshall Place, the small, leafy park dominated by the statue of Justice Marshall and sandwiched in between the Canadian Embassy and the enormous footprint of the U.S. District Courthouse. Vincent could no more picture a commute hour mugging of Grace here than he could imagine the old chief justice climbing down off his pedestal.

He walked north through the park and in two blocks, came to the National Law Enforcement Officer's Memorial at Judiciary Square just past the U.S. Court of Appeals. Beyond that, on 4th Street, the Federal Bureau of Investigation loomed. These edifices projected the somber face of law enforcement Two blocks further north at 4th and K Streets, the urban feel could not have been more different. In that short space, development had changed from monolithic governmental architecture to public housing. It was an area in which urban renewal had brightened and civilized portions of the neighborhood, but there was no mistaking the fact that poor and desperate people could be found here.

So this is where they came from.

Vincent had what he came for—a feeling, an understanding on a gut level of how such random acts of violence occur. Grace was probably wondering where he was. He headed southwest, zigzagging from K to 5th streets toward Chinatown, when he passed a young black man leaning on a tricked-out Honda with a cell phone to his ear. It was the backpack that stopped him. It had an old, peeling, iron-on patch of the pink breast cancer ribbon. Then man on the phone was wearing Grace's backpack. Vincent heard the young man speaking numbers. They could have been weights or sums or anything. Something about the voice sounded familiar. He stopped and looked at the back of a muscular youth wearing bling around his neck and on his ear. Pretending to look in the window of a pawn shop, he waited for the player to compete his call.

When he did, Vincent dialed Grace's cell phone number. The player's ring tone went off.

"'Lo."

Vincent spoke into his phone while closing the distance between them. "I have a message for you from Grace, asshole. Turn around."

As the player turned, Vincent sucker-punched the young man hard on the side of his face, splaying him across the side of the Honda. Vincent took a second, roundhouse swing at the same spot high on his victim's cheekbone. He was pretty sure he heard bones breaking this time. Then he brought a right hook down on the bridge of the youth's nose, shattering it and starting a cascade of blood down into his mouth. Vincent shoved the semi-conscious gangster onto the pavement in the space between the Honda and the car parked behind it. He lay there moaning. Vincent reached down and picked up the cell phone now lying on the sidewalk and put it in his pocket. As he walked off, he passed a matronly black woman with a startled look on her face.

"Ma'am," Vincent said with a nod.

What's he going to do, call the police and complain that his stolen phone was stolen? That he's a mugger who got mugged?

On the Metro from Chinatown, he got out his list and scratched off getting a new cell phone.

Nice. I ought to play the lottery. What are the odds of that happening?

That left only the driver's license replacement, and the Arlington office would be open tomorrow.

Sitting across from Vincent on the Metro car was a young man concentrating on the screen of his tablet. He looked up wide-eyed and made eye contact with Vincent.

"We've invaded Venezuela, for chrissakes. Over oil contracts or some shit." Then he began to read out loud what he was looking at.

"Venezuela's President told the American Ambassador three weeks ago that he had voided oil deliveries contracted for sale to American refiners on the grounds of coercion. The oil was instead going to be delivered to tankers belonging to the Peoples' Republic of China. Early this morning, Eastern Standard Time, elements of the 82nd and 101st airborne divisions were dropped into major oil fields in Venezuela. Also, the Second Marine Division, part of a Naval Expeditionary Force, had arrived to take control of the government buildings in Caracas, the Venezuelan capital. The White House will make an address to the American public at 3:00 pm."

Vincent exhaled deeply.

So that's their goal. If the President of the United States was now a part of it; it's policy and no longer a conspiracy. McMasters and company had gambled by acting early and their actions were sanitized when the President ratified their initiative.

He logged onto his own device and started reading the details.

***

When he got back to the apartment, Grace was asleep on the couch. He glanced at her open laptop on the kitchen table and touched the keypad. The screen lit up and he could see that she had completed only two paragraphs of her article.

She opened her eyes and stirred, feeling his proximity. Seeing him looking at the screen, she said, "Not good stuff. Can't seem to write through this … fog."

He leaned over and kissed her. Then he raised her legs and sat down where they had been, placing them on his lap and massaging her feet.

"This is going to take some time. The docs said maybe two or three weeks. Even more. Don't get discouraged."

"It is discouraging. It makes me feel panicky; like it's going to be permanent. My face isn't nearly as sore, though."

"Well, I've got to tell you, my little aubergine, you look like hell. We're talking full-on eggplant, here. I mean you could scare the bark off a tree with that face."

Grace started laughing. "Ouch," she winced. "Will you shut up, please? You're a big confidence builder." She twisted her grin to the uninjured side of her face to avoid the soreness.

"No, really. I think it may take five or six plastic surgeries before people will stop recoiling in horror when they see you. Going to have to get some dark sunglasses."

"Sunglasses won't do any good, dummy. They won't hide the side of my face."

"No, I didn't mean for you. For me. So I can just see shadows and not have to look at you."

Giggling with her mouth twisted, she picked up her feet and pummeled him in the chest. He caught them and started tickling the bottoms of her feet and triggering another round of giggles.

They sat for a time, enjoying the restorative effect of hard laughter.

"That's better," Vincent said. "You're not as ugly when you laugh."

She kicked him again. "Don't start."

Capturing her feet again, he resumed his massage.

"I've got some news. I got your phone back. In a Twilight Zone incident."

He related the basic details of his encounter with one of her tormenters, omitting most of the violence. He made it sound like the man gave the phone back when confronted with the fact that he answered the phone that Vincent just called. When she saw the inflamed knuckles on his right hand and looked like she was going to ask questions, he handed her the phone.

"If you get any calls from numbers you don't recognize, just answer, 'This is Sergeant Pulaksi at Central Station. Who is calling please?' That should do it."

"But that's not the big news," he hurried on. "While you were napping and I was sightseeing in the nation's capital, the United States invaded Venezuela."

Vincent could see the confusion on her face.

"Venezuela? You're kidding, right?"

He lifted her feet off his lap high enough to reach over and pick up the TV remote. The news channels were in full vacuum-filling mode with too little information to fill their airtime. The one Vincent clicked on involved a panel discussion among tangential experts in international law, world oil markets, and U.S.-Venezuela foreign relations speculating on the significance of this breaking story. Apart from the information Vincent had learned from the hipster on Metro, there was little that was new.

There were no news personnel imbedded in the assault force, so the news media were only getting the operational information the Defense Department spokesmen were putting out, which was not much. The President was to speak in fifteen minutes and the network promised to cut to the President's live address to the nation.

Vincent muted the television, and they stared at each other in amazement.

"I'm guessing that China isn't going to take this lying down. We don't know when, or how, but they will do something ugly."

Grace looked worried. "They said the Marines were going in. I guess I always knew that you weren't going to be able to stay here with me, but I'm not ready for you to ... be called back."

He tried to think of something reassuring, but couldn't come up with anything that made sense.

"Let's see what develops. This is going to be full of twists and turns. We'll just try to be prepared for everything."

Vincent walked to the pantry and got two Bordeaux glasses and a bottle of premier Napa Valley cabernet sauvignon he had picked up at Dulles to celebrate his return from what he then considered a well-executed and potentially important, clandestine mission. He intended to expense the bottle to Jerry McMasters, and since he still had all the money McMasters gave him, he supposed that he already had. He carried it and the glasses to the coffee table and opened the bottle.

"You're off pain medication, right?"

She nodded. "Medicate me."

The camera shot on the muted television shifted to the White House.

"Looks like they are getting ready," Vincent said. "Are you prepared for an updated Monroe Doctrine larded with Manifest Destiny?"

"There's nothing new under the sun," she replied, raising her glass to clink his.

The screen showed the President walking down a corridor in the White House alone toward a podium. She wore a navy blue pant suit with a brightly patterned gold scarf loosely draped around her neck. Vincent unmuted the audio.

The President spoke of the special leadership role the United States had historically borne in the Americas. She spoke of the sanctity of law in inter-American relations and of China's wrongful inducement of Venezuela's breach of its contractual obligations with American refiners. It could not be allowed to stand. In a court of law, she said, such conduct would give rise to legal action and in relations between governments, a similar response is appropriate. The United States sought nothing more than the full and fair satisfaction of its contractual expectancy from the Government of Venezuela. Once such assurances had be obtained by the Government of the United States, the "timely" withdrawal of American troops from the oil fields, which, she announced, were presently occupied and controlled by American forces, could be expected as soon as the circumstances on the ground warranted.

The Government of Venezuela was admonished not to allow or to perpetrate any acts of violence against the American Embassy in Caracas or any of its consulates, or to interfere with the U.S. Marine force in Caracas protecting American citizens and their property there on penalty of "severe consequences."

The President concluded her address by urging mainland Americans to conduct their affairs in normal fashion pending resolution of this "bilateral policy dispute." The television network then quickly moved its coverage back to the panel of pundits moderated by the network anchor. A legal expert began to explain the President's reference to what the President had referred to as China's wrongful inducement of Venezuela's breach of contract with the United States. It was something called "tortious interference with contractual relations," giving rise to civil liability, including punitive damages. The lawyer went on to say that no parallel exists between a remedy under American civil law and a remedial attack on another sovereign nation under international law. Venezuela is not bound by American law, and private American oil companies are the ones injured by these developments, not the American Government. Other panelists quickly pointed out that whatever the legal niceties may be, the American Government has served notice that it will use military power to protect the energy sources it relies on for its military and industrial uses.

Vincent muted the audio again. "Well, the oil companies owe this President big time. She is off the fence now, and the Defense establishment has got to be feeling more secure. The conspirators have just gone mainstream. Their funding of Aaron Grey as a challenger to the President may be the first casualty. They were probably either hedging their bets with Grey to insure Presidential support of their energy objectives, whichever party won the White House next. But now it looks like the Grey phenomenon forced the President to give in to the oil hawks. The oil companies support the President, and the administration takes care of them."

Vincent looked at Grace, trying to read her face.

"I'm thinking that you are going to need a new subject to write about," he said. "Grey is toast."

Grace nodded. "He started as a crusader for the consumer and wanted to manage scarce energy for the nation as a whole. I couldn't quite get this notion that he was the Defense establishment's best hope."

Grace quaffed the last of her wine.

"Medicinal purposes."

Vincent laughed. "You go, girl. It seems to have revived you."

A long time passed leaving them alone in their thoughts.

Vincent spoke first.

"You owe Grey an answer, don't you?"

Grace nodded. "I'm dreading that. If he calls me, I'll plead injury. My face is too discolored to be seen in public and all that, which happens to be true. But yes, I've got to have closure with him. Meanwhile, I'll write my article."

Dusk obscured the tree tops visible through the window and the room grew dark and stuffy. Grace switched the end table lamp on and nothing happened.

"Rats," Vincent said. "No air conditioning. I'm hungry. We got anything?"

"Hot dogs that have thawed and been refrozen a couple of times. We should either eat them or throw them out."

"Got mustard and relish?"

"Got mustard and relish."

"Got candle?"

"Got candle."

"Perfect."

Neither moved. They continued to sit, sipping the last of the wine.

"Grace, I'm thinking we should have a contingency plan. You know, what are we going to do if things get so bad that we can't survive here in the city anymore? I'm thinking the Los Alamos ranch. There's game and fish and local produce like maize and squash. Wood for fires and fresh water from the year around stream. Good, basic survival stuff. Not sure how we'd get there."

Grace looked appalled. Vincent's parents had lived in the Santa Fe National Forest a few miles north of Los Alamos. It was where she and Vincent honeymooned. The property was beautifully situated below a forest of aspens and conifers. The house sat a hundred yards upslope across a meadow with a stream that intermittently drained into the Rio Grande ten miles to the east. But it was very remote. The idea of living there indefinitely was panic-inducing. Vincent could read that in her eyes.

"You can do the thinking for both of us on that score, major. I don't do apocalypse."

***

They slept late the next morning. When Grace woke up, she noticed how quiet it was. She heard none of the drone of the commute hour on a Thursday from the expressway in the distance. When she got up, Vincent rolled over and stretched mightily. By the time she came out of the bathroom, he had progressed as far as a sitting position.

"We have electricity," she said. "Let's see what the news cycle is putting out today."

The earnest-looking, immaculately dressed and coiffed female anchor interviewed a retired Army general about the events of the last twenty four hours. He characterized the surprise airdrop into the oil fields at Boyacá and Carabobo as an outstanding success. Marines had taken the President into custody as well as control of the oil refineries at Caracas and Jose. Venezuelan army attempts to retake the refineries were stalled by drone strikes close ahead of the advancing Venezuelan columns. A no-fly zone over the affected areas was being enforced by aircraft from the American carriers offshore. The American military presence was a *fait accompli* and military and State department officials had made contact with Venezuelan government officials to discuss the American terms for withdrawal. Casualties on both sides were reported to be fewer than a hundred.

Vincent got up and went into the bedroom to call General Yin's private number. His assistant confirmed that the General was available. Several minutes later, General Yin came on the line.

"Major Long, I have just a minute."

"Sir, as I understand things, I am still attached to the Commandant's office. I'm wondering if you have orders for me in light of these developments or whether I should check in with the G-1 in case I can be useful somewhere else."

"Ah, yes, I see. You must feel adrift, major. Well, events have overtaken us and the matter you had been discussing with General Forest recently has obviously been mooted since the special op you were involved in has resolved itself into this operation. General Forest remains concerned about the response of our trading partner across the Pacific, however."

"I understand, sir. We can be certain that there will be a response. My recent mission for the NSA appears to have been designed to temporarily pause the cyber-attacks, but this action will erase all that."

"It is what it is, major. The question is what are your orders now? I'll have to check with General Forest on that. We'll get back to you. Can you shelter in place? I assume your paychecks are still arriving so you've got money for living expenses, right?"

"Yes, sir. I'm fine on that score."

He didn't go into the matter of the large cash advance he'd received from McMasters. He would have to take that up with his NSA paymasters.

"I'll call when I have something, major. It might take a while. Things are on overload here."

Vincent hung up and walked back into the living room. Grace looked at him anxiously.

"I'm in limbo. Can you believe it? This invasion has scrambled everything. I report to the Commandant, and he doesn't have time to nursemaid some major who has gone off the grid on business that no one wants to admit to. The personnel office might plug me into some billet somewhere, but I'm off of their radar as long as I report to the Commandant. General Forest is rightly worried about what the Chinese will do. Anyway, I'm without orders until he can get back to admin stuff."

Relief was on her face now. "So, we are 'recalculating' like the lady on the GPS says. Would it offend you if I said that I'm delighted?"

***

Grace combed her hair so that it covered most of the injured side of her face. A Dashiell Hammett-style fedora, inclined to that side, kept her hair in place and cast that side of her face in shadow.

"*Ciao bella,*" Vincent offered.

"Heck with it. I've got to get out. I'm going to the bank. I have zero money. The power's off, and I can't do any banking electronically."

"I think I'll mosey over to the bicycle shop over on Clarendon and replace Jody's bike if I can," Vincent said. "If she ever gets some insurance proceeds, she can pay me back, but at least she'll have a bike again."

"Jody's going to love you for that, and then it will be my turn to be jealous."

He winked and kissed her on her good cheek on his way out.

It felt good to get out and move, so Grace strode confidently to her bank four blocks away. She had no ATM card. Her credit card was linked to her account, but the card was missing also. They were both in her purse when she got mugged. She went inside and waited in a short line for a teller. When the woman in front of her got to the counter, Grace overheard the woman being told that the ATM machine was not working because the bank's system crashed and she had no way of knowing when it would be back up. The woman left and Grace stepped to the counter.

"I overheard you say the bank's operating system is down. I need make a withdrawal, but my wallet was stolen with all my bank cards in it. I've reported the loss to your customer service line, but I need to make a withdrawal to get by until my new debit and credit cards arrive. May I make a withdrawal from my account manually? I'd like three hundred dollars, please."

"I'm very sorry ma'am, but I have no access to your account information with the system down. I'm so sorry," she repeated.

Aware that she was getting angry and also that she was on shaky ground, Grace nevertheless persisted.

"I have no cash. I need to make a withdrawal of my funds and the bank's doors are open. There must be a way for you to make a manual record of it. Then you can enter it into your system when the system comes back up."

"Just a minute ma'am. Let me get an officer to speak with you."

She walked to one of the desks in the rear area and spoke quietly with an elegantly dressed Asian woman, glancing occasionally at Grace.

The Asian woman approached Grace. Her rank obviated any need to smile at her customer.

"Hello, I'm Emily Wang, the Branch Vice President. I understand that you would like to make a withdrawal but lost your debit and credit cards. Do you happen to have a copy of your latest statement?"

"No, your bank kept badgering me to go paperless and accept my statements electronically. Like a fool, I did. So, I have no paper statement to give you."

"And you didn't print it at home, either?" Ms. Wong was not so much asking a question as putting Grace in her place.

"If the statement should be printed and kept manually as a safeguard against the bank's computer malfunctions, then you should keep sending me printed statements and keep them yourself so that you can do your job when your computers are down."

"I see," she said, ignoring Grace's sarcasm. "Do you have your driver's license and check stub with you?"

Grace saw the absurdity of her position. She was standing in a bank lobby asking for money with no ID or bank records. Her militancy was unwarranted under the circumstances. Without ID and bank cards, she was a non-person.

"No, as I mentioned to the teller, my wallet was stolen. *All* of that stuff was stolen. I was mugged over in D.C. on the Mall, in broad daylight." She pulled back her hair giving Ms. Wang a glimpse of the side of her face with her eggplant colored skin.

Ms. Wang's face registered shock. "Oh, dear, I'm so sorry Miss ...."

"Long, Grace Long—Mrs."

"Does your husband have an account with the bank, Mrs. Long?" Ms. Wang asked brightly, suggesting a possible way out of their predicament.

Grace shrugged abjectly. "No, no. He doesn't. He is in the Marines," she added irrelevantly. So, the fact that I have been banking here for three years doesn't count? None of you know anything about me?"

"I know, Mrs. Long. It's frustrating. We lose a lot of customer contact when our customer's use the ATM's."

Grace let that one go. "So that's it? The bank's open and solvent, but I can't access my money until your system comes back up and I can print your own records?"

"I'm afraid so. And some ID."

"How do I do that since my ID was stolen? Catch 22."

"The system should be back up before too long," Ms. Wang said ignoring Grace's logic.

"Great. What if the system doesn't come back up? Does the bank just collapse?"

"Oh my," the bank manager said, smiling good-naturedly at the idea. "Let's hope it doesn't come to that."

CHAPTER

24

Vincent was not at the apartment when Grace returned, and the power was off again. The apartment would be habitably cool until around noon, but her tablet's battery charge had run out. She sat down and began to write in longhand the article she had in her head. It flowed easily and clearly, for which she thanked the writing gods. She had her brain back. The article traced the trajectory of Aaron Grey's campaign from its quirky origins to the present where his popularity and successful fund raising made him a leading contender to oppose the President.

Grace found herself sifting through euphemisms when describing Grey's visionary approach to the energy shortage crisis. She made no mention of his likely personal motivation to confiscate Big Oil assets or his mental state. That made her uncomfortable. It was a conflict of interest, but she had agreed that what she knew on those subjects was off the record.

When the article was finished, she noticed that the power was on and plugged in her laptop and cell phone to charge them. As she opened the home page of her browser, the top three headlines jumped off the screen. The leading headline screamed that the computer operating systems of the Federal Reserve and six major U.S. banks had all crashed simultaneously. The article reported that most of the retail banking and inter-bank transactions throughout the country had come to a complete halt. Crowds were forming at isolated branch offices of the retail banks in several states, even those that were still functioning. Federal authorities were said to be fearful of a run on the banks when their systems came back on.

The next headline capped an article explaining that air traffic control systems were down at several major airline hubs around the country. Passengers were stranded at airports throughout the system, and no one at the Transportation Security Administration or any of the airports reached by reporters had any information on the cause of the system crash or when it might be remedied.

The third headline was a query. Had China launched another, or a series of new cyber-attacks? And, if so, was it triggered by America's invasion of Venezuela? There was no article following this headline. It appeared to be an open query raised by the website's editor based upon the blindingly obvious coincidence of the invasion followed by what had all the earmarks of a coordinated cyber-attack on vital elements of America's infrastructure.

Grace grabbed her partially charged cell phone and speed-dialed Vincent.

"Yes, darlin'," he answered. "Are you reading these postcards from our Asian friends?"

"I am. In fact, I was on the leading edge of this story and didn't know it. I couldn't get any money out of the bank this morning because its system was down."

"Yeah. I suspect we are in deep do-do. I'm just walking into Madsen's grocery and I plan to buy as much non-perishable food as I can carry. Say, can you drive over and pick me up. That way, I can get more stuff."

"Unh, okay. Is that ethical? Hoarding like that?"

"Ethics? I think ethics will be the first casualty of collapse. This is going to be life-boat ethics. I say we get enough groceries for a safety cushion. Things could get dicey fast."

"Roger that, major. You're the Armageddon officer. I'm on the way."

"Are you good to drive? Is your head clear?"

"Yes, dear, I am, and it is, thank you. I seemed to have made a V-shaped recovery. I had no problem finishing my article. Car has gas, thanks to you. See you in a bit."

Vincent got a large shopping cart and headed for the canned goods section. When he got there, he passed a banner sign apologizing for any shortages due to interruptions in deliveries. The store's stock was indeed low. The frozen food section was essentially empty, partly because of customer hoarding, but also because of curtailed deliveries. It was too hard for the market and its customers to keep goods requiring refrigeration under circumstances when the power to their refrigeration units were off for long periods of time, so, perversely, the store ordered less and customers bought more frequently. A decent selection of canned goods was still on the shelves and he began to pile canned meats, fish, vegetables and fruits into his shopping cart. He did so in close proximity to several other, single-minded shoppers doing the same thing. None of them made eye contact or yielded position to the others.

This is embarrassing.

He hurried to the housewares isle looking for candles and found only small birthday candles. He grabbed a couple of packs of those. At the meat counter, he picked up the last pre-roasted chicken. They would have that tonight and tomorrow. The hamburger was grey, and there were no steaks or chops. He passed on the hamburger, but grabbed two packages of pork sausages. They would probably have enough industrial nitrates in them to stand thawing a few times.

Lastly, he picked up three sorry-looking onions, a half-dozen garlic bulbs, a gallon of olive oil, salt, pepper and several bags of legumes. He knew from his survival training that beans were a good source of protein. The onions, garlic, salt and pepper would make them palatable. The sausage would be the topper.

Just then, Grace appeared at his side. She was not wearing the Fedora and didn't seem to notice the quick stares of the other shoppers.

"No greens?" she said scanning the cart's contents.

"I didn't see much when I got the onions, but you have a look."

She walked through the display bins, scanning them and confirming Vincent's report. She picked out some desiccated corn on the cob and some potatoes.

"They're not vegetables, but they are good calories."

Finally, in the candy and snacks aisle, Vincent got corn chips and Grace got bars of semisweet chocolate. They looked at each other and shrugged.

"Let's go."

At check-out, a thin, disheveled, woman with uncut grey hair blocked one of the checkout lanes. She was yelling at the store clerk about sky-high prices and poor quality produce. Her eyes were bloodshot and her fury seemed unwarranted since she had no groceries items to buy.

The store manager appeared at her elbow and took her arm.

"Mrs. Kelly, we have talked about this before. You can't block the store's checkout lanes. I'm going to have to ask you to leave or I'll call the police."

She looked chagrined and allowed herself to be led to the door. Near the door, the manager reached into the charitable donations food barrel and pulled out a can of tuna fish and a package of corn muffin mix and gave them to her. She grasped them eagerly and hurried off without speaking.

Seeing Grace and Vincent watching them, the store manager nodded.

"She's one of the talkers—you know, the crazies who stand around screaming at no one in particular. But she's got enough moxie to figure out that if she makes a scene here, I'll give her something." He hunched his shoulders. "What are ya gonna do? There are more people begging every day."

Vincent signaled approval of the manager's handling of the situation silently with two thumbs up. After clearing the checkout stand, Grace reached into one of their bags and dropped two cans of chili into the donation box on their way out.

Vincent loaded the groceries into the trunk and got into the passenger seat. Grace stared vacantly out the windshield.

"It's a good thing you had some money. I've got eleven dollars. Did you spend all of yours?"

"Not by a long shot."

He told her of the travel cash he still had from the China trip. "I don't think I'm going to be in any hurry to turn it back in either until this banking situation resolves itself."

"I felt so helpless at the bank. I had no ID, no credit or debit cards, no bank statement, and I'm standing there outraged because they wouldn't hand me over some money. What an idiot!"

At the next corner, they passed the branch bank Grace had visited earlier. A sizeable crowd had formed outside the bank and the bank's doors were closed. A woman was backed up against the front door with her palms out, as if pleading.

"That's her. Emily Wang. That's the bank manager I talked to this morning. There was no crowd at all then. Wow."

"No air travel and no major banks. Oil and gasoline in short supply. A military invasion of Venezuela is underway." Vincent was recapping the situation out loud. "Let's get this stuff home and think."

Grace nodded, craning her neck to look back at the bank.

Vincent rubbed his forehead and grimaced.

"If the hackers want to really make their point, they will go after the power grid again. Then Americans will have no news, no money, power blackouts and no transportation. Scrounging and hoarding will be everyone's top priority."

Mercifully, the elevators were working, and they didn't have to haul their groceries up five stories to the apartment. Grace turned on the television while Vincent put their supplies away. The anchor listened to the feed of a reporter standing on the corner of Wall and Broad Streets in New York. He described the odd quiet that had settled over lower Manhattan. People flowed out of offices, speaking in subdued voices and sometimes congregating in small groups before moving toward the transit modes that brought them from home that morning to see if they were operating.

The reporter corralled a middle aged man walking by and asked him what was going on in his workplace. He said he was a lawyer from Los Angeles in New York to close a Port of Los Angeles funding deal. The transaction couldn't close because the banks were not able to wire transfer funds. He didn't know when the close would happen, and he was unable to fly back to LA because air traffic control was out. He was going to try to check back into his hotel.

The news feed then switched to Chicago's O'Hare airport. The reporter at O'Hare showed camera shots of long corridors of gates normally teaming with travelers at this hour, but virtually devoid of them other than stranded passengers camped out in departure lounges. He interviewed an elderly couple whose aircraft had made a harrowing emergency landing at

O'Hare without the benefit of tower control. The pilot landed the plane, low on fuel, between thunderheads coursing through the Chicago area, and was unable to take off again due to the fuel shortage. The couple had no place to stay, and spoke of their concern because the woman's supply of medication was nearly exhausted.

The anchor cut off the feed from O'Hare and announced that the President was going to address the nation. The White House news room lectern appeared on the screen, and the President entered the room. She was freshly coiffed and handsomely dressed in a bright fuchsia jacket, but her eyes showed the strain and dullness of lack of sleep. She made no greeting.

"Late last night and continuing today, the United States has come under cyber-attack from multiple locations around the world. The nation's Air Traffic Control system has been compromised and because of malfunctions in its operating software, it had to be shut down. Please be assured that we are doing everything humanly possible to ...."

Then the screen went blank. Vincent saw that the LED lights on the computer and kitchen appliances were also out.

"No power," he said. "And if I were a betting man, I'd wager that this is no blackout. I'll bet that it stays off. It's the other shoe. The timing is a dead giveaway. If someone were to want to embarrass the President, I can't think of a better way to do it that to show that she can't control her own country's infrastructure. Hell, she can't even address the nation during an emergency without interdiction by foreign agents. Gracie, things just got ugly."

They sat down together on the sofa, and Grace reached for Vincent's hand. All the windows were open to a bright, mildly tropical afternoon. The scent of lilac filled the still air above the building's common area. Their fifth floor view overlooked deep green treetops from which a cacophony of birdsong emanated without pause, chronicling the hope of a still abundant and harmonious natural world even in an urban setting.

"What do you suppose they are saying out there?" Grace mused.

"Who?"

"The birds." She looked at him.

"Oh, the birds." He listened for a minute. "I think they are saying, okay you arrogant, humanoid screws, let's see how well you do living off the land like us."

"How *can* we live off the land?"

"We can't do it here, that's for sure. No land. I was wondering what we would need for the ranch if this doesn't get fixed pretty soon."

"You mean the Los Alamos place."

"Umm," he said, nodding.

Grace frowned. "How do I write and transmit my articles?"

"In New Mexico? What articles?" He looked at her.

"No, not New Mexico. Here, without power every day. Vincent, I don't want to go to New Mexico. It can't be all that bad."

He sighed. It was a sigh with plenty of editorial content.

"Maybe the Chaos Theory will save us," he said. "A butterfly flaps its wings in the Amazon and enough oil for a millennium is redeposited in the depleted source rock."

"Sarcasm isn't helpful."

They continued to sit, deep in their thoughts, until Grace's cell phone began to play Pachelbel's Cannon on the coffee table. She looked at its screen and then scooped it up as she stood and started to pace.

"Hello. Oh, hi Aaron. Much better thanks. The swelling's gone and I seem to have all my marbles again. What do you make of all this cyber war nonsense? Why don't you throw your weight around and put an end to it?"

She leaned on the kitchen counter and listened for a long time, shifting from one foot to the other, and making no move to leave the room.

"Yes, we need to talk, Aaron. I do want ... we do need to talk. Ah, with the power out, it's so stuffy indoors. Can we meet maybe on the Capital grounds? You probably know of a good park bench somewhere."

"This evening? Well, sure, that works."

She listened some more and wrote notes on a notepad near the phone.

"Okay, six thirty. I know where that is. Yes, me too. I'll see you later."

Grace came back and sat down next to him.

"Can't avoid it any longer. I've got to tell him."

She looked over at Vincent who returned her gaze.

"It won't be the answer he wants," she said.

Vincent made a gesture as if wiping sweat off his brow, and she elbowed him in the ribs.

"How did he sound? I mean, did he say anything, you know, off-kilter?"

"Not exactly, but he didn't say a word about the cyber-attacks or any of the fallout. He just kept pressing for my answer. He said he wanted me to see something and tell him what I thought about 'it.' No idea what 'it' would be. God, I hope it isn't a ring."

"Um, given your recent experience, I'm not comfortable with you driving up to the Hill and walking around by yourself. Should I go over with you? I can stay out of sight somewhere. You can even use picking me up as an excuse to get away if you need one."

"That's sweet of you, Vincent, but I'll be fine. It's not like the town is burning. I don't want to have to worry about the time when I'm talking with Aaron. I have a professional interest in his candidacy apart from his proposal, and he may have interesting things to say about what is going on. It might be a short conversation or a long one. Don't worry about me."

Vincent didn't look convinced, but he shrugged.

"You da man, girl. It's your call."

***

At half past six, Grace pulled into Lower Senate Park off Columbus Circle on Capitol Hill, parked without difficulty, and walked to the Japanese American Memorial. The path took her to the monolith pool, a water and rock garden arrangement surrounded by cherry trees that, when in pinkish-white bloom, closely coordinated with the light grey stone of the pool's surround and passageways. There, on a granite block facing the water garden, Grey sat, his left leg bouncing up and down quickly as he gazed into the water. She noticed that he wore his hair differently. Usually combed back above the collar, it appeared longer and parted in the middle forming what might, in a matter of weeks, approach shoulder length.

He jumped to his feet as Grace approached. Smiling broadly, he preempted her hesitancy by hugging her closely.

"Hi there, pretty lady," he spoke into her ear.

Grace patted his back affectionately before pulling back.

"Hello yourself. How is the distinguished Senator from Oklahoma?"

"Oh no, my girl. We are way past the formalities. I mean, you called out for me in your time of need. I have bandaged your wounds. You have chronicled my charisma and heroics to the world. We are comrades in arms!"

He was clearly enjoying himself.

"Charisma and heroics? Is that what I chronicled? I guess it *was* to the World Wide Web." Grace began to relax. He seemed to be at his charming and nimble-minded best.

They sat down on the granite block together. He looked at the injured side of her face.

"Your face looks a lot better. A few more days and there won't be a mark on you. You say the concussion symptoms have gone away?"

"Yes. I seem to have a scar on the inside of my cheek, but that's minor."

"Heard from the police? They arrested anyone?"

"No, but, oddly enough, Vincent had a run in with one of them."

She told Grey the story of how Vincent recovered her phone while being used by a drug runner.

"I don't think he told me the whole story, though. I don't suppose the guy just handed it over. Vincent's knuckles were all red."

Grey's countenance grew more pensive. Her remark reminded him that she lived with her ex-husband.

"Well, the Marines don't have a reputation for finesse, do they? They just do whatever it takes to accomplish their mission."

Grace noted the left-handed praise. She decided to divert the conversation.

"Speaking of the Marines, I hear that they have expanded the Marine security detachment at the Embassy in Caracas by about a division. The American government has nationalized an oil industry as you have been advocating, but it's Venezuela's, not America's. What is your take on all this?"

In an instant, Grey's countenance moved all the way to the dark side.

"That bitch in the White House has done this as blatant political calculus. She's appeasing those Judases in the NSA ... at Defense. She knows full well that they supported me, and now they've cut off my funds. And it's all to *save* the fucking oil industry."

His features were now twisted with fury as he stared at the pool. In the middle of the pool, two bronze Japanese cranes hung in agony, trapped in barbed wire at the top of a pylon. They symbolized the blundering internment of Japanese Americans during World War II. Grey hurried on.

"Well, I'm not done with them. I've got plans for overcoming their treachery."

Grey's hands were clenched, and he punched the air in front of him as he spoke. Then he looked at her and returned to the moment.

"That's why I wanted you to see it. I wanted to get, you know, your opinion on it. Do you notice anything different about me?"

He rotated so that Grace could see his full face, his eyes wide with expectation.

Confused, Grace looked back at him.

"It's the hair. Do you get it?"

Grace shook her head slowly.

"Oh, I know it has to grow some more, but I think you can begin to see it."

His left leg bounced rapidly again on the ball of his foot like it did when she first saw him.

"Imagine it longer, like down to my shoulders. Parted in the middle. Does it remind you of anyone?"

Perhaps unconsciously, he extended his arms, hands palm up, toward his front as he faced Grace. It was an unmistakable clerical gesture.

Grace's face registered her shock.

"Aaron, do you mean … Jesus?"

His face lit up with joy. Giddily, he clapped his hands.

"I knew it! I knew you'd see it!"

Then he dropped his voice and continued in a confidential tone.

"I came to realize that, in chaotic and threatening times, people need to feel comforted, even loved, by their leader. If they associate my image with that of Jesus, they will be quick to follow me, vote for *me* over these nitwits. My image alone will be more powerful than all the campaign funds in the word. Posters! They cost nothing! We can just print millions of posters and put them up all over the country."

Grace involuntarily recoiled, stunned. Grey was no longer in the moment; he was seeing something beyond his present surroundings.

"Diane will look at that image everywhere she goes! She does love her Methodist Jesus. Well, let her gaze upon it every time she goes out—every time she turns on the TV!"

Grace's shoulders slumped in pity and concern. She was unable to speak, unable to put what she was witnessing in perspective. Grey's candidacy was over. Her currency as a rising cross-media reporter with her finger on his campaign was valueless. Her sense of where the country might be headed, at least within certain parameters, had vanished.

"Grace ...."

His voice broke the awkward silence surrounding her thoughts.

"Don't pay any attention to my remarks about Diane. It's not like I'm fixated on her or anything. It's you I care about. It's you I want to spend my life with."

Grey's mind seemed to be back, as if a switch had been flipped. She wondered how the miraculous and mysterious processes of the human mind could function both normally and abnormally in parallel. She spoke to him as to a cogent, comprehending mind.

"Aaron, you have made me a very flattering and attractive offer of marriage, and I owe you an answer. I'm sorry to have to tell you that I'm not in love with you, and that I am in love with Vincent. He and I have unfinished business together, and I have to follow my heart. I wish you all the best and hope you have a long and distinguished career in politics."

Grey sat on the hard granite block with his head down. He seemed to have expected Grace's answer.

"Grace, I know that sometimes I have trouble keeping some thoughts ..., um, straight in my mind. I wouldn't ever want to hurt you or embarrass you, and I take comfort knowing that you are in a, you know, happy relationship. I'll just have to keep doing the best I can, you know, doing what I believe in. For as long as I can, anyway."

It was obvious to Grace that he knew on some level that something was askew in his mind.

Grace was crying as she put her hand on his face and kissed his cheek.

"There is life after politics, Aaron. If things get too ... chaotic, too stressful, think about your options. There must be some good fishing holes around Ardmore. I'll bet you have a few good books in you, too."

He nodded, averting her gaze.

"Then they win. They've already begun to ...."

He started to get agitated again.

Grace stood and cut him off.

"Take care of yourself Aaron."

Grace turned and walked back up the path toward Columbus Circle in the long shadows of the setting sun. As she got into her car, she saw that Aaron had followed her, keeping a half block's distance. When he saw her surprised look, he gave her the windshield wiper wave.

"Just wanted to make sure you got back safely this time," he called.

She got through Columbus Circle before pulling over to the curb a block before the I 395 South on-ramp. She couldn't see through her tears.

CHAPTER

25

As Grace drove over the Potomac on her way home, she could see billowing smoke rising against the sunset in her rear view mirror. It came from the section of the District beyond North Capitol Street, past where she had been mugged. She turned on the radio to see what was being reported. The all-news station was broadcasting an interview with the Deputy Fire Chief on scene. He was saying that a large group of youths were roaming the area and starting fires at liquor stores, fast food outlets and small markets, which, in the relative absence of chain store supermarkets, were preponderantly owned by Korean and Pakistani immigrants.

The news anchor explained that the closing of the banks and their ATMs, together with the indefinite furloughing of many municipal employees, added up to a perfect storm in the poverty-stricken neighborhoods. The residents' access to cash and food stamps had evaporated, leaving them desperate. Unfocused mob anger was taking over, he said.

Grace took the off ramp onto the Barack Obama Expressway on the Virginia side and headed toward Arlington. Grace smiled at the name. The Expressway had formerly been named the Jefferson Davis Expressway, but Virginia's second black governor renamed it, saying the former name celebrated the wrong man.

The news anchor switched to the next story in his news recap. An encampment of migrant Americans from around the Eastern Seaboard estimated to be several hundred homeless people, preponderantly families, had set up a loosely consolidated campsite adjacent to the Viet Nam and Korean War Memorials. Police were negotiating with unofficial spokespersons for the group trying to get them to relocate to an athletic field at Gallaudet University in Northeast Washington. The campers refused, saying they believed the police were trying to shuffle them out of sight. Moving them to a university for the deaf reeked of a cynical intent to lessen the effect of their demonstrations, they said. Moreover, the very same Northeast neighborhood where Gallaudet is situated was presently aflame and unsafe for the families. The police have so far acted with restraint, the announcer said, and negotiations would continue.

Unh oh. Is this going to stop?

The broadcaster next reported on a television spot that had just surfaced. He said a group calling themselves Americans for Energy Independence were blanketing the Northeast with a hit piece on Senator Aaron Grey's controversial Presidential campaign. It disclosed that Senator Grey had a history of incapacitating mental illness, and that his father before him had been arrested several times for threats of violence against public figures. A spokesman for the group was quoted as saying, "Crazy people, I'm sorry to say, have crazy ideas."

Grace recalled that Aaron had said "they" had started to attack him. He'd probably seen the spot.

She turned into the garage of her apartment complex and parked the car. She felt emotionally exhausted by her meeting with Aaron Grey and frightened by the apparent breakdown of law and order in the District. She didn't know what to say to Vincent. Her heart was full, and she was sure to start crying when she talked about it. She just sat staring at the concrete wall in front of her car.

***

Vincent stepped out on the balcony of the apartment in the gathering dusk and looked at this watch. He called Grace.

"Where are you? Can you talk?" he said when she answered.

"Downstairs. I'm getting out of the car." She sounded whipped.

"Whew. I was getting worried."

He listened for a response but heard the line go dead.

In a few minutes, Grace came in the front door and dropped her keys in the small basket on the hall table. She unslung her purse and dropped it on the edge of the table next to the basket and missed. It fell to the floor as she walked over to the sofa and sat down, out of breath from the five flights of stairs.

"How'd it go?"

"I'll come back to that in a minute," she said weakly, patting the cushion beside her. "Have you been listening to the news?"

"No. Power's been out all afternoon and evening. Why?"

He sat down and put his arm around her.

Grace told him about the neighborhood fires in Northeast Washington. Then she told him about the growing encampment of migrant Americans on the Mall between the Viet Nam and Korean War Memorials. Finally, she related her entire, devastating encounter with Aaron Grey. She did the latter in a halting, quiet voice.

The bare fact of having glimpsed, up close and personal, the mental disintegration of a man she viewed as a distinguished and promising statesman shocked her. He got that. The added circumstance of the man's proposal and her refusal would have been upsetting for anyone. Hell, even he was shocked. He would give her lots of room about it. She could talk about it when it felt right.

He went to the kitchen, and returned with a lit candle, two champagne flutes and a lukewarm bottle of Prosecco from the now-thawed freezer compartment. He opened the cork with an explosion of air and filled two full wine glasses, putting one in her hands.

"Hardly an occasion for bubbly," she said.

"It seems like we resort to the sauce every time something stressful happens, which is often these days. Anyway, it tastes good and has alcohol in it that will put things slightly out of focus. Since we aren't going to be needing our fight or flight response tonight, that might be a good thing."

She smiled weakly.

"You're a good man to have around in a crisis, major."

He refrained from any wisecracks, clinking her glass.

"You said encampment? Of migrant Americans? Is that the way they put it?"

"Their words exactly. It's like Aaron's stories about the Great Depression," Grace said. "That's the last time people spoke of 'migrant Americans' that I remember reading about."

They were quiet for a time. Grace broke the silence.

"You have that slush money from your trip, right?"

Vincent nodded and drained his glass.

"Haven't a clue how to do an expense report and return it, and there's no one to ask because I'm in limbo."

"Do you still think New Mexico is an option?"

"The best one by far."

The silence between them returned. This time it was broken by the lights coming back on in the kitchen.

Grace looked up.

"Do we dare listen to the news?"

Vincent answered by picking up the remote. They were just in time for a summary on the hour. First, a naval task force of the People's Republic of China with four new carriers and their squadrons of attack aircraft had been dispatched to the Caribbean. It was not clear whether the Panama Canal would be open to them, given the American military presence in the area, but the new Nicaragua Canal had been funded, built and operated by a PRC company. The Chinese fleet would be in the Caribbean in a matter of eight or nine days.

"We've been operating our warships in the South China sea for decades. Now let's see how our government likes them apples," Vincent said.

The second story being previewed was that long lines for gasoline were being experienced all over the country, with the States in which oil refineries were located doing a bit better than those with few or no refineries. The Northeast and California were experiencing the worst delays because of the greater demand from their large populations.

"There was a shortage like this back in the seventies," Grace said. "I remember my folks talking about it. It was caused by an OPEC embargo that kind of woke Americans up to how dependent they were on imported Middle Eastern oil. My folks always drove small Japanese cars after that until everybody relaxed and mostly went back to SUVs and muscle cars. Hybrids and electric cars never did win a major market share."

Next came a report about the increased number of deaths in cities throughout the country and in areas of rural poverty due to the power outages. Ironically, many deaths were occurring in hospitals due to shortages of medical personnel unable to get to work to care for the most vulnerable. The elderly living alone without air conditioning, as well as increased vehicle accidents due to inoperative traffic lights accounted for many more. Malnutrition was becoming a problem causing a spike in ER visits.

In an almost celebratory tone, the news anchor chronicled the ongoing failure of the air traffic control system in the People's Republic of China, along with that of the operating system for the Chinese national railways. Power outages were also reported in the huge south Chinese cities of Shanghai, Guangzhou, Shenzhen, Wuhan, and Chongqing. The commentator reported that demonstrations against America had broken out in those cities, accusing it of having caused the grid failure through a cyber-attack. Demonstrators also carried signs condemning American imperialism in Venezuela. A former Cabinet secretary blogged that, even if American cyber-attacks had taken place, "what's good for the goose is good for the gander." His implication was that any such cyber-attacks, if true, were likely payback for China's reported attack on America's Western power grid earlier in the month and the unexplained and still partially unrestored system failures in America's largest financial institutions.

The final story was of widespread panic buying of consumer goods and foodstuffs throughout the country.

"One man's hoard is another man's emergency supply of necessaries," Vincent said, somewhat defensively.

Grace looked troubled. "Great, now we are a new cultural stereotype. Save yourselves."

They sat transfixed as the broadcast broke for a commercial interruption consisting of exactly three commercials announcing clearance sales by local stores and car dealerships. This contrasted with the normal programming breaks for up to twenty commercials plus network promotion spots in a half hour broadcast.

"If the lack of commercials is an indicator of the fall-off in business activity generally, I'd say we are headed into the New Great Depression. Or worse," he added.

Grace took Vincent's hand in both of hers, and he was surprised by the hardness of her grip. He looked over and saw that she was crying. He couldn't think of any way to sugar coat what they and the country, even the world, was confronted with, never mind the prospects going forward. Instead, he disengaged a hand from her grip and reached for the champagne bottle.

"A little toleration medicine," he said, refilling her glass.

"This is like a turning point in a novel or a play," she said. "It's the place where the reader says 'Aha, the plot thickens'. It changes everything, sets all the action in a new direction of ever-increasing tension and danger. Only this isn't fiction; it's our lives and we've become the actors. I wonder what the chances are for a happy ending."

"Isn't that always the case with a good story? The suspense builds to an unbearable level before it is finally resolved in the hero's favor. That's why you should never lose hope."

She looked at him. "Is that some Marine crap you are giving me? Never give up? Tough it out? I'm not big into the Marine thing, as you will recall."

"You brought up the fiction writing analogy. Writing is your thing. I'm just pointing out some convenient and possibly relevant learning from what little I know about it," Vincent said with the hint of a grin.

Grace snorted and weakly poked him in the ribs. A smile crept across her face.

"Is this how you're going to be? Always with the pep talks; the locker room exhortations to overcome?"

"Afraid so. We call it gung-ho. Can do. Never give up. Onward and upward."

"Enough already. Point made. I won't let you down, sir. You can count on me. I've got your flank. Victory is ours!"

Vincent was laughing now.

"Excellent. We laugh at danger. Just what the doctor ordered. We're good to go."

"Yeah, bring it on!"

"Banzai, man!"

Vincent reached over and took a swig from Grace's champagne glass.

"What the hell? Leave my bubbly alone."

"Well, we're all out." He pointed to the empty bottle. "I just thought that you wouldn't mind sharing."

"*You're* all out," she giggled. "*I've* still got some, so keep your shit hooks off, jarhead."

Grace was clearly feeling the effects of the half bottle of Prosecco she had consumed on an empty stomach. Vincent was glad that she was still in the game. She would be resilient, and she would need to be.

CHAPTER

26

"I don't get it. There you were, writing potential Pulitzer Prize winning articles one right after the other about the most interesting Presidential candidate in recent years. And then you just stop? I know you got knocked in the head, but you seem fine now. It can't be that."

Grace was sitting in the office of Raj Patel, founder and publisher of *Insider On Line* e-news magazine. He had asked for the meeting.

"I know, Raj, it is disorienting for me too. To shut down something that consumed me for so many weeks."

"So what happened? What is Grey up to? I'm hearing nothing from anyone."

"What happened? You mean with me? Or with him?"

"Both."

"For me, it got personal," Grace said offering nothing more.

"Got personal? These political guys make passes at government girls, journalists, lobbyists, hell, any tail that moves. So what's the big deal? You dodge it and keep going. You didn't fall for him did you? You didn't get involved with him?"

"No, Raj, but my personal ethics are at the center of this. Off the record, he did try to, ah … start a relationship, but I am not, nor have I ever been involved with him romantically. More to the point, and still off the record, you can take it from me that he will not be the next President and his non-campaign will turn out to be just that, a non-campaign. He isn't going to be news any more. Not political news, anyway."

"Great. Well, that still leaves a couple of hundred questions unanswered. There are a lot of people out there who want to know what's up with him, so that does make him news. Can't you just write something that will tie all this up so that we can save some professional face?"

"That's a reasonable request, Raj, and I feel like I've let you down. I feel like I have been somehow unprofessional about this, but no, I can't write that article. It isn't up to me to declare Senator Grey's candidacy over, and I'm certainly not going to write a disclosure about an arguable conflict of interest that necessitates my withdrawal. Why don't you just call around to the wire services and get whatever reporting on Grey you can. They'll be happy to sell you something."

"That's it? That's all you're going to give me?"

Grace nodded. "I'm afraid so. When the yeast rises a bit you'll find out what happened to Grey. Someday, maybe we can revisit the subject in some satisfying way. In the meantime, the country is falling apart. *That's* the story. What is *Insider's* approach to that story? What kind of content are you looking for going forward?"

Patel got out of his chair and went to the window facing 17th Street and the back side of the Mayflower hotel.

"You're not wrong there. And as bad as things are here, it's even worse in India. My aunts and uncles in Bangalore are starving. Mind you, Bangalore is India's Silicon Valley. It's a pensioner's dream location. Only now, people there are starving."

According to the bio on Patel that *Insider* published, his father was an engineering graduate of the Indian Institute of Science in Bangalore who came to America on a green card to join the team in Palo Alto that was developing the router. Grace knew that Patel's father became wealthy from the developer's stock options. His mother was a doctor.

Raj Patel himself was a graduate of MIT, but he developed a love for journalism and saw a market niche for an Internet based publisher of news and opinion. *Insider* was the result. Grace met him on a trip to San Francisco at a Friday night entrepreneur's "meet up" to which she had been taken by college girlfriend who regularly attended. Meet-ups were freeform, ad-hoc gatherings in those days and young women were an always welcome minority. Grace and Raj had exchanged email addresses after Patel mentioned that he was working on a business plan for a startup e-news publication and Grace expressed interest in writing for it. She called Patel three years later when she moved back to Washington after the divorce. He'd set up an office in DC to be close to the source of American political news and took Grace on as a stringer.

"Starving?" Grace asked. "If Bangalore can't manage, what city in India can?"

"Bangalore has been riding the prosperity that flowed from tech development and out-sourcing by Western corporations for years. But tech runs on energy, and India is a big importer of energy. The worldwide oil shortage has thrown the Indian tech industry into a catastrophic down-turn. It has a lot of natural gas, but like in the U.S., it doesn't help in the transportation sector. There are few oil pipelines into India. Food imports into India have fallen off as transportation stalls. Domestic production has been slashed along with energy usage. Add hoarding to the mix and you have complete market failure. Even people who have money can't get food that originates from outside the immediate area. Big cities like Bangalore are vulnerable, as they are here, only worse because of the more primitive infrastructure. An urban population can't survive very long if its logistics fail. I hear terrible things about bigger, poorer cities like Mumbai and Delhi."

"That's exactly what is happening here. I don't hear people talking about solutions, Raj. Well, no one except Aaron Grey. It's as though every-one bought into the paradigm of perpetual, self-correcting free enterprise. How does urban civilization survive?"

Patel turned to look at her, and he saw the worry in her eyes. He merely shrugged. "I think we have all been delusional. The idea that there could be sudden, irreversible collapse was too awful. There *are* no good answers."

He sat down and absentmindedly rolled a magic marker between his fingers, although he had nothing to edit with it.

"I'm afraid we are day-to-day here, Grace. Advertising has dried up completely. Subscriptions are being cancelled. We are insolvent, as the accountants would say. I'm using my own money to stay open now, and my parents aren't willing to contribute to a losing operation. Forget about a bank bridge loan. Banks are looking at growing defaults on their loans so they have big problems of their own. I can't pay you your guaranteed salary anymore, meager as it is, and if you submit free-lance pieces, I can't honestly say there will be money to pay you for those. That's why I was hoping for something electrifying from you on Senator Grey's ideas and prospects. I thought we might get a subscriptions boost if we had exciting, hopeful stuff from him."

"I see, Raj. I'm sorry. But, quite apart from my own reluctance to write about him, I'm afraid that Grey isn't going to be our savior. You can take that to the bank, as the saying used to go."

Patel absentmindedly traced a declining line in the air with his marker.

"People have assets out there, of course, but the value of them shrinks as markets collapse. Some people have garden produce and clothes and chickens and eggs—stuff people need to survive and that can be exchanged for necessaries. Some sort of order will form around that kind of barter economy where local security can be established. I think we are going back to city states, only without the cities. Our national population levels just can't be sustained in a collapse scenario. I fear the coming period as society transitions from inter-dependency to small and self-sustaining groups. A lot of people are going to die, and they are not going to do it without putting up a struggle. The fortunate people, the ones with liquid assets like cash and gold, have another problem—they have a target on their backs."

"Write about that, Raj. Write about how we have a lot of collective memory. Our societies can reinvent the crucial things that brought human culture into the modern world. Order can be restored after collapse by bringing back the most helpful of the great inventions, only it won't take so long this time."

"You may be right, Grace. Societies can reform after collapse, and their progress will be more rapid than with original evolution. They can remember the useful things, things like paper, penicillin, steam engines, hell, the Gutenberg printing press. That was maybe the greatest invention ever. It allowed knowledge to replicate rapidly across great distances and independently of local aristocracy and religious orthodoxy. Maybe that is the best way we can contribute going forward."

Grace sighed. "It's going to be hard to submit my articles without email, though. I don't even have a Gutenberg press."

Patel laughed. "We'll just have to reinvent email, that's all. After we reinvent electronics, of course."

Grace stood up and extended her hand.

"Thanks for giving me the chance to write for you, Raj. It meant a lot to me. Good luck."

"Grace, you produced the best stuff out of all my writers. You're twenty four carat gold in my book. Stay in touch."

They shook hands and Grace walked out and down the stairway. She could tell by the silence in the building that the power was off and elevators weren't working.

***

Vincent sat on the bar stool at the kitchen counter and scratching his two-week-old beard. He'd trimmed it for the first time that morning and was surprised at how different he looked. The dark beard even came in with a few gray hairs. His haircut looked just plain unkempt. He looked like a civilian. If he got a call to appear at the Pentagon, he could shave the beard in a matter of minutes, but he couldn't go there with this haircut.

Later.

He picked up his phone and keyed the number he had for General Yin. He was surprised when the General's secretary put him right through.

"Hello, Major Long. I've been thinking about you. Are you in town?"

"Yes, sir. Still standing by. I also want to change my paycheck arrangements to cash disbursements if possible. The bank direct deposit arrangement isn't a good one anymore. I expect you want me to take it up with the G-1, but I thought I'd check with you first since this has to be a systemic problem and maybe you have some guidance for me."

"Well, the good news is that you have orders of a sort. The bad news is what they are, and they will moot your question about bank deposits. The President and the Appropriations Committees in the Congress have been able to reach rare agreement on something. In light of the suddenness and depth of the recession into which we are falling, the Federal Government's revenue has dropped off a cliff. Treasury can't borrow either in this market. The Chinese are boycotting T-bond sales and dumping their existing holdings. The dollar is falling like a stone.

"Under orders from the White House, DoD has been prioritizing parts of the budget to be cut rather than having Treasury print money, which is inflationary. The Marine Corps is going to have to do its share. As a first step, General Forest is furloughing one regiment in each of the three divisions and one squadron in each of the air wings, along with some headquarters types. You are in the latter category, as am I. Effective immediately, you are furloughed. You will be given a month's salary by way of severance. That isn't much, but that's the deal."

Vincent slipped off the stool and stood up as General Yin spoke, running his free hand back and forth over his abundant hair.

"Wow. Didn't see that coming, sir, but I get it. Ah, if I understand the dictionary meaning of furlough, it means leave of absence. That implies that it is temporary. Is this temporary?"

"Good question, major. The answer is I don't know. That's because the White House and the bean counters on the Armed Forces Committees in the House and Senate don't know either. They are unwilling to make our Defense Establishment cutbacks official because it directly translates into a lasting loss of national military power. I suppose the furlough idea gives them a legal string to pull people back if the situation improves. I don't think you can count on that, though, so if I were you, I would do whatever you need to do to take care of yourself."

"Aye, aye, General Yin. Guess I'll have to store my uniforms somewhere and get some more civvies."

"Now, as to your severance pay. I can't do anything about the direct deposits already made to your bank. That is between you and the bank, but we can provide a letter certifying which deposits were made to give you something to show the bank if their computer "loses" them. We've been getting a lot of that. But for people here in the Pentagon receiving severance, we've made arrangements for the severance to be paid in cash. There are problems with cashing checks. Something about the inter-bank check clearing system when the power is off. So you can come over here and pick your severance money up at the G-1's office. I'd do it sooner rather than later in case they run out of cash."

"I'll do that, thanks. It's been a pleasure working with you General Yin."

"And with you, Major Long. This will all make a good story to tell your grandchildren."

He hung up.

Holy Crap! I just went into personal DEFCON 2.

Vincent was unable to sit down. He paced the limited square footage of the apartment and the deck overlooking the green belt. His mind raced, but made no traction. He went back to the kitchen counter and picked up his phone again. This time he dialed Commander Jerry McMasters. He answered the phone immediately.

"Vincent!" McMasters' voice boomed. "I thought you'd be down in Caracas guarding our new oil reserves about now."

"No, Jerry," Vincent said. "I'm just hanging out here in case you need me to go spin a new yarn to Superintendent Liu before their four carriers arrive."

"We'll have *five* carriers there to meet theirs. I'm sure we can all have a nice government-to-government chat about torts and remedies for interference with contractual relations. They'll learn something about a government of laws and not of men."

"I'll bet. Maybe Sam Johnson can moderate the discussion."

McMasters ignored the remark.

"Anyway, Liu is dead," he said casually.

Vincent was stunned. "He's dead? How did that happen?"

"He was killed in a train wreck. It seems that the operating system for the Chinese National Railways suddenly and mysteriously ceased to work not long after our banks were attacked. The Chinese rely on their railways to move around all those hundreds of millions of people this way and that—so much so that they continued operating their trains manually. Liu was sitting up in the front car with some Communist Party VIP's going to Shanghai when their train crashed head-on with a northbound train."

Vincent paused only a moment.

"And do you have a contingency plan for countering China's invasion of Taiwan? One that works with a furloughed Defense Department and scarce fuel?"

"Taiwan? That island doesn't have any oil," McMasters said dismissively. "Anything else? That why you called?"

Vincent knew he had become suddenly irrelevant to what was playing out on the world stage now. He felt incredibly discouraged. This isn't how he expected to serve his country. These people are not the ones he expected to serve with.

"Just one thing. I've been furloughed from the Marine Corps. I just wanted you to know that I'm out of this."

"No strings to us. It never happened. Oh, and that wad of cash we gave you when you went to Beijing? You can keep whatever is left over. Our records show it expensed for field operations. You will probably need it."

A flush of embarrassment washed over Vincent. He hadn't asked about it first. "People are going to want to be paid in chickens, not dollars," Vincent said, trying not to sound lame.

"Oh, Vincent, by the way, they found that tanker that had been hijacked. It was on the beach in India waiting to be cut up for salvage. The seller was some shell outfit with no real offices or employees. I suppose we'll never know who took it, but it reinforces the Indian connection."

McMasters seemed to be rubbing it in.

"And I suppose the Chief Engineer was never found."

"No, that remains a mystery. He was in the wrong place at the wrong time, I suppose. It happens."

"Tell me Jerry. What was up with the flash drive recovery trip and the nonsense about going to Beijing to deliver disinformation to Liu. None of that made any sense."

"Sure. The fact is that you were a little too good in your guesswork about what was going on. We wanted to hook you, string you along so you wouldn't go off the reservation prematurely and be a distraction. You are a bit of a boy scout with your Marine straight arrow mindset, so it wasn't hard. Besides, who knows, the disinformation you gave Liu may have actually helped keep them from further cyber-attacks until we were ready with the Venezuela operation and our own cyber-attacks. So, mission accomplished and well done."

"Jerry, you have taught me the meaning of the word regret. I hope I run into you in a dark alley some time."

Vincent hung up.

He would have to live with the knowledge of having allowed himself, against his judgment, to be ill-used by rogue agents. Still his actions appear to have been harmless. Maybe he did temporarily prevent a cyber-attack on America. He would never know.

Anyway, he had more immediate problems.

CHAPTER

27

"Well, the decks are cleared," Vincent said as he and Grace finished exchanging reports on Grace's meeting with Raj Patel and Vincent's calls to General Yin and Jerry McMasters. "We're free to do what's best for us."

Grace said nothing and didn't move from her position on the sofa with her knees pulled up to her chest gazing at the clouds sliding over Georgetown. She was fighting the problem.

"In fact, we *must* take care of ourselves now. You with me on that Grace?"

She swung her feet to the floor and straightened her back.

"Yes, I'm with you. But to be honest, I'm pissed. This didn't have to happen. Some people who should have known better screwed it up, and now we all have to go into panic mode or, like, die."

"Yeah, well, you're not wrong, although, it was sort of inevitable. When you don't have enough resources to support the population of the world, something like this has to happen. The players and timing might vary, but the competition for scarce resources quickly becomes deadly, since, as you say, life itself is at stake. Besides, I'm not sure you and I don't belong in that category of those who screwed things up. What did we do to prepare ourselves for peak oil?"

The smell of acrid smoke from the rubber tire fires across the river intensified in the room, and Grace got up and closed the door to the balcony.

"Must be a wind shift," Vincent said. "The fires haven't been put out because the mobs keep attacking the fire trucks. You wonder why they burn the tires, though. They have to breathe that poison more than we do."

Grace worried the forming scar inside her mouth with her tongue and nodded. "It's going to get hotter and stuffier in here with the door closed. Let's work on a plan while it's still bearable. I assume you are still thinking New Mexico?"

"I am."

"Rather than Denver?"

"Denver? You want to live indefinitely in your parents' spare room?"

"No, but we could get a place and keep tabs on my folks."

"A place costs money. We will have no source of income for the foreseeable future. Denver is a city. Cities are collapsing. Your parents may have to come and live with *us*. The high desert in New Mexico is distant from urban centers and so should have relatively fewer desperate types around wanting to take everything of value. The house is big enough for us. It has a guest house for your parents in a pinch. And there are trout streams and a national forest nearby. Dad kept fishing gear and a shotgun and a rifle."

"My God, you expect pitched gunfights?"

"No, no," he said and laughed. "The shotgun is for hunting ducks, geese, wild turkeys, pheasant—you know, birds. The rifle is for deer, raccoon, squirrels. We are going to be hunter-gatherers if we can't get groceries, and we don't know what will be available in local markets. Also, we might have to barter fish and game for other things we need when the money runs out. I just hope Joe has been able to care for the place. We'll need it to be weatherproof. It will be getting cold there as we head into fall."

He referred to the Taos Pueblo Indian caretaker that had helped his father around the place. Vincent paid Joe to keep the property up and vagrants from moving in. Vincent said he heard from Joe once a month by email from the Taos Internet Café and always delivering the same report.

"House OK. No problems." Joe never asked for reimbursement for maintenance and repair expenses or anything else. They would need his help.

"So how do we get from here to there? I assume we take the car. Pack as much stuff as we can into it, and head west like the Joad family?"

"I think we have better options that they did. Let's noodle this."

By the time the apartment became too stuffy and too dark to continue, they'd compiled a list of things to do that that was surprisingly short and not overly daunting.

Grace would advise the utility company when to turn off service and the post office where to forward mail. She would contact the management company that ran the apartment building and terminate her lease. They would be asked to forward her deposit refund by check to the Los Alamos address if the management wouldn't return it immediately when they moved out. She was resigned to losing it if they didn't follow through.

Vincent would buy a pistol and ammunition. Grace was concerned about that item on the list, but Vincent said it would be prudent to have it for their self-defense as they traveled across country. He told her of his experience in Honolulu's Ala Moana Park en route back from China and reminded her of her own mugging.

Vincent had devised a loose plan for traveling to New Mexico. The plan was to sell Grace's hybrid car in Washington, converting the value of the car into cash. Then they would travel by Amtrak from Washington's Union Station to Albuquerque, paying cash for one way tickets. They would take as much luggage containing winter clothes and useful small household items as they could manage. The plan would save them the expense and uncertainty of gasoline availability if they were to drive a car. It would take less time and also avoid the danger of driving on their own such a long way. Once in Albuquerque, they would buy an SUV or pick up—preferably a hybrid. They would need something suitable for New Mexico country roads in the winter. They would then drive with their possessions and as many groceries they could buy in Albuquerque to Los Alamos via Santa Fe.

An exodus from the metro Washington area would likely be developing creating demand for used cars. They assumed that Grace's hybrid car would be in demand since it could operate on either gas or an electric charge. They also assumed that cars would be available in Albuquerque since people hurt by the recession would be selling used cars to raise money or to reduce gas expenses. They had no idea what the demand side would be for cars in Albuquerque.

Vincent called Amtrak and determined that the trains were running, though on a reduced schedule, and that seats were more readily available on the southwest route than on the north-south routes.

Grace had successfully made a withdrawal from her branch bank before her meeting with Patel. Her bank had been successful in retrieving depositors' account information from data storage during the periods the power was on, but its computer system still seemed to be remotely controlled and could not perform interactive functions. Her bank manager told her she could not withdraw the entire balance because of "accounting problems," but Grace suspected that the bank was really trying to moderate a run on the bank as depositors flooded it with withdrawal requests. She now had fifteen one hundred dollar bills and another two hundred dollars in twenties, tens and fives.

That money, together with the proceeds from selling her car, Vincent's severance pay in cash from the Marine Corps and the bulk of his $10,000 travel advance he'd received from McMasters, would give them nearly $30,000 in cash. That much cash would enable them to meet any expense shock they ran into.

***

It took them five days to sell the car. They had no initial responses to their on-line ad, likely, Vincent surmised, due to the long periods that computer service was not available during rotating power outages. They were close to taking a dealer's below-wholesale offer when they were contacted by a woman recently furloughed by the State Department who eventually saw the ad on line. She needed a car to move to Pennsylvania to care for her parents. She and Grace hit it off, and the car was sold for cash just below retail value.

Vincent had no trouble buying a .45 caliber pistol and five boxes of ammunition. Grace terminated the apartment lease, but the management company insisted on keeping a portion of the deposit to cover possible outstanding utility bills. She gave them the furnishings in the apartment and hoped that they would follow through with the deposit refund.

Vincent stood in line at the Amtrak sales office to buy hard copy, one-way rail tickets to Albuquerque. They packed his suitcase and sea bag, her two suitcases and two others they bought at a flea market with clothes, shoes, coats, personal effects, small kitchen utensils, a few books and their important documents. Vincent convinced Grace that eating utensils and dishes would be in the ranch house, but she took two sets of flatware anyway "in case we have to eat *al fresco* along the way."

They packed one of the bottles of wine Grace had left in her wine rack and gave the others to Jody. Jody said she would take the replacement bicycle Vincent had bought with her when she moved back in with her parents in upstate New York. Jody had just received the insurance settlement for the theft of her bike and reimbursed Vincent for the cost of the replacement bike. Jody and Grace promised to stay in touch, but both knew they were saying goodbye for good.

Grace phoned the car mechanic she had used to service her car and arranged for him to drive them to Union Station at two o'clock for a three thirty departure. He had offered to do it for fifty dollars, but Grace had insisted on paying him seventy five, hoping to motivate him to follow through. Vincent thought it an inspired move.

On the day of their departure, Vincent surveyed the luggage piled by the door one last time. Grace sat across from him at the kitchen table. In perhaps a foretaste of their new life in the American Southwest, they munched the last of their blue corn chips and store-bought salsa.

"Ready?" he asked.

A tear spilled from the corner of her eye, and she wiped it away with the back of her hand.

"Yes," she said, with a tight smile.

It was just before two o'clock. Vincent and Grace carried all six luggage items to the elevator and down to the front door. They didn't have long to wait.

***

Vincent looked out the rain-streaked window of their first class coach at the passing countryside. The leaves on uneven clumps of sumac growing along the railroad tracks shined glossy wet. Grace had gone to check out the menu and food service hours in the dining car, and Vincent let his eyes drift among the passing sights. The gentle sway of the train gliding along welded track lulled him into a deeper state of relaxation than he'd known for weeks. He didn't want to think about the events that precipitated the trip. He wanted to think about he and Grace together on the ranch.

From Washington, the Capitol Limited would take them to stops at Pittsburg, Cleveland, and Chicago. They would change trains in Chicago to the Southwest Chief for the trip to Kansas City and Albuquerque on its route to Los Angeles.

The trip to Chicago was scheduled to take seventeen hours. That meant at least one meal on this leg of the trip. The layover in Chicago was six hours and the trip from Chicago to Albuquerque would take twenty six hours. That's if there were no delays. Vincent had splurged on a sleeper compartment for the Chicago-Albuquerque leg.

Vincent joked that they would pretty ripe by the time they got to New Mexico, but, with one or two Minnesota Fats-type freshenings-up in the sleeper, they should arrive more or less rested and ready to cope.

Not knowing how long it would take them to find and buy a car, Vincent had booked a room for three days at the Hotel Andaluz not far from the Amtrak station in Albuquerque. The reservationist had taken the reservation, but said she could not guarantee the room with a credit card until the credit card system was restored. No-shows resulted in cancellation of the booking. She said that the train schedules had been erratic lately. Vincent assured her that he could pay cash for the room, and they would try to advise the hotel of any delays by phone. The reservationist pledged to do the best she could.

Grace came through the automatic sliding door at the head of the car, swaying with the railcar as it traced the rails.

"It's not great," she said sitting down close to Vincent.

"The dining car is in 'limited service' mode. Most of the menu items are not available due to 'on-going interruptions in supply.' The porter said the snack cart would come around. It's stocked with chips and cans of soft drinks."

The dining room was open during the three meal hours, she reported, but the menu choices were few and a little primitive.

"Spam and hash browns for breakfast and chipped beef on toast for lunch. Oh, and hot dogs with succotash for dinner," she said.

Vincent clapped his hands and hooted.

"Chipped beef on toast? Shit on a shingle? Are you kidding me? I haven't had that since boot camp! Outstanding! That's comfort food for me."

Grace opened her mouth and stuck her finger in, making a gagging sound.

"We'll have dinner tonight and breakfast tomorrow on the train," he said. "Scrounging at the Chicago station and maybe local vendors in the neighborhood should be a bit better. Maybe we can score some good snacks for the last leg. Anyway, that menu sounds doable."

"Says the guy who eats in Marine mess halls."

"Oh well, if you're going to get all high maintenance on me, this is going to be a long trip." Vincent exaggerated rolling his eyes.

"We shall overcome, darlin'" she said, punching her sweater into a shape that fit behind her neck.

"I didn't sleep well last night so I'm going to take a nap."

She turned sideways and contorted herself into as close to the fetal position as she could manage and still remain sitting upright and then closed her eyes.

Vincent pulled out the copy of last month's *Atlantic* he found in the luggage bin near the door of the car when they entered. His eye fell immediately on an article about the top one hundred inventions of mankind over recorded history nominated by a panel of distinguished scientists and thinkers. He scanned the top rankings. The Gutenberg printing press. Electricity. The steam engine, and so on. He tore the article out and folded it to fit in his pocket.

We'll have to remember what has to be recreated.

***

Vincent awoke when Grace put her hand on his thigh and shook it. Grace pointed out the window. He saw in the dusk that the train was creeping along.

"It's been like this since I woke up twenty minutes ago. I don't see any lights, but I saw some buildings go by."

The porter came through the sliding door at the head of the car, and was immediately stopped by a woman seated in front on the aisle. They couldn't hear her question, but they could hear his response.

"When the signal lights don't work and the traffic control system goes dark, we have to slow way down. Yes, ma'am, it puts us way off schedule sometimes."

Vincent immediately thought of Superintendent Liu's fate.

I didn't even consider this when we made our plan. Idiot!

Grace groaned. "We're going about 10 miles an hour. This trip could take a week. Surely they can go faster than this."

"It's almost dark, Grace. They can't see the track ahead and the signal lights are off. Trust me, my love, if we are going to collide with another train on the tracks, we want to be going as slowly as possible. I just hope the trains behind us are doing the same thing."

The porter had worked his way down the aisle checking tickets and got to them.

"Excuse me, where are we now?" Vincent asked. "Are these slow rolls frequent?"

"We're not too far from Pittsburg. The yard is pretty congested with all the new coal trains going to the utilities, so it will take a couple of hours to get to the station at this speed. If the system is still down then, the train will probably be able to leave, but we'll have to maintain this speed. With the system down, we can pick up speed some if it's a clear day tomorrow, but probably not more than about thirty five miles per hour, tops. Once the system comes back up, we can open her up again. It happens a lot."

The porter moved on to the passengers behind them. Vincent and Grace quickly ran the numbers and realized that they would miss their connection in Chicago. Vincent got up and caught the porter as he was about to leave for the next car.

"Excuse me again. I'm thinking that we will probably miss our connection in Chicago to the Southwest Chief. Is it company policy to give priority to delayed connecting passengers on the next available departure over passengers who originate in Chicago?"

"I understand your situation, sir. Mostly, they give priority to the people getting on in Chicago. That way, they don't have to do this cascade of rebooking for everybody—they just have to reschedule the ones delayed. But, if there are a lot of missed connections from a lot of delays, then it gets chaotic. I've seen 'em do first come, first served. If I were you, I'd get to your train as soon as you can and if your assigned seats are empty, just sit in them. It's easier to shut out the ones who haven't settled in. The company don't have the time or the people to do all the arguin' and packin' people back up and all that."

Vincent glanced at the man's nametag.

"Many thanks, Arthur. That's good scoop." He slipped a five into Arthur's hand.

"Thank you, sir."

Vincent related Arthur's advice to Grace. She looked deflated.

"This is going to be an ordeal, isn't it?"

"It's shaping up that way. But don't think of this as a setback," he said theatrically. "Think of it as an opportunity, an opportunity to think outside the box and have an adventure. You know, like a reality show on TV. It will be fun to test our limits."

The barest hint of a smile crept onto her face despite her best efforts to suppress it. She leaned over, conspiratorially glancing to both sides.

"Vincent, how would you like for me to knee you right in the balls. You won't know when or where, but I will get you if you keep up with this gung-ho stuff."

Satisfied that Grace was back, he looked at his watch.

"The dining car is open. How about some of those hot dogs with succotash. Maybe a pretzel *brule* to finish?"

"God, I hope they have alcohol."

***

By the time the train pulled into the Pittsburg station near the convergence of the Allegany and Monongahela Rivers that formed the mighty Ohio River, they'd finish their strange and Spartan meal. Still sitting in the dining car, they were working on their third lager each. Vincent bottomed out on his and Grace pushed her mostly full bottle over to his side of the table.

"I'm done. Go for it."

"Look at all those people," Vincent said, pointing to the clumps of people that sat on the platform between their track and the next one. The groups, perhaps families, sat in circles facing each other across blankets and towels spread out on the platform with their gear piled around them. "What do you make of that?"

The steward in the aisle overhead him.

"Those are the new homeless," he said with what Vincent took to be a Latin accent. "The station's waiting room is too close to the parking lot to be safe. The criminals swoop into the cupola area and run inside with guns, taking money and yanking off jewelry, watches, computers and phones, grabbing everything they can. They even do it when there is a police car out there. They just run off in every direction. It's like the beaches in Rio de Janeiro when I left, only worse."

"So, out there on the platforms is safer?" Grace asked.

"Much. It's too far from the waiting room for the bad guys, and there's stairs. The criminals can be cornered out here, and the mob will beat them up. It's colder at night outside here, but no one bothers them, and it's out of the rain."

"You're from Brazil?" Vincent asked, guessing at the accent. "What are conditions like there?"

"It's not too bad there, I think. Brazil produces much oil—enough to export. China financed development of a lot of deep water wells so it gets first export rights. I think America has been cut off. My government is corrupt, and the oil money is taken by the officials before any gets to the people. The *favelas*, excuse me, the poor areas in the cities, are bad. But there is electricity a lot of the time, and people can live cheaply on government subsidies. I'll go back if I get laid off from Amtrak. It will be bad here, I think."

Grace reached up and offered her hand.

"I'm Grace. This is my husband Vincent."

The steward's eyes brightened, and he shook hands with both of them.

"Ah, I am Vincente, the same."

"Good luck to you, Vincente."

"And to you Vincent and Grace. *Boa sorte!*"

He left to wait on another couple who had entered the car.

"Did I just hear a Brazilian immigrant say that he liked his chances better in the *favelas* of Rio than here?" Grace whispered.

"I am ...," Vincent finally came up with the word, "speechless." He pulled on the last of Grace's beer.

The train began to move slowly forward, and Vincent continued to look out the dining car window at the people on the platform. Suddenly, a bottle of liquid smashed against the window opposite his face. Involuntarily, Vincent ducked. Then he looked down into the face of a disheveled man whose face was twisted into a snarl. He could faintly hear the man screaming at him through the window glass and could read the man's lips easily.

"Fucking plutocrat! Did you have a nice dinner? Do we look quaint?"

Grace's eyes were wide. Neither of them said anything. Vincent cupped his hands against the spattered window as he tried to look out of the moving train. At the end of the platform, a pile of eight or ten bodies lay stacked together. Out in the switching yard, he spotted an unlit signal light pole and then another as the train passed them in the dark.

"No signal lights. I guess the train creeps all night."

He said nothing about the image of the pile of bodies now etched into his mind. They got up from the dining car and went back to their seats.

***

The train resumed full speed after an all-night crawl to Cleveland. The stop in Cleveland had been quick, but it involved a memorable vignette. Early that morning, after the train pulled to a stop and the doors opened onto the quiet platform, a woman in rough but exotic clothes with a lined face boarded the car. She pushed ahead of her a boy of perhaps ten with a dirty face and wearing frayed clothes. The boy pulled the crew neck of his long t-shirt down over his left shoulder, exposing a stump where his arm had once been. Vincent had seen a Roma mother and boy begging on the streets of Marseilles once, and noted the similarity in dress, look and *modus operandi* of this pair.

The mother held out her hand and asked for "help for my hungry boy" in a voice and with an expression on her face that were studiously pitiful. The boy himself extended his good arm, palm open, but was silent as he stared at each passenger he encountered. The look in his eye was one of shame and anger. That he should have to expose his maimed shoulder to strangers in order to get money for food was humiliation for which he could not excuse those better off. Vincent folded a five dollar bill and slipped it into his hand. The boy's expression changed momentarily to one of relief, then, without a word of thanks, pocketed the money and continued to worm his way up the aisle through the standing passengers.

"Welcome to the third world," Grace said softly.

***

The train got under way again and proceeded to Chicago at normal speed, arriving in Chicago fifteen hours after the scheduled departure of their connection to the Southwest Chief.

At Chicago's Union Station, they gathered their six pieces of luggage and struggled out of their sitting car and onto the platform. Vincent looked around without success for a baggage-handler. By stacking smaller suitcases on larger ones with rollers and slinging the sea bag across his shoulder, he and Grace were able to pull all of them to the main lobby.

Checking the giant electronic schedule board, they were delighted to see that the Southwest Chief had also been delayed and would be boarding in two hours. Both Grace and Vincent were exhausted from their two days of sitting upright with only fitful sleep, and this news was exhilarating.

"We've got two hours to scrounge for something decent to eat, and then we get our sleeper car seats."

"Hold on, major dear. Before you get too Pollyanna-esque, it's not like we can check these bags safely and go off and do lunch. And, I'm not going to be able to relax until we know that our ticketed seats are really going to be there."

"That's ex-major dear, dear. And, you have a point."

Vincent looked around at the crowd of people in the main waiting room.

"I'm not comfortable with leaving you with all the bags alone, and I'm not comfortable with you going off to explore on your own while I stay with the bags. It is a conundrum, yes?"

"Why don't I take a seat over here with the luggage in plain sight," she indicated an empty bench. "You, in turn, can walk over there to the ticket booth and see if they will confirm our connection. I would feel a lot better if they do."

"Ah ha. Slicing up the elephant, are you? I like your problem-solving style. No flies on you, missus."

They piled the luggage close to the open bench and Grace sat down wearily.

"Let me just step over to the ticket window and see if they will confirm our tickets, shall I?"

Grace gave him a look.

"*Eeetaii*," he said, making the Japanese sound for "ouch."

Vincent hadn't been in the short line to the ticketing window long when he heard Grace calling his name. He turned to see a large man and a woman standing over Grace and beside the luggage. Both the man and the woman turned and watched him approach. Vincent noted the breadth of the man's shoulders as well as his greater height and girth. Using his best drill instructor voice, he ignored the woman and addressed the man.

"Can I help you?"

"Oh, is this lady with you? That's good," the man said, with a look that was not reassuring. "The way things are these days, we thought she might need some assistance. So, where are you folks trying to get to?"

The woman had a vacant look on her face, and they both reeked of BO.

Ignoring the question, Vincent said, "We're good, thanks. Everything's under control. How about you? Are you traveling, or just hanging out?"

There was no mistaking the suspicion in his demeanor.

"This man was asking me if I needed a ride somewhere," Grace offered.

"Lech, let's go. I don't feel that well." The woman looked at the big man with fear in her eyes. "Please?"

"In a minute," the man said. "Say, bud, I'm just trying to be helpful. Are you sayin' I'm a crook or some'pin?"

Vincent saw that the man's eyes were bloodshot and he was blinking rapidly.

"Cause we could settle this if you want."

Vincent stood perfectly still and stared into the man's eyes.

"My wife doesn't need any help. We're good. You can leave now."

The woman had turned and was pulling on the man's jacket to come with her. He allowed himself to be pulled away, but continued to look back at Vincent with his hand in his pocket.

They could hear the woman hissing at him.

"Only the easy marks, you said. Are you crazy?"

"Not a cop in sight," Grace said, watching the couple walking out of the vast waiting room through the main entrance.

"And we haven't even arrived in the Wild West yet."

Vincent looked around and saw no one that looked concerning.

"Let's try this again," he said and walked back to the ticket windows.

***

With their tickets confirmed, they waited on the near end of the platform for track six as the Southwest Chief slowly backed into the shed. Their plan to score some tasty food at one of the many food purveyors in and around Union Station had been largely frustrated by the need to stay with their luggage. That, together with the fact that many places were closed due to "supply interruptions."

They had found a piroshki stand operated by a local Russian man and his wife who proudly advertised that they made their own. They were doing a land office business, and Vincent and Grace had each relished one of the deep fried buns. Now they just wanted to board as soon as possible and climb into their bunks.

They located their car and cabin and piled their luggage into the cabin space. Two upholstered adjoining seats faced forward with a fold-out table attached under the window in front of them. The seats could be converted into a small double bed. A space above the seats contained a second berth that could be lowered. A small half bath was behind a door on the opposite side next to the luggage space.

After luxuriating in their cabin for a half hour, Grace noticed that no one else seemed to be coming down the platform to get on the train. She walked through the rest of the car and found it empty.

"This doesn't seem right, she said. Are you sure ...?"

Vincent didn't let her finish.

"Yes, I'm sure. This is the right track and the right train and the right car."

Just then a porter walked in from the next car. As soon as he saw them he stopped.

"You folks going to LA?"

"Albuquerque. This is the Southwest Chief, right?"

"Well, it was. You must have boarded early or you would have seen the notice on the schedule board that it has been delayed and the departure track changed. The Chief is going out of track nine later. This train is being diverted to New Orleans. The City of New Orleans train derailed this morning, and we've got to get a lot of refinery workers to Metairie in a hurry. You'll have to pack up and go back to the waiting room until your train is called."

This news was like being kicked in the stomach. Grace looked to be on the verge of tears. She would have to trade her sleeper bedroom for unidentified accommodations after an unknown amount of exertion for an indeterminate amount of time. She didn't receive a gung ho prompt from Vincent, though. His instinct told him not to try it. This was gut-check time.

They made the slog back to the waiting room and reprised their last drill. She sat on a bench within sight of the ticket window, and Vincent got in line to find out what was happening. The electronic schedule board listed the Southwest Chief to Los Angeles, but its boarding track was blank. Ominously, the boarding time read "to be announced."

Grace could see Vincent speaking with animation and at length with the ticket agent. Finally, he picked up his tickets and headed back toward her scowling.

He sat down and looked at his shoes. She could see he was trying to figure out what to say—or rather how to say it.

"Out with it, dude. Just give it to me straight. Are we back to the Joad family mode, only without a car?"

He straightened up and shook his head.

"It's not that bad. They have moved the departure time of the Southwest Chief train to the next regularly scheduled departure time. That is twenty four hours later than the train departure we were booked on yesterday. It's six hours from now. The people who are booked on that train today from Chicago get first priority over us. All the sleeper car accommodations and all the regular seats are sold out. However, we can get out tomorrow at this departure time on the same train in a sleeper car. I've got new tickets for that."

"Well, I have an idea. You were urging me to think outside the box, to think of adversity as an opportunity? Well, I've done just that."

Vincent knew he was being messed-with and started grinning through his fatigue. "Yo, lay it on me."

"Let's go out to platform nine and three quarters. Instead of going to Albuquerque, we'll go through the wall and catch the train to Hogwarts. Find a place to bunk on Diagon Alley."

Vincent looked confused. "I've heard of Hogwarts but can't quite place it."

"Not a reading man, eh? Harry Potter ring a bell?"

"Ah, no. Never read him. What did he write?"

"Philistine! Muggles! You've never ...?" She saw he was laughing at her.

"Bunking on Diagon Alley gives me an idea, though," he said. "Let's just get a room in a nearby hotel, sleep until we wake up—only horizontally rather than diagonally— pun intended, heh, heh—and resume our sojourn tomorrow. What do you say, pard?"

"Brilliant, absolutely brilliant," was her Hermione-esque response.

"Okay. You stay here where I can see you, and I'll go over and check out those phone books and find us a room. Then we'll schlep and sleep."

"Brilliant. Altogether."

"Wait right here."

CHAPTER

28

The Southwest Chief departed from Chicago's Union Station only three hours late, and Grace and Vincent were thoroughly rested from their stay at the Holiday Inn three blocks from the station. Moreover, they had their sleeper cabin all the way to Albuquerque. Things were looking up.

The train left Chicago in the system-down, slow-roll mode, but somewhere south of Mendota, Illinois, the computers rebooted, and the train resumed full speed to Kansas City, Missouri. Vincent awoke in the lower berth when it arrived at Kansas City's Union Station around midnight. It was quiet at the station and the train made the brief stop without incident.

Just before dawn, they were awakened by screeching wheels as the train braked suddenly, followed by a jarring shock to the car as the train slowly came to an emergency stop. Vincent raised the window curtain in their unlit cabin and looked out. He saw the jerky movement of a line of flashlights converging on the train out of the dark. The glow of what appeared to be a fire flickered from the front of the train.

"Stay calm," he told Grace. "I think this might be a stick up."

Vincent jumped up from the lower berth and pulled his sea bag to the front of the luggage pile. He quickly clawed the contents out until he found the vinyl portfolio containing their money. He pulled out all of the cash except $500 from the portfolio and restuffed the contents back into the sea bag leaving the portfolio on top. He then handed the cash to Grace to hide inside the recess from which her upper berth had been pulled when the room was made up. He also pulled the pistol out of his duffle and shoved a loaded clip into the handle recess. A quick back and forth movement of the slide put a round into the chamber. He'd bought the .45 caliber gun because its low velocity round provided maximum impact at close range.

They didn't have long to wait. They heard the sliding entry door to the sleeper car and loud male voices.

"EVERYBODY UP! Open your doors and turn your lights on. This is a robbery. We want your valuables. If we get them, no one will be harmed!"

Grace gathered the covers around her and sat in the middle of the upper berth. Vincent saw his Rolex watch on the table and quickly put it in the toe of his shoe. He secreted the pistol behind his scrotum before he opened the door to their cabin at the end of the car. Standing in his t-shirt and underwear, he confronted two men.

"Move out in the passageway," ordered a tall thin man with matted hair and a several weeks growth of beard. He smelled strongly of sweat and urine and carried a shotgun. The other man, older and also disheveled, held a semi-automatic pistol on Vincent in the corridor.

Vincent did as he was told, taking small steps so as not to dislodge the .45. He could see three other men carrying pistols further down the corridor.

A firefight would get a lot of people hurt.

The thin man pointed to Grace.

"You stay where you are. Where's your purse?"

Grace pointed to it on the end table. Vincent's wallet was next to it. The man quickly rifled through both removing some two hundred dollars in cash, but leaving credit and debit cards—worthless to thieves since corneal ID technology had been introduced.

The thin man pointed his gun at Grace's head and turned to Vincent in the hall. "Now where is the rest of it? And don't bullshit me, man. I know you've got some more stashed."

"Sir, it's all we have. We can't get money out of the banks ...."

"Shut the fuck up. You, the fat cat in the sleeper cabin, are telling me that times are tough? My heart bleeds for you, dude. Where is the stash!" He made a move closer to Grace's head with his gun.

Vincent pointed to his sea bag. "It's on top. In the plastic folder."

"Get it out. Fast."

Acutely aware of the tenuous position of the .45, Vincent moved back into the cabin and uncinched the top of the sea bag. He retrieved the folder and handed it over. The robber pulled out the $500 and pocketed it. He saw the stenciling on the sea bag.

"Marine Corps, eh? Well, semper fuckin' fi, major. I was a jarhead myself once. Three tours in Iraq and Afghanistan. Never had much use for officers. Saw too much of the inside of a brig thanks to officers. Never saw one that didn't have a God complex. Be a pleasure to take officer money."

He opened the two floral patterned suitcases and combed roughly through Grace's things while the second man in the corridor kept his gun pointed at Vincent. The robber opened and cast aside a zippered pouch containing cosmetics, then stuck his head into the lavatory space. Seeing nothing more of interest, he stepped out the door, brushing by Vincent.

"I see jarheads still wear the same skivvies," he grinned.

The other man told Vincent to shut the door and stay there. As Vincent closed the cabin door, they heard a woman crying hysterically down the passageway and men yelling at her to shut up. Vincent liberated the .45 from his crotch, and put on his pants and shoes. He put the .45 in the waistband of his pants behind him and covered it with the tail of his t-shirt.

After three or four minutes of shouting commands and throwing bags against walls, all went quiet in the rail car. Vincent turned off the lights in their cabin and looked out the window. Just then the robbers outside started yelling.

"Smokey's coming, man! We gotta get the cars out before they're blocked!" shouted one.

"It's too late! We need hostages!" yelled another.

Vincent could make out red and blue flashing lights speeding in the distance on a course that seemed to parallel that of the tracks. He told Grace to get in the bathroom, lock the door, and sit on the floor. She did so quickly. He heard heavy footsteps in the corridor again, and the door to the cabin flew open. The thin man with the shotgun stood there leveling the barrel at Vincent's torso.

"Where's the missus?"

He looked at the closed bathroom door, and tried the handle, but it was locked. "Get out here, lady, or I'm going to blow the major's head right off!"

"Don't do it, Grace," Vincent said loudly.

The thin man had sweated through his dirty green t-shirt and the headband of his gimme cap advertising Toby's Feed and Grain. Panicking at the proximity of the highway patrol, he screamed at Vincent to get out in the corridor.

"You'll do as a hostage! Get movin'!"

As Vincent moved through the cabin door sideways, his body masked his right hand movement. Pulling the .45 out of his waistband in a continuous arc that left the pistol pointed directly at the robber's forehead, Vincent faced his adversary. The startled, sweating man instinctively crouched with the shotgun pointed at Vincent's chest in a standoff he hadn't expected.

Behind Vincent in the corridor was a row of windows to the outside. A shotgun blast in that direction would hurt no one.

Vincent stared at the robber.

"You've got a couple of precious minutes to try to get away, friend. You can stay here dead with me or leave alone. The hostage thing isn't going to happen."

"I used to shoot you officer fucks in the back over in Helmand!" the robber screamed, his lips curled in sneer. "They're all, like, 'follow me, men,' and they'd be all full of themselves, the first to charge the enemy. We'd shoot 'em in the back, the arrogant motherfuckers. You want to end it here?"

Vincent fired into the man's forehead and simultaneously spun away from the cabin door. The .45 caliber round snapped the man's head and upper body back violently, yanking his rigid finger on the shotgun's trigger. The shotgun blasted a 12 inch round hole in the corridor window opposite the cabin, raking the small of Vincent's back with peripheral buckshot a split second after he twisted to the side. Then all was quiet.

"It's okay, Grace," Vincent called. "I think it's over, but stay in there to make sure. He pulled up his shirt and looked at his back in the mirror. A cluster of bloody striations ran sideways across his lower back from which blood oozed in thin sheets.

I'll live.

In the distance, he could hear bull horns telling the robbers to drop their weapons and walk forward with their hands on their heads. A staccato burst of gunfire erupted and then stopped.

Vincent picked up the dead man's shotgun and pulled a handful of shells from the man's pocket. He reloaded as he ran to the end of the sleeper car and down the stairs to the track bed. A swath of shoulder high weeds grew on the right-of-way between the track bed and a field of sunflowers. First light showed in the east allowing him to see the length of the train. He took a position crouched in the weeds facing the train. If any of the robbers came back to the train for hostages to leverage a getaway, he would see them.

He heard the men running before he saw them. Two of them came out of the stand of sunflowers and weeds not twenty yards in front of him. As they started to run for the stairs at the other end of the sleeper car, Vincent stood up and fired the shotgun over their heads.

"FREEZE!" he ordered. They did.

"ON THE GROUND!" They dropped onto their stomachs.

"ARMS AND LEGS OUT!" They assumed the position.

A spotlight behind them suddenly washed first over the men on the ground and then Vincent.

A voice ordered, "POLICE OFFICERS. YOU, STANDING UP. DROP YOUR WEAPON."

Vincent raised his left hand in the air and slowly placed the shotgun on the ground with his right hand. Then he raised his right hand in the air, and smiled into the flood light.

"Welcome officers. For the record, I'm a passenger on the train, and those two are bad guys."

The two men on the ground were swarmed by men in SWAT gear. Two other police officers faced Vincent.

"Are there any other bad guys on the train?" one asked.

"There's one down in this car. Dead. The shotgun was his. I haven't seen any others," Vincent said.

"Did you kill him?"

The officer jerked his head toward the sleeper car and the other SWAT officer ran over and boarded the car.

"I did."

"It looks like you are hurt."

"Some of the dead guy's buckshot grazed my back. It's not bad. By the way, I've got a .45 in my waistband. That's the weapon I used to kill the guy inside."

The officer on the train returned and said, "One dead." He patted Vincent down and took the .45.

Vincent lowered his hands. "The shooting didn't start until you guys showed up, and by then, the robbers were trying to get away. There was some hollering among them about taking hostages, and the dead guy and those two came back to take some, but ... that didn't go well."

It was lighter in the east now, and the officer holding the flood light on Vincent switched it off.

"When the medic gets here, he'll take a look at your wounds."

Grace peered out from the window of their cabin at them and then disappeared. In a few seconds, in her jeans and t-shirt, she came running down the steps and onto the gravel shoulder beside the tracks where they stood. She stared at the blood on Vincent's t-shirt.

He beat her to it.

"It's not bad, Gracie. Really, it's minor."

She was shaking as she spoke to the SWAT officers.

"This is my husband. He is a major in the Marines, and he was a hero here tonight."

The one asking the questions grinned and looked at Vincent, raising his eyebrows.

"Well," he said. "In that case he should get a medal. Let me see your back, sir."

The SWAT officer could see that the blood was oozing rather than running or pulsing.

"Why don't you folks go back to your seats, and we'll be coming through to check on you and ask some questions. Well done, sir."

CHAPTER

29

As they returned to the passageway outside their cabin, Grace stepped over the body of the robber, making a face. Vincent, however, stopped and searched his pockets. In one, he found their $700 and pocketed the money.

"Being a righteous man and to paraphrase the Bible, I'm rendering unto Vincent and Grace that which is theirs."

A minute later, deputies arrived and, after searching him, took several photographs of the dead man before placing him in a body bag and removing the body from the train.

Vincent retrieved the stack of bills Grace had stashed inside the fold-out berth cabinet and placed it and all but two hundred dollars from their wallets that had been taken by the robber back into the folder. The folder was returned to his sea bag, and he handed the two hundred to Grace. Finally, he folded the upper berth into the cabinet.

Grace sat down on the lower berth, still shaken. Vincent walked the length of the sleeper car. Doors to the cabins and curtains to the sleeper berths opened cautiously and heads peered out. Vincent explained that a sheriff's SWAT unit had surprised the robbers and had them in custody. The officers would be coming through to check on everyone shortly, he said.

The porter entered the far end of the car and was immediately peppered with excited and angry questions. He held up his hands and asked everyone to be quiet. A woman in the berth where Vincent was standing started screaming about the lack of security and railroad mismanagement and how they would pay for this outrage. Vincent recognized her voice as the one crying hysterically during the robbery. The heavy lines of mascara running down her face seemed to confirm it. Vincent calmed her by patting her on the shoulder and placing his finger over his lips.

"We need to hear this," he said.

Grace came up beside her and put her arm around the woman.

The porter was a large, powerfully built black man, with the hint of an accent Vincent guessed to be African. His graying hair revealed that he was older than his bearing indicated. He had what was known in military circles as "command presence." He immediately asked whether anyone needed emergency attention. There being no response, he spread his arms and beamed.

"Congratulations," he said cheerfully. "You are the first victims of an Amtrak train robbery. So far, only one passenger has been reported with injuries."

He looked at the blood on Vincent's t-shirt.

"And that would be you, sir? Are you the Marine officer the SWAT Team talked to?"

Vincent nodded.

"An EMS vehicle is on its way from Dodge for you. Be here in a couple of minutes. Are you okay till then?"

Vincent nodded again, then stopped, his eyes going wide.

"Did you say Dodge?"

"Yes, sir, we are about eight miles east of Dodge City, Kansas."

A smile spread across Vincent's face, and then he began to laugh along with the others.

"A train robbery in Dodge City, Kansas? You couldn't make this stuff up."

"I've got this story written already," Grace said, grinning.

The porter continued. "These officers are all Sheriff's deputies for Ford County. The Sheriff's office had a tip that some robbers—basically desperate, hungry people—that have been active in Western Kansas were planning something around here, so they've been on the ready. When our station master in Dodge got the SOS from our engineer, he called it in. I gather that some of you also called 911. Anyway, the SWAT guys high-tailed it out here and surprised the robbers.

"Taking a page from Willie Sutton, I guess, they robbed us because that's where some money was. They put up a big pile of railroad ties on the tracks and set it on fire when the train came along. When the engine hit it, we had to stop rather than take a chance on derailing. That's when the robbers moved in.

"The ties are being removed from the tracks, and the police have all the robbers in custody except those in one vehicle that escaped down a section road before the police arrived. Deputies are in hot pursuit and they'll probably get the perps.

"The Sheriff has asked us to pull into the station in Dodge City where EMS people can check you out while the Sheriff can put these sinners in jail. The train station is right on Wyatt Earp Boulevard, a block from Gunsmoke Street and a couple of blocks from Boot Hill—well, the museum anyway." He chuckled low in his throat. "This will all make a heck of a story for the folks back home."

The woman who had been hysterical was quiet but shaking uncontrollably. Grace asked her name and she said "Gillian."

Grace took the woman's hand in both of hers.

"I'm Grace, Gillian, and this is my husband, Vincent. You're safe now. Anyway, who wouldn't be upset with all those guns pointed at you? Maybe your excitement distracted them and helped more than you think."

"Well, he wasn't scared, thank goodness," Gillian said, indicating Vincent who looked embarrassed.

"We're all glad the excitement is over and no one on the train got hurt," Vincent said diplomatically. "Porter, how soon is the bar going to be open? We need to buy Gillian a tall one."

The porter flashed a broad grin.

"I am personally going to the bar and see to it that the drinks are flowing. And, while we're making the trip into town, I suggest that you all make a detailed inventory of anything you lost to give to the police. That will help them identify the stolen property they've recovered and return it to you."

Vincent and Grace started to walk back to their cabin, but the porter called to him.

"Sir, I'll need for you to come with me to the EMS vehicle. They'll take you to the ER from here and treat your wound."

"I'm going too," Grace declared.

Vincent protested. "You should stay with our stuff, hon. Besides, if the train leaves before I get back ...."

Grace's look told him the matter was decided.

The porter placed his hand on Vincent's shoulder.

"Major, you have my word that your cabin will be locked and safeguarded, and that this train will not leave Dodge City without you and your wife on it."

***

Vincent lay on his stomach facing Grace in the EMS vehicle gurney en route to Dodge City. The medic examined his back and pronounced all the buckshot wounds as superficial except for one that might have to be stitched up. Grace sat close by him and held his hand.

"Vincent, that was very quick thinking to hide most of the money, and leave some money in your bag to fool them. How did you know it was a train robbery, of all things?"

"I didn't know. Something about the way the lights were moving in a line toward us make me think ambush. Condition reflex, I guess. I saw some al Shabaab moving like that once in Somalia."

"Well, I'm very impressed, big fella. Bravo Zulu. Isn't that code for 'well done'?"

"It is. Hey, you remembered that from Lejeune. And Bravo Zulu right back at'cha. You kept it together real steely-like when that guy was pointing a gun at your head. You avoided any drama that might have gotten the robbers all a-twitter. Not to disparage Gillian's, ah, contributions."

"I sincerely hope our future life is not going to be full of adventures like this, although I'm beginning to realize that we're not in Kansas anymore."

They looked at each other.

"Oh, wait, yes we are."

He and Grace fell into a fit of the giggles. The medic groaned and shook his head at them.

Their giggling subsided, and a shadow passed over Vincent's face. "What?"

"Oh, I was thinking about that guy I shot. He was probably at the end of his rope. I could have let him take me hostage. He could have shot me first, but he didn't."

"Coulda, woulda, shoulda," said Grace. "It was a split second call. Besides, did you hear what he said—about shooting officers in the back? Does that ever happen?"

"It happens. Not often, but it does. Combat deaths to officers by so-called 'friendly fire' are troublesome for the command, so they have an incentive not to investigate those incidents too much. It's bad for morale, and the facts are hard to identify with all the battlefield chaos. Anyway, I'll always wonder how much those comments of his affected my decision to shoot him."

"Nobody made him pick up a shotgun, rob people at gunpoint, try to take hostages at gun point, and threaten to kill you. Even poor, desperate people can be cold blooded killers, you know.

"And then you had the presence of mind to go outside to stand guard and prevent those other two from taking hostages. How did you know to do that? You know what I think? I think Wyatt Earp really was there taking care of things. I think he was you."

The medic chimed in. "Me too. You were lucky, though. That shotgun blast could have spoiled your whole afternoon. I've seen some of those in the ER. Nasty."

"I had the advantage of knowing what would happen and when, so I spun out from in front of the barrel at the instant I pulled the trigger. If I weren't so slow, fat and uncoordinated, I could have been in the clear," he said.

He and Grace lapsed into another fit of the giggles as the ambulance pulled into the ER unloading zone at the Western Plains Medical Complex. The medic grinned and shook his head again.

In the ER, the traumatic medicine doctor painted all the stripes made by the buckshot with disinfectant and decided to put butterfly bandages on the part of the deepest wound that cut across what the doctor called the *latissimus dorsi* muscle—the big broad one on either side of the spine. He didn't think the wound was likely to tear or open up, and the butterfly bandages would fall away in a week or so after the scabs had formed solidly. That would save Vincent the trouble of trying to find someone to remove stitches while he was traveling. Vincent liked the call. The cuts would be sore for five days or so, though, and he was told to avoid stretching his back muscles.

Vincent asked about handling luggage. The doctor looked doubtful. If it hurts, don't do it, he said. Vincent had trouble seeing how he was going to sit on a train seat for hours at a time with a raw back, let along lump the luggage around.

Once discharged and standing outside, they looked around for some sign of public transit. Just then, a gray haired man pulled up to let off his wife, a nurse starting her shift. Grace took the initiative.

"Sir, are you going anywhere near the Amtrak station? We don't know how to get from here to there and we have to catch the train."

The man told them to hop in; he would take them there. He told them they'd missed some excitement on Amtrak. He'd just heard on the radio that the Southwest Chief had been robbed east of town. Grace volunteered that they'd been on the train at the time, and that her husband had been shot. He'd had just been treated for his wound at the hospital.

"It was a minor wound," Vincent said.

Grace explained that Vincent was a hero who had preventing hostages from being taken. The man congratulated Vincent for his quick thinking and bravery. When he dropped them off at the train station, he asked Grace to take a picture of him with Vincent.

"Wait till I tell my golf buddies about this," he said. "Nothing exciting ever happens in Dodge City."

***

When Vincent and Grace rejoined the train, the Sheriff's deputies were finishing up their interviews with the passengers and train crew. The two of them were the last to tell their stories. To minimize the chance of being asked to return for a coroner's inquest into the cause of death of the robber, they were each videotaped giving their statements and took an oath administered by a deputy that he said invoked the laws of perjury. Then the train pulled out and resumed its westward roll at full speed.

With strong wireless cell phone coverage from the tower in Dodge City, Grace called her mother to see how her parents were faring and to update them. Vincent lay face down on the pulled out berth trying to read a how-to book on farming he picked up in the Amtrak station in Dodge City.

'Hello mom," she said when the familiar voice answered. "Please tell me you and dad are okay."

There followed a long and animated conversation about the conditions under which her parents were living. When Grace told her mother that she and Vincent were on a train to Albuquerque and the about the robbery, her mother was incredulous. "Gobsmacked" was the word she used, Grace said later when recounting the conversation to Vincent.

When her father came on the line, Grace's tone of voice was less inflected and more hesitant. She seemed to be listening a lot. At one point, Grace's voice seemed to catch.

"Thank you, Dad. It means a lot to hear you say that. Yes. It would be wonderful to all be in the same neighborhood and able to see each other more often."

They exchanged goodbyes and promises to stay in touch. Grace put her phone away, extended her arms high in a long stretch and exhaled deeply. It had clearly been a cathartic call for her. Vincent waited.

She explained that her father had followed her articles on *Insider On Line* and thought they were outstanding. He said she had distinguished herself as a journalist in the series, and he was very proud of her. She stopped her narration at that point and wiped her eyes with the back of her wrists.

"Are they coping with the shortages and banking problems and the like?"

"Pretty well, I gather. Their neighborhood has banded together and they keep in touch and help each other out with food and money and rides when people don't have gas. Dad is staying busy because the railroad is hauling a lot of coal and oil from Western Colorado to the West Coast. They're pretty well off so they can pay the high prices for the things they need so far. They said everybody was counting on these conditions being temporary, though. Mom said they couldn't keep it up forever."

"Oh, and Dad was over the moon about our being back together. He was very unsupportive when we got divorced. He thought I'd just screwed up again."

"He got that part right. Horsewhipping would have been too good for you."

"Shut up. He said he understands now."

Vincent reflected on what she said.

"So, would I be wrong if I were to think that the problems we had in LeJeune were not a hundred percent about the protocol for Marine officers' wives? Maybe your situation there triggered some deeply felt anger about being treated summarily again? Disrespected again? Unloved again?"

"It's a fair question. I can't honestly say how much my urge to get back to Washington on my own was honest ambition and how much was a knee-jerk reaction to being told who I was supposed to be and how to act. I don't think it's possible to separate the two."

"That's good to know. If some semblance of normal life returns, we—that is, I, will have to keep that in mind. It's in your DNA."

"No, 'we' is the right word. We'll both have to pay attention to the little neuroses each of us have."

"Hey now, if you are suggesting that *I* have any neuroses that have to be monitored, then forget it. I'm a hero, remember. Joe Cool doesn't have neuroses. Get out of town," he said, snorting.

"Have you forgotten that I have to apply the salve and change the gauze on your back tonight? Would you like me to be careful with my fingernails when I do it?"

"Oh, yeah. Maybe we can, you know, be considerate, mutually, going forward. What I meant was, I'm all for that."

CHAPTER

30

The Southwest Chief crossed Western Kansas, the southeastern tip of Colorado's high plains, over Raton Pass and into the beautiful New Mexico headwaters of the Arkansas, Purgatoire, and Pecos Rivers, through Apache Canyon, and lastly glided over the Turquoise Trail and past the Scandia Mountains into Albuquerque. En route, Vincent and Grace considered their next moves, but too many elements of their new lives were unknown. Their plans were contingent on local circumstances, so they would just have to take things as they came. Joe Martinez' name came up a lot. Vincent counted on Joe to help them hit the ground running.

They spent two days in Albuquerque shopping for the car and necessaries, as best they could guess what those would be. Vincent's painful back regularly reminded him of his limitations. On the second car lot they visited, they found a canary yellow, eight year old Jeep Cherokee hybrid. It was relatively inexpensive, had moderate mileage, and was suitable for ranch terrain. They paid cash and closed the deal quickly. The rest of the time they spent in big box stores buying toilet paper, soap and other household items Grace thought vital, plus a lot of non-perishable canned and packaged foods and dried fruit. There seemed to be more inventory in the Albuquerque stores than in Washington. In a nod toward civilized living, they also bought some beer and wine.

***

The Cherokee containing Vincent and Grace, six suitcases and eight grocery bags turned off Highway 4 onto gravel Indian Service Road No. 201 and followed it around the point of a mesa and up into a hanging valley on the flank of Cerro Grande. The high hill stood as a remnant of the old Valles Caldera four miles west of the town of Los Alamos as the hawk flies. An undesignated right fork in the road led to what was simply known by its few, distant neighbors as "the Long Ranch", a half section parcel covered with scrub mesquite, pinion and juniper. The Long homestead stood within the National Forest boundary but it pre-dated that designation; hence, was grandfathered for private ranch use.

Grace watched the spare, scrub vegetation along the driveway transition into lush mesquite, aspen and pepper trees around a small lake that Vincent's father had created by bulldozing a dam across a narrow channel in the wash below the wide meadow. The lake filled from a stream carrying winter and spring run-off from high ground to the west. Later in the season, the stream slowed to a trickle and then disappeared into the unseen water table under the talus slope on which the ranch lay. A hundred yards above the lake stood a single story main house and a separate guest cottage, both adobe reinforced with *viga* timbers and ornamented by French windows and shutters. The once blue-green shutters were now faded into pale lavender with cedar weathered to a silver color exposed where the paint had worn off. The guest house sheltered behind an outcropping of sandstone rocks as big as the house. An unbroken view to the horizon where the sun rose featured a dark, jagged gash in the earth's surface that ran north-south across the landscape eleven miles away. It was the shadow cast by the canyon walls of the Rio Grande River in the mid-morning sun.

"I'd forgotten how spectacular this place is," Grace said. "Arid and remote, but spectacular."

"Dad used to keep the lake stocked with trout. I hope there are still some in there."

They pulled up to the side of the house and parked alongside a dusty green Ford pickup.

In the truck, Joe sat waiting for them. They exchanged waves as Joe climbed out of his truck. Joe was in uniform—faded denim jeans and jean jacket over an off-white cowboy shirt with pearl buttons. He wore a straw cowboy hat with a "Calgary roll" in which the front and back brims were pulled down severely to form almost a half-circle of hat. Joe hadn't aged much in the seven years since Vincent's parents' funeral.

Vincent wore a big grin as he shook hands with the older man.

"Great to see you, Joe. You're looking well."

"You look sharp yourself, General, sir," Joe said and saluted, but managed to convey a wry, elder-brother nuance.

"You're driving the wrong Indian, though."

His joke meant that the Cherokee were plains Indians. Joe's people were Pueblo Indians whose ancestors were remnants of the Anasazi culture than dispersed at the beginning of the 14th century due to prolonged drought.

"Well, they were all out of the Kokopelli SUVs in Albuquerque, so this is the best I could do."

Vincent referred to the powerful shaman, magician and trickster of Pueblo legend. Kokopelli was customarily depicted as a hunchback playing a flute by which, according to the old ones, he played the whole world into being.

Vincent put his arm around Grace's shoulder.

"You remember Grace? We were just married when we came here last."

He didn't complicate the introduction with an explanation of the divorce and the fact that they were not technically married.

Joe removed his hat exposing dark, sun-weathered skin up to his forehead and a much lighter shade above that—a two-tone trademark of farmers and ranchers. His hair was black with three blazes of gray running backward from both temples and the cowlick at the crest of his forehead.

Grace shook hands and smiled. "*Ya-ta-hey*, Joe."

"Good memory. That's Navajo," Joe beamed. "Hello yourself, Grace. I sure do remember you. I was glad to know that someone was going to break Vince in and civilize him a bit. Welcome home, ah ..., back."

"The place looks great, Joe," Vincent said. "It looks lived-in. I hope it hasn't been too much of a hassle for you," Vincent said.

"Naw, the house was well built, so it holds up. Had to run some squatters off a couple of years ago, but no real problems. Guess I let the paint on the shutters go, but I sort of prefer them faded-like. Not that bright penny look."

He thought better of having expressed such an opinion in front of the new mistress of the house.

"'Course, Grace gets a bigger vote than I do."

Grace put him at ease.

"I agree with you, Joe. In fact, people pay decorators a lot of money to recreate this authentic, weathered look, and they never get it quite right. You have the soul of an artist."

Joe was not sophisticated enough to be immune to feminine wiles, and so he blushed through his deep tan and looked at the ground.

"Indian life is full of what you might call art, I guess."

Then he looked up at Vincent.

"Things have been hard at the pueblo, so I been living in the guest house. I can vacate, though if ...."

Vincent and Grace interrupted in unison.

"No, no ...,"

Vincent said. "You stay right where you are. We have a lot of figuring out to do, and we need your help. We hope you'll stay and help out so us tenderfeet don't embarrass ourselves."

Smiling, Joe nodded, "Well, sure. That'd be fine with me."

After Grace studied the kitchen layout, they unloaded the Cherokee's contents into the house.

Vincent queried Joe thoroughly about local sources of supply. There was a supermarket in Los Alamos that had a cyclical supply of fresh meat and produce, but their stocks sold out quickly. A farmer's market was held on Saturday in Los Alamos and on Tuesday night in White Rock further down Highway 4. The produce at the farmer's markets also sold out quickly. Prices for everything were high—a lot higher than they'd been before the trouble.

As Joe talked about how he was getting by, it became clear that he had little income. Work for farm hands and in construction had all but dried up. He had no food stored in the house and his diet, like that in Taos Pueblo, was pretty much limited to corn meal and squash that he got at the trading post in Taos when he had money from the Pueblo casino distributions. He also trapped rabbits and ground squirrels on the property.

Grace asked whether the children in the Pueblo got sick from their diet. She mentioned pellagra, a disease caused by lack of green vegetables in the diet.

Joe shrugged.

"Indian kids get sick a lot. But I don't know about that sickness."

The refrigerator worked when the power was on, but the power could be off for a day or more, making it a guessing game in handling perishables. Joe said he usually made smoked jerky from any meat he got trapping. That way, the meat would still be okay if the refrigerator went off for a day or two at a time.

The ranch needed propane for heat, but the tank had been empty for years. Vincent said he'd try to find a service that would come check the tank and make periodic deliveries to fill it. Joe wasn't sure if there was still a service in Santa Fe, but if there was, he thought it would be expensive.

Joe showed them the fire pit he'd made beside the rocks by the guest cottage. It was covered with a lean-to made of old corrugated sheet metal he liberated from an abandoned Navaho hogan. It kept the rain and snow off the fire in inclement weather. The grate he put on top of the fire pit came off of the opening of a drainage culvert that didn't appear necessary to keep debris from clogging the culvert. For firewood Joe just picked up pieces of dead trees on the property, in the National Forest, and pretty much anyplace he happened along and saw wood lying around. He said you could see a lot of fresh stumps higher up in the National Forest where people were poaching firewood. Joe, however, didn't think that was right, and he picked up only dead wood. But, he allowed, there might come a time.

The ranch had a deep well and the water was good. The periodic power outages wouldn't be a problem for their water supply since the pump could top off the three thousand gallon water tank when the power was on, and they would conserve for showers, toilets, and cooking when it was off. There was no external landscaping of any kind that required water, but Joe said they should think about using runoff for a garden in the spring to save money and augment the supply of produce at the store.

When the sun went behind the hill, the temperature dropped noticeably. The kitchen stove was inoperative without propane, so they cooked a meal of spam, canned green beans, and warmed-up packaged tortillas on the outside grill using some of Joe's firewood. While the meal was cooking, Joe and Vincent each drank a luke-warm beer, and Grace nursed some red wine from a coffee cup. They ate inside at the dining room table. Joe said it was the best meal he'd had in six months.

Grace located the linen closet and found all of Vincent's mother's linens and a big down comforter packed in plastic bags. She marveled at the fact that the fabrics all seemed to be in perfect condition. She made up the bed in the master bedroom with sheets, pillows with pillowcases, and the comforter. It looked luxurious to Grace.

My joys are getting simpler.

Joe said he had wool blankets in the guest house and didn't need anything else.

After dinner, they decided to save the remaining firewood and sat in the living room chairs talking—Joe in his fleece-lined duster and Vincent and Grace in sweaters and wrapped in blankets. They started a list of the things they needed to acquire starting with propane and several cords of firewood.

"It all comes back to energy," Vincent said.

***

They drove into Los Alamos and over to White Rock to reconnoiter the stores that were operating. Store proprietors talked about their supply chain problems and how the shortages had become chronic and seemed to be getting worse. Imported goods were almost non-existent now that the international transportation infrastructure had contracted so dramatically.

They were surprised to learn that the Los Alamos National Laboratory's historic mission included the development of alternative energy sources and identification of national security issues, in addition to their core mission of designing and safeguarding the nation's nuclear weapons. The ongoing energy and cyber-security problems now devastating the country had greatly stimulated the scientists at Los Alamos to study and remediate the energy shortage. As much as they could, anyway. They had no substitute for the rapidly fading, hydrocarbon-driven Industrial Revolution. Federal government support, however uncertain, promised to keep the laboratory operating.

The trickle down effects from the support of the National Laboratory and the salaries paid to its scientists perpetuated the economies of Los
Alamos and White Rock. It was said that it wasn't the absence of need or
demand that caused markets to collapse; it is the absence of the ability to
pay. For that reason, the residents of Los Alamos fared better than most
Americans. Grace and Vincent understood their chances of survival were
better than most. Their daily activities, however, would still be subsistence-driven.

A propane truck delivery service out of Santa Fe was indeed still supplying the National Laboratory facilities and population. Propane was a
by-product of the shale fracked in the Raton and San Juan Basins in
Northern New Mexico and the Permian Basin in Texas, so it was available.
It was expensive and subject to the availability of gasoline for the delivery
trucks, but the delivery man estimated that the three of them could made
do with two tank fill-ups over the winter. Vincent ordered the service. The
price of cordwood was high, but less expensive than propane, so he bought
two cords of mesquite. There was cheaper fir available, but Joe suspected
the softwood came from poaching in the National Forest, and Vincent
yielded to Joe's sensibilities about that. Besides, mesquite had the added
benefits of burning clean and adding flavor to meats cooked over it.

Vincent quickly reacquired the visceral, atavistic attachment to the
land which had grown latent in his years away from it. The New Mexico
land, air and vistas had been incorporated into his being as a boy. He'd
learned to hunt, fish, and camp here. He'd learned to survive outdoors
here; it was an affinity that served him well in the Marine Corps. The
harshness and dislocation brought on by the recent economic collapse
were mitigated by his sense of having returned home.

He knew that Grace felt no such attachment to this land. She seemed
frightened by the elemental life they faced and worried about their future
prospects for a return to what she considered normalcy. But the legendary
enchantment of the land was already beginning to have its effect on her.

In some pillow talk the night before, she'd commented on the irony
that modern Americans, an amalgam of descendants of Europeans who
tyrannized American Indians to take their land were now being forced to
adopt much of the hunter-gatherer, agrarian way of life of the aboriginal
people they had vanquished. It was as if the American Indians lost all the

battles but eventually won the war. Locally, at least, their lifestyle and their traditional uses of the land were to be the final refuge of modern Americans. Grace marveled at how it all happened so quickly.

Vincent reminded her that he, as Chief Armageddon Officer, formulated the plan to put them in the circumstances they now enjoyed. Because, he crowed, he had facilitated, defended and protected their exodus in various and sundry ways, he hoped Grace would credit his exemplary efforts from time to time. Grace rewarded him with laughter at his shameless self-aggrandizement. Then, throwing her leg over him under the comforter and sitting up, she bestowed one of the many credits she freely acknowledged he was entitled to.

CHAPTER

31

A late spring storm passed over leaving a dusting of white on the low mountains behind the Long Ranch. The air was brittle under the hard light of the brilliant blue sky as they bounced down the track in the Cherokee to Highway 4 and beyond to Los Alamos. In the six months since they'd arrived to make new lives on the ranch, they had settled into a comfortable, if subsistence-driven routine.

Grace looked pale to Vincent and seemed slow to undertake things that required effort. She said she was fine, had no fevers or respiratory or GI tract symptoms, and went through her routine normally. Still, Vincent was concerned.

They were on their way to the town meeting at the National Laboratory. In a spontaneous group dynamic fostered by social media, a majority of the Los Alamos community had come together following the collapse in response to two phenomena spread on the still-functioning World Wide Web, accessible intermittently as electricity permitted.

The first was general consensus on a fundamental premise that would guide their community. It was, quite simply, that the collective memory of the survivors, written and otherwise, was their biggest asset. It was the only thing that would prevent survivor communities from consignment to the random, brutish subsistence that had characterized the evolution of *homo sapiens*.

The second phenomenon crucial to their survival had caught on at the social-media-spread urgings of a group of volunteers on the memorial Liberty ships, one each in San Francisco and Baltimore. Their advocacy had gone viral as they called for a reprise of the "Greatest Generation"— the American generation that united across all occupations and social strata to work collectively and single mindedly to overcome the Great Depression and defeat fascism in Europe and Japan in World War II. It was the only instance in American history, until now, in which such single-minded effort was required, and it had been successful.

The Los Alamos tribe and many other communities across the Web were quick to adopt the example of the Greatest Generation for the current, even more extreme crisis. A blogger had given the phenomenon a name—GreyGen 2.0. The abbreviation for "Greatest" was coined by the blogger as "Grey," a tribute to former Senator Aaron Grey who had been the first to publicly and persuasively warn of the dangers to which the country's economy ultimately succumbed. Grey had delivered his prescient advocacy in a bid for the Presidency that had ended prematurely by his institutionalization for mental illness.

The term GreyGen 2.0 stuck. It stood now as shorthand for the collective effort to reboot the American nation under the limitations of its new economic reality. Spontaneous formation of GreyGen 2.0 communities, or "tribes," all over the country followed. Groups of interested citizens formed workshops to solve local community problems of food, shelter, sanitation, transportation, medical treatment, education, conservation and the like.

In time, the community groups followed a practice of nominating a leader who would meet with other community leaders in their region, irrespective of former state, county or municipal boundaries, to share their learning experiences and successes. The term "loya jurgas" was adopted to refer to these inter-tribal meetings after the Afghan tribal councils of the same name, and that name also stuck.

Vincent contributed the *Atlantic* article he'd found on the train cataloguing the one hundred most important human inventions. Working groups of the many scientists in the Los Alamos tribe continuously evaluated and prioritized these objectives to fit the needs of the community and also to avoid the environmentally harmful applications used by the pre-collapse world. Grace had been elected to the Steering committee of the Los Alamos GreyGen 2.0 tribe, largely because of her celebrity arising out of her former professional nexus with Aaron Grey.

In no small part due to Vincent's exploits during the Dodge City train robbery, published at every opportunity by Grace, Vincent was elected to head up the section on security. That section, in the absence of actual law and order issues, morphed into a focus on energy security. Cyber-interference with the local and regional power grids was largely absent now, although rotating blackouts and brownouts were still common due to growing obsolescence as maintenance and repair of hardware diminished over time.

Shales below tracts of public land in the Southwest produced both oil and natural gas. Fracked well drilling by skeletal remnants of the oil and gas exploration companies could occur only by Department of the Interior permit. These permits were issued only if the drilling applicant could demonstrate a source of water other than local water needed to sustain local housing and agriculture. Wells then drilled were tested for methane and fracking chemical leakage. Any wells shown to be leaking were sealed, and the driller was required to pay for any environmental remediation necessary through insurance funded by a tax on fracking operations.

The washboard surface of their private road caused the Cherokee to vibrate so hard that Vincent had to slow down, and he glanced at Grace, noting her pallor.

"What is your section up to?" Grace asked. "Are you still looking for pipe?"

Vincent nodded. "Iron or PVC pipe. We can make do with some clay pipe. It's easier to make—sort of like the Romans did."

Vincent referred to a project underway to "store electricity." By using electric pumps at night when demand was light, they intended to pump water from a reservoir in Los Alamos up through a pipe to an alpine lake above town. The next day, during the peak electricity demand, the water in the lake could be released to cascade down a parallel pipe to the generator before flowing back to the reservoir. The upper lake would be charged by rainwater and snowmelt.

"We can use clay pipe for the line flowing down from the lake to the generator. But for the uptake line from the reservoir to the lake, we need welded or sealed pipe big enough to carry the water, and it needs to be air-tight so the suction pump can work."

"That's cool," Grace said. "You said someone found a spare genera-tor in the Laboratory's power plant that would work, so all you need is the pipe?"

"That and some valves, yeah. Iron pipe is scarce because of the energy needed to make it and lack of demand. PVC would be better because it's light enough to pack in off-road. But PVC is made from oil, so its production has fallen off too. One of our guys has a line on some good sized, surplus plastic pipe over in Roswell. He inspected it, and he's going to report his findings today."

The Cherokee eased onto the hardtop surface of the highway and pointed downhill toward town. Vincent drove faster, but had to dodge the plentiful potholes that had developed over the winter. Oil based asphalt needed for repairs was as scarce as the county highway crews to make the repairs.

Grace pointed to several fresh cut fir stumps as they drove past.

"Look at that. The poachers did that just since we went to town on Saturday. I'm going to suggest another project for the committee. We should make a plan for tree seeding to insure that the tribe's use of timber is sustainable."

"Speaking of planning, is the Steering Committee functioning? Do you have confidence in it?"

Vincent glanced over at Grace. Her eyes were closed and she seemed to be waiting for whatever she felt to pass. Vincent frowned and started to say something, but just then Grace's eyes opened and she rallied.

"It pretty much functions. The job of long range planning is so frus-trating when we can't count on getting needed supplies to support the liv-ing standards we are all used to. There is a good deal of unfocused discussion about a million problems.

"There is one thing we are going to take up today, though, that sounds interesting. There's a member of the Lab's faculty who knew about some pre-collapse studies indicating that the human brain is hard-wired for empathy, but only on a tribal level. Humans evolved within that experience, allowing them to readily wage war without empa-thy on humans of other tribes while mutually supporting and emotionally attaching to individuals of their own tribe. So to overcome this aspect of human evolution, and to prevent evolutionary history from repeating itself, the regional *loya jurga* is making a priority of teaching empathy for other tribes across the Southwest and beyond to foster cooperation among them when competing for scarce resources. Failing that, the hypothesis goes, we who survive the collapse will re-experience the same unending wars and slavery practices that our city-state predecessors did."

As they drove to town, Grace marveled at how important a discrete scientific insight like that could prove to be if humans could overcome such a basic evolutionary defect by socialization and education. However, they both agreed that it was, as Vincent put it, a low percentage shot if things get desperate.

"Say, Vincent, whatever happened with the standoff between the American and Chinese carriers off Venezuela? I don't hear anything about war, so it must not have come to that."

"I gather that after the collapse, the need for oil by each side fell way off. When the markets collapsed, Americans and Europeans stopped buying Chinese manufactured stuff, so China didn't need it for manufacturing. On the American side, demand fell as the cities emptied out. Less employment, less economic activity, and less transportation of all kinds resulted in much less refining. The oil news website I check into when I can said the carriers had been withdrawn, and our occupation of Venezuela is over. The dispute was mooted by Venezuela offering each country roughly half of Venezuela's output. Ironically, neither country is able to take that much now.

"We're still living on borrowed time, though. We can't put Humpty Dumpty together again after markets collapse. Also, we can't just resume the old ways because with recovery, oil scarcity returns and it is too expensive to use the way we used to use it, even with the cutback in global infrastructure. Oil—what's left of it—will be rationed by the market from here on out. So, we have oil and gas, but not enough to sustain all of us as we used to live. Even that is being exhausted—either rapidly or slowly—depending on the rate at which we continue to use it."

Abruptly, Grace commanded, "Stop the car."

Vincent quickly pulled over in time for Grace to open her door and vomit onto the shoulder of the road.

"That's it," Vincent said. "We can't keep ignoring this. You aren't well, and I'm taking you to the clinic."

When she finished retching, Grace flopped back into her seat and groped for rags in the glove box. With one in each hand, she proceeded to wipe off her mouth and blot the sweat from her forehead.

"You mean we can't just ignore *him*," she said weakly, turning to face him.

Under her steady gaze, Vincent's expression dissolved into one of realization.

"You mean ... you're pregnant?"

Grace smiled and nodded.

"I asked Joe to start thinking of name suggestions."

"You have discussed this *with Joe*? Before telling *me*?"

"Yeah, well, unlike a clueless former Marine who we all know and love, Joe connected the dots. He asked me this morning when the baby was due."

Vincent sat stunned, stroking his beard.

"Holy bloodline, Batman! We're gonna be parents!"

"Have you noticed me taking the pill lately? I ran out of those a long time ago. Anyway, I was going to fix a romantic dinner tonight and tell you."

She wiped her mouth again and waited for a lesser wave of nausea to subside.

"Him? You said him." Vincent grinned broadly. "It's got a tassel?"

"Or not. It's just a feeling. I guess we'll have to wait and see."

CPSIA information can be obtained at www.ICGtesting.com
Printed in the USA
BVOW08s0337080915

416763BV00003B/269/P